DANGEROUS OBSESSION

A SOPHIE STAR SERIES BOOK ONE

L. J. WEBB

DANGEROUS OBSESSION
A Sophie Star Series Book One

A special thanks to **Andrew Scott, my editor**, for all his help.

Cover by Plumstone Book Cover

eBook ISBN 978-1-7330939-0-3
Paperback ISBN 978-1-7330939-1-0

Library of Congress Control Number: 2019907042

Thank you to all those who took time to help me get my first book published.

L J

TABLE OF CONTENTS

"For I know the plans I have for you," declares the LORD, "plans to prosper you and not to harm you, plans to give you hope and a future.
Jeremiah 29:11

DEFINITIONS

Abbastanza/enough

Addio/goodbye

Anch'io/me too

Ascolta fratellino/Listen little brother

Buona notte/good night

Calmati/calm down

Capisco/I understand

Certo/Sure

Certo che/of course not

Che ne dici/ what about it?

Ciao/Hello

Consigliere/advisor

Dimenticarlo/forget about it

Dove sei/where are you

È che una minaccia/Is that a threat?

Fratellino/little brother

Figlio/son

Fuori di qui/get out of here

Grazie/Thank you

Grazie, miei cari figli/ thank you my dear children

Mi capisci/you understand me?

Mi dispiace fratellino/

 I'm sorry little brother

Non buono/not good

Ora /NowPazzo/idiot

Promesso/promise

Si/Yes

Solo io e te/just you and me

Tesoro/sweetheart

Ti amo/I love you

Ti amo fratellino / I love you   little brother

Ti fermerà/I will stop you

Va bene/OK

Zitto/shut up

CHAPTER ONE

A thick, dark fog was lifting off her. She was groggy, confused, like coming out of a heavy, dreamless stupor. *Where am I?* She could hear something, no, maybe someone. She tried to open her eyes but couldn't make them move. *What's wrong with me, why can't I open my eyes? Maybe they're open and it's just dark out. Who's calling out?* Her body wouldn't respond to her commands. Panic began to set in. *No, I need to stay calm. Think. Maybe I've been in an accident, and they are looking for me. I need to make some noise.* She tried to move her arms, but they wouldn't move. She tried opening her eyes again. This time, she was able to see from a tiny slit. *Light! Why is everything so blurry? I need to call out so they can find me. HELP! HELP!* She couldn't hear herself. Her jaw wasn't moving. *HELP! I'M OVER HERE.* All she could hear was moans coming from her mouth. She could hear someone moving. Maybe they heard her. The voice...it was saying something.

"I'm so sorry Sophie, I love you, I love you, forgive me."

Who is saying that? A soft whisper — she couldn't recognize the voice. Another moan came out of her. Then she heard someone yelling.

"She's waking up, get the doctor!" She heard a door open.

"Ms. Star can you hear me? My name is Velma. I'm your nurse. You're in the hospital. If you understand, can you nod your head?"

She barely nodded, her head started spinning and stabbing, fiery pain started shooting through the back of her skull. *The hospital — what am I doing in the hospital?* She tried to open her eyes again, but the lids barely moved.

"That's great, Sophie. Now, can you move your fingers?" Sophie moved her fingers on both hands. "Can you wiggle your toes?" The nurse waited. "That's great. Excellent job. Now, Doctor Jones will be here shortly to check you out. Don't try to talk — your jaw is wired shut."

Wired shut?! Why is my jaw wired shut?

Then she heard that voice. "Sophie, it's me — Nikko. You're going to be fine. You have some cuts on your face, but I'll get the best cosmetic surgeon to make them invisible. I don't want you worrying about scars."

It took a while for the doctor to come. "Sophie, my name is Dr. Jones. I am going to shine a light in your eyes for a moment. I want you to follow the light — can you do that?"

Instantly, another debilitating pain shot through her. She closed her eyes and moaned. "It's alright — can you answer some questions by nodding or shaking your head?" Just the nodding motion made her nauseated.

"Do you know where you are?" He could see a slight movement and took it as a nod. "Good, do you remember what happened to you?" She shook her head to indicate no. Speaking to Nikko he said, "That's not uncommon. She probably has short term amnesia. Her memory should come back as the swelling in her brain from the concussion diminishes." He returned his attention to her.

"Sophie, the reason you can't open your eyes all the way is that they are swollen. You won't be able to talk for a while because your jaw is broken and wired shut." When he said that, the heart monitor started making sounds; her blood pressure and pulse were skyrocketing.

"Doctor, what's happening?" Nikko was startled.

"She's reacting to what I just told her. I am going to have to give her a sedative. Nurse, give her a boost of morphine and a

4

sedative. I'll finish with this tomorrow — she needs to get some more rest. Now that she is no longer comatose, we can run more tests to check for any permanent damage. I'm ordering a new CT scan and an MRI to make sure the swelling is going down."

"Yes sir." Nurse Velma noted his commands in the chart at the foot of Sophie's bed.

It didn't take long for Sophie to go to sleep after the sedative and pain killer were administered. Nikko sat by her side for a few more minutes, gently stroking her hair. One of the nurses had taken a wet washcloth and tried to sponge the matted blood out of her long, auburn hair. Her five foot six inch slender curves silhouetted under the thin hospital blanket. Nikko got up and went over to the window, rubbing his knuckles as he gazed outside. He watched the rain coming down, the wind blowing from the Southeast causing the rain to run down the glass like teardrops. *Even nature cries for her,* he chided himself. Both hands were red and swollen with cuts from his fists hitting her teeth and bone, and he was sure that more than a few knuckles were broken. He accepted the pain in his hands as punishment for his transgression. He could remember feeling the pain as he kept pummeling her, but it didn't stop him. When his right hand hurt too much, he switched to hitting her with his left. Total exhaustion was the only thing that made him stop. When he thought about it, it was like an out of body experience, like he was watching the beating happen from somewhere above it. *I could have killed her. What got into me?* He leaned against the window, his forehead touching the cool glass, and wept.

Thomas had just gotten back into town when Nikko's driver, Ben, ushered him to the hospital. Ben told Thomas that Sophie was injured, but Nikko instructed him not to provide any details. Although, Nikko and Thomas' Italian heritage made it evident they were brothers, Nikko stood 6'1" to Thomas' 5'11". Nikko's hair was thick and wavy, and he wore it to his collar, where Thomas' straight black hair was in more of an Ivy League cut. They were both handsome by any standards. Thomas entered her room and stood at her bedside; he was shaken. The swelling completely distorted her oval face, and her round hazel eyes were shut up behind lids that puffed out like marshmallows. Her normally suntanned skin was covered by bruises of assorted colors from red to blue to purple. Inside of Thomas, an explosion was brewing. He took a few deep breaths — he couldn't let his brother read his reaction.

"Nikko — what happened to her?" He turned to face his brother. "Did you do this?" Nikko barely nodded his head, but he couldn't raise his eyes to meet his brother's gaze.

"Why?"

"Thomas, it was like some *thing* possessed me. I was so excited Saturday night when I came home with the ring. It was beautiful — I knew she would love it. But when I asked her to marry me, she said she wasn't ready to answer me yet. She thought it was too soon. I told her I was okay with it...and I thought I was. But when we went to what was supposed to be our announcement dinner, I saw her talking to Jimmy. They were laughing, and then she put her hand on his arm. I just got so jealous; I lost my mind. I grabbed her and brought her down to the wine cellar and just started hitting and hitting, I just — it wasn't me. It wasn't me." He buried his head in his hands, "I just love her so much, I couldn't stand the idea she might not feel the same."

"This isn't love, Nikko. This is insanity." Nikko's face turned red with both anger and embarrassment, and he turned his gaze out the window with his back to his brother.

After a moment, Nikko spoke. "Don't judge me."

"I have every right to judge you. I'm family, and you know this isn't right. I've never seen you this crazy for any woman.

6

You've always been about chasing the girls, then when you get what you want, you dump them. But, with her, you seem to be out of your mind." Thomas moved to where Nikko was watching the rain fall against the window and put his hand firmly on his shoulder.

"Sophie's not like the others," Nikko answered. "She's smart, and beautiful, and engages me in ways I can't explain. I guess I am obsessed. I don't think I can let her go. If she leaves me now, I don't know what I'd do." He walked back to her bed, brought her hand to his lips, and kissed it. "You know I have to go to Florida. Will you take care of her while I'm gone? I'm sure someone here will report this, and you'll have to handle the police." He turned to Sophie and whispered, "I will make this up to you."

"Alright," sighed Thomas. "I'll take care of everything here." He started toward the door. "Are you going to stay here tonight, Nikko?"

"Yeah, I haven't left her side since the accident. I'll stay until I have to leave tomorrow."

"Then I'll come back in the morning around 9 with some breakfast. I'll see you then, certo?" Thomas moved for the door while Nikko walked to Sophie's bedside and patted her hand.

"Va bene." Nikko replied and sat back down in the reclining chair next to her bed. He leaned over to her and whispered in her ear.

"You have to forgive me. I can never let you go. It would kill me—and you," Nikko whispered.

Then he took hold of her hand, leaned back in the recliner, pushing up the footrest and closed his eyes. Behind her swollen eyes, Sophie's sedative addled mind struggled to grasp onto that last statement.

Did he just say he would kill me? Then she drifted out again.

The next morning, Nikko went into the bathroom and cleaned up. Ben had brought his clothes and toiletries the first night in the hospital. He stretched and looked out the window, the weather had cleared, and the sun was shining. He knew what he had to do the moment she woke up. He took the velvet box out of his pocket and set it on the nightstand. He had thought about it all night.

Sophie's mind was starting to clear up now, and the pain began to register. The night before, other than the pain in her head, she could feel only numbness, but now she could feel everything. Her heartbeat pulsed in her ears, her whole body ached, and even the hospital gown touching her skin hurt. She felt a sickening pain in her jaw and right arm, and her face felt like someone had crushed it.

"Mmmmppphhhh!" Nikko heard Sophie groan through her teeth and called for the nurse.

"Sophie are you in pain?" he asked. She attempted to nod. "The nurse is coming. She will give you something." The nurse came in to check on her and was met by Nikko's irritation.

"She's in pain! I told the doctor she was to be medicated all the time, so she wouldn't feel the injuries! Can't you people do anything right?"

With a professional composure, the nurse replied, "We are limited by protocol on how much pain medication to give, and she is on the maximum dose allowable. Only the doctor can order supplemental medication. You don't want her to end up addicted to the pain medication, do you?"

"Then get the doctor in here, now!" Nikko was angry, his intimidation usually fixed these things. But in this situation, he was powerless, and he knew it. The helplessness just made his anger grow.

"I understand your frustration, Mr. Morano. I promise we are doing all we can to keep her comfortable. I'll tell you what— there's a cafeteria downstairs if you would like some coffee.

They even have an espresso bar. I'll stay with her. I need to bathe her now anyway." The nurse needed to speak with a patient alone when injuries were suspicious, like these. But this man wouldn't leave her alone long enough for her to do it.

"No. my brother is bringing breakfast for me, you can just pull the curtain I won't leave her."

"Now, Mr. Mora..."

"I said no! Just do what you have to do, and then go." Nikko wasn't leaving until he had a chance to talk to her.

Half an hour later the nurse pushed back the curtain and left. Nikko moved closer, sitting on the edge of Sophie's bed. Her eyes were a little more open this morning. She looked at him, quietly bearing the pain. *Why can't I remember what happened to me? And why is this man acting like he's responsible?* She wished desperately that she could speak.

"Sweetheart, I know you can't talk right now, so I'll talk for both of us. I love you so much. I know you said you wanted some time to think about my proposal, but I don't think we should wait. I have no doubt you love me. It makes no sense to put it off." He anxiously took the ring out of the box and slid it on her finger. "With this ring, I thee wed." He laughed. "It may not be official, but as far as I am concerned, you are my wife, now and forever." As Sophie tried her best to voice a protest, Dr. Jones entered the room.

"Ms. Star...Sophie how are you feeling this morning?" He checked her chart for the most recent set of vital signs, then physically and visually examined her eyes and her jaw. When he finished, he perched himself on a rolling stool and folded his hands in his lap.

"Sophie, you took quite a fall. You were in a coma for two days. Luckily, the swelling on your brain is going down, but you

9

still have a broken jaw, your right arm is broken, you have two fractured ribs, and your left ear drum has burst. There is also deep bruising over 65 percent of your body and you have lacerations on your face." His eyes darted momentarily to Nikko then back to Sophie. Nikko didn't notice the glance. "I must say this is one of the worst fall injuries I've seen in a woman of your age."

As the doctor continued to discuss her healing time and physical therapy, Sophie's mind suddenly flooded with memories. She remembered the *would be* engagement party, and she remembered that Nikko grabbed her in the middle of her conversation with Jimmy; which puzzled her at the time. He took her to the basement wine cellar. She remembered him asking why she was flirting with Jimmy. "Flirting with Jimmy," she laughed, "don't be ridiculous he's your cousin." She started up the stairs, and that's when it happened — the first punch struck her face. She couldn't remember ever feeling such pain, shooting pain that went straight down to her knees, almost crumpling her. Then another hit; searing pain behind her eyes. And another; her vision became foggy.

He had slapped her a couple of times in the 16 months they had been dating, nothing hard, and she felt that the rush of the lifestyle he offered her was worth overlooking a few minor flaws in her character. But this — he had never done anything like this. She never even imagined it. She was screaming at him to stop but he started hitting her in the ribs. Now on the ground, he wouldn't stop even when she begged and pleaded. Her screams went unanswered by anyone upstairs. He just kept hitting until, even after losing consciousness, she felt blow after blow. So much pain, excruciating pain everywhere; it all came back.

Suddenly, her stomach lurched, and she started throwing up through the small opening where her jaw was wired. The pain from her involuntary reflexes was like someone was stabbing her in the ribs. The doctor sat her up and moved her to

10

clear her airway so she wouldn't choke on her vomit. He called for help, "Nurse, get a suction tube so we can clean out her mouth, stat!"

Nikko moved out of the way. He heard the blood pressure warning beeping. He couldn't take it. He stepped out the door. When he looked up, he saw Thomas coming.

"What's going on?" he asked.

"The doctor was explaining her injuries, and she started throwing up. They have to clean her airway. She's in so much pain." He put his head in his hands, as he leaned his back against the hallway wall.

Thomas felt his brother's discomfort. "Here… go to the cafeteria." He handed his brother a sack and an espresso. "I'll stay here and call you in a bit." Nikko said nothing; he just headed for the elevator.

Pazzo! What did he expect would happen after beating her like that? There was no doubt his brother was sorry, and he promised he would never do anything like that again. But Thomas knew other men like him. They got off on controlling women because they liked the feeling of power and the rush that a woman's fear brings them. Leaving is the only way for a woman to get free from a man like that. *But who could leave Nikko Morano and live to tell about it?*

Nikko came back twenty minutes later, and he and Thomas went back into the room. The nurse had cleaned Sophie up, and the doctor was talking to her again. "It will take about six weeks for your jaw to heal and about the same for your arm. The other injuries and bruises will heal in due time. Also, a physical therapist will come by to help you get your strength and muscle tone back. A cosmetic surgeon will be in to look at your cuts. I'm going to recommend that you stay here for two weeks so I can keep an eye on you…"

"No, I can take care of her at home," Nikko interjected. "I have the best doctors and nurses available. We can take care of her pain and make sure she's comfortable." His face showed that he was insistent.

"Is that what you want, Ms. Star?" Sophie started to respond, but Nikko objected.

"You talk to me, Doctor. I am her fiancé, and I will take care of her."

"Mr. Morano, she is my patient — my obligation is to her, not you." He turned back to Sophie. "Ms. Star, is that what you want? Do you want me to release you into the care of your fiancé?" She nodded. She would have to figure out what to do later. "Alright. But I insist she stay here for *at least* seven days. No argument."

Nikko relented and said, "alright. Now leave us so I can talk to my fiancé." The doctor touched Sophie's arm and left the room.

Nikko moved over next to Sophie where the doctor sat moments before. "You know I can take better care of you," he said. "I will make sure you feel no pain while you're healing, and you will be more comfortable in my home. Well, it is actually your home now, too," he added with a smile.

The last statement took Thomas slightly by surprise, but then he noticed the ring on her finger. Nodding to the ring, Thomas asked, "When did *that* happen?"

"This morning, I told her I love her, and I *know* she loves me. She wanted time, but there is no need for that. We are destined to be together, so why postpone it? We'll get married as soon as she's healed." Nikko turned and stroked her hair. She was trembling. She couldn't control it—her very insides were shaking.

Thomas shot a side glance at Nikko. "Shouldn't she get a say in this?"

"Are you saying she doesn't love me?"

Thomas moved him away from her and whispered. "No. All I'm saying is that you nearly killed her. Don't you think she might be a little leery about marrying you?"

"No. She'll forgive me. There's no need to wait." He moved back to her bed and sat on the edge. "*Tesoro*, I have to go finish that business in Florida. I will only be gone for a week. I hate to leave you, but Thomas will be here. I wouldn't go, but my father doesn't trust anyone but me and Thomas, you know that. And since I'm the one handling this transaction, I should be the one to finish it. But as soon as I get back, I will take you home. Don't you worry about a thing." He leaned down and kissed her on the forehead. He lingered there, stroking her hair, then lifted her left hand and kissed her finger just below the ring. "*Ti amo*. I will be back in one week."

The brothers turned when they heard the door open. Two men came in, the older of the two was about 6' tall in his mid-thirties. The other had red hair, shorter, in his late twenties. The dark-skinned man put his hand out to Thomas, who reciprocated.

"My name is Detective Cartwright, and this is Detective Mahoney." He reached out to Nikko, but Nikko didn't respond. His gaze remained fixed on Sophie. "We need to talk to Ms. Star, alone." As they moved toward Sophie, Nikko rose and stood in front of them.

"What do you want with my fiancée?"

"We need to talk to her about her *accident*."

"If you know it was an accident, why do you need to talk to her?"

"Sir, it's standard procedure. Whenever a patient comes in with these types of injuries, the hospital is required to call us, and we are obligated to get a statement."

"Well, you can see she is in no condition for an interview right now. Her jaw is wired shut. You'll have to get permission from her doctor before you can talk to her. Until then, I will have to ask you to leave." Detective Cartwright moved closer to the bed.

"Is that what you want, Ms. Star?" She nodded weakly.

"You got your answer," Nikko said. "Now, please, leave us."

Detective Mahoney turned to Nikko, "And just who are you to Ms. Star?"

"I am her fiancé. As I said."

"And were you there when this incident happened, mister...?"

"I am Nikko Morano, and yes, I was there. She had gone to the wine cellar at my restaurant to get more bottles for our guests. When she didn't come back for a long time, I went to check on her. I am the one who found her at the bottom of the stairs and called the ambulance. It was obvious she tripped in those stilettos she wears and fell." As Nikko was talking, he took hold of Sophie's hand. Detective Cartwright noticed his swollen knuckles but said nothing.

Detective Mahoney turned to Thomas. "And you are mister...?"

"Thomas Morano, Nikko's brother."

"Were you there too?"

"No, I was out of town when it happened, so I can't really add anything to his statement."

"Mr. Morano, we will speak with her doctor, as you requested. I also need to get statements from any others that were at your restaurant that night."

"I will have my attorney get in touch with you. Do you have a card?" Both detectives handed him a card. They bid the two brothers and Sophie a good day and left the room.

Dangerous Obsession

CHAPTER TWO

A s the detectives stepped on the elevator, Cartwright said, "well I wasn't expecting to see the Morano brothers there."

"Me either. The nurse I talked to just said the boyfriend wouldn't leave her side, so she had no chance to ask her what happened."

"I thought he was the 'love um and leave um,' type," Cartwright responded.

"Maybe she's the lucky one to get the brass ring — If you call being beat to a pulp lucky," Detective Mahoney said.

"Yeah, there is no way those injuries came from a fall. The ER doctor who called it in said she had deep bruises over 65 percent of her body. I can't even imagine that."

"Her face was almost unrecognizable," Mahoney shook his head thinking about how she looked.

Cartwright paused for a moment then said, "I saw Nikko's hands. His knuckles are red and swollen, maybe even a couple of broken ones. There is no doubt he did this." He thought for a moment, "isn't Ms. Star an accountant?"

"That's what my notes say. We will have to get with DEA and see if they are aware of her place in the Morano family. Maybe we can get him locked up for assault. I know they would love to get him behind bars for something." As they left the building, the two men were already making phone calls.

"I knew they would be coming." Nikko never took his gaze away from Sophie. He kissed her on the lips gently and whispered in her ear. Then he turned to Thomas and nodded to the door. Thomas looked at Sophie. She looked terrified. How could his brother not see that? They started moving toward the elevators.

"Thomas, I am trusting her to you. Get her prepped for the police and make sure the doctor keeps her doped up, so she doesn't get any crazy ideas."

"Like what?"

"Like thinking she wants to leave me or telling the police about our spat."

"If you think she would do that, why are you insisting on marrying her?"

"Because I love her. She might be mad at me for a while — I get that. I have to protect her from herself until she can get over it. She knows we belong together. I'll never hurt her again."

"I know you believe that, and you're right. I've never seen you do anything close to this, to any other woman. But you are obsessed with Sophie. I'm worried about you — I don't want you going off the deep end again. Can't you see this is a dangerous obsession?" He looked Nikko straight in the eyes, "does papa even know what you've done? You know, he would be livid if he thought some woman, even Sophie, as important as she is to this organization, had this kind of control over you! You better talk to him before someone else does." There was true concern behind Thomas' stern eyes.

Nikko grabbed his brother firmly by the arm. "Ti amo fratellino, I know you're just trying to look out for me, but don't get in my way. I *will* marry her. I'll explain it all to papa in due time." Nikko put his arm around Thomas' shoulder. He always liked being taller and slightly bigger. As the older sibling, he thought it appropriate, and he felt that it punctuated his dominance over Thomas. What he didn't know was that Thomas wasn't afraid of him and never had been. He was the levelheaded one of the two. More like his mother.

Thomas relented slightly, for now. "I'll take care of everything. I packed your bag for you, and Ben is out front with the car to take you to the airport."

"Grazie. I'll call every night. I know she can't talk, but you can put the phone to her ear, so I can talk to her." They stopped walking when they got to the elevator, and Thomas turned to give Nikko a hug.

"Go. Finish your job and get back home."

"Love you, fratello."

"Anch'io." Thomas waited till the elevator doors closed. *How far am I going to have to go to protect her from him?*

Thomas walked into Sophie's room and sat in a chair by her bed. She looked at him, and tears started rolling down her face. He took her hand. "Sophie, I'm so sorry that I didn't see this coming. If I had been there, you know I wouldn't have let it happen. I wish I would have had the nerve to ask you out when you first came in applying for that accountant's job at the restaurant. I knew I liked you the minute I saw you. I just didn't have the nerve. How could I have known that Nikko was interested? But you know him; he doesn't hesitate. Once he asked you out, I couldn't say anything and betray him. I'm so sorry."

He lowered his head for a moment and took a breath. "If I had asked first, he would have left you alone. He wouldn't have infringed on my interest." He knew she couldn't respond, but he had to say something. His words revealed his guilt over his inaction.

She moved her hand to his face and rubbed away a tear. That sweet gesture broke him, and he put his head down on her bed and cried for her. It was at that moment he knew he had to get her away; she had to disappear. He knew Sophie would never agree to marry Nikko now, and he would kill her for that. One way or another, Nikko would be the death of her.

Thomas stayed by her side and fed her every meal. With her jaw wired shut, she could only sip through a straw. For the first couple of meals, just the act of sipping took all her energy. When she slept, he would get on the phone and contact men who could help him get her a new identity. He would get everything she needed to make her disappear. He couldn't use his regular contacts for fear it would get back to Nikko. He only had one man he trusted with his life and that was his bodyguard, Franco. Franco would attend the meetings that Thomas set and exchange money for papers.

Thomas only had a week to work out every detail. He found a private physical rehab clinic in Virginia. She would go in under her new name. He couldn't take money out of his own account because it could be traced, but he always kept at least $500 grand in his safe for emergencies. He also knew she had about the same amount in her savings account, but she would have to leave it. The family had paid her very well for being their confidential accountant. He just had to make this work without casting suspicious eyes on him. He also needed photos for her new passport and driver's license. She would need to change her hair color and maybe wear some glasses or colored contact lenses — and all this had to be done in just five days. If Nikko didn't come home early, Thomas' plan might work.

As he reflected over the details, a bittersweet feeling arose. He would miss the time spent with her. She was getting stronger, eating a little more each day. She had graduated to sitting on the edge of the bed. He would talk to her, and she would respond with notes. It was good she was ambidextrous, or she would be forced to scribble illegibly with her injured hand. He hadn't told her his plan yet, but he would today. He always took their notes and put them in the hazardous waste bin so no one would find them. As he returned from disposing of the day's notes, he heard his phone ringing.

"Hello?"

"Thomas. How is my girl doing today?"

"She's doing well, Nikko. She sat up on the edge of the bed today. I might try to get her in a wheelchair tomorrow and take her outside." It was hard for Thomas to keep his voice from betraying his true sense of anger.

"That should be me," Nikko stated, rather coldly.

"Yeah, but you want her to get better as soon as possible, don't you?"

"Yes, of course. I'm just jealous that you get to be with her, and I'm stuck here. She needs to be leaning on me, trusting me."

"You'll be back soon enough. She has a long recovery ahead of her. Do you want to talk to her?"

"Well, you don't think I called to talk to you, do you?" Thomas held the phone to her ear. She started to tremble, and he could see her blood pressure going up on the machine. It happened every night when he called. He didn't want Nikko to hear the beeping of the machine; he can't know how afraid she is. He reached over to turn the volume off.

Thomas saw her eyes watering as Nikko spoke to her. He hated to put her through this, but he had to keep up the ruse. If Nikko thought something was amiss, he would drop everything and come home. After a few minutes, Sophie signaled to Thomas, and he hung up the telephone. He reached over to turn the volume back on the machine, and she grabbed for the notepad. She furiously wrote for a long time, tears streaming down her cheeks. The last words barely legible as she became exhausted. Thomas read her note out loud.

"I won't marry him, Thomas, I don't love him. I don't think I ever did. It was just exciting being in his world. I never thought he would fall in love with me. If he takes me to his house, he will keep me drugged up so I can't leave. If I tell him I won't marry him, he will kill me someday. I can't take another beating like this. I have to get out of here before he gets back." Thomas choked back tears and steadied his voice.

"Sophie, I know. I have a plan worked out." He told her all that he had arranged so far. "I have a guy coming in to take your picture. He's gonna create new identification for you. He will get you a blonde wig and green contacts, but we will have to dye your hair as soon as you are out of here."

She wrote again on her pad. 'If he finds out you helped me; he will kill you.'

"Let me worry about that. I have my tracks covered, but he wouldn't dare touch me. Nikko knows that our father would retaliate. Obsession is weakness in my father's eyes, and he does not tolerate weakness." Thomas stared down at her with a reassuring gaze.

Sophie reached over and timidly touched his hand. "Sophie, if we do this, you have to leave everything. You can't take anything with you. You will have to leave your bank accounts untouched, and everything you've worked for will be gone. Can you really do that?"

She wrote. 'What's my choice? My money is no good to me if I'm dead. And if I stayed, being married to someone I fear and don't love would be just as bad. But before I go, you must promise to keep working on the legitimate family businesses. I don't want to see you drawn into the underworld Nikko lives in. You're too good for that.'

Thomas smiled. "Don't worry about me. My hope is to totally get the family out of the drug business. It's mostly Nikko who stands in the way. Papa is retired; he would vote with me, but he doesn't want to abandon his firstborn son. Papa understands how powerful the allure of that world is. It's what got him into it, and Nikko is just like him." Sophie nodded, and he suggested she rest for a while.

The nurse brought in Sophie's liquid dinner. Thomas got up and disposed of their notes in the usual manner. He then returned to her bedside to hold the straw and encourage her to eat. He knew that she was well enough to do it herself, but he also knew she would only take a few sips without encouragement. She'd already lost too much weight. His real motivations, however, were stronger; the act of helping her was an intimate one, and he loved the time that he spent with her.

Thomas' bodyguard, Franco, came into the room later that night. He looked at her and his eyes showed his shock at her condition. He hadn't seen her since before the incident.

"Mr. Morano, I brought the clothes you asked for."

"Grazie, Franco. Is everything set for tomorrow?"

"Yes. The photographer will be in and out quickly." He stepped over to look in the bathroom. "The bathroom in here has a nice white wall we can use as a backdrop. I didn't use our usual guy. I called in an old favor just like you asked.

"Sir..." Franco hesitated for a moment, considering his question. "Did Nikko really do that to her?" Thomas turned and glared at him. No matter how upset he was at his brother, he would not let anyone else judge him.

Thomas leveled his gaze. "Fuori di qui."

"Yes, sir. I, uh...I meant no disrespect." Franco backed out of the room and into the hall.

"Okay, Sophie." Thomas walked over to her bedside after Franco left. "After the physical therapist brings you back in the morning, I'll tell the nurse you'd like to get dressed, I have a makeup artist coming. She will try to cover all your injuries. Then Franco will bring in the photographer who will take some pictures. So, get some rest—you will need your strength if we are going to pull this off." She just nodded. He could see she was tired. Her eyes closed, and he went to his chair and resumed making phone calls.

The next morning, everything went just as Thomas had planned. The nurse helped her change into the black slacks and a silk top Franco had brought for her passport and driver's license photos. The makeup artist helped her put on her wig and contacts and did wonders with her face; she almost looked normal. The photographer arrived, and they took the photos against a clean, white wall in the bathroom. It wasn't perfect, but it would do the trick. After the photographer left, Thomas took her outside in the wheelchair, she hadn't been out of that room since the beating, she needed fresh air. When they got back the nurse helped Sophie change herself into a pair of pajamas instead of the awful hospital gown and slipped back into a restful sleep.

Nikko would be back Saturday, so plans needed to continue as smoothly as they had so far. Thomas had planned carefully, and he knew he was ready, but he was less convinced that Sophie was up to the entirety of the tasks involved. *She is still so weak*, he thought to himself, *but time is not a luxury we can afford.* As he reviewed the plan over and over again in his head, her eyes opened, and he moved closer so that she could see him.

"Good afternoon, sleepy head."

Sophie smiled, or at least attempted to. With the wires fixed to her jaw, she could only move her face muscles so much without pain. But he saw the smile in her eyes. He was going to miss her.

"We need to go over the plan again. We have to do this on Friday, or it will be too late. Are you sure you can do this?" She nodded.

He continued. "I have set up a time to meet with the police at 3 pm on Friday. They have been trying to get me to come in and put my statement in writing even though I wasn't there. I think they want me to turn on my brother. Sophie, you know you can never go to the police about this or anything else involving the family organization. The only hope you have of my father not searching the four corners of the earth for you, is if he wholeheartedly believes that you won't betray him. Even then, I'm not sure Nikko will ever stop. His interest in you is something entirely...different." She motioned for a pad to write on. He read the question she wrote.

'**Do you think I should leave a note saying I have no intention of betraying them?**'

After a moment, he replied, "I'm not sure it will do any good. There's gonna be a big ruckus at first either way. I think only time and your silence will convince them."

The door opened, startling the two allies. As Detective Cartwright and Detective Mahoney moved into the room, Thomas stood to his feet covertly crumpling the note paper and putting it in his pocket. "Detectives. I thought I was clear when I said I would see you Friday."

Det. Cartwright spoke while Mahoney stood like a sentinel at the door. "We are not here to speak to you Mr. Morano. We never got a statement from Ms. Star."

"You know she can't talk." Thomas stared at the two officers with incredulity.

"The doctor said she was well enough to answer questions. She can nod or write her answers on a notepad, so long as we get some answers from Ms. Star, firsthand." Cartwright turned to Sophie, "Is that alright with you, Ms. Star?" She nodded. She knew she had to do this if she was going to get them off her back. Detective Cartwright took out his pad and pen.

"Maybe you should go grab a cup of coffee, Mr. Morano, so we can talk to her alone." Sophie shook her head and took hold of Thomas' hand.

"Nuh! Nuh!" Sophie sounded through the aluminum wires around her mouth. She let go of Thomas' hand and placed her palms together in a pleading motion. "Stay," she managed the basic sounds for the detectives.

"Okay, ma'am, if that's your wish. Now, can you tell us how you got these injuries?" She made a tumbling motion with her arms.

"Are you saying you fell?" She nodded. Cartwright glanced toward his partner at the door, then back to the hospital bed. "Ms. Star, Doctor Jones assured us these injuries could not have come from a simple fall." She took the pad from Thomas to write on.

'**I bounced down the entire flight of concrete steps and into the basement. I tripped on the first step.**'

Cartwright replaced the cap of his pen with a sigh. "You know, Ms. Star, I've been doing this job for a long time. Your injuries are consistent with someone who took a severe beating. Is anyone forcing you to lie to us?" She shook her head no. "We can protect you, Ms. Star, but only if you tell us the truth."

"I think that's enough detective. You asked, and she answered. It seems obvious that you are trying to get her to blame my brother for this. Now, you got her statement, and I will be down on Friday to give you mine. Why don't you guys take a hike and let the poor girl rest?"

They largely ignored Thomas' words but moved toward the door, nonetheless. Before they left, detective Mahoney spoke; "Ms. Star, we are only trying to help you. Whoever did this to you will likely do it again unless he's stopped."

Sophie wrote on the pad and held it up for Thomas to read to them. "Thank you for your concern, but this was an accident. That's all."

"I'm sorry you don't trust us." Cartwright held up his card, "in case you change your mind." He walked over and set it on the nightstand, then the two men opened the door and walked out.

Thomas drew in a heavy breath. "You did good Sophie." He pulled the notes from earlier out of his pocket, dropped them in the hazardous waste bin like the others, then plopped down in the chair.

A few steps outside the door, Mahoney and Cartwright stopped to regroup. Mahoney spoke first. "She will never talk with a Morano hovering around her — we have to get her alone."

"Well, the DEA says Nikko's out of town," Cartwright answered. "We better act soon or we might not get her to talk at all. Let's try again on Friday. While you take Thomas Morano's statement at the precinct, I'll come visit Ms. Star."

"Sounds like a plan." Mahoney replied. "You hungry? Let's get outta here."

Thomas paced the room, trying not to let his nerves get the better of him. After Sophie had finished her breakfast, a physical therapy assistant wheeled her down to the exercise room to see if they could get her upright and walking a few steps. She was still weak, but she must be able to walk out on her own to the rendezvous where he can pick her up and take her to the private hospital. His alibi only works if she leaves while he is somewhere no one can dispute. He can't trust even Franco with the location of the rehab. Nikko will be home on Saturday, so this must go off without a hitch. The phone rings.

"Ciao?"

"Thomas. I'm glad you're there, brother."

"Where else would I be? You told me to take care of her till you got back."

"Right, you're a loyal brother and I appreciate you, but I called to tell Sophie that I'll be home Friday night. Put the phone to her ear."

"She's at therapy right now."

"I've chartered a plane. I'm so anxious to see her! Well, maybe I will just surprise her—in fact, don't tell her. It'll be a great surprise."

"Sure, that will be a great surprise." Thomas whispered with his hand racking through his perfectly coiffed hair.

"See you Friday, fratellino."

Thomas threw the phone across the room. *This is impossible!* He had given himself an extra day to mitigate circumstances if she couldn't physically walk out on her own. But now, there was no choice. She had to do this exactly the way he planned.

Sophie was back in an hour. The therapy assistant had to help her into bed because she was so weak from the session. When the assistant left, Thomas looked at her and made the decision. "You can't do this. You'll never be able to walk out of here on your own."

Sophie motioned for her pad, and he read what she wrote out loud. "I can do this." He put his head to hers and just held it there for a moment. He couldn't tell her Nikko was coming home early. He was hoping, if she failed Friday, one more day of therapy would improve her odds of making it on Saturday. But the added pressure of knowing there was only one shot wouldn't help her frame of mind.

There was another piece of bad news, however, that Thomas felt he did need to tell her, and now seemed as good a time as any.

"Sophie, I need to tell you something, but first, I have to ask you if you trust me completely."

Sophie grabbed her pad and quickly scribbled, 'of course!'

Thomas drew a breath and continued; "In order for you to follow my instructions to the tee, your head will have to be completely clear. I'm going to tell the nurse that you want your pain medication cut. I'm going to tell her that addiction runs in your family and that you are concerned about the amount of pain meds you have been taking."

Sophie soaked this information up for a moment before putting the pencil to her pad with resolve. She simply wrote, 'whatever it takes.' Those were the words that Thomas was hoping to see.

With him and her both on the same page, Thomas returned his attention to Sophie's physical strength. He stood her up and tried helping her walk a few steps at a time, hoping to build on what therapy had done. Watching her struggle to just take three or four steps, shot fear through him that his plan wasn't going to work. He began to insist that she eat more at each meal. He stayed with her that night, knowing that it would be their last time together.

Dangerous Obsession

CHAPTER THREE

Thomas woke early, his mind racing with details. When breakfast came in, he encouraged her to eat it all. "Sophie, you have me worried. If you can't do it, then just stay here. I'll look for you at the rendezvous point first, but if you're not there, I can come back here and get you."

'You know you can't do that. If people see you taking me out of here, Nikko will find out,' she wrote.

He took her hand, "I don't care. You're not going back to him."

She looked in his eyes, **'I can do this,'** her hand dropped the pen.

The therapy assistant returned to take her for her session. She came back just before lunch, exhausted. He wouldn't let her sleep until she ate all her food.

After lunch, he waited until she fell asleep, then he went to the nurse's station. He looked for Velma, and he found her working on the computer.

He got her attention, "Can I talk to you in private for a moment."

"Sure." They moved to a quiet spot.

"I have to leave for a few hours this afternoon, but Sophie expressed to me a concern about her pain medication. She confided in me privately that her father was addicted to drugs in her childhood, and the affliction seems to run in her family. She told me that she would like to start reducing her pain medication unless she specifically asks for more."

The nurse smiled at his compassion. "Well, I don't think that will be a problem, the doctor's orders say to give as needed. We have many patients who share her concerns." Velma had kind eyes. In them, Thomas could imagine the young girl who once dreamed of becoming a nurse.

Thomas added, "and she also said she would like to change into a pair of pants and a loose top instead of the gown – that is, if the examinations are basically over. She said it would help her feel more human again." Again, Velma said that she saw no reason that she couldn't oblige the request. He thanked her and she started to leave, but then she turned and put her hand gently on his arm.

"I see how much you care for her. She is lucky to have you." He could tell she knew something was afoot amidst all these requests. Nevertheless, maintaining his stoic air, he went back to Sophie's room to find her still sleeping. He hated to wake her, but he had to leave, and she had to be awake so she could get ready.

"Sophie, you have to wake up." Her eyes fluttered open, and she turned to face him with those beautiful hazel eyes filled with sparkling green flecks. "I'm leaving in 5 minutes. I asked the nurse to cut your pain medication. I know it's past time for another dose, I'm sure you're starting to feel it." She just nodded. "I hate to do it, but you have to be alert. You know where to go. It's only two blocks down, and you must be there by 4:30. If I'm held up at the police station, just wait. I will be there." She took his hand and kissed it. He swallowed the lump in his throat.

Thomas walked out of the hospital knowing there was no turning back.

The nurse had just left after helping Sophie into her change of clothes. Sophie was watching the clock, waiting for 3:30 pm, and trying her best to rally the courage needed for this trek. In physical therapy that morning, she had only walked ten steps before collapsing, from pain and exhaustion. Her therapist thought she did great, but they had no idea what she was planning. She could certainly feel a difference in the absence of the pain killers, but she was thinking clearly for the first time since the beating. Sophie looked at the ring on her finger, slipped it off and slapped it on the nightstand by the bed.

Sophie had carefully and attentively studied the layout of the fourth floor every time they took her out in the wheelchair or down to physical therapy. She knew that if she took the elevator from this floor, she would have to pass the nurses' station. That wouldn't work for her, which meant she would have to go down one flight of stairs and catch the elevator on the third floor. Finally, ready to make her move, she peeked out the door, looked both ways, and slipped out to the right. Leaning on the wall for support, she made it to the stairwell door.

At the same time Sophie was making her escape, Detective Cartwright was opening the door to her room. In his peripheral vision he thought he saw a familiar figure moving carefully through the stairwell door. He glanced in Sophie's room, noticing that she wasn't in there, and chose to discreetly pursue the woman on the stairs. *Where could she be going?* He knew from his conversation with the nurses that she was in no condition to be leaving the hospital.

With every jarring step down, shooting pain tortured Sophie's body. She leaned on the cold metal handrails to help support her body. *Just one step*, she kept telling herself. *Just one more step.* Sophie could feel herself growing woozy. She couldn't afford to faint; she had to keep going. *You can do this, Sophie.* Finally, the last step. She opened the door and rested for a minute. She made it this far.

Detective Cartwright heard the echo of a door closing on the level directly below him. He continued quickly down the stairs, skipping as many as he could.

After a brief rest, she regained enough energy to move to the elevator. The doors opened with a clinical sounding bell, and her eyes met hospital patrons packed in the elevator. She felt them staring at her as she waited for them to exit, but she quickly stepped in and pushed the button for the first-floor parking garage. She was thankful she didn't have to take the stairs three more flights down, and she doubted that she could have.

Cartwright couldn't see Sophie anymore, but it was clear now that she intended to leave the hospital. He heard the elevator doors closing as he ran to catch up to her. Cartwright didn't know which floor she was going to, but common sense dictated that she would have to be going down to leave the hospital. She was clearly trying to be discreet. He decided that waiting for the elevator was an exercise in futility, and he dashed back to the stairwell.

Sophie leaned against the elevator wall. Her face reflected in the polished brass interior. It was the first time she had seen her face since the beating. Her own reflection startled her; she didn't recognize herself. Her eyes and face were still badly swollen, even after a week. The bruises were a rainbow of colors. She looked like a monster, and her mouth maintained an awkward shape from being wired shut. She wanted to scream, but she had neither the energy nor the physical capability. The doctor kept telling her she would fully recover, but she wondered if one's face ever looked the same after a traumatic beating like this. Tears started streaming down, and she began to emit muffled sobs. Then she realized how much unwanted attention she would get if the elevator doors opened and there were others waiting to get on. Sophie had to stop crying, she couldn't draw attention to herself. She wiped away her tears just before the elevator doors opened, keeping her head down and her eyes focused on the floor. Taking a tentative step outward, she looked to see which direction led to the ambulance bay. She turned left through two glass doors and kept on walking, just as Thomas had told her to. She made it as far as the southwest entrance to the ambulance bay and stopped to rest against the cold cement structure. Suddenly, the exertion caught up with her; *I can't do this Thomas. I can't take another step. Just let me die.*

Detective Cartwright stepped smartly out of the stairwell and glanced in all directions. *Where did she go?* It was obvious now that Sophie was making an escape, but why, and to where? He would have to make a guess and hope that years of experience and a detective's intuition would serve him now. There were two exits from the parking garage on the northeast side. He ran out onto W. 114th street facing Notre Dame and looked around. He didn't see her. *What now?* He thought about calling Mahoney, but there was clearly no time. He ran back into the structure.

No matter how much she wanted to quit, Sophie knew she had to keep going. Seeing her face in the elevator solidified the reality; it was only a fluke that Nikko hadn't killed her. No matter what, there could never be a "next time." She remembered Thomas' promise that he would pick her up at the hospital if she couldn't make it to the park but getting back upstairs would be an unthinkable ordeal. Regardless, she felt comforted in knowing that Thomas wouldn't let Nikko ever get to her again.

Sophie straightened herself and headed down the street toward Morningside Park. Franco hadn't brought her any kind of jacket. It could have been an oversight or maybe he thought it would arouse suspicions.

Although the sun was out, it was early April in the upper west side of Manhattan, and a damp spring chill hung in the air, moving across her skin, through her muscles, and settling into her bones. Thank goodness that the towering cathedral of Saint John the Divine blocked the south wind. She stared wistfully up at the high gothic buttresses. *Are you watching up there?* Sophie was barely managing to put one foot in front of the other. At the intersection of W 113th and Morningside Drive, she looked to her left and saw an empty bench against the stone wall, marking the entrance to the park. *I can make it that far, Sophie...right?*

It had taken the detective a few minutes to put himself in Sophie's shoes and figure out there was only one other exit she could have taken from St. Luke's. Eventually, he emerged from the ambulance bay of the emergency department just in time to see Sophie crossing the street for the park. *There she is! Where is she going?* He grew more confused with her journey; he could see she was struggling just to walk across the street. As Cartwright grew closer, he could see she was mere seconds from collapsing. Even in her clearly pathetic condition, none of the Friday afternoon pedestrians or commuters offered any help. *That's New York for ya.'* Even here on the upper west side, most people were too afraid to help a stranger in need. He ran toward her and wrapped his arm around her torso to support her weight. She groaned through the wires as he touched her ribs, but the two kept moving forward across the street. They soon reached the bench, and he set her down.

"Ms. Star, where do you think you're going? You're clearly not ready to leave the hospital yet. Did you clear this with your doctor?" She looked up, not knowing who helped her. When she felt herself being helped across the street, she suspected divine intervention and was surprised to find Detective Cartwright next to her on the bench. She motioned for the notepad that the detective kept in his jacket. He removed the pad and a pen, handing both to her.

Cartwright read her words as she wrote. "**You know he will kill me someday if I stay.**"

The detective quickly replied. "No, we can protect you. If you tell us what really happened, and you find the courage to face him in court, we can put him behind bars for a long time."

Sophie wrote frantically now with what was left of her energy. '**Nikko's family has money and lawyers. This would be the first offense on record. He will only get a slap on the wrist.**'

"Look at you, Ms. Star. You can't even walk. How can you do this without our help?"

'**Just two more blocks,**' she wrote. '**Someone is coming for me.**'

"Who is coming?"

Sophie pointed to the word she already wrote. '**Someone.**' Cartwright could see that the writing had drained her.

"You won't make it, you know that?"

'**Then help me, please.**' She looked at him through those watery, swollen eyes. Tears falling down her cheeks and off her chin, from the pain she was in.

The detective forgot who he was for a moment. He was breaking a cardinal rule; letting himself get personally involved.

Sophie wrote again, but more slowly and with a strained effort, now. '**Just help me to the park. I'll be okay.**' She started to get up on her own. He could see that her plan was going to happen with or without his help. Cartwright took an oath a decade ago to protect and serve, and he planned to make good on both promises today.

"Alright. Where are we going?"

'People's Garden. Two blocks south. Bench by Peace Fountain.' He read her now barely legible writing, aloud.

Cartwright got up, put her left arm over his neck and wrapped his right arm around her waist. They moved up W 113th street and took a left down Amsterdam Ave. Sophie dragged her feet one in front of the other until they got to the location. For a moment, he thought about the comedy of their appearance. They looked like two old friends stumbling home from a late night out. Within a few difficult minutes, they reached the fountain, and he sat Sophie down on the circular cement bench which surrounded the sculpture. She motioned for the pen.

'Thank you,' were the only two words she had the energy to write.

"I really hope you have made the right decision. It's not too late for you to..."

She touched his arm gently. Although her jaw was wired in a fixed position, he knew she was smiling at him underneath. Her smile was one of relief, gratitude, and perhaps a little sadness. But her energy was waning fast.

Cartwright sat by her for a few moments, lost silently in thought. It was likely true that Nikko wouldn't see much jail time for this; maybe none. And for all their good intentions, there was no reliable and durable way for the police to protect her. If the FBI got involved, they might put her in witness protection, but not unless she was vital to their ongoing investigation of the Morano family. A domestic violence charge was a fourth-degree assault in New York State, and that would certainly fail to spur the interest of federal investigators. As far as the FBI, DEA, and any other organized crime investigators were concerned, Sophie Star was no more than an accountant for a family restaurant and Nikko Morano's new toy. These positions hardly warranted federal protection.

Sophie tapped his arm, pulling him from his thoughts. She pointed at the pad she had written on. **'Please leave now. You can't be here.'** Despite the brusque nature of her words, he knew it was from fear he'd see who was picking her up, not lack of appreciation.

"Okay, Ms. Star. As you wish. Here is my card if things don't work out as..." She put one hand up and pulled out the card that he had left in her hospital room from the pocket of her pants. She showed it to him. He smiled meekly. That's when he noticed the engagement ring was no longer on her finger.

Cartwright walked away as she asked, but he had no intention of leaving her alone in a public park until he could assure her safe departure. He would stay out of sight until her ride came. There was a small sloping hillside behind the benches which led to a sprawling, beautifully manicured lawn. Detective Cartwright leaned against a tree behind this hill and watched as Sophie waited. Nearly an hour passed before he saw any movement by the bench. It was hard to see who it was from this distance, but his height and the way he carried himself seemed familiar. When the stranger arrived at Sophie's side, he scanned the area revealing his face to the watching detective. It was Thomas Morano. *What in the world is he doing getting between Nikko and his fiancé?* Cartwright watched as they spoke for a moment, then Thomas scooped her up in his arms and carried her to his car. As Thomas opened the rear passenger door and placed Sophie on the back seat, it looked to Cartwright like Sophie might have been unconscious. Thomas quickly jumped into the driver's seat of the car and drove off.

Detective Cartwright was more confident now that he did the right thing by aiding her escape, but what to make of Thomas Morano's involvement, he wasn't sure. He also realized that his partner, Detective Mahoney, would likely have questions but

Cartwright could never tell him what he knew. One thing was sure; if Nikko Morano ever found Sophie, or if Nikko found out that his brother helped her escape him, Sophie, or Thomas, or both, would wind up missing or turn up dead. Just like his cousin Jimmy, whose body they found this morning. Time of death was determined to be the night after her beating. He tore out all the notes that Sophie had written in his book and put them in a dumpster on the way back to his car and headed back to the precinct.

It took almost three hours to get to the private rehab center. Sophie slept for most of the trip, but Thomas had lots of information he still had to tell her before they got there, so he woke her up with about thirty minutes left of their trip.

"Sophie...wake up." He heard her groan. "We're almost there. I've called ahead, and a man named Dr. Gladstone will be out back to take you in. He's a very old friend of mine, but others who work there know my father, so I can't be seen. You can trust him completely, but you must do *exactly* as he says. Some of the staff aren't as trustworthy. He's going to have one of his nurses dye your hair tomorrow. I have a bag for you in the trunk. It has a new driver's license, passport, social security card, and an airline ticket inside along with a few changes of clothes, a new purse, and a few other things. You know, the movies make these relocation things seem so easy, but it is nothing short of a miracle that this came together the way it did."

Sophie waved her hand in a writing motion. Thomas leaned over to his glove box and pulled out a notepad, then took a pen from the middle console. He handed it to her.

Sophie wrote on the pad. **'Where am I going?'** He tried to read while keeping his eyes on the road.

"You're going to a small town on the southern border of Washington state, called Lake View. There are five burner phones in the bag. You can call me every Sunday while you're here. Only use the phone a few times then throw it away. I bought my own burner phone and put the number on the contact list of each of your phones, but I put it under the name "Angel." Once you move to Washington, we can't have any more contact. You understand, this only works if no one knows how to track you. The rehab center has been paid in full for three months. The doctor said you should be fully recovered by then. I had a copy made of your medical records with your new name on it. You just be careful and keep repeating your new name over and over in your mind. You also have an account set up at a small community credit union in Lake View. Stay away from national banks; my brother has connections to most of the big ones. The account number is in your bag. There is three hundred thousand in the account and twenty thousand cash, in your new purse. That should be enough to set you up with your own accounting business if that's what you want. Just keep a low and local profile."

Another note came over the seat. **'I can't take it. It's too much.'** Thomas knew she would object, but she needed the startup money to build a new life. Besides, she was leaving at least that much behind. He would have given her more, but after paying for a new identity and the private hospital, it was the last of the cash from his safe. He didn't dare make any suspicious withdrawals from his account.

"I know you have a problem with this, but you are going to need that money. Besides what use is it to me? I've blown more than that on a trip to Rome or Paris. You are so much more important to me than the money. You know that don't you?"

Sophie was sitting up now looking at him through the rearview mirror. She was beginning to tear up and she simply nodded her head. If only things could have been different.

41

Thomas pulled up to the back door of the facility and saw the doctor waiting. He turned off the engine, opened the trunk, took out her suitcase, and opened the rear passenger door. Gently, he picked her up again and carried her to a nearby wheelchair. Her arms were around his neck and her head was on his chest. She was fully crying now. He started to put her down, but she tightened her grip. Tears of his own escaped his eyes and started down his face. He swallowed the lump.

"Sophie, I have to go, I need to get back to pick Nikko up at the airport. I must be with him when he discovers that you are missing. He is going to be furious, and I should be there."

Sophie let go and wiped the tears from his eyes and he gently kissed her on the lips. He knew the tears weren't just for him. She was leaving everything she had and everything she knew. She was going to be all by herself starting over from scratch. The fact that she was an only child of dead parents would make it easier to disappear, but she now had no one to turn to for help, either. "I will truly miss you," he said. He turned away from her, got back in the car and drove off.

As the car sped away from the rehab center, he whispered to himself, "I will always love you."

When he returned to the island three hours later, his phone was filled with missed calls from the hospital. He had waited to put the battery back in so it wouldn't ping off any towers as he traveled. The hospital had discovered that Sophie was gone. They searched the hospital and all the grounds but hadn't been able to find her. With her daring escape now in his past, Thomas returned to his role of brother and confidant and waited for Nikko as his plane landed.

When Thomas told Nikko that Sophie had disappeared from the hospital, he insisted Thomas take him there immediately. Thomas accused the hospital staff of incompetence—luckily, Velma had been at lunch when Sophie left, but the glance she gave Thomas let him know she would never tell his part in it. They assured him that there was no reason to believe she was kidnapped. She had left her engagement ring in the room, which indicated that she had likely left of her own volition. At this news, Thomas smiled to himself.

Dangerous Obsession

CHAPTER FOUR
EIGHT MONTHS LATER

Lexi didn't know how long she had been sitting in the corner on the floor, with a knife in her hand and her eyes wide open. The reflex seemed automatic when the lights went out. Fear... no, pure terror, kept her paralyzed to that spot. Lexi was sure that this was it; Nikko had finally found her. She remembered hearing someone knocking on her door a couple of times and calling her name, but there was no way she was moving from that spot. Lexi's mind kept replaying that cold, April night lying on the cellar floor, beaten to a bloody pulp, her mind replaying the beating over and over again.

Lexi's mind was slowly beginning to release her from the fear paralyzing her. The lights had come back on, and the thunder and lightning stopped. She heard banging on the door accompanied this time by Suzie's voice franticly calling her name. Lexi got up, saw the knife in her hand, set it down, and walked to the door to let her in.

"Lexi. Hi! Are you alright? I know how jumpy you get when a bad storm comes. I came to check on you when the power went out, but you didn't answer."

"I'm fine Suzie. Thank you."

"You don't look fine. You look like you just saw a ghost. Look —you're shaking!" Suzie took hold of Lexi's arm and directed her to sit on the couch. She went into the kitchen to get some water and noticed the butcher knife sitting on the table.

She came back with the water. "Here, drink this." Lexi obliged her.

Lexi Westin bought this duplex a month after coming to Lake View. She used some of the seed money Thomas had given her as a down payment. She had been staying in an old hotel turned apartment complex in the city center, called the Hotel Monticello. When she found herself needing to move out, she got into the duplex right away. It was only ten years old with a sturdy brick construction. Each half had two bedrooms, a larger than average kitchen, and a nice sized master bathroom. She left its management to a management company so the other tenant wouldn't bother her with maintenance issues. Plus, collecting rent would be awkward if she ended up being friends with a tenant. The arrangement was working out great so far. She received Suzie's application a month after she moved in. and Suzie turned out to be a great tenant and an even better friend.

"Lexi, I know you're afraid of someone. Have I ever told you that I hear your nightmares through the wall?" She had told her. Many times.

"I even heard you scream a few times. I came to check on you once, but you didn't answer the door. You know you can talk to me about anything, right?" But Lexi knew she couldn't talk to anyone, ever. Instead, her solution would be to get soundproof insulation installed in her bedroom walls when Suzie went to visit her folks next month.

"I pray for you every day, Lexi. I know how crippling fear can be. I suffered with anxiety for years before I left it all at the foot of the cross. If you would just come to church with me, I know you can be delivered from all this fear."

"Suzie." Lexi took a deep breath. Suzie had been inviting her to church every week since she moved in. "Let me think about it."

"Okay. You do that. But I just know you'll find the peace you need. Anyway, I have to get to work. That was quite a storm last night, huh?" Lexi just nodded, but her gaze was fixed at a nearby wall. Suzie gave her a hug and left.

Lexi opened her accounting office in a little strip mall with a faux-Germanic motif. Or was it Swiss? She couldn't really tell. It was a little odd, but the buildings were new, and it was on the busiest street in town. She had only been open for eight months, but she had already managed to get enough clients to break even. *Maybe in a few more months, I might actually make a profit*, she thought to herself. As long as she had the business built up enough to support herself when Thomas' money ran out, she would be fine. Or, at least, she hoped.

"Thomas, are you telling me there is still not one shred of evidence indicating where Sophie went?"

"That's right, Nikko. I talked to the FBI last week. Their kidnapping investigation is still open, but no leads. They keep saying that women like her walk away all the time. Without some hard evidence soon, they will close her case file and assume she doesn't want to be found."

"They said 'women like her', what's that supposed to mean? Someone had to have helped her. No way did she have the street smarts to disappear like that."

"You've looked at everyone, Nikko. Our competition had no reason to take her. You would know by now if they did. You've interrogated everyone in our organization, some of them rather brutally I might add. And if she had gone to the law with all she knows about us and the organization, we would all be in jail by now. It appears she just wanted out of the relationship. If you can't find a way to let this go, it's gonna eat you up inside."

Nikko jumped up from his seat and lunged at Thomas, red faced and pointing his finger a few inches from Thomas' chest.

"Don't ever say that again! Non sempre!"

"Come on, Nikko. Why else would she stay gone? Papa has told you to let this go. If he finds out you are still obsessed with her, he won't be happy."

"Well, be sure not to tell him then."

"Nikko, I don't get you. You're dating Sylvie now. Papa wants you to marry her, and so does mama. She will make a great wife and mother."

"That's not what I want. I want more than that from my wife. I want what's mine. I want Sophie."

"Well, she's gone, and I'm getting tired of wasting my time looking. I got a job to do in this family, too, ya know?" Thomas walked away from the family kitchen table where they ate breakfast with their parents every morning. Their mother and father had already finished breakfast and were preparing for their day, upstairs.

Thomas walked outside to his car. He had almost convinced his papa to dissociate from the criminal side of the family business and expand the legitimate side. He had been slowly trying to coerce his father toward completely legitimizing the organization. It was only his brother, and some of his unruly "associates" who stood in the way of that plan. Nikko loved the adrenaline rush of being his father's second or more like a consigliere in their family run organization.

Thomas hadn't heard from Sophie since she left the rehab center. He missed hearing her voice even though he was the one that insisted they cut all contact. One private investigator got close to finding her in those first three months. One of the nurses reported that someone who matched Sophie's description was staying there. But, by the time the investigator got to the center to question her, she no longer worked there. He then thanked the investigator for the information and told him he no longer needed his services, giving him a large severance check.

Across the continent, Lexi finally gave in to Suzie's pleading and agreed to accompany her to church. "Come on Lexi. We'll be late if we don't get moving." Lexi emerged from her bedroom in a soft mint top, something she could never wear with her natural auburn hair, and a pair of black slacks. When she saw that Suzie was wearing a more conservative skirt and blouse, Lexi wanted to change. But Suzie said there was no dress code.

The parking lot was small but full. The church building was very old, but it was well maintained. Suzie led her to a seat about halfway back from the raised platform which held a well-crafted, white, wooden pulpit. It appeared that the sanctuary held approximately two hundred people, and it was nearly full. It wasn't extravagantly decorated like the Catholic churches she went to with Nikko a few times, but it had a nice soothing color scheme. There were large windows lining both sides of the building which were covered with vertical blinds that matched the chairs. When the praise music started, the words were displayed on two large television screens so that everyone could sing along if they wanted.

After the music director sat down, the minister stepped up to the pulpit. He was a fit looking man who must have been in his late fifties.

"This morning," he began, "I would like to continue my sermon on King David, a man after God's own heart. Now, I discussed all his strengths last week, but now I want to introduce you to some of his weaknesses. Even though David loved God with his whole heart, he was a man, and he made mistakes. Sometimes big mistakes, but David knew how to repent. You see, that's the key! He knew, when he failed, how to get down on his knees and turn back toward God." The minister went on to preach about David's affair with a married woman and how David arranged to have her husband put to death when he found out the woman was pregnant.

"David knew there would be a consequence for his sin. Even though he knew God had forgiven him, sin has consequences. And sometimes you have a chance to make them right, and sometimes you can't undo the worldly damage of your actions. In David's case, he couldn't bring back the woman's husband."

Lexi could relate to that idea—all sin has its consequences. In fact, she was paying right now for the lifestyle she had chosen. The lifestyle she had lived in New York was not what one would consider righteous. When she started working for the Morano family, she didn't know the way they truly made their vast fortune. It didn't take long to figure it out. But when she started dating Nikko, she certainly knew his reputation, and she dated him anyway. She did not consider herself a bad person, but consequences for actions were now her reality. Forgiveness is what she wanted—to be forgiven and start over fresh. She wanted to be born a new creature, just as Suzie had said.

The minister went on to remind his congregation that only God can give you eternal peace and deliver you from your sin. He sent His son to pay the price for our sins on the cross, to face the ultimate consequence so that we didn't have to. The minister explained the pain and the torture that Jesus suffered as he was whipped and crucified. "He took it all for you," he said. "Even if you, alone, were the only one who needed to be saved from your sins, he would have done it."

For some reason that thought made her cry. Suddenly, Lexi felt something like warm honey inside of her, and it flowed from the top of her head to the tips of her toes—it was peace. It was like nothing she had ever felt before. She didn't know how she knew it was peace, but she knew it. Near the end of his sermon, when the minister asked if anyone wanted to come forward and give their heart to a Savior who had given His all for them, she stood up and came forward.

As Lexi and Suzie were leaving the sanctuary that day, an older woman stopped Lexi and handed her a box with a new Bible in it. "The Lord led me to buy a new Bible this week and bring it to church. It must be for you." She gave Lexi a hug, then turned and left.

The ladies went out to eat after church. Lexi suddenly had so many questions for Suzie. Salvation had been offered to her, and she welcomed it in. Somewhere in the recesses of her mind it felt like coming home, familiar, and new at the same time. She had questions and Suzie had an answer for most of them.

"Lexi," Suzie resolved, "the best thing I can tell you is this — 'My people are destroyed for lack of knowledge' [Hosea 4:6]. That scripture was drilled into me as a child and it's true. You must read the word of God. If you want to know about Him, it's all in there. It also says that, 'the Word became flesh and dwelt among us' [John 1:14]. Jesus and the Word are one. If you want to know the Man, get to know the Word." When she got back to her living room, Lexi sat down on her couch and opened her new gift.

Dangerous Obsession

CHAPTER FIVE
ONE YEAR LATER

Mark was coming toward her. "Lexi! We're over here. What took you so long?"

"Suzie and I had to clean up the mess that the kids made in Sunday school. The project was fun but messy." Suzie and Lexi looked at each other and laughed.

They followed Mark to the tables where everyone was already seated. The waitress was there taking orders. Lexi thought that these Sunday lunch gatherings were so much fun. She considered these people her very close friends. And to think that, less than two years ago, she barely knew anyone in this new place.

Lexi often thought of the pure joy and peace this was, compared to the drama of her old life. Today, her mind had been wandering during Pastor's sermon; it kept going back to the first sermon she heard. He had said when we repent and lay our sins at the Cross, God forgives because the price to cover those sins was paid in full by His Son. He never remembers them again. But he also went on to say some sins have consequences on this earth; sometimes jail, sometimes divorce, sometimes worse. He said some mistakes can be fixed and some can't. And that was the part that her mind wouldn't let go of. Lexi was the accountant for the Morano organization, but she was also Nikko's chief strategist, she found more stable suppliers, and she extended his reach further while doubling his business. She couldn't undo the harm his drugs had done with her help, but maybe she could undo the organization that she helped to build in order to prevent further harm. That thought had been haunting her as she wondered whether it was a pipe dream or could be made into a reality.

Suzie elbowed her, "the waitress is waiting for your order."

"Oh."

Lexi spent the rest of the day asking God for direction. There had to be a way.

Thomas got out of the limo and reached back to take his mother's hand and help her out. Nikko came out behind her. He wrapped his arm around his mother, escorting her up the steps and into the foyer of the home she would now occupy without their father.

"Grazie, miei cari figli. I don't know how I would have made it through today without you." She patted Nikko on the cheek and went to Thomas and did the same. "I'm going upstairs to rest."

"I'll come get you when dinner is ready, Mama," Thomas called out to her as she was ascending the stairs. She just raised her hand in acknowledgement.

Nikko followed Thomas into the den. Thomas took off his suit coat, folded it, and laid it on the back of a chair. Next, he took off his tie and put it in the coat pocket. Nikko hung his coat in the foyer closet. He always took meticulous care of his possessions. He loosened his tie and went to the built in bar to pour himself a drink. "Want one?"

Thomas held up a hand. "No, grazie."

Thomas was lost in the memory of a promise. His parents had called a family meeting less than a year ago to let the boys know that their father had been diagnosed with cancer. He laid out his last will and testament, and he explained his reasons for what was in there. He told them that if they had objections, they should bring them up now because he was not going to have his family fighting over it when he was gone. The house and all his money went to their mother. All the businesses, legal or not, were to be run as an equal partnership between the two brothers. There were a few conditions, however.

"Thomas when I'm gone, I want you to be Nikko's consigliere until he can find someone you both feel you can trust."

"Papa," Thomas protested, *"you know I don't want anything to do with that side of the business."*

"I know, but we're a family first, and he will need you. Be a good brother and do it just until he can find someone." Thomas still didn't like the idea, but he knew he needed to respect his father's wishes.

"Nikko, I want you to consider your brother's proposal of going legit. You could open some casinos together since neither of you have felony convictions. The gaming commission won't dare deny your application without apparent cause."

Now it was Nikko's turn. *"Papa, you know my side of the business has brought in half a billion since I took over for the family, while Thomas was lucky to clear $135 million!"*

"You mean since Sophie restructured and reorganized the business for you. Don't you?" Nikko didn't respond. He just slumped into a chair. His father walked over to where he sat.

"Nikko, my boy, if you get caught, what good is your money in jail? Now, I don't judge you for wanting to continue what I started; it's how we got were we are, after all. But maybe your brother is right. And you've already made more money than you'll ever be able to spend in two lifetimes."

"You know it's not about the money, Papa."

His father smiled. *"I know that all too well, figlio. I can still taste the adrenaline rush and feel the power like it was yesterday. capisco."* He returned his attention to Thomas for a moment. *"Thomas, do you promise that you will do as I have asked?"*

"Promesso, Papa."

"Nikko, I have one other stipulation." Mr. Morano went back to his chair before continuing. He knew this would cause some conflict. *"You need to get married. You think I don't know you are still looking for Sophie? Your obsession with that woman has to stop right this minute!"*

His mother chimed in, *"Sylvie is a nice Italian girl."*

Nikko's tone perceptibly changed, now. *"I can pick my own wife, grazie Mama."*

His father was quick to snap to her defense. *"Don't talk to your mother that way! You are to marry in the next two years, or I will shut you down! Mi capisci, Nikko?"* Thomas could see this coming; his father had become increasingly agitated with Nikko because he was still searching for Sophie.

Nikko hadn't answered his father, so he continued. *"Sophie hasn't gone to the police or the FBI. She just left because of your foolish actions. Her leaving was a great loss to this organization. But that can't be undone. The future is what matters. Now... have I made myself clear?"*

Nikko relented. When his father spoke, he meant business. *"Si, Si, Papa. I get it."*

"Alright, then. It's settled, va bene?" Thomas looked at his brother and could tell he was not happy with the tongue lashing. But both nodded their heads and affirmed that they would comply.

It doesn't seem possible that this was only eight months ago. Their mother was there through it all, she loved and took care of him until the end. She stayed with him in the hospital, day and night, after his operation. The doctors thought they might be able to get the tumor out when radiation and chemotherapy both failed to work. But when the opened him up, it had spread too far. They did what they could, closed him up, and made him comfortable. Mama Morano brought him home and nursed him. At one point, her own health began to decline, and the brothers suggested that she check into the hospital, herself. The boys even offered to hire a nurse, but she scoffed at the idea. Everyone deserved to be loved the way that mama loved her dying husband.

The sound of ice cubes hitting the bottom of Nikko's tumbler yanked Thomas back into the moment. "Ya know, Nikko, I didn't agree with papa when he told you that you had to get married in two years. Every man should have the right to marry whomever he wishes, so I won't hold you to that... on one condition."

Nikko looked disinterested, but he engaged. "Okay. I'll bite. What condition?"

"You have to stop obsessing over Sophie. Stop searching for her. Get on with your life. I have already terminated the private investigators."

Nikko stiffened and glared at his brother. "What?! You had no right to do that!"

"Yes, I did. And it wasn't my decision. Papa ordered it over a year ago. And you need to quit sleeping in her penthouse. If papa knew you'd been doing that, he would have gone ballistic."

Now Nikko looked perplexed. "How did you know about the penthouse?"

"One of the accountants was curious about a payment for property taxes on an apartment that wasn't in the family name. I never said anything to papa about it."

"Which accountant?"

"Dimenticarlo, Nikko."

Nikko slumped in his chair and stared into the bottom of his drink. "I don't think I can stop. No woman I have dated ever held a candle to Sophie. This one isn't as pretty... this one isn't as smart... this one doesn't make my heart race. I've tried to get her out of my head, but I just can't."

"That's why they call it an obsession. You've seen it with your own eyes. Men obsessed with gambling, drugs, porn. It never ends well. Most of them lose their families, many their fortunes, some lose their lives. Remember Joey Fratelli? He owed the bookies all that money from the horse track. He knew something bad was going to happen to him, but he still couldn't stop until something or someone stopped him *for good*. He was obsessed. You need to get ahold of yourself. Your reputation with women is starting to spread around the organization, and beyond. I heard that you dumped a woman on the side of the road because you got tired of her before the date ended. Did that really happen?"

Nikko set his drink on the table next to him and stood. "Who are you, Mr. Manners?"

Thomas stood to meet his brother's towering gaze. "And that's not all I've heard. Did you get rough with one of the waitresses you dated? This is your brother talking, Nicky. This isn't like you. Give it up before you cross a line, and you can't come back."

Nikko grabbed his suit jacket out of the closet by the door, turned, and said, "I'm leaving. Tell mama I will see her at breakfast in the morning." Thomas started to say something but ended up just letting him go. He knew when Nikko got like this, the only answers were time and space.

CHAPTER SIX
TWO MONTHS LATER

L exi loved to fly first class. She had gotten accustomed to it
when she was with Nikko, but this time she needed the extra
elbow space to help curb her anxiety about seeing him again.
God had delivered her from fear, but she still struggled with it
from time to time. God was helping her overcome it bit by bit.
And now, her contacts were beginning to bother her. She hadn't
worn them since the rehab center, but she had to be very careful
once she got to New York. She didn't think she'd ever go back
there again. Lexi chose La Guardia because Nikko hated that
airport, he always flew into JFK. She couldn't take the risk of
running into him by accident even with her disguise.

Lexi pulled out her notebook. It took her two months to get
everything in order. She found a retired accountant at the church
to keep her business open and take care of her clients until she
got back. She estimated it would take sixty to ninety days to
ensure the complete demise of the Morano family's illegal
enterprises. She paid her housing and heating bills for three
months in advance and told Suzie that she had to go take care of
some unfinished business. Naturally, Suzie started asking
questions, but Lexi told her that she would explain everything
when she got back. Finally, she spoke with her Pastor and asked
for the church to keep her in their prayers. She couldn't tell him
much, but he understood and promised they would do as she
asked.

As Lexi read over her cover story to see if she missed anything, it really did look convincing. Now she just had to convince federal law enforcement agencies to go along with her plan. The Drug Enforcement Administration, the Federal Bureau of Investigation, and Immigrations and Customs Enforcement all had open cases on the Morano family. Any of them would love to have the information she possessed. Perhaps if they all worked together, they could stop Nikko and his soldiers once and for all. As the gravity of the situation set in, she set her notebook on her lap and prayed to herself. *Oh Lord, am I really being led by You or is this just crazy? Please, close the doors if this isn't of Your making.* She put her things back in her Gucci purse. It was the one Thomas had given her the last day she saw him. *I hope you kept your word and stayed legit, Thomas. I don't want to hurt you. Will you ever forgive me for taking down your brother?* But she knew the answer; Thomas was fiercely protective of his brother, and he would never forgive her. But she had to try to make things right if she was ever going to move forward. Lexi looked at the beautiful ring Thomas had put in the purse he gave her. It was beautiful and she chose to wear it on the way back to Manhattan. She closed her eyes, but there was too much running through her mind to sleep.

A taxi took Lexi to The High Line Hotel, just a few blocks north of the DEA's New York Division. She didn't want to have very far to travel in the daylight. She hadn't made an appointment with anyone at the DEA because she couldn't afford to have her presence leaked out to the Morano family. There were always moles and leaks in an organization the size of the DEA.

Lexi opened the door to her room, put her suitcase on the rack, and set her Chinese takeout food on the end table. All she wanted right now was to get out of these clothes, take a shower, get into her pajamas, eat her dinner, and read her Bible till she fell asleep. Tomorrow would be a long day if things went the way that she planned.

Lexi awoke about 5 am and instantly felt that she needed to pray. She could sense that the fear was trying to take ahold of her. She had to fight it. It had taken months of praying and of the church laying hands on her for her to overcome the fear that had a steely grip on her. It was the kind of fear that paralyzes. It's like reliving the pain of something before it happens, and it happens over, and over again, in your head.

Lexi left the room on Tuesday morning at 8 am and took a taxi to the nondescript office building on 10th Avenue. She was stopped in the lobby, and she told the security detail that she needed to see the Supervisory Special Agent in Charge of the DEA offices, James Hampton. The security guard asked if she had an appointment, to which she replied, "No. But please let him know that Sophie Star is here to see him."

The guard scoffed and said, "people don't just walk in off the street and ask to speak with Agent Hampton, ma'am."

Sophie replied again, telling him to say that Sophie Star is in the lobby. "I'm sure he'll want to speak with me."

The guard begrudgingly called upstairs; a woman answered. "Agent Hampton, please." The secretary asked who was calling. The caller said he was security on the first floor. She put him on hold. After a long pause.

"Agent Hampton."

"Sir, this is Murray on the first floor. There's a woman here named Sophie Star who said she...yeah. Star...Okay. Yes sir.

Right away." He hung up the phone, spoke a few coded words into the radio on his shoulder, and motioned for Sophie to step through the metal detector. Setting her purse on an x-ray belt, she stepped through the scanner with her hands above her head. There was no sound. The brusque guard motioned her forward, and a female guard suddenly appeared to pat Sophie down by hand. The female then gave her a visitor's pass, and two other armed guards appeared.

Murray spoke to the two security officers who answered his coded message. "Gentlemen, please see that this young lady gets safely to Agent Hampton's office." They replied affirmatively and stepped her around the corner and into an elevator. One of the men used a key from his utility belt to activate the buttons on the elevator, and they ascended to the third floor.

When the doors slid open, the men walked Sophie through the bull pen, consisting of a collection of small dividers that separated the big room into many makeshift offices. In the back were two conference rooms and a few private administrators' offices. The armed escort stopped on the far side of the bullpen in front of SAC Hampton's secretary, seated behind her desk outside his office, she got up and opened his office door. He waved Sophie forward, "Ms. Star. Please have a seat. There are a lot of people who will be glad to know you're alive."

Sophie quickly responded. "I'd like to keep my presence quiet for as long as possible."

Hampton paused for a moment, but he clearly understood her request. "Ms. Star are you aware there is still an open case on your disappearance? There are many in law enforcement that believe Nikko Morano killed you, and others—the optimistic ones— think you were kidnapped and taken to Mexico for crossing him."

"I am aware of that, sir." She explained everything that had happened to her—except for divulging that it was Thomas Morano who helped her—and then went on to explain why she had come back. She laid out a portfolio of information that she had compiled over the last few months. It contained specific dates, account numbers, transactions, names, and secret locations of evidence to corroborate her information.

"We had no idea you had such intimate knowledge of the Morano's operations." He peered over the papers on his desk, shuffling through them a few at a time. Then he looked up from them, and asked her, "what makes you think this will work?"

"Well let's put it this way. Your *only* chance of getting to the Morano network is if I give him to you on a platter. He is untouchable, I made sure of that. But I can give you more than Nikko... I can give you his whole operation, local and international, from the lowest to the highest, including some crooked law enforcement if I can get my hands on the proof."

"Why now, after so long?"

"My reasons are my own. I do have a few conditions. We don't touch any of the legitimate businesses of the Morano family or Thomas and his mother. Also, I need complete immunity from anything I may have done that was illegal. We will need the cooperation of the FBI and ICE to do this, but *I* run this operation. She handed him a copy of her cover story and her plan step by step. You can see in there the budget will be high, that needs to be approved before we get out of the gate. There are also a few NYPD detectives I would like involved. One more thing, I pick my protection detail. "

"Those are a lot of demands, Ms. Star."

"Well, you have until 5 pm to decide, then I am going back where I came from, and you will never hear from me again. If you do decide to go through with this, I can't come in here again, we will have to have a safe house for tactical meetings. You will see there I will need a computer expert, too. Everything on my list is nonnegotiable. It's what I need to make this work."

SAC Hampton leaned back in his chair, putting his head back slightly. His mind was racing. They had been trying to take down the Morano's for nearly thirty years, since he first became an agent. When Joe Morano first started, he had made a few mistakes, they could have taken him down then, but the brass felt he was to insignificant and wanted to put their efforts into the bigger targets. As he got more powerful, he also got a lot smarter and the DEA along with the FBI and ICE have been trying to get something on him ever since. But the egos in the other departments weren't likely to move aside to let Ms. Star run the show.

Sophie watched as he sat and evaluated her offer. His hesitation made her think he was rejecting it. Sophie got up, reached her hand across the table, and said, "thank you for hearing me out."

Sophie's movement brought Hampton out of his thoughts. He sat up straight again. "Ms. Star, I'm willing to give it a shot, but you have to know it will be difficult to convince the brass even in my agency, let alone the others, to go along with this idea." He stood, "If you give me your number, I will call you an let you know."

"It would be better if I call you."

Agent Hampton shook her hand and handed her his card.

"I'll wait for your call." When she left, Hampton called out for his secretary. When she came in, he started barking orders, "Sarah, I need you to get me the Attorney General, the District Attorney, Agent Sam Cosby at the FBI NY field office, Agent Benson from ICE. Oh, and I need to talk to the NYPD Commissioner. In that order. If someone isn't in, just move on."

"Yes sir."

As she left his office, she noticed several of the agents were looking, no doubt wondering what was going on. She glanced up, and her eyes connected with an agent for just a moment. She walked past him and proceeded out of the building. By the time she reached her hotel room, she was shaking like a leaf. *Lord, what am I doing*?

Agent Houston Townsend turned to his partner, Agent Alfonso Rodriguez, and asked, "Do you know who she is?"

"No but put your eyes back in their sockets. We have a case to work." But Houston had felt something. He just couldn't put his finger on it.

When Sophie had decided to come back to New York, she did some research online to see what became of her condo. She owned it outright, so no one could sell it until she was declared dead. But the state could foreclose for unpaid property taxes. She wanted to see if it had been foreclosed on and what happened to her belongings. She found out that it was still in her name. Nikko Morano was paying her taxes.

Sophie decided she would go and see if she could get in her apartment; maybe he hadn't changed the lock. Her key had been with her at the hospital, and she had kept it, although she wasn't sure why at the time. With her blonde hair, green contacts, a baseball cap, and sunglasses, she was sure no one there would recognize her.

The taxi dropped her off in front of her building. The doorman wasn't at his desk. That was a stroke of good luck. She headed for the elevator and looked up as she turned the corner. Her eyes caught the side of a handsome man's face. "No, no, no, no this can't be happening, that can't be Nikko", she muttered to herself, but it was him. Sophie had to think fast. If she turned and ran, it would draw too much attention. She just kept walking right past him and Ben. She gave him as wide a birth as was possible in the common area. As she passed him, she heard his conversation stop, but she kept on walking. Once around the corner, she ran to the rear emergency exit. *This was a bad idea.* Sophie grabbed the first cab that came along and went back to her hotel, shaken by the incident.

Ben was just telling Nikko that staying at Sophie's condo against Thomas' wishes was a bad idea when Nikko noticed a blonde woman in the common area just walking into the complex. When she passed by him, a strange feeling came over him. He stopped for a second, turned, and saw her go around the corner. There was something familiar about her, the way she carried herself, her walk. He hurried to the corner to see if he could catch up with her, but she was gone. He tried to just shrug it off, but it lingered in his mind the rest of the day.

It was finally 5 pm when Sophie pulled out one of her prepaid cell phones and called Agent Hampton. He answered the phone himself. "Hello Ms. Star. I was waiting for your call."

"What's your answer, Agent Hampton?"

"I have to say it was a marathon on my part, but we got the go ahead from every department. It seems your Mr. Morano is on everyone's high priority target list."

"That's good news. I need the signed letter of immunity in my hands before we start."

"Understood."

"Where and when can you have everyone together? I only want to go over this once. The more times we meet, the bigger chance of this getting out. And Agent Hampton—you tell everyone involved to only bring in those they would trust with their own lives."

"Do you have a number that I can call you back on?" She gave him the number she was using.

"I will get everyone together by early afternoon tomorrow. Will that work for you?"

"Yes. And the Penthouse and the protection, they will be in place tomorrow? As I wrote in the info that I gave you, nothing can come from the confiscated assets of any of the agencies were using—not the penthouse, not the cars, nothing. You have no idea how easy it is to get that kind of information if you have the right software, and contacts, and are paranoid enough to check. And trust me, old Mr. Joe Morano made contacts early on in his *career* and the organization has kept them close ever since. How do you think they have stayed one step ahead for so long? I can tell you it wasn't dumb luck. His organization is compartmentalized. Each head only knows the information of his area and the areas under him, but never above. That way, if someone gets caught, they won't be able to squeal because he is the biggest fish in his pond. It's brilliant, really," Sophie said.

"I made that clear to everyone I talked to. The protection can be in place immediately, but the penthouse, I'm not so sure about. DOJ will be paying for that. That's above my paygrade."

"Well, I can't make a move until everything is in place."

"Everyone is aware of your conditions. They're willing to meet them wherever possible."

"Thank you, Agent Hampton. I know this is an extremely complex undertaking. I don't mean to make light of how difficult this is for all of you. I'm just..."

"I understand. I'll call you tomorrow."

SAC Hampton did understand. He had pulled her file, and saw the photos taken in the ER. He couldn't believe she recovered from all those injuries with only a few scars. He had no doubt she had emotional scars from which she might never recover. He had worked cases of women being abused or battered by men. He came to understand that most of them felt the good times outweighed the bad, but, unfortunately, it was an illusion. Many of them blamed themselves for the beatings. Too few ever take the chance and leave, making a new life for themselves and their children.

Hampton stepped to the office door the following morning and bellowed out, "Rodriguez, Townsend, Smith, and Kelly, in the conference room now." After they were all assembled, Agent Hampton said, "I don't know how many of you noticed the lady who was in my office yesterday." Rodriguez nudged Houston who in turn gave him a glare. "Her name is Sophie Star. Does that ring a bell for anyone?" He gave them a minute to connect. The mumblings made it evident they did.

"Where has she been all this time?" Kelly asked. He didn't reply, instead Agent Hampton handed out the file with the photos.

"What I need you to do now is understand this is to be a totally blacked out operation; it will not be on the books anywhere." Everyone nodded their understanding. "We only have until tomorrow to get together our first task force meeting. Townsend, I want you to find a secure facility to meet in over the course of the operation. Maybe find a warehouse so we can hide the vehicles, too."

"Yes sir, can do."

"Kelly, she asked for a guard dog and a handler to be with her 24/7. That's your department. Keeping this quiet means we need to keep the detail small, so how many will you need to make that happen?"

"Sir, if I can get Maxwell to agree, we can alternate, running twelve on and twelve off for the entire assignment."

"Can you trust him?"

"With my life, sir," She replied, then added, "sir, why has she come back now?"

"I have no idea, but the information she has is vital to taking down the Morano's operation."

Sophie took the green contacts out of her eyes, opened her suitcase, and took out the L'Oréal 'Darkest Auburn' box she had brought with her. "I guess it's time to be Sophie again," she mumbled. But did she want to go back to her old self; she liked who she had become in Lake View. She liked the new creature Jesus made her into. *No matter how you look on the outside, you're still the same on the inside.* The thought startled her, but then gave her peace, and she headed to the bathroom.

Agent Hampton made good on his word and called her late the next morning. She was up and ready for the call. "I will have a man come and get you at your hotel. His name is Agent Houston Townsend. Make sure he shows you ID. He is 6'1" with dark brown hair. He will be there at 1 pm."

"Thank you, Agent Hampton, I'll be ready."

At exactly 1 pm, a knock came on her door. She looked through the peep hole and saw the man that was described to her. She recognized him from the office. She opened the door with the chain on and asked for ID. He handed it through the door. Satisfied, she opened the door, handed him back his ID, and placed her Gucci purse over her shoulder.

"WOW".

She looked at him with a small grin.

Oh, Houston, tell me you didn't just say that out loud. You idiot. She'll think you have never seen a beautiful woman before. He had been taken by surprise when she opened the door and he saw her in her natural hair and eye color. She really was a beautiful woman, blonde or brunette. He escorted her to his SUV.

"Where are we going?"

"I'm sorry, ma'am. That is need to know."

"Don't you think I need to know?"

"Not my call, ma'am." She paused for a moment but decided that she could live with those precautions. They were only doing as she asked.

After about 25 minutes of driving, he made a phone call. She didn't recognize this side of town. They drove maybe another mile and turned into a huge warehouse, possibly an old airplane hangar. The drive thru entrance opened for them. Once they drove in, the door automatically closed behind them. The place was filled with cars, men, and equipment. On the left were some stairs that led to an office, but other than that, it was a wide-open space. It was overwhelming. There had to be 10 vehicles lined up on one side of the warehouse. She didn't think this many people would be involved. She looked for Agent Hampton.

"Agent, there is no way this many people can keep this quiet. I can't do this. Take me back to the hotel." She turned, but he grabbed her arm, and she pulled away with a start. He apologized for grabbing her.

"Look, these are all trained agents. This whole thing is top secret, and there is no paper trail. None of them will talk, but you should know that for every one person up front in an operation, there are always two behind the scenes making it work. You wanted secure; this is secure!" He could see the men

70

all staring at the scene they were making, so he took her over to a corner where they could have some privacy. "Please, Ms. Star, I can appreciate how afraid you are, but we know what we're doing."

"I certainly hope so, Agent Hampton." She took a moment to compose herself. "Do you have my immunity agreement?"

"Yes, it's over here." He took her to a table he had been using as a desk. After looking it over she accepted it and waited for the meeting to begin.

Dangerous Obsession

CHAPTER SEVEN

Agent Hampton was talking with the other agency heads when he caught her eye and waved her over. He told her the floor was hers.

Sophie was nervous, *whatever made me think I could convince these hard-core law enforcement heads to listen to me. I can't do this.* Sophie felt like she could throw up, it wasn't just her knees that were shaking, her whole insides were. *The minute I open my mouth they are going to realize, I don't know what I'm doing. If I don't act confident, they are going to sit me down and take over. But I am confident of one thing. None of these experienced men will ever be able to take Nikko down. I'm the only one that can get close to him.*

Sophie walked to the head table where all the agency brass was looking at her. She moved to stand in front of the small tabletop lectern and looked out. She opened her mouth, but nothing came out. *Lord, please help me, don't let me fail.* She looked at all the people in the warehouse. Her eyes locked on Detective Cartwright, he nodded to her and smiled. This time when she opened her mouth, words came out.

"I'm sure you all have been briefed on this operation but let me make one thing clear. I am the one who will make the decisions on how this goes down. You may think you know the Morano operations, but I promise you, you do not. We are going after the criminal enterprises only. We are not going after the legitimate ones or the brother who runs them, Thomas or his mother. Is that clear?"

Special Agent in Charge Cosby from the FBI replied, "I'm not convinced there is a line clear enough to separate the businesses. If the criminal enterprises support the legal ones, then they're all fair game along with Thomas Morano. I don't believe the mother has ever been involved."

Sophie knew there would be push back. If she weren't able to handle the first test to her leadership, they would sit her down and take over. "You may not know there is a line, but I do. I was the organization's top accountant, and I know exactly what went on and where. This is my condition for helping you take down Nikko's criminal enterprise. If we are not all on board with that, tell me now."

The place went silent. Agent Hampton knew this would happen. He watched as the Supervisor of the FBI tried to control his hot temper. He knew, just as well as Agent Hampton did, their only chance to get this done was with her help, so Cosby reluctantly nodded his bald head in agreement as did the other supervisors.

"Okay, then let's move on. Has a penthouse been secured?" Someone spoke up with an affirmative. "I am going to pass out my cover story, where I've supposedly been, and what I've been doing. It will pass muster but only if all of you are able to get your contacts and your CIs to start passing these rumors around as if they've been facts for years. I understand you have a network of your own already in place, so let's use them. It will give me more credibility. While you're looking those over, I'd like to pick my security team."

The FBI agent stood up, "Mathews, has the penthouse been wired yet with sound and picture?"

"Yes, sir."

Sophie stopped in her tracks. "Wait a minute, I never authorized that."

"Ms. Star, you don't think we are going to put all these resources and money into an operation and not be able to produce the evidence we need to prosecute?"

"No, of course not. I just need to be able to shut them down if I need to. Can you do that?" By the look on his face, he didn't like it, but he agreed.

Sophie moved over to a small table in the corner and asked Agent Hampton to bring over the K9 handlers, Officer Cody Maxwell and his dog Bully and Officer Ann Kelly and her dog Titan. Sophie spoke to Officer Kelly, "Titan is a strange name for a female dog."

"Most people are more intimidated by a male dog. I knew Titan was as powerful and as smart as most of her peers, so I wanted to give her an even playing field. When she's off duty, I call her Tani so she can connect with her feminine side." Sophie couldn't help the laugh that came rolling out of her.

"I like the way you think, Agent Kelly." When she was satisfied the handlers were on board with the operation. She decided that Agent Houston Townsend and Agent Alfonso Rodriguez would also be a part of her security team, along with two FBI agents who would be set up outside.

"Agent Hampton." He turned from what he was doing and met her halfway.

"Are you done with your interviews?" he asked.

"Yes, and I want to thank you for making my choices easy. You have done far more than I thought was possible."

"To tell you the truth, we have never put together anything like this in so short a time. I'd say you have a friend upstairs."

"Well, I actually do—just not who you think," Sophie smiled. Agent Hampton laughed. "I'm nervous about so many people knowing our plan. How soon can I get into the penthouse under protection?"

"If you would like, I will have one of the men take you to your hotel room, and we should have everything set up by evening. I'll call you with a time and send a man to pick you up and escort you there. Are you ready to go now?"

"No, I have one more thing to do. I need the list of all the vehicle vin numbers you're using and the address of the penthouse. Then I need to talk with your computer tech." He led her to an agent setting up a series of computers.

"Agent Mathews, this is Ms. Star. She will be asking you to do things from time to time. You are approved to do whatever she asks."

Hampton turned to her, "I'll go grab the vehicle information."

Sophie sat next to the agent. "Are any of these computers online yet?"

"Yes ma'am, this one."

"Please call me Sophie." She explained to him how to get into the site she needed to access then handed him the information Agent Hampton just brought over. "Check each one of these vin numbers and the address on the penthouse and see if you get a hit."

"Where did this site come from?"

"I paid someone a lot of the Morano's money to come up with it. In turn, the family makes a lot of money from other criminal organizations for access."

"This is incredible. It's going to take months for us to come up with counter measures for this."

"Maybe I should give up the name of the man who built the site for me," she laughed.

"Would you do that?"

"No," her demeanor serious, "he is totally loyal to the Morano family." After a few minutes, Agent Mathew's got a hit. Sophie went to Agent Hampton.

"I told you no vehicles from confiscated assets."

"I made that clear to everyone," Agent Hampton assured her.

"Well, someone didn't get the memo, because we got a hit." Agent Hampton walked over to the tech who showed him the site and the hit.

"How long has this site been in operation?"

"I had it set up the first year I worked for them, so it's probably been 3 years now."

"Well, that explains a few failed operations. I'll get a clean SUV to replace it." She talked a few more minutes with Agent Hampton and indicated she was ready to leave. Agent Townsend was assigned to take her home. Just before she left, she stopped to talk to Detective Cartwright.

"Detective, I never really got to thank you. You helped me escape. I don't think I would have made it to the park on my own."

"I often wondered about you. I prayed you made it to your destination. But I can see you are no longer that scared young woman lying on a hospital bed."

Sophie lowered her head, her eyes cast down at the finger that once held Nikko's engagement ring. "No, I'm not. Thank you for your prayers, they made a difference in my life."

"You asking for me and my partner to be on this task force gets our names in front of the NYPD brass. Thanks, Ms. Star." Detective Cartwright had kept her secret all this time and would continue to do so—some secrets were worth keeping.

Houston walked Sophie to the door of her hotel room and told her he would be back to pick her up when the penthouse was ready. She packed and read her Bible while she waited for the phone call from Agent Hampton. It finally came at 9 pm.

Sophie was quiet all the way to the penthouse. He carried her suitcase for her. When she got there, the guard dog and handlers were there along with Houston's partner. She insisted everyone call her Sophie unless the circumstances required otherwise.

The penthouse was at least four thousand square feet. To the right, it had a conversation pit with a fireplace. It was decorated with an expensive leather couch, matching leather chairs, and a heavy-duty coffee table sitting between them. You could see a dining room with french doors that opened to a large balcony. To the right of it was a large chef's kitchen. You could see part of it through the archway. He took her suitcases down a hall to the right to the master bedroom, which housed a large four post bed set up with a feminine touch. The master bath was equally lavish.

Houston went back to the dining room where everyone had gathered. After Sophie retreated to her bedroom, they discussed the best plan to make things run smoothly.

Sophie took her clothes out of the suitcase, put everything away, and stored the suitcase in the back of the closet. She had to make this feel like home. She needed to feel safe. After her bath, she put on her pajamas and went to bed. As soon as she shut her eyes, she was asleep.

She woke up at 5 am and knew she needed to pray. So, she rolled out of bed and onto her knees. By 8:10 am, she was showered, dressed, and had her hair and makeup done. She knew there were agents out there awake, so she headed to the kitchen to make coffee for everyone. When she stepped out her door, the smell of coffee and bacon hit her. Someone was cooking.

"Hey there. Want some breakfast? We have eggs, bagels, bacon, orange juice, and coffee—all on the DEA's dime," Agent Rodrigues lifted the spatula he was using.

"That sounds so tempting, but only coffee for me," Sophie responded. Ann Kelly, Max, and Houston all sat around the table. Pleasantries went back and forth. Kelly was just going off duty, and Max was coming on.

"What's the plan for today?" Houston asked.

"Around 10 am, I want to go to a little cafe where I might be recognized. I want the word out in town, but just bit by bit—rumors. Then I need to go to the Citi Bank downtown. Today, the plan is just to be seen. I would still like one of you to come with me."

The cafe was within walking distance of the penthouse, and since no one knew yet that she was here, she felt safe walking. That was what today was all about--exposure. Houston sat across from Sophie facing the door while they ate. It had to look like they were conducting business rather than him just being her bodyguard.

"Sophie, is that you? Where have you been? The whole world's been looking for you." Sophie turned her head and saw Chelsea Milton's shocked expression on her pretty face.

"Chelsea, have a seat. Do you mind Houston? I would like to talk to my old friend."

"Not at all Ms. Star. I'll finish my coffee at the counter."

"Thank you." Chelsea slipped into the booth where Houston had been a moment before.

"Really, Sophie, where have you been? I went to see you at the hospital, but they weren't allowing visitors."

"I had to get away for a while to think, and I didn't want anyone to find me. But now I'm back."

"Sophie, I couldn't believe what Nikko did to you." Chelsea was one of the few women Sophie considered a close friend. When she got the job with the Morano family, Chelsea tried to warn her off. Sophie didn't see the trap she was falling into; she only saw the huge salary and the glitzy lifestyle, the kind she read about in the magazines as a kid. Even though she was in college when her father died, without his constant influence in her life, she started wanting things a little on the wild side. Chelsea was her last anchor to a stable life. But after Sophie got the job, she found herself spending less time with her friends.

"I have really missed you, Chelsea. I'm only here for a few months on business."

"What kind of business, Sophie? You're not going back to Nikko, right? He almost killed you!"

"No, don't worry about me. I finally have things under control. And if you haven't noticed, my associate is also my bodyguard."

"Does that mean Nikko is still looking for you? You know he tapped my phones and had me followed for nearly a year. He even threatened me once. He thought for sure you would get in touch with me."

"I'm so sorry you got dragged into that."

A little smile came across Chelsea's face. "It wasn't all bad. The NYPD put security on me for a while, a gorgeous man named Steven. We have been dating now for almost a year. I think he is going to ask me to marry him."

Sophie let out a laugh. "That's wonderful! Congratulations."

"I hope you have time to meet him while you're here. What about you? Have you found someone?"

80

"I have some male friends, but no one of a romantic nature. Chelsea, what's Cody doing?"

"He got married last year. He's now managing partner at the Kirk and Manchester law firm. You know he had a crush on you?"

"No, I didn't, but I never thought of him as more than a friend."

"Yeah, he finally figured that out. But he was distraught at what Nikko did to you. He was glad you disappeared even though he missed you."

Chelsea looked at her watch. "I'm sorry, I'm only on a break. I have to get back to the bank." Sophie got up to hug Chelsea goodbye. As she watched her leave, Sophie realized that it seemed like someone else's life they had been talking about. So much has happened since then. A moment later, Houston came back, "Are you alright?"

"Yes, she was a friend from a long time ago. She works at the Bank across the street. Word should start spreading. She won't tell many people...only people who knew me then. But it will start things rolling."

"Are you ready to leave?"

Sophie smiled. "Yes." Houston put down a tip, picked up the check, and went up front to pay. Sophie grabbed her purse and went outside.

The next stop was personal. She was willing to let her money go when she had no choice, but now she planned on retrieving it before she left town. "Where to now?" Houston asked.

"Can you call Rodriguez to come with the SUV? The bank is downtown, too far to walk." Houston called Rodriguez, and soon she was walking into Citi Bank. She walked over to the customer service desk and asked to talk to the manager. The girl behind the counter asked for her name and what her business was regarding. Sophie answered her questions. The manager came down, his expression showing that he knew exactly who she was.

"Ms. Star! What a surprise. It's been a while since we've heard from you."

"Yes, it has. Can we go somewhere to talk?"

"Of course," the manager moved his hand in the direction of his office. Houston waited in the lobby.

"Can you please tell me how much is left in my account?" The manager got on his computer and brought up the information she asked for.

"There is $474,900.22." She reached in her purse and handed him an account number.

"I would like you to transfer all the funds in my account to this number. It's an overseas account. Can you do that?"

"Yes, we will just have to take the red flag off your account and see the proper ID." Since her driver's license in New York hadn't expired yet, Sophie ordered a replacement card before she left Lake View. She knew she would need some sort of ID. It came a week before she left.

"How long will this take?"

"Shouldn't be more than 30 minutes. You're welcome to wait in our VIP lounge, Ms. Star."

Sophie got up from her chair. "No, I will be fine out here, I have an associate waiting for me. But thank you." She left his office and sat on the couch in the lobby. She knew exactly what she was doing. She set up this overseas account before she left Lake View. If anything went wrong, and she had to run again, she wouldn't be able to go back and sell everything; she needed a nest egg just in case. And, if everything went well, she could transfer all the funds to her account in Lake View. That brought up another thought—*if Nikko was behind bars and the organization crushed, would I want to move back here?* No, there would always be someone with a vendetta against her for taking the organization down. She was still better off staying gone.

Thirty minutes later, the manager came out to meet her with a receipt for the transfer. He shook her hand and said, "I am pleased to see you're alright." She raised her eyes.

"Thank you." She slipped her receipt into her purse and walked out with Houston.

When they got back to the penthouse she turned to Houston and said, "I need another tactical meeting with everyone this afternoon." Houston looked a little confused.

"Now I have to put pressure on Nikko to search us out." Houston made the calls and by 6 pm, they were pulling into the warehouse.

Sophie walked over to the tech she met last time and handed him a thumb drive. "Would you please put this information up on the screens?"

"Yes, ma'am." She noticed Detectives Cartwright and Mahoney and spoke with them until she saw the information was up. She excused herself, went to the table, and took a seat while the others read what she had displayed for them.

"Ms. Star, how accurate is this information?" Agent Hampton asked.

"This is incredible." She heard some of the others mumbling to each other.

Sophie stood. "For this operation to work we have to create a vacuum that only I can fill. As you see on the screen, I have traced the operation back to Southern Mexico where Nikko owns the coca farm. You now have the rotated trafficking routes, the locations of their storage warehouses, and the exact methods by which they cross the border. Some of this may have been altered, but since the enterprise has been untouched by law enforcement, there is really no reason for them to have changed it. Hitting the warehouses will be tricky because Nikko keeps the stuff moving until it's in the hands of the street distributors. He insists on payment up front in case the dealer get busted. That way it is the dealer's loss.

When I pressed him to try it that way, the street handlers were very unhappy because they had always been granted time to pay. But I told him to only work with those smart enough to have money up front. They're the ones who will be most careful because they have something to lose. Once the decision was made, their losses went down substantially. We need to hit the field, burn the crop, confiscate the product in the warehouses and the trucks in route simultaneously. If word gets out, they have emergency procedures. All the mules that transport for Nikko are undocumented illegals, which is where ICE comes in. If you can capture the product and get the mules transported back to Mexico before word starts spreading, we may have a chance to make this thing work."

"We can take care of that," Agent Benson responded.

"Agents Hampton and Cosby, do you have counterparts who will work under your supervision in Southern Mexico?"

Cosby looked at Sophie with a slightly displeased look on his face. "Let us worry about that, Ms. Star."

She was quiet for a moment then replied. "I'm not challenging your ability, Agent Cosby. I just want to know if it's possible. Because if it's not, then there is no need to proceed. In order for the rest of my plan to work, Nikko must be cut off from his own source to start looking for someone else. The fields have to be burned."

"I am confident we can do that."

"Thank you, Agent Cosby. Agent Hampton, who will take the lead on this?"

Hampton replied, "DEA has an SRT that has authorization to work internationally with the approval and co-operation of Mexico's Federal Judicial Police. Agent Aguilar will be the lead."

Agent Aguilar stood in response to his name being mentioned. Sophie turned to him.

"Agent Aguilar how long do you think it will take to get geared up for this?"

"My best estimate would be 4 days to launch."

Sophie continued. "I have spoken with Detectives Cartwright and Mahoney, and they will have their informants start dropping word about the new supplier in town. Agent Mathews has been entering the cover story about Viktor Tsvetkov — where he was born, when he immigrated, when he became a citizen, and personal history to support the rumors. Are there any questions?"

With no questions asked, Agent Hampton dismissed the group, and the separate teams immediately started working among themselves, the room soon filled with noisy chatter.

Agent Hampton approached Sophie. "Ms. Star, can I speak with you?"

"Yes of course, Agent Hampton."

"How are things working on your end? Do you foresee any holes in your plan yet?"

"Not yet and with the grace of God, I'm praying it stays that way. If the operation to take down the fields works, Nikko should be looking for someone to temporarily replace their product until he can rebuild. And unless we can catch him red handed, which is what we're trying to do, he will rebuild. He makes 100 million dollars a year from those fields in Southern Mexico alone, and if he doesn't produce product for his dealers, they will move on to someone else."

"It's a sound plan, we all agree. But some of the men have expressed their concerns of whether or not you will be able to hold up under the pressure."

"Have I given you any indication I can't handle this?"

"No, and I'm not one of them questioning. It's just that so much money and resources are hanging on your ability to make good on all your promises."

"I am aware of that, and I won't let you down."

"I have confidence that you won't. You are a strong woman, Ms. Star. You have already survived…a lot."

"I appreciate that, thank you. Unless you need me, I would like to go now."

"Certainly, we have a lot of work here to do, but you've supplied us everything we need."

Sophie was quiet for the entire return trip. When she got to the penthouse, she went straight to her room.

"Is she alright?" Rodriguez asked Houston.

"I'm not sure. That was quite the operation she laid out there."

"No kidding! She might be the smartest criminal I have ever met," Rodriguez quipped.

Houston glared at Rodriguez, "She is not a criminal; she's an accountant."

"Not now, but she was when she helped the Morano family cook this all up." Houston didn't reply because he knew in his head, if not in his heart, that Rodriguez was right.

CHAPTER EIGHT

The next few days went by slowly. Sophie would get up shower, dress, then go out to the balcony to sit for hours reading her Bible or, occasionally, another book. The days were warming up with no rain like a typical mid-spring in New York. She had a sweater on this morning. Max was done with his sweep for this hour.

"What's wrong with her? She has been like this for days." Rodriguez noted to Houston.

"I don't know. I've tried to talk to her. She's polite and responds but won't take up a conversation," Houston replied.

"Here, take her this sandwich and milk. Maybe you can perk her up." Houston took the food to her and sat it on the little wooden table in front of her.

"Sophie, what's going on with you? Are you alright?"

She raised her hazel eyes with green specks to him. "I'm just wondering if I'm doing the right thing. What if this doesn't work? What if one of your teams gets killed? What if Nikko gets away? I'm not sure I can live with any of those results."

"Look, Sophie, Rodriguez and I have been on a lot of operations, and I have never seen one as well thought out and organized as this one. We usually go in with fuzzy intel at best. You have given us a road map. As far as someone getting injured or killed, this is the risk that we take every day. Every agent in that room knows it when he signs up."

"I appreciate you telling me this, but I do feel responsible."

"Is there anything I can do?"

"Well..., actually there is. Do the police dogs ever go 'off duty' and just get to be petted and played with?"

Houston smiled. "Yes, of course. Max and Kelly both take their dogs home with them and once the vest is off, they are great family pets."

"Do you think Max would take Bully 'off duty' and let me spend some time with him on the balcony?"

"Max would have to clear it with Agent Rodriguez since he is the senior officer on duty, but my guess is he would." Houston went in and explained to Max and Rodriguez her request. They talked it over for a while and decided Max could make his rounds for a few hours without Bully.

Max brought Bully out and let Sophie get comfortable with him, then he placed a tennis ball on the little wooden table and went back inside. She just sat there petting him for the longest time. Dogs are so intuitive; he could feel her somber mood and just laid his big head on her lap. The agents went about their assignments and simply kept an eye on her. When Houston came back to the penthouse from another task force update, he saw her throwing the ball for Bully. The dog ran for it like it was a steak then padded back, so proud of himself. She would bend down and praise him. He'd drop it at her feet, and the entire process would repeat. And then he saw it—a smile. Bully had put a smile on her face, and that smile warmed Houston clear to his heart.

Sophie came in for dinner, Bully padding in right by her side. She asked if there had been any news or developments. Rodriguez noticed that her demeanor was better as he caught her up to date. Things are on track to start at zero four hundred, our time, tomorrow morning. They will all hit at the same time no matter their location—the fields in Southern Mexico, the southern US border, or the East Coast. They have a Special Response Team working with the Mexican Federal Judicial Police in Southern Mexico, one also working with ICE on the borders, and another Special Response Team working on the east coast. They plan on moving swiftly, arresting and deporting the illegals on down the chain as they go. It's a solid plan.

Sophie politely interrupted. "Will you be able to get any real time intel?"

"Yes, ma'am."

"Would you mind keeping me up to date."

"My pleasure, ma'am."

"Thank you, Agent Rodriguez."

"Please call me Fons if you like." His tone was inviting, but his face demonstrated the seriousness with which he took his job.

Sophie smiled then responded, "Maybe I will when this is all over. But I appreciate the warmth of your offer." After dinner she went to her room. She wanted to get some sleep, but she planned on setting her alarm clock for four, so she could be in prayer during the operation.

At four o'clock, Sophie's alarm went off, and she grabbed her Bible, got on her knees, and began to pray aloud. "Jesus, I plead the blood over all these agents and officers involved with this operation. In You there is victory, and You shine down on those who stand for right and truth. Confuse the enemy, as you did for your chosen people throughout the Old Testament, for You are no respecter of persons...."

Houston wasn't on duty, but he had gotten up to get a drink of water and sat with Rodriguez and Kelly, listening in real time to the comms, when he heard something coming from Sophie's room. When he got closer, he realized she was praying. That realization made him so ashamed of himself. He was raised Christian, loved the Lord all his life, and was convinced that he was walking the walk. But it hadn't even dawned on him to pray for his colleagues. He realized he had gotten out of the habits of praying, reading his Bible every day, and going to church. *I wonder when that happened*, he pondered to himself. A tear came to his eye, and he figured now was as good a time as any to renew his faith. He closed his eyes for a moment — *Lord, forgive me for my arrogance in thinking I can do this job without your help. Bring me back to a closer walk with you*. He went back to the kitchen, not wanting to eavesdrop on her prayers, but he could hear the soft sound of her praying for hours. He knew she was tortured over the idea that someone might be injured.

At about 6 am, Sophie put on her robe and came out to the kitchen, hoping there was some information she could get on the operation. Rodriguez turned up the volume on the comm radio. There was a lot of static, but she could make out what was being said. It appeared that the raid on the field went well, and they were now burning the crops. On the East coast, they had arrested warehouse workers at three of the locations on her list and had confiscated the product. Immigrations and Customs Enforcement now had the men in their custody. The men at the border were in a chase with a U-Haul truck loaded with product. The driver was trying to get back over the border to Mexico, but the team has the Mexican police tapped in, and they were waiting in case they made it. Hearing it live was exciting and frightening at the same time.

"This is SRT team 5 heading west on I10 in pursuit of a black SUV the license plate number is obstructed, they are firing on us from the vehicle! We are headed into a small town... there could be civilian casualties if we don't get help stopping them, who do you have available?"

"SRT 5, this is command. We have Highway Patrol on standby. They are coming in from the south and setting a blockade ahead of you. Be ready for them to deploy a spike strip."

"Ten four" The chatter had been going on for several hours. Rodriguez made breakfast while they listened.

"Command, we see the blockade. They are turning off Interstate 10 and heading into the desert. We are in pursuit. The Highway Patrol is right behind us." They could hear the drama continuing.

Other agents were in pursuit of a pickup truck on its way to a warehouse in Brooklyn. The driver abandoned his vehicle and ran into a home. The fear of hostages became highest priority. Support teams were searching property records to see who owned the home and how many lives were in jeopardy. They heard command give them the information, "SRT 8, the house is owned by a former Navy Seal, Arthur Benedict."

You could hear a few chuckles, "Big mistake," someone on the command team said.

Apparently, the owner was home. He subdued the man, opened his door, threw the man out, and said, "get this man off my property."

With one driver now in custody, the pursuit in the desert was still under way. By 9 am the chatter was slowing down. Some pursuits didn't end well, including the one in the desert; the suspects tried to shoot their way out and one was killed the other injured. Fortunately, no officers were injured in the shootouts.

Sophie decided to go take her shower and get dressed. She thought it would be a good idea to make another appearance in Nikko's neighborhood.

"Houston, can you get ahold of Agent Hampton and ask how soon they will have the stats on the raid?"

"Sure."

"I need to be seen again. Can we get a driver to take us to the Carnegie Deli by Times Square? I used to go there for lunch sometimes."

"Rodriguez can take us."

Sophie shook her head. "No, he's off duty and needs some rest. Is there anyone else?"

"No problem. I'll get someone else. What time do you want to leave?"

Sophie looked at the watch on her arm. "How about one hour?"

About 90 minutes later, Max waited outside the restaurant with Bully, as Houston and Sophie went inside. The deli was very busy, but Houston spotted a table butted up against the east wall. He led her to it. The waitress came with water and menus. Sophie didn't recognize her, but the woman gave her a strange look. She took her time and lingered at the restaurant for maximum exposure. When Houston went to pay the bill, a man came over to her table. She recognized him as someone who had worked as a waiter at Nikko's restaurant, Morano's. He leaned in close and whispered, "Ms. Star, you know Nikko is still looking for you. Are you safe coming in here?"

"Nate! It's great to see you. Can you sit for a moment?" He nodded affirmatively and sat across from Sophie. "Are you still working at Morano's?" she asked. When Houston saw a man at her table, he hurried over, not knowing the circumstances.

Sophie looked up. "Houston, this is Nate. He works at Nikko's restaurant." Houston acknowledged him, then stood behind Sophie.

"Worked," Nate added.

"You left?"

"Yup. Right after he nearly killed you. You were always so nice to the staff, and when we found out what happened, we figured if he could do that to someone he loved, he could do the same to any of us. Several of us left after that."

"Where are you working now?"

"Actually, I work here. This is just my day off. The tips aren't as good, but the atmosphere and the people are great." Sophie got up and reached her hand out to him. He got up and took it, holding it a few extra seconds.

"It was really nice to see you again, Ms. Star. And I might add you are as beautiful as ever." He smiled and Sophie smiled back.

"That is such a nice thing to say. I'll stop by here again when you're working."

"Just ask for my section. I will give you the VIP treatment."

"I know you will, Nate."

They made it back to the penthouse after stopping at a few stores for some items she needed and some fresh baked treats for the agents.

"Agent Hampton said there will be a debriefing at 6 pm. Some of the teams will debrief by secure live video conferencing," Rodriguez informed her as she came into the kitchen.

The warehouse was buzzing when they arrived. She went to sit at her regular place and waited for the briefing to begin. Agent Cosby brought everyone to order.

"As everyone here is aware, the operation started at zero four hundred, eastern time. I'm happy to report that the coordinated efforts were largely successful. In some instances, clean up and CSI are still working the warehouses, but the bulk of the raid was over by noon. Our team, imbedded within the Mexican Judicial Police, are debriefing us by live video.

Cosby pressed a button on the console in front of him and turned to a large screen on the wall. "Agent Aguilar, are you online?"

"Yes, sir," his face appeared on the large screen.

"Please give us your report."

Agent Aguilar continued speaking. "The operation started on time with the Mexican police taking lead, as agreed. We went into the bunk house and the main house on a 'no-knock' warrant. There were shots fired, but none of our men were injured. A few of the ranch security were wounded and taken to the hospital. After everything was secured, we covertly burned the fields and any stockpiled leaves that had been harvested. They had a processing plant built on site too. We confiscated all that equipment and the finished product ready to be shipped. Or I should say the Mexican police did. From a tactical perspective, it went as planned, sir."

"How long before your men get back here?"

"We should be moving out in the morning, sir."

"You and your men are to report to command after you go home and get some rest. I look forward to reading a more detailed account in your report."

"Yes, sir. I would like to say one more thing. I see Ms. Star is present, and I would like to let her know that I believe the accuracy of her intel was a big reason for our lack of injuries and success of the mission."

Sophie did not respond to the compliment. She knew that the praise for the success of the mission belonged solely to God. Cosby spoke again. "Thank you, Agent Aguilar. Compliments on a job well done."

"I'll pass that on to the team, sir."

"Please do." Agent Aguilar stayed on the line while Cosby asked for the other team's report.

"Agent Hampton, do you have a report yet form your men at the border?"

"Yes. I will defer to my man on the ground, Agent Dalton, for the initial report. Agent Dalton are you online?"

"Yes, sir." Agent Dalton's face replaced Agent Aguilar's who was now in a small box at the top of the screen.

"Go ahead."

"Sir, things got a little messy here. We have one suspect dead, and one smuggler injured. The U-Haul truck that we were chasing crashed about a mile north of the US border. The driver died, and the passenger was injured. In total, from all the raids, we confiscated approximately 10 tons of pure, uncut cocaine, maybe slightly more. The street value could be close to a billion dollars, sir."

"How many suspects do you think escaped the drag net?"

"Not many, if any. We had this wrapped up tight with the help of the Mexican Police. ICE took all undocumented immigrants into custody relieving us of that responsibility. That was a big help. We even captured a drone flying over the border with 30 lbs. of cocaine. We're not sure if it's Morano's product, but it got caught in the raid nonetheless."

Agent Hampton spoke up. "Well, it sounds like you and your men did an excellent job, Agent Dalton."

"They did, sir. And I would like to echo Agents Aguilar's comments to Ms. Star."

This time Sophie nodded her head in appreciation of his comment. Hampton continued, "Thank you. What is your ETA, Agent Dalton?"

"We will be done here by this evening and fly home tomorrow morning."

"Can your men be at command tomorrow night to write up your AAR reports? DOJ has us on a short leash because of the enormity of this operation."

"Yes, sir."

Agent Hampton got up and addressed the room. "I believe that is all we have right now. More will come in through the night. We will meet up again tomorrow night. Ms. Star, do you have any questions before we close?"

"Yes, but first I would like to say I thank God that none of your men were injured," Sophie turned to Detective Cartwright, who was sitting with the other men. "Do you know if word of this bust has filtered into the streets yet?"

Cartwright stood up and spoke. "Yes, and we heard a few rumors about Nikko going ballistic when he got a call from his ranch manager during the incursion there. He does know the fields and harvested crop were burned."

"I expected as much. Do you know if the rumors about Viktor Tsvetkov have circulated?"

"A few CIs are saying his name has been spreading among the dealers. The street level dealers never want to be out of the loop, so they act like they know who he is. The word is he never leaves the west coast, but he has been seen in town."

"Thank you, Detective. That's good news." She turned back to Agent Hampton. "That's all I have, sir. Thank you."

With that, Agent Cosby dismissed everyone to continue with their duties. On her way out, many of the support team came to her and thanked her for her part in the success of the mission.

Sophie knew how important correct information was to a successful raid, and to raid a network this size, there couldn't be a flaw in the data. But she knew in her heart that it was God that truly kept the men safe, and it was that coupled with the men's training which made the whole thing come together. Even though law enforcement would consider this a success regardless of whether Nikko took the fall, the point of this, for her, was to stop Nikko. He would be back up and running in less than a year if the second part of her strategy didn't go as planned, and then all of this would have been for nothing, at least in her mind.

Sophie's demeanor was lighter on the way back to the penthouse. She had already reconciled the cost to her if this went lopsided, but the burden she carried for these men on this first leg was heavy. High ranking officials all over must carry this sort of weight every time they are forced to put men in harm's way. Sophie now had a better understanding of how to pray for them. She looked over at Houston and wondered what it would be like if she met him some other way.

Now that there was some room to breathe, Sophie's mind was free to wander. "Houston, I'm afraid I have been very rude to you and the others. I have never even asked about your family or why you chose the DEA."

"Ms. Star, you have been nothing but considerate to all of us." Houston smile was genuine.

"That's generous of you but my mind has been so wrapped up in this first stage," Sophie said.

"I just thank God that the operation was a success, and no one was killed," he said.

"There was a death, just not on our side," she reminded him rather stiffly. "I was praying no one would die. But those things are in God's hands, not mine. I have to let it go." A smile returned to her face, and she sighed. "Please tell me about your family, Houston."

He sat back rather comfortably in the driver's seat and began. "Well, I grew up mainly in Houston, Texas, in case you didn't guess." Sophie let out a little chuckle as he continued.

"My dad was working on oil rigs when he met my mother. She was a waitress at a little greasy spoon diner. Both came from poor families who couldn't afford to pay for a college education for their children. We went through some very destitute times when we were little, but my folks were strong Christians and trusted God to put food on the table or pay their rent when they couldn't. God never failed them."

"And does their faith live on in you today?"

Houston hesitated, but only briefly. "Yes, but I have found recently that I have not kept up my prayer life as well as I used to. It's so easy to let your walk with God slide to the back burner, but that's not what I want for myself. When I realized it, I decided to do something about it."

This brought a very warm smile from Sophie. "Good for you! Few people recognize their own need for God. Do you have any brothers or sisters?"

"Two brothers and one sister. She is engaged to a wonderful man. He is the bank president of Chase Bank in Trenton, New Jersey."

Sophie nodded, took a sip from her Styrofoam cup, and said "tell me more about your parents."

"Dad would have to move the entire family whenever the job ended, whether it was a gusher, or it was a dry hole. If it was a dry hole, trying to get his last paycheck was a turkey shoot. If it was a gusher, they generally got a bonus. Feast or famine. When dad got hired on at CBJ Oil, he started rising through the ranks until he ended up managing all their fields. That meant he still traveled a lot, but he made it a point to be at all our big events. What he really wanted was to go out on his own. Mom promised when their last child's college fund was fully funded, she would support him in his dream. We were living in Houston, but when dad was working for CBJ, his last promotion moved our family up here to Trenton.

About ten years ago, dad got his wish. and it paid off for him, big time. Now he works 8 months of the year, and he and mom travel the other 4 months. He plans on retiring this year.

My folks are still just as in love as ever, maybe even more now that they get more time together. I'm hoping I can find what they have some day." He smiled self-consciously and wondered if he'd said too much.

Sophie replied, seemingly unphased. "Being a Christian and marrying another Christian is your best chance of that. As far as finding someone, I'm sure you will have little trouble in that area. You're a born protector; I can tell that it's in your very nature. Women respond to that, but you still have that gentle side, too. It seems that so few men manage to keep that in your line of work." Houston didn't know why those words meant so much to him coming from her.

As she paused to take another sip of tea, Houston turned the conversation "What about you? Tell me more about Sophie Star."

"You know all about me from my file, I'm sure."

"Well, up to your disappearance."

Sophie tried to hide the pain on her face. "I'm sorry Houston, I can't tell you anything about where I've been. If this goes awry, I'm hoping to be able to go back there and get my belongings before I disappear again. It's not that I don't trust you. It's just that I had to leave everything behind last time, and I don't want to do that again. My privacy is how I ensure that. I'm sorry." He was a little hurt that she still couldn't trust him, but her being able to trust anyone after what she had been through would be even more of a surprise.

"I understand," Houston replied, hiding his hurt feelings.

When Sophie's protection team returned to the penthouse, she asked to speak with them. "I know you were all at the same briefing as I was, but I wanted to thank you all individually for taking on the job of protecting me. I don't think I could have gone through with this if I didn't feel safe.

"The next stage of this plan is on us. If Nikko doesn't bite, I'm not sure where we go from here. If I go seeking his business rather than him coming to me, it gives him the upper hand. This doesn't work unless he comes to me. Anyway, I hope I get an opportunity to learn a little about each of you before this is all over, but I promise you one thing—I will always be praying for you, no matter where I am." The group sat and talked until dinner then ate together. After that, Sophie went to the balcony with her Bible and read.

CHAPTER NINE

Nikko was screaming at whoever was on the other end of the phone when Thomas walked into his office at the restaurant. "You're telling me they burned our fields and confiscated the processing equipment at Puebla, and no one had a clue it was coming?!" Thomas couldn't hear the other end of the conversation, which sounded very one-sided. "Which warehouses?" A second of silence. "What do you mean all of them?!" Apparently, Nikko didn't like the response because he threw the phone across the room.

"Thomas, the Mexican police raided our farm in Puebla this morning. I got a frantic call from Sisco a little after four, moments before they arrested him. They burned everything, took the processing equipment, and arrested all my workers. The DEA had to be behind this! The local police in Puebla have always turned a blind eye to my crops because they bring hundreds of thousands of dollars into the local community. It will take months, if not years, to get the ground ready for a new crop after being burned like that." Nikko cursed under his breath and bared his teeth.

"Calmati Nikko," pleaded Thomas, "you're going to have a stroke." Nikko didn't even hear him.

"They got to our warehouses too. Everything is gone, Thomas, just like that!"

"Nikko, I am sorry. Even though I'm not crazy about what you do, I would never wish this on you. What are you going to do?"

Nikko stared straight forward as he replied. "First, I'm going to find out who betrayed me. There's no way the DEA is smart enough to wipe me out like this. Then I have to find a temporary supplier until I can get another crop going. If the street dealers can't rely on me to keep the flow of drugs coming, you know they will go somewhere else. Junkies aren't the kind to wait patiently."

"Maybe this is the universe telling you it's time to get out of the business, have you thought of that?"

"Don't be ridiculous."

"I'm serious Nikko, no law enforcement has ever gotten this close to us. I won't let you take all papa worked for, down with you."

Nikko glared at his brother. "Zitto, Thomas. They can't get to me, you know that. No one in the entire organization, except for you and Sisco, knows enough to connect me directly to any of this. Sisco will never talk, he knows what would happen to his family if he did." Thomas knew Nikko was right, and the idea both comforted and concerned him.

"Papa talked about you opening some legal casinos. I'll support you in that, and I'll help you in any way I can, but I want us out of the drug business."

There was a tinge of exasperation in Nikko's voice mixed with subdued anger. "It isn't going to happen, Thomas. You know the wealth I've brought into our coffers through the years with those drugs."

But Thomas persisted, lowering his voice now. "You know that at the end papa encouraged you to get out. Nikko how much money do we need?"

"It's not the money; it's the power, the connections. Money is just a byproduct, albeit a big one, and, Thomas, you also know that papa told you to support me until I find someone else that I can trust."

"I remember, Nikko, and I will keep my word."

Nikko sat down at his desk and put his head in his hands. Thomas went over and put his hand on his shoulder. This was his brother regardless of their differences.

Nikko glared at a picture of his late father on the wall. "I *am* going to kill whoever did this."

"Nikko, I don't want to know about it. Come on. Let's go have dinner. We will discuss the avenues open to you at this point."

Nikko's gaze did not budge. "I thought you had a date tonight."

"I wasn't looking forward to it. Mama set me up," Thomas said.

Nikko let out a small, uncomfortable chuckle. "Okay, fratellino, I'll rescue you."

At dinner, Nikko spilled his biggest concerns. "What I know is this—the street dealers who buy my product won't wait for me to regroup. They'll just go to my competitors. I've got to find someone who's willing to sell me a harvested crop. It will probably cost me a bundle because I'll have to take it out from underneath another customer. They will surely gouge me because they know I have no other options."

"Do you have any idea who you could work with?" Thomas asked. "Is there someone maybe you worked with before you got your own farms?"

"All the ones I worked with are in new hands. Those kinds of turnovers are common in this business. But Ben told me he got word from a reliable source that a man name Viktor Tsvetkov is in town looking to expand the sale of his crops. Apparently, he bought or took over another farm."

When they were on the way home, Nikko turned to Thomas, "I heard another rumor. Guess who's back in town?" Thomas looked at him quizzically.

Nikko's voice hesitated. "Sophie. Someone saw her at the Café we used to go to in the morning on the way to work."

"Nikko, you know how many sightings of Sophie we've followed up. It always ends up the same. Pointless rumor. People looking for the reward will swear they saw her face in the clouds."

"I know," Nikko responded, audibly disheartened.

It took several days before the final reports came in for what had become known as "Operation Extermination." Rodriguez came in with a summary report in his hand.

"Sophie, Detective Cartwright asked Agent Hampton to get this info to you." She took it and sat down to read it.

"Agent Rodriguez, have we ensured that there is a way for Nikko to contact us."

"Yes. We haven't made it easy, but we have made it possible for him to find Viktor Tsvetkov." It was not lost on her that she would soon be coming face to face with the man who caused her so much physical pain and nearly killed her.

Off to one side, Rodriguez was quietly voicing his concern to Houston. "Keeping her safe from now on will be a lot more complicated."

"I know, I was thinking the same thing. Do you think we should bring on more men?"

"I don't think that would be wise at this point. Ms. Star is beginning to trust us, and I doubt she will let anyone else in now," Fons said.

Houston nodded in agreement. "You're right. Maybe we should overlap shifts at critical hours."

"That's a good plan."

It was only a short time later when the call from Nikko's camp finally came in. Ben was the one who eventually called, unknowingly reaching Houston who posed as Viktor Tsvetkov's right hand. They agreed to meet on the top floor of a garage at a mall on the lower east side. Houston pulled into a parking spot and noticed a well-groomed man in a pair of blue jeans and a distressed denim shirt made by Yves Saint Laurent which probably set the man back a grand. Houston got out of the car and walked over to the concrete retaining wall where the man waited.

Ben left his hands in his pockets, tightly wrapped around his favorite revolver, a gift from Nikko for his 34th birthday. "I'm Ben. Are you Houston?"

Houston looked around, checking his surrounding in case Ben might be setting him up. "Yes. Thanks for meeting me here."

"I get it, we don't know each other or our respective bosses. It makes sense to meet in an open space." Ben took his hands from his pockets and leaned against the wall next to Houston. "We heard a rumor that your employer has recently come into possession of a farm and has a crop he would like to sell," Ben said.

"Your information is accurate. It's why we're here in New York. With our new acquisition we are able to expand our sales. But I've got a bit of bad news...I'm afraid we already promised the crop to someone else."

Ben winced. "All of it?"

"Yes, my boss only deals with those who can handle copious quantities."

Ben stepped away from the wall and turned to face Houston. His face showed concern. The last thing Nikko had told him was not to return with bad news. "Has any money changed hands yet?"

"No, but my boss wants to keep a sterling reputation, and believes a handshake is still as good as a done deal."

Ben began to wave his hands as he spoke, betraying his cool façade ever so slightly. "Look, Mr. Morano wants this crop. I'm sure he would be willing to pay more than the offer you have now. Can you at least get us a seat at the table? This is New York, and in New York, a deal ain't over until money has exchanged hands."

Houston pretended to be thinking carefully. "Give me a minute." He moved away from Ben's earshot and called Sophie, "He's on the hook, he wants a seat at the table. I told him the crop was already promised but he's pushing."

"That's what we want," Sophie replied. "Ben knows that he can't go back to Nikko empty handed. Reel him in, Houston." Houston hung up and walked back over to where Ben was standing.

"Viktor Tsvetkov will only meet with Mr. Morano. He doesn't do business with middlemen. If he wants a seat at the table, he can have it, but the seat belongs to him and him only." He was worried he was pushing Ben too far. But Nikko had to be the one who came.

At this, Ben hesitated, then replied, "wait a minute. Now it's my turn to call my boss." Ben called Nikko, "Nikko, they have a crop, but it's been promised although no money has exchanged hands yet."

"Then offer them double, just get that crop."

"I offered more money, but this guy says his boss won't renege on a handshake. He did say we could meet with his boss and try to make a deal, but that's another thing...Mr. Tsvetkov will only meet with you."

"Okay. Then get me a meeting. I'll go."

Ben hung up and turned his attention back to Houston. "Mr. Morano has agreed to a meeting with Mr. Tsvetkov. Can you set it up?"

"We were planning on leaving as soon as this deal is done in a couple of days but let me ask." He called Sophie back letting her know it was a go.

"Okay, you have a meeting set for 6 pm tomorrow," he informed Ben.

Ben was clearly relieved. "Where?"

"We will text you tomorrow and let you know." They finally shook hands and went to their cars.

Back at the penthouse, Agent Rodriguez called Agent Hampton and let him know that the meeting was set for 6 pm the following day. This was it! There were just a few more hurdles to leap over. They had to make an agreement, set up a time for money and product to exchange hands, and Nikko had to be the one to hand her the money in order to incriminate himself. She told Agent Hampton she was going to need a large enough sample for Nikko to test. He told her that this was already arranged with the DOJ. Sophie went to her room early. She needed time alone with God.

The team had gone over the plan several times. Kelly and Titan would stay with Sophie in the conversation pit by the fireplace, and Houston would be by her side. Rodriguez would stand by the door, and Max would have Bully at the door to the balcony. All cameras and microphones would be on, and backup agents would be on the ground floor but out of sight. Everything that happened would be broadcast back to support at command. Both Agent Hampton and Agent Cosby would handle tactical command in case anything went wrong. Sophie asked for Detective Cartwright and Mahoney to be in the building too. This operation was running on all cylinders. Once the plan was approved by the higher ups, Houston was given the go ahead to text the address to Ben in the morning.

Sophie spent the afternoon getting ready. She wore a Norma Kamali dress, black, which was fitted to the waist then flared out at the bottom to just below her knees. Two wide tan stripes were separated by two wide black stripes from the hips down. She looked feminine, gorgeous but also subtle. She had her hair in a chignon at the nape of her neck. Her makeup was flawless. She had a one carat diamond earring in each ear and a two-carat sapphire on her finger. She knew Nikko liked her in dresses, and she needed him to be off guard. She had to shake him up so he would make a mistake. It was her only chance. If he were working at full capacity, he would see through her façade, and her confidence would crumble.

At 5:30 pm, she came out of her room to speak with the team one more time. The sight of her took Houston's breath away.

108

Max whistled, and Sophie chuckled. Men always seemed to like seeing women in dresses.

"You look great," Houston told her.

"Thanks, Houston."

"Don't worry about anything. We have your six."

"My what?" she asked.

"Your six. It means we have your back." They shared a laugh.

"I know you do," Sophie assured him. They all talked for a few minutes, then Sophie went to the leather chair in the conversation pit that faced the door. The FBI told Rodriguez through his earbud that Nikko just handed his Porsche keys to the valet and that Thomas was with him. Rodriguez was the only one with a hidden earbud, and it was risky for even one of them to have it. But they needed a way to communicate in case things went bad. He relayed the message to Sophie.

"Thomas? He said Thomas is with Nikko?" Sophie inquired.

"Yes." Rodriguez opened the door when he heard the knock. Nikko was scoping the penthouse out for threats when his eyes fell on Sophie.

"Sophie?" His voice was so weak it barely came out. His knees almost went out from under him, and Thomas reached a hand out to support him. Thomas looked like he was in shock.

Sophie had intended to stand, but suddenly her legs wouldn't move, and she was shaking. She felt like she was the same naïve young woman back in the hospital.

Lord, no, please, I can't let fear take me over. Give me strength, she prayed to herself. Houston noticed she didn't move. She didn't say anything—this wasn't the plan. Houston was somewhat startled by her reaction. She hadn't given any indication before this that she was scared, and he wondered what was going on in her mind. He could see the same confusion on his partner's face. Nikko started rushing toward her. Titan growled at his sudden movement.

"Sophie, sweetheart…" Houston stepped in front of her and put his arm out to stop him.

"Get out of my way! That's my fiancé!" Sophie finally found her strength. She stood up and put her hand on Houston's shoulder. It was a good thing that her dress came down over her knees because they were shaking so badly.

"It's alright Houston, I'll take care of this." He moved to the side.

"Hello, Nikko. It's nice to see you, but let's get one thing straight right away—I am *not* your fiancé!" Her voice had a small, almost imperceptible quiver. She saw Thomas move forward.

"Please, Nikko, have a seat." She motioned to the couch.

"What's going on here, Sophie? Where have you been? I looked everywhere for you," Nikko questioned her.

"We will catch up later. First, let's take care of business."

Nikko was visibly puzzled. "I don't get it…I'm here to see Viktor Tsvetkov."

Sophie smiled meekly. "I am Viktor Tsvetkov…or, I should say, I took over his name for business purposes when he died. But the crop you seek is mine. The only reason I agreed to meet with you was because of your father. He was good to me. I heard he died recently. I'm sorry for your loss."

"Thank you," Thomas responded when Nikko didn't.

Sophie got right to business. "Nikko, I have already promised the crop to someone else. I'm sorry. I can't sell it to you."

"Sophie," Nikko began, "I've had a setback. The DEA burned my crop in Puebla and confiscated all the product in my warehouses."

"How is that possible?"

Dangerous Obsession

"I don't know but if I don't get this crop I will be out of business."

"If the DEA is onto you, that puts my organization in the cross hairs if I do business with you. What makes you think that I want to take that kind of a risk?"

"No, there's no risk. They still can't attach any of it to me, or else I would already be in jail. Only the farm manager knows who I am, and he would never give me up."

"Even if that's the case, I have promised it to someone else." *This is one smooth lady*, Houston thought from his station at her side.

Nikko insisted, "I'll pay whatever you want, double the other offer, even. I have the money. You, of all people, know that."

Sophie sighed aloud and feigned deep thought. After a moment, she relented. "Okay, Nikko. I don't know how I will make it right with my buyer, but you can have this crop. It's 8 tons uncut. I won't sell it in pieces you either take it all or none."

His eyes lit up at this news. "I need it all! How much?"

"Well, why don't we let Thomas and Houston work out the details, and we can talk." She turned to Houston and nodded. Thomas and Houston moved to the kitchen table. Nikko got up to move closer to her. Titan lurched at him. Sophie held up a halting hand. "Nikko, I wouldn't come any closer." Houston was on his feet, and Rodriguez was moving toward her. She waved them away, signaling that she was fine.

"Can't we have some privacy?" Nikko pled.

"No. Nikko, what you did to me was unforgiveable. We will talk here in plain view."

"No, Sophie, nothing's unforgivable if you love someone."

Sophie's face remained stoic. "You don't beat someone nearly to death if you love them."

Nikko was almost stuttering now. "I know, but it wasn't me. Something just got a hold of me when I saw you with Jimmy. I

111

was already upset because you said you needed time to answer my marriage proposal. I don't know why...I just got so jealous." He ran his hand down his face.

"If you did that to me, what did you do to Jimmy?" He didn't answer, but only stared at the floor. She gasped. Houston looked over to see if she was alright. "Tell me, Nikko!" Sophie demanded. "What did you do to Jimmy?!" She almost shouted the question this time.

Hesitantly, but fearing that she might withdraw her offer to sell him the crop, he relented. "After I saw what I had done to you, and you were laying in the hospital in a coma, I was so angry. I blamed it on him. If he hadn't been talking to you and making you laugh, none of it would have happened. I went to his house...and...I slit his throat."

Sophie let out an emphatic scream. "NOOOOO!" Houston shot to her side. Sophie stood. "Get him out of here."

"Sophie! We can get through this, sweetheart!"

"I said get him out of here, right now!" Rodriguez took Nikko by the arm, but he pulled away from the agent and tried to get back to Sophie. Houston grabbed his arm and twisted it behind his back to take control of him. Thomas jumped to Nikko's side facing off Houston.

"Get your hands off my brother. I'll take care of him, let him go." Houston turned his glance to Sophie, who nodded, so he let him go. Thomas walked Nikko out the door.

When the door closed behind them, she turned to Houston, her anger palpable. "Did you know?"

"Know what?"

"That he killed his cousin, Jimmy."

Houston looked dumbfounded. "I thought you already knew." She turned and ran to her room, sobbing.

Houston called after her. "I'm sorry, Sophie! We thought you already knew."

The comm in Rodriguez's ear was alive with chatter, and Houston's phone was ringing. They knew this whole thing just blew up in their face, and their boss' wanted answers. The big question was whether they could provide them or not.

Dangerous Obsession

CHAPTER TEN

The rest of the night was spent fielding calls from the DOJ, the FBI task force, and their own boss at the DEA. Throughout the night, they could still hear her sobbing. Houston asked Max if Bully could go in and be with her, so Max removed the dog's vest. Houston didn't knock; he opened the door quietly, just wide enough to let Bully in, then closed it behind him. Bully jumped on the bed and snuggled up to her. He sat down on the floor just outside the door, his arms across his bent knees, for the next few hours as he listened to her sob. Finally, she quieted, and he went to the kitchen.

No one had left. They were all worried about her.

"What happens now?" Kelly asked Rodriguez.

"I'm not sure this is salvageable, even if we could bring Ms. Star back from the edge. What do you think, Houston?"

"I don't know, Fons. You didn't see her reaction when he came through that door. She was paralyzed, shaking like a leaf. I couldn't believe she even rebounded from that. I don't know how much more we can ask of this woman."

Agent Rodriguez leveled his gaze at Agent Townsend. "The boss is giving us 24 hours to decide if this operation is salvageable. Otherwise, he is dismantling the joint task force. Every day that warehouse is open, it's costing the DOJ a mint not to mention what they are paying for this penthouse. They feel like they have had a successful operation even if they don't get Nikko. We shut down an entire network of drugs coming into the US. That's a big win for the DEA, DOJ, ICE, and the FBI. It can end now as far as they are concerned."

"Yeah, but you know that's not what she got into this for. She wants Nikko in jail." No one responded to Houston's comment because they all knew it was true.

Houston placed a hand on the shoulder of his friend. "Fons, I don't think I'll get any sleep tonight. I'll take this watch. Go get some rest. You too, Max. The FBI put some extra security on the penthouse doors for the night."

"Alright, but I'll relieve you at 4 am, so you can at least *try* to get a few hours of sleep. All of us need to be alert," Fons countered.

"Thanks." Rodriguez went to his room and Max used Houston's room. He didn't want to take Bully away from Sophie, so he decided to stay the night.

Kelly did her sweep. Houston started his rounds too.

Thomas had taken the keys because Nikko was too shaken to drive. "What on earth happened in there, fratello?"

"Sophie asked me about Jimmy. I guess she hadn't heard that he died."

"He didn't die Nikko...he was murdered around the same time that you put Sophie in the hospital. But you swore to me that you didn't have anything to do with that."

Nikko looked at his brother then back to the dashboard in front of him. "I told you already that I didn't." His voice went soft now, "Thomas, she's back, Sophie's back. There is still a chance for us."

Thomas looked at Nikko in shock. *Does he really have no clue she will never let him touch her again? Is my brother, who's so smart in so many ways, really that blind when it comes to Sophie?* It was then that Thomas started thinking Nikko might need psychiatric

116

help. This had gone from obsession to delusion. Thomas took Nikko home, but he knew he couldn't leave him alone. He most certainly would try to go back after Sophie. Thomas knew this as certainly as he knew his own name. They left the car in the porte-cochère and went inside.

"Nikko, what are you going to do about getting more product? It looks to me that Sophie's crop is out." Nikko went to the bar, poured himself a drink and sat down on the couch by the window. He stared out the window for a long time, thinking.

"Thomas...you have to go back and talk to her. I *must* have that crop. Did you and her man settle on a price before we were escorted out?"

"He says there is 8 tons in the warehouse and their willing to sell it for $108 million."

"Pretty reasonable," Nikko mumbled, "under the circumstances." Thomas moved to the chair across from his brother.

"Nikko, it's still not too late to change direction here. Maybe this is a sign, or maybe it's papa trying to tell us something. Let's move out of the drug trade. This seems as good a time as any." For a second, Thomas thought Nikko might relent and give up this craziness, but then he stood up moving toward Thomas.

Nikko pointed at Thomas' chest and spouted, "You promised papa, you would support me. Well, I need your support now. I need you to go back to Sophie and get me that cocaine."

Thomas stood up. It was his turn to chastise. "Be careful, fratello. I want to honor my promise to papa but make no mistake; if I feel your putting our family's overall interests in jeopardy, Ti fermerà."

At this, Nikko got right in Thomas' face. "È che una minaccia?!" Thomas moved away from his brother a full step.

"Not a threat, Nikko. That's a promise." Now Thomas' finger was raised and pointing back to his brother. "And if I ever

117

find out you had *anything* to do with Jimmy's death, I will sever all ties with you! He was family too."

Nikko took Thomas' promise seriously. Thomas did not anger easily, and when he did, he meant exactly what he said. "Calmati, fratellino. Nothing is going to go wrong. Please Thomas, at least try to talk to her." Thomas let out a long breath.

"Okay, I will make one attempt. Then I'm done with all of this. That business is all yours. I'll get our attorney to separate our businesses. It's time we go our own ways." Thomas had threatened that before, but this time Nikko saw he meant it. Maybe it was time to leave his little brother behind. It just meant more money and autonomy for him.

Nikko's sense of indignancy returned somewhat. "I'm alright with that, but I want the restaurant too."

"Nikko, I won't argue with you over it. You can have whatever you want. You will always be family. I just can't worry everyday if this will be the day we're taken down by your illicit exploits."

Nikko set his empty glass on the bar. "I'm going to bed. You're welcome to use the spare bedroom if you want."

"Thanks. I think I will." Thomas was not leaving Nikko tonight.

At 1:20 am, an ear-piercing scream came from Sophie's bedroom. Houston was the first one there, his weapon drawn. Then Kelly, Max and Rodriguez came up behind him. They searched the room to make sure no one was there then holstered their guns. Sophie was coming out of her nightmare but still feeling the effects of it. Bully was still lying next to her, nudging her awake. Houston sat on the side of her bed and noticed she was shaking.

"You're alright, Sophie. You just had a nightmare. We're all here...no one can get to you."

He took her head and gently brought it to his chest. She relaxed into him and sobbed. The others filed out of the room. Sophie lifted her head when she was done crying. "Please tell the others I'm sorry for scaring them. And thank you for your shoulder to cry on."

Houston spoke softly, "I want to be here for you."

"Thank you, Houston, but I'm okay now. I need some time alone." He got up, and left her alone, but he didn't go further than his spot outside her door. He heard her get out of bed. She was praying, "Lord, I can't live through this again. The nightmares, the fear. You delivered me from all of that. I can't let it get a foothold on me ever again. You said, 'true love casts out all fear,' and you have shown me that kind of true love. Deliver me from my enemies, as you did for David," she continued to pray.

He knew he was invading her privacy, but he was glued to that spot. His arms felt empty now that she wasn't in them anymore. It felt so right, her in his arms even for those few minutes. He wondered when his heart got involved, but he knew the answer. He was smitten from the moment their eyes met when she stepped out of Agent Hamptons office. Then — the first time he saw her smile, the first time he heard her laugh, and when he watched her holding her own against Agent Cosby at the briefing. Yes, he could track it from its origin. He wanted her to trust him, to know he would keep her safe, that he would never again let anyone hurt her like Nikko did. He knew she had no plans to stay here when this was done, and he also knew his heart would be broken when she left. But he had no intention of building a wall around his heart. He was going into this with his eyes wide open, knowing coming out would be painful. He was just grateful he had an opportunity in this life to care for someone like her. He'd never felt this way for any other woman.

119

He just hung his head and began praying quietly. He needed to find that closeness with God he once had. And he needed guidance on how to keep this woman safe.

Rodriguez came and relieved him at 4 am. He got up and went to his room. No sounds had come from Sophie's room for a few hours now, but all the same, he just hadn't felt like leaving his spot outside her door.

By 8 o'clock the next morning, the whole team was regrouping around the kitchen table and eating bacon and eggs. Kelly had made the coffee. Hers was much better than Rodriguez's, so she took over that job. All the chatter stopped when Sophie came out of the room with Bully by her side.

"Max, thank you for letting Bully stay with me last night." She squatted down and rubbed Bully's face.

"It was our pleasure. Come here, boy!" Max called his dog over to him.

"I'm sorry about last night...all of it. I don't know where we go from here with this operation. I might have blown it with Nikko." Rodriguez came over to her with a cup of Kelly's coffee.

"That's alright, Ms. Star. Where we go from here is up to you. We're with you either way. If you don't think you're able to continue, we understand. DOJ is plenty happy with the results so far. Shutting down his network and confiscating over 10 tons of cocaine, besides burning a crop in the field, is a bigger bite than they ever hoped to take of the Morano operation. If you walk away now, no one will hold anything against you."

"Thank you, Agent Rodriguez. That's very kind of you to say. But I need to finish this. I just don't know if I can. I blew it last night. What is Agent Hampton saying?"

"He said he would give us 24 hours to decide."

She nodded. "Could you please see if Detective Cartwright would come up to see me this morning?"

"Yes, of course." She made small talk with everyone for a few minutes and went out to the balcony.

Houston watched Detective Cartwright talking to Sophie. He was sitting on the little wooden table facing her. He reached out for her hand, and she let him take it. He wondered why she trusted him. What was their connection? It wasn't romantic; it was more like there was some history between them.

"Why didn't you tell me about Jimmy, Don?"

He sighed. "Well, I knew you would take the guilt on yourself. But there was nothing you could've done to stop it. You were in the hospital when we found his body in a ditch."

"Did you know Nikko killed him?" Sophie asked.

"During our investigation, we talked to some of the guests that were there the night you were assaulted. We pieced together that you had been talking to Jimmy when Nikko rather abruptly snatched you away. I put the puzzle together and was pretty sure that Nikko had gotten jealous for some reason. We had absolutely no forensic evidence, no eyewitness, and Nikko had a rock-solid alibi."

"He admitted it to me last night."

"I know. I could hear through the comm, now it's on tape but..."

"Any smart lawyer will get these tapes thrown out. You know my testimony alone won't get him convicted."

"And his lawyers are good."

"If I can find a way to get this sting back on track with enough iron clad evidence, maybe Nikko would make a deal with the DA. If the DA will clump the murder with the plea, even if Nikko doesn't do extra time for it, it will still be on his

121

record. I want that justice for Jimmy. I want to hear Nikko admit it out loud in court."

"Sophie, I will talk to the DA and help him find a way to convince Nikko to take a plea if our evidence is strong enough."

She looked up at him. "I couldn't hold it together last night when he confessed. I thought I was doing well. Then when I found out..., I'm sorry." She hung her head covering her face with her hands. Detective Cartwright took her hands away from her face and held them again.

"You did great last night. The success of the raid on Nikko was all because of your intel. You have nothing to apologize for." He got up to leave. She put her hand on his forearm. He looked down at her.

"Tell the others I'm going to try to figure a way to salvage this. When I pray, I know that's what I need to do. I just don't know how yet." He nodded and patted her hand.

The Detective went inside and told the team what she said. "She wants you to let everyone involved know that she'll do whatever she can to salvage the sting." Rodriguez nodded his head.

"She is a strong woman, Detective," Agent Rodriguez said.

"That she is."

Houston walked Cartwright to the door. The detective was surprised when Houston stepped into the hall with him and closed the door behind them.

"Detective, she trusts you. I know you and your partner were the detectives on her assault case, but it seems there is a deeper history there. Can you tell me?"

Cartwright was quiet for a moment, looked Houston in the eyes, "I guess. There's no reason to keep it a secret any longer." He went on to explain how he and his partner were trying to talk to Ms. Star without Nikko or Thomas in the room. They were trying to get her to bring charges against him. He told Houston the account of Sophie's brave escape from the hospital and how he helped her to the rendezvous point. Houston cringed as the detective relayed his tale. Cartwright finished by telling Houston, "I know you saw the pictures in the file, but it's not like seeing it in the flesh. You can't imagine how awful that beating was. I almost lost my lunch the first time I saw her."

"Did you see or know the person who picked her up?"

Cartwright looked at the agent with resolve. "Now, that is a secret I intend on keeping. I never even told my partner any of this. She doesn't know that I know who it was."

Houston reached out to shake his hand. "Thank you, Detective. I appreciate you telling me."

Rodriguez brought Sophie's lunch to her around noon. "What do you need us to do, Ms. Star?"

"I don't know — an opportunity has to present itself. I can't just call him after that fiasco last night." She looked up at him, took the sandwich and the iced tea, and said, "thanks for the lunch."

Rodriguez soon got a message from the FBI through his comm. He got everyone's attention; "the FBI says Thomas just handed his keys to the valet downstairs." He went to the balcony door and called Sophie in, "Ms. Star, Thomas is on the way up. What do you want us to do?" Her eyes got wide.

"This is the way back! I can make this work!" She looked straight into one of the camera's, "I want all of the cameras and microphones turned off for this." Chatter started screeching in Rodriguez's comm.

"Command says no, ma'am."

"You tell them that isn't a request. It's the only way that I can make this work." She looked him right in the eye.

Sophie turned her attention to Houston now. "When you let him in, put him in that chair." She pointed to the one facing the balcony in front of the fireplace. She wanted to be on a higher elevation when he first saw her. She needed the upper hand, and that started with him having to look up at her. *It all starts in the mind.* Nikko taught her that.

"I'll take him out to the balcony." Rodriguez turned to Kelly, "you and Titan are with her."

"No," she said. "I need to be alone with him. I'm in no danger with Thomas."

"Sophie, I don't think that's a good idea," Houston added aggressively.

"Really, it will be fine." She headed to her room to get ready. Rodriguez went to deal with command who was going crazy in his ear. Kelly took her position at the balcony doors, and Houston took a position by the front door.

Houston escorted Thomas to the designated seat and told him Sophie would be with him shortly. It looked like he was in the same expensive Italian suit he had on last night. About ten minutes later, Sophie walked out in a titanium colored, silk draped blouse with ivory colored silk slacks and black pumps. She had the same sapphire ring she always wore, but her earrings were small gold hoops. Thomas got up to greet her. Houston started to step in, but Sophie waved him off. Thomas hugged her and kissed her cheek.

"Sophie." He sounded relieved to see her.

"Hi, Thomas," She turned to the balcony and led him through the doors. As much as Houston hated to admit it, a small tinge of jealousy hit him. They sat close on the wicker couch at an angle that allowed them to look at each other.

"Sophie, why did you come back here?"

"I had business here, and I felt it was time to face my demons. Thomas, what are you doing working with Nikko? You promised me you would only work the legal businesses. You were the family's only hope to get out of this life."

Thomas took her hand. "Before our papa died, he made me promise to be Nikko's partner until we could bring in someone we could trust. But after last night, I told him I was done. We're splitting the business and going our separate ways."

"Thomas, that's wonderful."

Yeah, well he asked me to do him one last favor. He wants me to convince you to sell him your crop." She pulled her hand away from his.

"You know he killed Jimmy, don't you?"

"Who told you that?"

"He did. Last night." Houston saw Thomas get up. He looked angry, and Houston was ready to go intervene, but he saw that Sophie's face was calm.

"I asked him when they found his body if he had anything to do with it. He swore he didn't and last night, he lied to me again." Thomas turned back to look at her. She had to pull back a little bit or Thomas would be so angry with Nikko that he might just walk away from the deal. She had to remember her goal here.

"Look, Thomas, I know how much you love Nikko. He's your brother, so if you promise me that this is the last time you will have anything to do with his drug trafficking, I will sell him what I have." Thomas sat back down. He was quiet for a while.

"Sophie, how did you get back into this life? I thought for sure you would go straight after what you went through." This was it; she had to sell her cover story to a man to whom she hated to lie.

"That was my plan. When I got to Lake View, I used your money to open an accounting office just like you said. That's how I met Viktor Tsvetkov. I did his personal taxes." She went on to tell him how Viktor was a distinguished Russian about 25 years older than she. He knew she had no family, so he befriended her. He would cook for her, or they would go to a show together but nothing romantic.

"Sophie..." Thomas raised a single eyebrow in skepticism.

"Alright, maybe he was interested in me, but he never acted on it." She went on to tell Thomas that, as they became closer, he told her what Tsvetkov Enterprises' product really was. He had a coca farm in Peru and a network similar to Nikko's but not as secure. She started giving him some advice and strategies to grow his business, and he turned all the books over to her. One day, he asked if she would like to be a 50/50 partner with him. He said he had no family to whom he could leave his enterprise. A few months later, he collapsed at dinner. He had a heart attack and underwent triple bypass surgery. She nursed him back to health, but he never really regained his stamina. A year later, he died in his sleep. When the will was read, she found out he left everything to her — the farm, the house, and all of his money.

"Why didn't you retire then? Thomas inquired of her.

"The same reason you and Nikko don't. We're too young. What would I do? I have no husband, no kids, and no extended family. I figured I would build it up for the next ten years then sell the whole network to someone and open a restaurant. I always loved being at Morano's." He took her hand again.

"You know Nikko thinks he can win you back. He thinks you will forgive him."

"I have forgiven him, Thomas. It was the only way to make the nightmares stop."

A gentleness came through in Thomas' voice, now. "I thought of you every day, Sophie."

126

Dangerous Obsession

CHAPTER ELEVEN

Houston saw Thomas put his fingers under her chin and lift her head. He kissed her gently on the lips, and then he leaned his forehead on hers. That's when it hit him like a thunderbolt. Thomas *must* have been the one that helped Sophie drop off the face of the earth. He knew it had to be someone with lots of money and contacts. Both brothers were in love with her, but Nikko made the first move, and that made her off limits for Thomas. But after Nikko nearly killed her, Thomas made her disappear for her own good.

"Sophie, do you think there is a chance for us?"

"Thomas... how would that work? Nikko is still your brother. You would never betray him like that, and I'm leaving as soon as I complete this deal. It's time for us all to move on." He moved his head away from hers.

"You're right. I just wish…"

"I know. Me too."

"What are you going to do about Nikko?"

"I will meet with him once more at the exchange and make it perfectly clear that I have no intention of seeing him again, ever. And Thomas, you must promise me that you won't back down and let him talk you into coming with him. You're out of this, or the deal is off."

"No, I told him if I found out he had anything to do with Jimmy's death I would sever all ties with him, and I meant it." They sat there talking another hour. Then Thomas kissed her again and walked out the door without saying a word to anyone.

Sophie walked to the railing and looked over the city with her back to the French doors. Houston thought she might be crying. Rodriguez asked, "should one of us go see if she's alright?"

"No," Ann Kelly said, "she'll come in when she's ready."

About 15 minutes later, she came in. Everyone was already sitting at the kitchen table, waiting.

"I just lied and betrayed the man who saved my life. Someone I care about very deeply," she sighed. "But the deal is back on."

Normally, the team would have been celebrating that the operation was a go. But her sorrow at what she had to do to accomplish it, kept their excitement at bay.

"Agent Rodriguez, will you let command know we need 8 tons of cocaine and a place to make the exchange. I know they will need some time to set up cameras and microphones but see if we can get this done tomorrow so I can go home and be done with this," Sophie requested.

The last part of her statement yanked at Houston's heart, the thought of not seeing her again. Rodriguez went to make the arrangements. No one knew what else to say, so they went about their duties. Only Houston stayed at the table with her.

"Sophie, you don't have to go through with this."

She looked up at him and replied, "it's too late. The deed is done, and this is what I came to do—to put Nikko behind bars."

"Is Thomas the one?" Her eyebrows scrunched together.

"What do you mean, 'the one', Houston?"

"Is he the one who helped you disappear?" He thought maybe she wasn't going to answer.

"Yes. Thomas was livid at what Nikko had done to me. He swore that he would never let Nikko touch me again, and the only way to do that was for me to be out of reach. While Nikko was gone to Florida on business, Thomas stayed by my bedside and made all the arrangements. He paid for everything, set me up at a private rehab to recuperate for three months, and gave me a ticket to a new life. He gave me money to start over because I had to leave everything behind. If there was any money trail, Nikko would have found it."

"Was he in love with you?" She paused, and he wanted to reach for her hand like Thomas had, but he stopped himself.

"Maybe, but he would have done it anyway. He never approved of Nikko's lifestyle. He says Nikko still thinks he can win me back. You must tell Agent Hampton that no one can ever find out I was involved with taking Nikko down. His mother is fiercely protective of their family. She may seem meek, but she lived this life for years, and she would put a bounty on my head until there was proof that I was dead."

"I'll confer with the task force to make sure." He was afraid to ask this next question for fear of the answer. "Will you and Thomas pursue a relationship after this?"

"It's time for all of us to move on. I'm a different person now. I will always love him because he took care of me, saved me, but not in a romantic way. What feelings I once might have had for him have morphed into a concern for his soul." Houston didn't realize he had been holding his breath. "Houston, do you think I could get out of here and go out for dinner?"

"I don't think that will be a problem." She got up and went to her room. Houston sat for a minute and considered what she had told him.

Sophie had a craving for Italian food, and her favorite place in New York for Italian, besides Morano's of course, was Pellegrino's Ristorante. She could already taste the Fettuccini Giovanni on her tongue. It was a little more upscale, so she dressed appropriately. Houston was in a suit. She was reminded of how handsome he was, and she was surprised when her heart skipped a beat. She had invited Max and Bully to eat with them instead of waiting outside. That wouldn't be a problem since Bully was a service dog. Max had on a suit, too.

"You guys are all dolled up." Sophie said and laughed as they did the mandatory twirl, and Bully copied. She reached down and cupped Bully's face. "And they thought I was talking to them," she cooed. Everyone laughed. Houston held out his arm to her; "my lady?" She chuckled and took it.

Pellegrino's was busy, as always, but they had reservations, so they were quickly escorted to a booth. Houston looked up the blueprints of the restaurant before they came; he had to know the escape routes in case of trouble. He also visually swept the perimeter of the inside to see if anything felt off. The waiter handed them menus and offered them alcoholic beverages, which they all declined in favor of coffee or tea. Sophie was excited to be here. Max asked her, "so, what's good here?"

"Everything, but I'm having Fettucine Giovanni. But if you're looking for something heartier, the Filetto di Manzo or the Carre D'Angello are superb."

"Eaten here once or twice, have you?" Max teased.

"Yes." The waiter brought their beverages and garlic bread sticks.

"Are you ready to order?" The waiter asked.

Houston nodded then said, "the lady will have the Fettucine Giovanni…" instantly he felt her look at him and tense up. Then, just as quickly, she relaxed and smiled. He continued his order, but he would have to ask her what that was about later. "…and I will have the Filetto di Manzo, medium rare."

"I will have the Carre D'Angello, medium, please," Max finished the order.

"Okay, if one of us eats these garlic bread sticks, which are fantastic by the way, all of us have to, or we won't be able to talk to each other. Deal?" Sophie bartered.

Max and Houston looked at each other, "deal." Max went to grab some bread and Houston slapped his hand, "what, were you raised by wolves?" Houston picked up the basket so Sophie could take the first piece then put it back down. Sophie laughed at the look on Max's face. Houston realized that he loved that laugh if he could only keep them coming. It almost felt like he was on a date with her. The thought sparked his insides.

"Sophie, can I ask you a question?"

"Sure, Max."

"Why did you come back here? No one would have ever found you."

"You're right. My cover was good." She wondered if she could explain her conviction. Sophie continued. "When I left New York, after my body healed, my mind was still a mess. I jerked away at any touch, male or female. I had nightmares that I woke up screaming from. One night, the lights went out, and I sat in a corner with a knife in my hands expecting Nikko to come through my door any minute.

"A young woman who was my neighbor befriended me, and she would constantly invite me to church. She had heard me screaming night after night."

Although Sophie didn't remember much of her past, she did have a vague memory of going to church. "Suzie, my neighbor, continually talked about Jesus. I finally decided that if Jesus could help me, I was desperate enough to give Him a chance. I ended up turning my life over to Christ and laid all my sins at the foot of the cross so His redeeming blood could cover them. It took time," she said, "but I was delivered from my fears. I still have to fight some of the things that try to hang on, like over questioning someone's motives. Are they being polite or are they trying to control me?" Houston realized that he just got his answer. "I really was a new creature; it was like all those horrible things happened to someone else. The pain of it was gone. Part of being delivered was forgiving Nikko, which was a challenging thing to do. But the pastor reminded me that Christ tells us we must forgive because He first forgave us. One day, I understood that forgiving Nikko didn't make what he did to me right. It released me from the hatred that was keeping me bound."

"But why come back?" Max asked.

"It was something I heard in one of the sermons. Pastor said that when we do things wrong and repent, God forgives us and never remembers them again. But here on earth, there are repercussions for our immoral behavior. He said that there are some things you can make right and some that you can't. I started thinking of all the harm I inflicted by helping Nikko's organization grow and how I set up the protections that kept him from getting caught. I knew I couldn't change what was past, but maybe I could stop it from continuing. I know taking Nikko down won't end drug trafficking in this country, but it will end the part I played in it."

The waiter finally brought their food. Sophie and Houston both bowed their heads in a silent prayer over their meals. Max waited out of respect. When she looked up Max said, "thank you for sharing that."

The food and the company were great. Houston and Max bantered back and forth, and it made Sophie chuckle. She wanted to take food back for Agent Kelly and Agent Rodriguez, so she had Houston place an order to go. Their plates had been cleared, and they were just waiting for the 'to go' order. Houston was still on duty, so he periodically swept the room with his eyes. Just then, Max heard a low growl from Bully. Houston raised his eyes and saw Nikko and Ben near the entrance. Nikko was talking to the Maître d'. Houston told Max to text the FBI driver and have him bring the car around.

Sophie hadn't noticed the two men at the door yet. Ben's eyes met Houston's as he swept the restaurant, then he bent down and whispered in Nikko's ear. Nikko jerked his head in their direction. Houston whispered to Sophie, "Nikko just came in." She looked up and noticed that he was headed their way.

"Sophie, sweetheart…"

"Nikko! Please quit calling me that."

"Sophie, I know you're angry with me right now, but we need to talk. Thomas said you planned on leaving soon. You can't leave without letting me talk to you, privately."

"Not right now, Nikko. Maybe after our business is done. Thomas said you still want to go through with the deal. I will keep my word, but only if you and I do the exchange face to face. If you are exposing my organization to the DEA because of your troubles, then you are going to be exposed right along with me. Understood?"

"Of course, Sophie. I would never put you at risk." Sophie put her hand on Houston's knee. He knew she was getting nervous, and he had to get her out of there.

"Houston will get in touch with Ben tomorrow and provide the location." Houston stood and said, "Ms. Star, we need to leave. We are attracting too much attention. Max will take you to the car. I'll pay the bill."

Nikko turned to look at Houston while still addressing Sophie. "Do you let your help tell you what to do, Sophie?" She stood up.

"Houston does what I pay him for, and that's to watch out for me."

Houston knew she was playing a role, but, for some reason, treating him like "the help" still hurt. Nikko grabbed her wrist as she started to step away. Bully growled.

"We need to talk."

She wiggled from his grasp. "After, Nikko. I said after!" He moved out of her way and Max escorted her out. The waiter brought the 'to go' food, and Houston gave him his credit card.

Nikko stepped closer to Houston and spoke beneath his breath. "You stay out of my way. She belongs to me...do you hear me?"

Houston was unmoved. "She doesn't belong to anyone. She's not property. And I have no intention of letting you get near her unless she says so." The waiter came back, and Houston added the tip and signed the slip. He picked up the food and started to leave. Nikko put his finger on Houston's chest, his face now red and the veins in his neck visibly bulging.

"I will get her back one way or the other. If you want to stay alive, don't get between us." Nikko and Ben finally moved toward their table. That was a threat, and Houston had no intention of taking it lightly.

Sophie was quiet on the way home, but she didn't want the evening to end on a bad note, so she tried to come back from that confrontation with Nikko. She handed the food to Agents Rodriguez and Kelly, getting them cloth napkins and china coffee cups so they could experience the food the way it was intended. She insisted on visiting with them as they ate. When they were done, she went to her room.

Houston told Rodriguez and Kelly what had happened at the restaurant and told them of Nikko's threat.

"I have no doubt he will kill her if she doesn't agree to go back to him."

"Well, it's our job to see that doesn't happen." Rodriguez replied. "I heard from command while you were gone. They have a location set up for the exchange tomorrow. They want it to go down at 5 pm."

"I'll tell Sophie in the morning," Houston affirmed.

"Command was angry that she turned off the cameras and mics. They chewed me out for allowing it."

"They agreed to her conditions when this all started. They'll just have to get over it. You did the right thing, Fons."

"I know. I'll take the late shift. You're off until zero five hundred," Fons said.

"Thanks. I'll be in the bedroom."

Houston couldn't help thinking about how much he enjoyed Sophie's company this evening. But the last few minutes with Nikko shook him up. He wasn't afraid, but the darkness that Nikko displayed, and the severity of his threat, were not something he could dismiss. She was in danger, and if the task force couldn't get Nikko behind bars, she would have to go into hiding for the rest of her life. And to Houston, that meant he would never get to explore the possibility of getting to know her outside his assignment.

Rodriguez had gotten the message that everyone was to meet at the warehouse at 8 o'clock in the morning. Sophie was up and ready by 7. He could tell she was nervous. They all rode together, with Rodriguez driving, Max riding shotgun, Kelly, Sophie, and Houston in the backseat. Bully and Titan were in the luggage area. When she got out, she went straight to her favorite tech, Agent Mathews.

"Can you do a search to see where these 8 tons of cocaine came from? I want to make sure Nikko can't trace it to a DEA raid that's on the books."

"I don't have to look, ma'am. I know where it came from."

"Where?"

"The raid on Nikko's warehouse in Texas and Brooklyn."

She looked around for Agent Cosby. Houston could see she was upset. "What's going on, Sophie?"

"They're trying to sell Nikko's own product back to him."

"Is that a problem?"

"Are you telling me the DEA never figured it out? I had Nikko place a distinctive trademark on his bricks when they were processed in case another syndicate stole it. That way, he'd be able to recognize it if it every came back around."

"Well, that's a problem. I'll go inform Agent Cosby."

She saw Detective Cartwright and went to talk to him. "Detective, will you be there?"

"Of course, Sophie, you know I'll watch your back."

"Thanks Don. I'm just a little scared that this may not work."

"It's a good plan, Sophie. We have everything covered."

Agent Cosby interrupted. "Ms. Star, we were not aware of any trademark on the product. There is no way we can come up with 8 tons from other sources. We only keep small amounts around for sting operations, a ton maybe two if we get some from other agencies close by. The rest is destroyed."

"Well, we can't sell him his own product back. He'll know immediately, and we'll all be dead."

"What if we replace the top two layers and the visible outer bricks?" Agent Hampton asked.

"Ben is the one who would choose the brick. Nikko is usually not at the exchange. He's only at this one because I forced his hand. Since Ben knows me, I doubt he would be too suspicious. That could work." Agent Cosby went to get his men. This fix could take some time, and time was something they had precious little of.

Sophie was huddled up with the DA, Anthony Stihls, the DOJ prosecutor Franklin James, Agent Hampton, and Agent Cosby.

"Agent Hampton, how are you going to handle the arrest?"

"My men will take you, Agent Townsend, Agent Rodriguez, and Agent Maxwell into custody. We will book you all on suspicion of drug trafficking and keep you in our holding facility. We will have you go to court in the morning, and the district attorney will ask for a 10-million dollar bail and your passport. When this is all over, we will totally delete all of it from your records. Nikko will go with the FBI out the other side of the old auto repair shop that we set up for the exchange and be held in their facility. They want to charge him federally for racketeering, the DEA wants to charge him for drug trafficking, and NYPD wants to charge him for Jimmy Cantore's murder. The murder is the charge they hope will keep him from getting bail, although they don't think it will stick unless he takes a plea."

"If he gets bail, we have no doubt he will leave the country. We plan on freezing all his assets," the DA added.

"Freezing his assets won't deter him too much, as he has overseas accounts that you can't touch, and he has a walk-in safe that he keeps copious amounts of cash in," Sophie explained.

"If this goes as planned, we should have plenty of evidence to keep Nikko Morano behind bars for years. This should also cripple his whole network so no one else can step in and just move on," Agent Cosby added.

"We want murder charges included with any plea he takes," DA Stihls, added.

Agent Hampton addressed Sophie. "Ms. Star, we will have an offshore account set up for you to make the exchange."

"No! His accountant will be doing the transfer, and before he lets go of those funds, he will do a check on the account. I trained him, and he will know instantly it's not mine! I set up my own offshore account during my time with his organization. I'll use that. I know your bosses will think this to be risky, but when you consider I helped to get nearly 10 tons of cocaine off the streets, I think they can trust me. I would also appreciate it if they would consider a small stipend as a reward. Maybe 10%?"

"Ms. Star, a CI reward is not out of the question, but all the funds will need to be seized as evidence. Plus, 10% of $108 million...well, that's a lot of money, and I didn't realize that was why you were doing this," Franklin James responded in a tone she didn't appreciate.

"Money *isn't* the reason that I'm doing this, but even with Nikko off the street, there is a good chance that a very large bounty will go on my head if it is ever leaked that I was the informant on this raid. If that happens, I will have to leave the country and be looking over my shoulder the rest of my life. I think I should be compensated for that, and Nikko is the one that should pay for it."

The others made a few comments to each other and agreed that this would be difficult to negotiate with the higher echelon, but they promised her they would see that it was done.

"You will transfer the money to the DOJ treasury when this is over, and we will return your stipend after the evidence is catalogued," the prosecutor ordered.

"Absolutely, but I want this agreement in writing before we go in tonight."

Agent Cosby went on with the briefing, explaining that even though they will have eyes and ears at the scene, there are a few key phrases to be used to alert them of problems. The phrase, *let's move this along,* would initiate a code orange putting everyone at the ready for an emergency breach. He went over a few more tactical items. Then they dispersed to see to the details.

Dangerous Obsession

CHAPTER TWELVE

As they were heading back to the penthouse, they opted to stop by a Subway sandwich shop so no one would have to cook lunch.

It was decided during the exchange with Nikko, that Houston and Max would escort Sophie. Bully would be kenneled but Agent Kelly would keep Titan and observe from the mobile command center. As part of Sophie's team, she will be able to recognize any indications of distress in Sophie's demeanor. Agent Rodriguez would drive the truck filled with the 8 tons of cocaine.

After they ate, Rodriguez briefed them on the Special Response Team's plan. "Houston, they want you to text Ben the address of the abandoned auto body shop about 3 pm. They want to have all their men and the command vehicles out of sight before you make contact. Because of the intel Ms. Star provided, they know that Ben sends men to sit on the location at least 2 hours ahead and that he generally has three men stay on the outside perimeter during the deal with 5 more inside. The SRT will have 3 men hidden on the roof. The rest will wait in the abandoned tire warehouse three quarters of a mile away with the mobile command unit. When command sees Ben testing the cocaine, via the cameras, that will be the cue for the SRT to move into their position hidden outside the auto shop. The men on the roof will have quick acting tranquilizer guns to take down the men outside when Houston gives the signal that the transaction is complete and the money has been transferred. The biggest risk we see is that one of the men might shout or signal a warning before they go down. Once they are secure, SRT will breach quickly and take down the others." He looked at Sophie. "Do you know what kind of weapons Nikko and his men carry and how many?"

"Ben always has a Glock 17 in his shoulder holster and revolver on his ankle. I believe he also carries a knife. Nikko normally has a Baby Glock in a holster in his back. That's it. Now, Lenny, his accountant who will come with him, will have a Smith and Wesson 9 mm. His soldiers all carry either AR-15 or SKS assault rifles."

"I'll be sure to pass that on. Do you have any questions, Ms. Star?"

"No. I just don't want any of you getting hurt, so please be careful." They all talked for a while and then carried on with their final duties.

Sophie spent time in her bedroom praying. She was scared, afraid something could tip their hand and get them all killed. But when she prayed, God gave her peace.

Bully was kenneled, and the rest of the team were on the way to the auto shop. Agent Kelly and Titan had already set themselves up at the mobile command unit. Sophie bowed her head and prayed that God would protect them.

Houston took her hand, looked in her eyes, and said, "you can still change your mind, you know."

"No, I have to do this."

They pulled in front of Stanley's Auto Shop. Rodriguez had already parked the trailer inside, loaded with the cocaine. He detached it from their truck, to give the impression Nikko's men could hook it up when the transfer was complete. His soldiers were outside, and it looked like Ben was there when they walked in, but she didn't see Nikko. Just as she thought Nikko had double crossed her, she saw him come from the back of the trailer. He had already begun checking out the product. Nikko had Lenny, his accountant, with him. Nikko saw her coming toward the table they had set up.

Nikko thought she looked beautiful in her straight black skirt and jacket and a pale pink silk top. He noticed everything about her, including her thin anklet and the fact that she wore her hair down. *She always knew what I liked,* he thought to himself, and that thought gave him hope. But when he saw that Houston had his arm on the small of her back leading her to the table, his nefarious jealousy flared. Sophie stepped to the table that was set up, and he pulled out her chair. Houston put her laptop in front of her but didn't sit. Neither did Max. Nikko and Lenny sat opposite her, while Ben and another man stood behind them.

"Ms. Star, it's so nice to see you again," Lenny said, as he put his laptop down.

"It's good to see you too, Lenny," Sophie responded.

Nikko looked at her, then looked up at Houston. He still wasn't sure if there was some romantic connection there. His temper was brewing, and Sophie could see the warning signs but wasn't sure what he was upset about. *Maybe he's suspicious about the cocaine,* she thought to herself, concerned.

Sophie spoke up, her voice echoing off the ceiling of the old auto shop. "Nikko, it would probably be best to get this over with as quick as possible. That's a lot of product, and we don't want to put it, or ourselves in any unnecessary jeopardy,"

Nikko held up a hand and pointed Ben toward the truck. Ben and Houston went to grab a brick to bring back for testing. Sophie and the team knew that this was the riskiest time because if Ben went too deep in the stack, this was all over, but the DEA had packed the truck tight so that Ben would be forced to take out one of the safe bricks.

Nikko leaned in toward her. "Let Ben and your man take care of business. I want to talk to you."

Sophie responded to Nikko's request, "I told you before—I will talk to you, just not alone. After we take care of business, I will go have dinner with you and we can talk." Sophie could see that he was calming down.

When Ben and Houston came back, Ben took out his test kit and stuck his knife deep into the brick. He put a pile of the fine white powder into the plastic packet with the testing liquid, and they all watched as it turned a deep shade of blue. He showed it to Nikko who nodded in approval. Sophie handed her overseas account number to Lenny and said, "now it's your turn."

Lenny looked at Nikko for approval, but Nikko kept his eyes on Sophie, looking like he was weighing something in his mind, then broke his silence. "Ben...go grab another brick."

Sophie leaned forward, trying hard to hide her anxiety. "What's the matter? You don't trust me, Nikko?"

"Of course, darling, but I don't know your men."

"If you know me, you know my men, but no matter. The cocaine will be yours in a few moments anyways. Waste all that you want." She motioned to Houston to comply, but on the inside, she was starting to worry he was getting suspicious.

Nikko got up and came around the table, sitting on the edge in front of her. Max made a move toward him, but Sophie waved him off; she couldn't act afraid if this was just a normal deal. He took her hand, kissed it, bent down, and whispered in her ear.

"I can't stand the thought of you on this earth without me." He slithered off the table edge and went back to his seat. She knew that this was a thinly veiled threat, but there was something about the way he said it that made her start shaking. *Lord, please help me. I can't fall apart. We're too close.*

Back at the mobile command, Agent Kelly called out to Agent Cosby. "I don't know what he said to her, but she's shaken up."

Houston and Ben came back. When Houston looked at Sophie, he noticed that she had turned ashen, and her eyes looked wan. He had no idea what had occurred a moment before. Ben tested the second brick and got the same result. Again, he showed Nikko. Houston shoved the account number closer to Lenny, and said, "let's move this along." The signal had been given, and the scramble began.

The command center initiated a code orange, and the men on the roof disabled the soldiers outside the shop without incident. SRT then moved into position for an immediate breach. There were three exits in the building, a garage door, a side entrance, and the front entrance. The majority of the team headed to the front and would initiate the breach. The men at the side and the back would grab anyone trying to flee. They couldn't all enter at the same time for fear of crossfire. As soon as the lead team breached, and the targets were disarmed they would call for the rest of the team to come in to contain the scene.

Lenny looked at Nikko, and this time he nodded. "This will only take a few minutes, Sophie. Lenny is very thorough, just the way you taught him." She knew that meant he was looking up her account to ensure that everything was legit.

"Nikko, I would expect nothing less."

"Where do you want to meet for dinner, Sophie?"

"How about Morano's? You know how much I love your food. Do you still know my favorite table?" Sophie feigned a weak but convincing smile.

"Excellent choice. I've kept a permanent reserved sign on our table," he laughed. Her body was still shaking, and her sight was getting fuzzy...*no, no, no, you can't faint, Sophie! Am I having a panic attack? Stay calm. God is with me.* She started taking some deep breaths while Nikko was busy watching Lenny.

Meanwhile, Houston was growing more worried. He could see her struggling to keep it together. She looked up to Houston, and he bent down. She whispered in his ear, "I can't let him see me shaking. Open my laptop to my banking site. My password is *mad$money_2136*." Houston opened the account. It would take about 3 minutes for the transfer to appear.

"Sophie, what time do you want to meet? And I want you to leave your goons at home."

"Nikko, I already told you I wouldn't bring Houston, but Max and his dog stay in the waiting area, or dinner is off."

Nikko relented. "Okay, what time?"

"How about eight?"

Before he could respond, the chime went off in her computer signifying the transfer was complete. Houston closed her laptop. Within 10 seconds of the laptop clicking shut, SRT flooded the building.

"FEDERAL AGENTS! EVERYONE GET DOWN ON THE GROUND WITH YOUR HANDS OUT TO YOUR SIDES! GET DOWN. GET DOWN ON THE GROUND NOW. GET DOWN!" It was loud and continuous as they took command of the shop. One of Nikko's men pulled his weapon and was shot before he could lift it high enough to shoot. Ben and Nikko saw it and knew it would be fruitless to have a shootout, they were outmanned and outgunned. Nikko trusted his lawyers to handle it from here.

The shop was in chaos, men running to exits, trying to escape. Only one managed to step out the side door and was immediately taken to the ground. The team had the others contained.

The scene was quiet now, All the bad actors were being cuffed and taken out. As an agent cuffed Sophie and lifted her off the floor, she looked at Nikko and teared up. "How could you do this to me?"

Nikko was struggling to get away from his captor, but he was shortly on the ground as well, yelling into the cold concrete. "Sophie, I wouldn't betray you! It wasn't me! You have to believe me!"

Sophie kept up the charade. "If this is some sort of revenge for me leaving you, I will never forgive you this time!" She yelled over her shoulder as she was aggressively being torn from the scene. She had to be convincing, and so did the agents. The officers escorted Max, Houston, and Sophie to an SRT transport unit, and as they were opening the back door, Sophie nearly collapsed, trembling to her core from the stress of the entire experience.

Houston looked at her just as her eyes started to roll, and she fainted. The officer holding her cuffed hands behind her back caught her, lifted her up, and handed her to another officer inside, who then laid her on the bench seat in the back of the wagon.

The others got in, and they closed the doors. But Houston was livid. "Get me out of these cuffs, now!!" He shouted.

They took Houston's off first, then they uncuffed Max and Rodriguez. Houston grabbed the key and rolled her on her side to get her cuffs off.

Rodriguez hollered to the driver, "We need some water. And get us to a hospital, fast!" He handed Houston a bottle of water, he put some on his hands, and he dabbed it on her face.

"Sophie? Can you hear me? It's over. You're alright. I've got you." He lifted her limp torso and slipped underneath her on the bench and held her head to his chest. Her eyes fluttered open.

"We're taking you to the hospital, Sophie."

She shook her head. "No, no," she strained to speak. "We've come too far. We can't deviate from our plan. It's my only chance to get free of him." Her voice was barely audible.

Houston looked at Rodriguez, but they all knew she was right. Rodriguez reversed his order to the driver. "Take us to the DEA holding as planned."

Houston kept her in his arms, giving her water and holding her head against his chest while her body shook. He leaned his head back against the side of the van and prayed silently — *Lord, her mind is strong, but her body can't handle any more of this stress. Please, Lord, be her rear guard, give her strength, and protect her. And give me wisdom and power to know what must be done to end this nightmare for her. I trust you, Lord, and I love You.* He looked down and noticed her body had calmed. She had stopped shaking.

The van was quiet, with no banter or high fives for a successful takedown. They were all worried about her. Rodriguez called his SAC to let him know Ms. Star's condition. When they were about 10 minutes from the holding cells, Rodriguez started explaining what would happen next.

"Sophie, I'm afraid this part will be very unpleasant for you, but we have to go through the standard procedure if we want this to be convincing."

"Please, Agent Rodriguez, just tell me the truth."

"A female guard will come out to the Sally Port and take you for initial processing. They will take a mug shot, fingerprint you, and then they will do a strip and body search." Houston felt her stiffen when he said that. "I know that will be humiliating for you, but it's standard procedure for anyone incarcerated. No one there has any idea this is an undercover operation; it's totally blacked out. It must be convincing because we have no way of knowing if Nikko has corrections officers on his payroll."

As much as Sophie hated this idea, she knew that he was right. Rodriguez continued. "Next, she'll take your clothes and give you the standard jump suit. Then you will have to walk through general population, in front of the other prisoners, and will be led into the high security holding area known as PC-SEG.

Once back there, it will just be you in one cell and Houston, Max, and me in the other. Normally, they would put you in a woman's facility, but the DEA made special arrangements citing the high profile of the case. They will take us to our arraignment hearing about 8 o'clock tomorrow morning, court starts at 9. They will decide on bail, which of course is already determined. DOJ will pay the bail through anonymous channels, and it will take about an hour for us to be released."

Sophie was still looking ill, but she smiled as best she could. "Thanks for walking me through. Knowing what's coming will help me to stay calm."

When the van stopped at the holding facility, the officers cuffed Max and Rodriguez. Houston told the officer he would cuff Sophie. He was hoping it would be less humiliating for her. Then he was cuffed, and they were all herded into the building, except for Sophie who was escorted inside by the female officer.

At the auto shop, Agents Cosby and Hampton were supervising the cleanup. They were heading back to command to determine how to close this operation down. The men back at the command warehouse were sifting through all the evidence, logging tapes and videos with short summaries to each one for easy indexing. It was very time consuming, but the tech, Agent Mathews had been keeping up on it daily. This set him at a good pace for a quick wrap-up.

The mood at the command center was upbeat. This had been an enormous success. Others were at the penthouse collecting the camera and mic equipment. DOJ wanted that place emptied as soon as possible because of the cost they were incurring, but Agent Hampton insisted that his team and Sophie be allowed to go and retrieve their personal items when they were released tomorrow. It would take days for every officer involved to write up their after action report, each accounting for their own part in the operation.

Agent Cosby was going to pull his FBI agents from the case once they were sure Nikko wasn't getting bonded out. It was really all left up to the DA now with the support of eyewitnesses, video and audio evidence, and any other physical evidence they could muster. Everyone knew that they would have to seal this conviction without Sophie's testimony because she had to remain a criminal defendant in order to protect her cover. Agent Hampton was going to release Agents Maxwell and Kelly, as well as Bully and Titan, to other assignments, as K-9 units were in high demand. But he planned on keeping Agents Houston and Rodriguez on Sophie's detail until they knew she was safe.

"I have to say, this task force accomplished more in two weeks than we normally do in a year," Agent Hampton mused in abject amazement.

Agent Cosby chimed in. "I hate to admit it, but that mostly was due to Ms. Star and her careful planning. She was very brave coming forward like that. Can you even imagine? After all that woman went through at the hands of Nikko Morano. To come back *by choice* when she was free of him already...that had to be a difficult decision. I heard the DOJ might even offer her a job as a strategist and forensic accountant. That woman certainly has a bright future ahead of her." Hampton nodded in agreement, and Cosby continued.

"Let's meet back her tomorrow after the bail hearing to finish shutting things down and see what Ms. Star's plans are."

"I'm good with that. Most of my men will still be here shutting down operations anyway."

Men in orange jumpsuits were hollering obscene comments and whistling cat calls as the guard led Sophie and the others down the main promenade of the jail and into the high security area. Rodriguez was walking behind Houston, and whispered to him, "I hate her being humiliated like this."

"Me too," he responded. The guard leading them was about 5'10" and looked like a weightlifter, a little top heavy. He had a military haircut and looked like he was trying to play a tough guy in a Hollywood movie. Once they passed through the steel door to the high security area, there were four cells, with bars. A concrete wall made up the back of the cells and the far wall on the last cell. There was a short pony wall that separated the toilet sink combination for the illusion of privacy, in each cell. There wasn't much need for more privacy since no one stayed here more than a day or two. Then they were either released on bail, sent to prison awaiting trial, or given over to ICE for deportation. The guard put the men in the third cell then slid open the next cell door and walked Sophie in. He pinned her against the wall, leaning into her space with his arm extended and his hand flat on the back wall.

"Well, aren't you a pretty one," he snorted. Sophie mustered up all the confidence she had and replied, "back off."

Houston, Max, and Rodriguez came to the bars between the two cells when they saw what was happening.

"Get away from her," Houston hollered, seething with rage that he couldn't reach her.

"Or what, tough guy?" The guard sneered at the men then started playing with her hair, twirling it in his fingers and smelling it. Houston was quickly losing his composure, but Rodriguez took over before he blew their cover. "Do you know who she is?"

"Yeah, she is my prisoner," he spat out.

"No, I mean do you know *who she is*?"

The guard turned, glared at the men, smirking, and said, "I told you, boy, she is my prisoner." He turned back toward Sophie.

"That is Nikko Morano's fiancé, you idiot. He killed his cousin just for talking to her. Can you imagine what torture he'll put you through before he kills you for touching her?" The expression on the young guard's face changed quickly, losing color. He backed up and showed her the palms of his hands in surrender.

"I'm sorry, miss. I had no idea." Sophie was a bit rattled, but she knew better than to show it. After all, if she could keep her composure while facing Nikko, this young punk wasn't going to shake her. He walked out of her cell and locked it. When the heavy metal door separating this wing closed behind the guard, Houston turned to Sophie. "Are you alright?"

"Yes, thank you all. That was quick thinking. Now, I think I'm going to lay down for a while, guys." Exhausted from the day's events, she fell onto her cot, covered up with the thin blanket they had issued her, and curled up into a fetal position. Houston wanted so badly to be able to hold her and comfort her, but only God could get beyond these bars. Everyone was tired. Rodriguez and Max each took to a cot—after offering one to Houston, who declined—and closed their eyes. There was only one set of bunks in each cell. A guard would bring in a thin mattress later that night for Houston to sleep on. He sat against the bars facing Sophie's cell, pulled up his legs, his arms resting on his knees, and he kept vigil over her.

CHAPTER THIRTEEN

Thomas got wind of the raid about 30 minutes after it went down. "How could this have happened, Franco?"

"I don't know, sir. There is nothing about it on the streets. They got all of the cocaine, and Nikko and all his men are in custody. They have Sophie and her men, too."

"Where are they now?"

"I believe Nikko is at FBI holding. I think Sophie is at the DEA holding. The word is that they are in lock up until they see a judge tomorrow morning. A street dealer who was in holding at the DEA saw them parade Sophie through to the high security cells. He called me, expecting that the information might gain him some favor."

Thomas clenched his teeth. "I can't stand the idea of Sophie in a cell. I'll send our lawyer over to Nikko and Sophie; he'll try to get them out on bail in the morning." He hung up and called the managing partners at *Fitz and Conner Law Offices*, the best criminal defense lawyers in town. Nikko always kept them on retainer for when his mid-level dealers ran into some trouble. He called Albert Fitz on his home phone. "Fitz, it's Thomas Morano. I need you over here pronto." When Fitz arrived nearly 45 minutes later, Thomas explained everything that had been told to him.

At just before 10 pm, a female guard came and woke Sophie, escorting her out of her cell. She looked over and noticed that the others, Houston included, were all sleeping. *Get some rest, gentlemen. You sure earned it today.*

"Your lawyer's here to see you." Sophie knew that as soon as Thomas got word that she and Nikko were in jail, he would send someone. This was part of the plan, keeping up the ruse that she was an offender like Nikko.

"Ms. Star, my name is Albert Fitz. Thomas Morano sent me over to represent you and your men." He wasn't what she expected; he was short, maybe 5 foot 6 inches, and balding with a paunch. She guessed that he was in his mid-fifties.

"It's nice to meet you, Mr. Fitz. Thank you for coming so quickly. I can pay you a retainer. I just need a phone call to transfer the money."

"Thomas insisted he will cover everything for Nikko and his men, as well as you and your men, Ms. Star. Please tell me what happened." She went through the whole story, blaming it on Nikko's recent run-in with the DEA.

"He must have led them to us, though I can't imagine how. Nikko is the most careful man I know."

"Well, this is your first arrest. Even though you were caught with an egregious amount of cocaine, I will try to get you and your men bail. Thomas said to tell you that he is calling in various favors owed to him in order to get you out. If they do grant bail, they will probably ask for an 'all cash' bail and hold your passport."

"I have enough money to pay any bail they ask for," Sophie reassured the man.

"Not if they have seized your assets."

"They have no clue where my assets are."

"Well, how about we let Thomas and my office figure the financial part out. Let's you and I focus on your defense, okay?"

He placed his notepad back in his expensive leather briefcase. Sophie noted that his initials were ostentatiously engraved on a gold plate under the handle. He stood and reached out his hand to her. "I will be at the arraignment in the morning. I'm on my way to see Nikko right now."

She stood and shook his hand, "I can't thank you enough, Mr. Fitz."

A female guard took her back to her cell. Houston was awake and, on his feet, waiting for her. When the guard left, he asked, "Who did he send?" When he woke earlier to find her gone, it scared him, especially after the episode with the young guard earlier. But when she returned safely, he knew she had to be meeting with an attorney. She went to the bars by Houston talking quietly so they wouldn't wake the others.

"Thomas sent Albert Fitz and said he's paying for everything, for all of us, just like I knew he would. Deceiving him is killing me, Houston." She placed her forehead against the cold metal bars and cast a pained expression toward the floor.

He reached for her hand through the bars. "I know Sophie, but it's the only way. If he caught wind that you perpetrated this whole thing to get Nikko behind bars, Thomas would tell him in an instant, and you know it." She gently drew her head back and banged them softly on the bars.

"I know you're right, Houston, it just hurts. That's all." She went to her cot and was soon asleep.

"Nikko sit down. Now, I can't guarantee you bail. I just got the indictment against you. If it had just been the felony drugs, I would be more optimistic, but they added this murder charge. Did you have any idea about this?" Nikko was pacing the room in front of Mr. Fitz

"They've been trying to get that charge to stick for years, but they have no evidence. It's just a trumped up charge to keep the judge from granting bail."

Fitz closed his notebook and leveled his gaze over his small eyeglasses. "Well, it could very well work."

Nikko leaned down and placed his hands on the table. "Listen, you get me out of here tomorrow, do you hear me? That is what I pay you for, right?"

"I'll do what I can."

Nikko sat down. "Did Thomas send someone over to talk to Sophie?"

"Yes, I went to see her."

"How is she? She thinks this is my fault. She was furious with me when they were taking her out in handcuffs."

"She still thinks you led the DEA to the shop."

"I can't think about her going to prison."

"Hopefully, I will get her out tomorrow."

Nikko handed Fitz an envelope. "I need you to call the number in that envelope and ask for Uncle Tony. Just tell him I said I lost my way. He'll understand." Nikko went up, knocked on the door, and told the guard he was ready to go back. Mr. Fitz took the envelope and put it in his briefcase. He didn't want to know what the message meant.

Things went as planned. Nikko was remanded to custody; his men were released on bail. Sophie and her team were also released on bail. She noticed Thomas in the courtroom as she was being taken back to holding to be processed.

When they stepped out of the building, she saw Thomas leaning on his town car talking to Franco and a nearby black SUV with a driver waiting. Thomas came up to Sophie, hugged her, and kissed her cheek. "Sophie, I have a car for your men to take them wherever they need to go, and I would like to take you to lunch. We can stop by my place if you want to freshen up first."

She took his hand. "Well, the FBI and DEA have searched the penthouse I leased. They have it taped off, so we can't go back there right now."

Thomas pulled her aside. "You know Nikko kept your condo up while you were gone? He was sure you were coming back."

She turned to Houston. "Houston, Thomas' driver can take you to impound to get our vehicles, then you guys can go get lunch. My lawyer says that we should be able to get our personal items from the penthouse in a couple hours. I'll meet you there."

Houston couldn't stop the jealousy that hit him watching them walk hand in hand to the town car. It hurt. Rodriguez patted him on the shoulder. "She's playing a role, Houston. Don't let it get to you." He hung his head for a moment as they walked to the SUV.

"I don't know about that. She really cares for him."

Thomas took Sophie to Morano's where they sat her at her favorite table and ordered her favorite meal. "You know me so well, Thomas. Thanks for this. I can be myself with you."

"I couldn't sleep last night thinking of you in that place."

"Well, I'm out now, thanks in great part to you. How did you manage that?"

"It was surprisingly easy to get you out, but Nikko...they really don't want to let go of him. They added Jimmy Cantor's murder to his indictment to keep him remanded. Fitz says there is no tangible evidence, but the judge wouldn't budge. Law enforcement has been trying to get him in jail for years. They probably put political pressure on the Judge."

159

"I'm sorry for Nikko, Thomas. I know how hard this will be for your family if he goes to prison."

"He'll never go to prison."

Sophie took a deep breath. "What do you mean?"

"When papa first started in this life, mama made him come up with an iron clad escape plan. She said she was not going to raise his children alone. If he wasn't smart enough to come up with one to get out of the country with her and the kids, he wasn't smart enough to be a successful criminal. That's when papa and Uncle Tony, in Italy, set up a war chest and several contingency plans depending on the circumstances. When Nikko and I each turned 18, he set up the same for us. Uncle Tony is the keeper of the chest and the overseer when the call comes in. Only Nikko can activate his own plan, but when he does, it means he leaves the U.S. for good. He can never come back," Thomas said. Sophie took it all in, not sure how to process it.

"What are your plans, Sophie? You certainly can't go to prison."

"I have no intention of going to prison. If Fitz can't find a legal flaw in their documents or procedure or get some of the evidence thrown out on a technicality, I still have the alias you made me. It will get me out of the area then I will leave the country. But it will be a year before any of us goes to trial, so I have plenty of time to go if I feel things aren't going as I would like. I'm hoping that if Fitz gets some of the evidence thrown out, the DA may offer a plea bargain just to get something on my, so far, pristine record...you know, in case they ever have another bite at the apple. I could live with probation. But Thomas, please understand that I will never testify against Nikko just to get out of jail. I would sooner leave the country." She laid her hand on his.

"I know Sophie. I'd hate to see you have to leave here again. Fitz is good. If anyone can get you off, he can."

"Thomas, if I *were* to jump my bond and you lose my bail money, I would reimburse you. You know I wouldn't leave you on the hook for it, right?"

Thomas smiled at her. "Somehow, I'm not all that worried. Nikko's legal fund is larger than the Gross National Product of most third world countries. Your bond won't even leave a dent."

She laughed. They finished their meal, and Thomas drove her to the penthouse to gather her things.

"Sophie, before you go, I need to ask if you would be willing to talk to Nikko. When I saw him earlier today, he insisted I ask you?"

"You know that's a bad idea. The Fed's will be bugging my phones for sure."

"He has access to a cell phone in prison and he could call one of my disposables."

Sophie thought for a moment then answered, "Okay. set up a time and come to my condo. I'm heading over there after I gather my things. I want you there when I talk to him."

"Thanks, Sophie. I know he's a criminal, but he's my brother, and he's in a bad way right now. He thinks you blame him for this."

Sophie sighed. "I said that when I was angry. I know he would never purposely bring the law down on us." She got out of the town car and headed up to the penthouse, she knew the DOJ wanted them out of there as soon as possible.

Franco escorted her to the elevator. He leaned into Sophie, and said, "Ms. Star, Thomas is a different man when you're around, ya' know. I don't think he ever got over what happened to you. He has never once committed to a serious relationship after you left, though he did date a few other women. I kinda' think he hoped you would be back someday."

Sophie smiled, almost a little uncomfortable to hear this coming from the big man next to her. "There is no way we could ever have a relationship. He knows how Nikko feels about me. He would never hurt him like that."

Franco nodded and turned his gaze back toward the elevator door. "Well, knowing it and getting your heart to accept it are two different things." The bell rang, and the doors slid open.

Sophie stepped in the elevator and breathed a prayer to herself. *Lord, forgive me for doing this to Thomas. Make a way for me so that I can tell him about you. I hate that I have to lie to him.*

While Sophie was gone, the others spent their time getting their reports in order and gathering their things.

Agent Rodriguez brought Sophie up to speed. "Sophie, the DEA has reassigned Agents Maxwell and Kelly, but Houston and I are assigned to you until this is over." She went to Agent Kelly, gave her a big hug, and thanked her for putting her life on the line for her. Then she bent down and gave Titan a big hug. She went to Agent Maxwell and gave him a hug as well, perhaps slightly more reserved, but she gave Bully some extra attention.

"I'm going to miss you, but you will always be in my prayers."

Maxwell and Kelly left. Sophie brought out all her luggage and put it by the door. Rodriguez finished his call with command and said, "Sophie, I have to go to the warehouse with our reports and debrief everyone. Houston will take the first watch. I'll be there at 10 pm to relieve him. Are you alright with that?"

"That sounds fine, but first I have some information you need to know. Today at lunch, Thomas told me that Nikko has had an escape plan in waiting ever since he turned 18 years old.

His dad, Joe, set it up for him. His uncle Tony in Italy is the one who puts it in play once Nikko gives him the go ahead. The only thing I know for sure is it includes him leaving the country permanently, and one thing I know about Nikko is he does not want to leave the country. It would mean giving up his empire."

"Wow. That's some news you're giving me. Thank you, Ms. Star. I will get it to the commander right away."

"Agent Rodriguez, you can tell Agent Hampton so he can take whatever precautions necessary. But absolutely no one else can know because it would instantly come back to me."

"I'll make that clear, Ms. Star."

A few minutes later Sophie told Houston. "I'm ready whenever you are." Houston took down their luggage then grabbed his bag of tactical gear and equipment. Houston opened the passenger door for her and then hopped in the driver's side. He knew the address from her file and headed there. She noticed he was being quiet, but she thought he might just be tired.

Houston glanced at her and said in a sad low voice, "Sophie, are you and Thomas..." His voice kind of tapered off in a mumble. She couldn't help but chuckle.

She took his hand which was resting on the console. "No, Houston. I told you I will always love Thomas for rescuing me and for all he is doing to help me now. He has no idea it's all part of the plan. But when I look at him, I have no romantic feelings. I did before I left and even carried them with me for a long time, but now I'm just comfortable keeping him in my heart as family.

"Once I became born again, my perspective on things changed. Thomas is a good man in many ways, but he's not born again. He lives on the edge of corruption. He knows what his brother does, knows that Nikko is a reprehensible, even evil, man. He also knows that Nikko killed Jimmy. But Thomas doesn't stop him, and his inaction and enabling make him guilty by association. Plus, he doesn't know the real me at all. I wouldn't fit into his lifestyle now. But it grieves me deeply the way I'm using him. Please understand that I don't have an ethical problem with what I'm doing. This is an undercover operation, and that is something I can compartmentalize. But it doesn't escape me that I am hurting a man I love, and it's scarring me. As far as a romantic relationship, I have to be able to admire any man who wins my heart, to know he would never physically harm me but would instead lay down his life for mine. That's not Thomas Morano. Does that answer your question?"

He took his eyes off the road for a minute and looked into hers. "You know he's in love with you, though, right."

Sophie let go of his hand. "I know, and I'm using that to my advantage. That's why this is so hard for me."

He realized she probably felt like he was judging her. "You're paying a high personal price to take down a criminal network. I admire you for that."

Sophie turned her head to the passenger window and looked out. *I hope I can live with myself when this is all over.*

After a few minutes Houston asked, "do you plan on leaving right away?"

She turned back to him. "I'm not sure what to do. I left home with everything in place for 90 days. I think it's too soon to leave. Things are still too up in the air. I have to be sure Nikko will never come after me again."

"Where is home for you?"

"I can't give up that information just yet. If I have to run, no one can know where to find me."

"I get it." He hesitated. "Sophie, it's no secret that I'm attracted to you, right? It seems to be obvious to everyone on my team based on the harassment I've been getting from them." He grinned a large grin. She laughed, but he continued. "Would you feel comfortable if I asked you out while you're still in New York?" He quickly added, "just to see if there's anything to this other than the fact that I think you are the smartest, most beautiful woman I have ever met. That is, if you feel it, too."

"That's quite the pickup line, Agent Townsend. Are you even allowed to date someone you're protecting?"

"No, but when I'm off duty, we both still have to eat dinner or go for a walk. Agent Rodriguez would be there to protect you, so it wouldn't be like a *real* date."

Sophie was intrigued. "I don't want you to compromise your job, but if you can figure a way to make it happen, I'm game."

A big smile crawled across the agent's face. She laughed and he grabbed her hand this time. Holding her hand gave him the best feeling. He couldn't get this stupid grin off his face. *She's going to think I'm an idiot*, he chided himself. He took her to her penthouse condo but left the luggage in the car. Houston needed to do a sweep of the condo first to make sure it was safe. He brought up only his equipment to check for listening devices and cameras. She had told him Nikko had been spending time there. When he reached the door of the condo, his whole demeanor changed, and he was all business. Agent Townsend took his job very seriously. He asked her for the key and instructed her to stand with her back to the wall away from the door.

"Where is the light switch?" It had turned dark on the drive over.

"Just to the left, about shoulder height." He got his flashlight out of his bag and took his gun from its holster." He stepped into a large, well furnished living room. Beyond that first room, there were a set of French doors which led to a dining room with a large table. The chef's kitchen was to the left of the table with a breakfast counter separating the two areas. There was a set of glass doors that slid into the wall expanding the living area out to the balcony. The rest of the condo was much like the other penthouse but just flipped around like a mirror image. Her master bedroom was to the left. She had a large en suite bathroom, but she didn't have to go through there to get to her walk-in closet. He noticed Nikko's clothes hanging on one side of the closet. He left her things untouched in there. He was waiting for her to come back. Houston wondered how many nights he stayed here. The den, bathroom, and two other bedrooms were to the right. He cleared the condo one room at a time then had Sophie come inside. He asked her to sit in the living room until he could do an electronic sweep of the rooms. As he was going from room to room, Houston began finding cameras. He decided he needed Mathews' expertise. He called Rodriguez. "Fons, are you still at warehouse command?"

"I'm done with the briefing but I'm still here. Why? What's going on?"

"I need you to send Mathews here. The place is riddled with surveillance cameras, and I need him to bring down his specialized equipment, so we don't miss anything. I'm not sure where these came from or how long they've been here, so you might also want to send Timms and Smith to come do a check on the roof, stairs, and common grounds. And you better send a locksmith, too. Let's keep it all hush, though, just in case these are Nikko's devices.

"Got it. we'll be right there." He didn't want to scare Sophie, so he told her she could move around but that Command was sending a team over to check out the place. She didn't seem to think that was odd.

CHAPTER FOURTEEN

Agent Mathews and the others came incognito. Houston was relaying his concerns to the men.

Agent Rodriguez asked. "What's your theory, Houston?"

"You wanna know what I think? I think Nikko Morano is one sick, depraved, and dangerous man. He's been watching every move Sophie makes for who knows how long." Timms hollered for them to come out on the balcony.

Agent Timms was looking over the railing from the roof and said, "heads up" as he dropped a rope ladder down in front of them.

"It's been up here a long time, attached to a large metal steam pipe," Agent Timms reported.

Agent Mathews came out of the apartment with something in his hands.

"There at least a dozen of these cameras that were spread throughout the house, mainly in the vents. But these aren't new. This model is at least three to four years old and, based on the amount of dust accumulated, I estimate they were brand new when they were installed. They've been here a while. I also found a few listening devices."

"Where *exactly* were the cameras located?" Houston asked. He had a bad feeling about this.

"There were three in the master bedroom, two in the master bath—one aimed at the shower and one at the tub—there was also one in the den positioned to see her computer screen and another one in the same area but aimed at her face. There were also two in the kitchen, two in the living room, and the rest were dispersed throughout the inside and out here."

"And where were the microphones?"

"One in the living room one in the master bedroom."

Houston thought for a moment. "Are you sure the place is clean now? Absolutely positive?"

"100%." Mathews responded.

"Can you tell where the images were being sent to?"

"They were all feeding into a hard drive hidden in the attic crawl space. It was connected to the building's Wi-fi in order to relay the signal. I'll take the drive back and track the signal. But this guy was good. It might have bounced halfway around the world and then right back here, but I'll find out." Pausing a moment, Mathews asked, "she has no idea, does she?"

"No."

Houston asked Timms and Smith to retrieve Sophie's luggage. He had to break the news to her. The locksmith was still working on putting in a new deadbolt.

Sophie came out to the balcony just as the other men were leaving.

"What's really going on here, Agent Rodriguez? This isn't routine, is it?" Houston led her to the wicker outdoor settee and sat beside her. Rodriguez sat in the chair next to her.

"Just say it. Your scaring me," Sophie insisted.

"Before we get into that, what was it that Nikko said to you that shook you up at the auto shop?" Rodriguez asked.

"He said 'I can't stand the thought of you on this earth without me.'" Rodriguez looked at Houston then back at her.

"Who lived in this condo before you bought it?"

"No one. It was one of Thomas' construction companies that built it. The penthouse was finished about two weeks after I started working for Nikko. One day, he came into my office and asked me to come with him. He brought me here. He said I could lease it for a fraction of its value as a perk for working for him. It took most of my paycheck, but I loved it. It was worth every dime. As I moved up in the company, my pay increased, and it became easier. About a year and a half later, I reorganized and made improvements in the organization which wound up saving them millions of dollars and strengthened their computer security measures. Joe Morano was so pleased with my work that he gave me the deed to the penthouse as a bonus. Nikko made a big deal out of it, taking me out to a fancy restaurant and handing it to me. We were dating by then."

"Sophie," Houston drew a long and careful breath, "we found cameras everywhere and a few microphones."

"What do you mean everywhere? Are you saying in my home? Where?" her voice was getting frantic. Houston grabbed her hand to calm her, but she yanked it away. "Where, Houston? Where were these cameras?"

"There were several in your bedroom, two in your bathroom, two in the kitchen…"

Sophie stood up with her hand to her mouth like she might throw up. She turned pale, and her eyes darted around looking for somewhere to run. She bolted, maneuvering around the locksmith still at the front door and ran. Timms and Smith were just coming in with her luggage. Houston took off after her, but she was already running down the stairs. He could hear her steps, and he could have caught up to her, but he gave her some room. He stayed close enough to protect her, but still give her space to breathe. She ran out through the back door and the common grounds of the complex, then through the garden and pool area, past some trees lining the property, and into a small grassy dog park. There were streetlights lining the park, so it was safe for families to walk their pets at night. She finally collapsed to her knees, put her hands to her face and cried. He stood watch over her, not saying anything. A few people glanced at her then moved on. She felt so violated and helpless. Her crying stopped, but she still just knelt there. He finally went to her, cupped her shoulders from behind, and lifted her to her feet. He turned her toward a bench, and they sat down.

"I was so naive. There were days I would wake up and feel like things in my home had been moved or touched. I just blew it off. One night, in what I thought was a dream, I felt there was someone in my room talking softly to me." She looked up at him. "It was Nikko, wasn't it?"

"He's the most likely suspect. He had a rope ladder that was secured and dropped down from the roof."

"How long was it there?"

"The ladder?"

"No, the cameras."

"Mathews thinks they were placed before you moved in."

She looked shocked. "I hadn't started dating Nikko yet. We barely knew each other."

Sophie turned white and bolted to the trees. He could hear her dry heaves. She came back and sat, putting her head on his chest. She couldn't face him. He just sat there with her, stroking her hair. It was nearly an hour before he insisted that she go back.

As Sophie approached the door, she said, "I always loved this place. It was the first place I ever owned. Now, I don't know if I can go back in there."

He lifted her chin until their eyes met. "This is still your home. Don't let Nikko rob you of that. He has already taken so much from you. I will be here as long as you need me, until you feel safe again."

She smiled. "That could take a while."

Houston returned the smile. "That's my greatest hope."

Sophie stopped again. "How do I look these men in the eye?"

"Sophie, you are the victim here. Their respect for you is not in question. However, I think some of them may want to beat Nikko into oblivion."

"Is one of them named Houston?"

"Absolutely." Houston opened the door, and they walked back into her penthouse.

Rodriguez was at the table talking to command. He hung up when he saw her.

"Sophie, are you alright?" She lowered her eyes. "Yes, I'm fine. Thank you for asking."

"Agent Hampton wants us at the warehouse in the morning. Does that work for you?"

She sat in a chair. "That should be fine, but I didn't have a chance to tell you that Thomas is coming over tomorrow. Nikko is calling him, and he wants to talk to me."

Houston looked upset. "You don't have to talk to him."

"I know, but he may give me more insight into his plans. I need to know if I have to get away from here."

"We can go to the warehouse early so we can get back and not miss his call. Will that work?"

"Sure, Agent Rodriguez, that will be fine." She looked at him. "Is it alright if I call the super and ask him to bring me some boxes? I want to box up everything Nikko left here when I was gone and have Thomas take it with him tomorrow. I don't want any piece of him in my home."

"Sure, but I can call him for you."

"Thank you, that would be appreciated." She got up and went to her room to start removing Nikko's things. She planned to go through every drawer in the house to make sure she didn't miss anything. Houston was off duty by the time Sophie was done. He would have offered to help her, but she needed this time to think and process all she just found out. She was struggling with the weight of the boxes when Rodriguez ran over to help.

"Where do you want these?"

"In the hall. They'll be safe, and Thomas can take them tomorrow. I want his stuff out of my home." He was surprised when she sat at the table.

"Agent Rodri… Fons, you must think I'm a terrible person allowing myself to be used like that," Sophie breathed out softly not looking at him.

He put his hand on her arm. "Sophie, none of this is your fault. You were victimized by a man with a seared conscience. Nikko's life experience and endless funds put you at a disadvantage. There was nothing you did that caused this."

Tears started streaming from her eyes. "I wish…"

He stopped her. "Sophie, you're a believer, right?"

"Yes. That's why I came back here. I'm trying to undo some of the wrong I did by helping Joe and Nikko."

"Well, scripture encourages us to *forget those things which are behind and reach forth unto those things which are before…* [Phil. 3:13.] You have to let it go, Sophie. The devil is the accuser of the brethren. He will plague you with guilt if you don't forgive yourself for being taken in, and it will eat you alive." Fons asked her to look at him, and she raised her eyes. "Not one man or woman who has worked with you hold you in anything but the highest regard and admiration."

"Thank you for that. I'll keep it in mind." She got up and headed to her room.

He called after her. "I will be up until 4 am if you want to come out and have coffee with me."

Sophie turned and smiled at him. "Looking for someone to keep you awake, huh? Isn't that cheating?" They both laughed.

Sophie was quiet all the way to the warehouse. Houston knew that meant she must have made a decision. She asked to meet with Agent Hampton, DA Stihls, and DOJ Prosecutor Franklin James. Houston and Rodriguez also sat in.

"I've made a decision." She started talking then took a deep breath. "You need to create an error in the process that allows Fitz to get the case against me dropped."

The DA was surprised. "Ms. Star, everything is going as planned. If we just let things progress naturally, it would give us the time we need to continue our investigation on Nikko. If we let you go, it puts our case against him in jeopardy."

"And what happens if he escapes, and I have to run? Some newbie police officer thinks he has a fugitive on his hands and ends up shooting me."

DOJ Prosecutor James' eyebrows furrowed. "What aren't you telling us Ms. Star."

"Nothing. You already know that Nikko has a lot of money. He has an expensive attorney who is trying to get the murder charge dropped for lack of evidence, which means Nikko could get out on bail. That puts me in harm's way. There are too many moving parts to this, too many chances that someone could leak word of my involvement. When I didn't think he could get bail, I was willing to take that chance. But even if he doesn't know I'm involved, you all know he is obsessed with me."

"There's got to be more to this new change of heart than you are letting on," DA Stihls chided.

Agent Hampton kept his promise and didn't tell what he knew. He sat there quietly.

"It really doesn't matter *what* is behind my decision. I have given you all kinds of computer forensic evidence tying Nikko to the farm, the cocaine, and the entire network. My part is done. I need to be gone when he gets out. I will stay until I get wind of him getting bonded, but I want these charges dropped so that if

I have to run, I won't be a fugitive. I will give you seven days, Mr. James."

DOJ Prosecutor James stared at her for a few seconds, "Ms. Star, I hate to change our plans at this point. It's very risky. But you have done an immense service for us, and I don't think I can deny your claims about him getting out and the danger that puts you in. We will come up with something."

Sophie stood. "Thank you. Please keep me in the loop." She turned and walked over to Tech. Mathews' desk.

Agent Hampton caught up with her. "Ms. Star, I know what they found in your condo, and the news that he has an escape plan. But doing it this way may draw suspicion to you that you really don't want. Please reconsider. I will put more men on your protection detail."

"Agent Hampton, you, and your team have done an excellent job with the information I've given you, but you don't know Nikko like I do. I have to protect myself."

Agent Hampton nodded. "Alright, Ms. Star. I will do what I can to help." He went back to the others.

Sophie addressed the technician behind his desk. "Agent Mathews, have you found out where that signal ended up?"

He turned to look at her. "Yes, actually. The end of the line was Nikko's condo." She didn't know why, but she was surprised. She knew the answer, but it still took her breath away to hear confirmation.

"Thank you for finding out. I'm sure it was difficult."

Houston and Rodriguez came up. "Are you ready to go, Ms. Star?"

"Yes, I'm ready."

In the car Houston asked her, "So, you've decided to leave?"

She saw his disappointment. "I'll wait as long as I can, Houston. But in light of Nikko's plans, I don't dare wait for him to get ahold of me again. We'll have time to talk before that happens," Sophie said. Houston just looked away and nodded his head.

They were at the condo about forty-five minutes before Thomas knocked. Houston peeped through the hole and let him in.

"Mr. Morano, Ms. Star would like you to take Nikko's things back to his place."

Thomas was not surprised at all. "Franco, will you go put these in the car."

"Yes, sir."

Houston looked at Franco. "I'll help you." Rodriguez was inside, and Houston thought maybe a conversation with Franco would give him some insight into the word on the street about the raid.

Agent Rodriguez escorted Thomas to the balcony where Sophie was sitting, her legs curled under her on the padded wicker settee. Thomas went to her, leaned down, and kissed her cheek. He noticed she was more aloof than normal. "Sophie, is everything alright?" He took a seat next to her. She had debated if she should tell him about the cameras. She decided not to.

"I'm fine, Thomas. This whole debacle has drained me."

"Fitz told me he is working through every document to find any kind of error."

"I know. I can't thank you enough for hiring Fitz for me."

"Nikko should be calling in about fifteen minutes." She nodded, and they chatted while waiting for his call. The cell rang right on time.

"Nikko?" Thomas answered curtly.

"Yes. Is she with you?" He handed her the phone.

"Hello, Nikko." She couldn't get too hostile with him. It would just spur him to try getting out even sooner.

"I had to talk to you Sophie. I couldn't let you think I had anything to do with this," Nikko said, hoping to vindicate himself.

"I was angry when I got arrested, but after thinking about it, it would make no sense for you to get back at me in that fashion. I had to spend the night in jail, Nikko."

"I know, sweetheart. I put the word out as soon as I could that if anyone touched you, they would answer to me."

"Well, I appreciate that gesture."

"What is Fitz doing for you?"

"He is trying to find some technicality to get me off. What's going to happen to you, Nikko? You are being charged with murder."

"Fitz said he has no doubt he will get that dropped. It might take a week or so, then I can get out on a bond."

She had to keep this up. "What happens if they convict you of the cocaine trafficking?"

"I will never let them send me to prison. I want to let this play out first, though, because my backup plan means we have to leave the country for good, and I don't really want to do that."

Sophie heard him use the term 'we,' and she knew what he was saying. She wanted to let him know that she had her own plans.

"I plan on waiting it out as long as I can, too. But if it looks bad, I'm gone." She realized she should have just let it go.

"Sophie, no. I will take care of you. You can't go without me. Don't you leave, Sophie, do you hear me?" His tone was harsh and demanding.

Sophie needed to back track. "Of course, Nikko. I'm sure your plan is better than mine." She heard him let out a breath and calm down.

"That's my girl. We'll wait it out as long as we can. I have to go Sophie. I just had to know you didn't blame me for this. I couldn't live with that thought."

"I know, Nikko. It's fine."

"We may not be able to talk again for a while. I love you, Sophie." She couldn't bring herself to say it, even pretending, no matter what the cost.

"I'm glad we were able to talk, Nikko." Sophie handed the phone back to Thomas who put the phone up to his ear.

"Nikko?"

"Fratellino," Nikko said brusquely, "whatever happens, don't let her leave until I get out."

"Okay, Nikko. I'll do what I can.," Thomas replied. Nikko hung up.

"Thomas, you know I'll have to go before he gets out."

"Sophie, is there ever going to be a chance for us?"

"How, Thomas, we've discussed this. As long as Nikko's alive, even if he were out of the country, you could never hurt him like that. And if he does get out, I have to go into hiding again if I'm not in prison. And you can't leave your mom and all your businesses. How could it ever work?"

Thomas took her hand. "What if I found a way?"

"Thomas, don't you think our time has come and gone? It's been too long. We're different people now, but I will always love you for rescuing me and taking such good care of me through all of this."

"I'm not willing to give up on us yet. A way could open up."

"You have a good heart, Thomas."

Thomas asked if she wanted to go to lunch. They left with Huston and Franco as their bodyguards and headed to Morano's again. Thomas always cheered her up. Houston knew it was ridiculous, but that made Houston heartsick. He and Franco were at the next table eating and watching over them.

CHAPTER FIFTEEN

The next day was calm. Everything was a waiting game now. Houston asked Fons if he could take Sophie to dinner and a movie.

"You know I'd have to go with you. What kind of a date is that?"

Houston rubbed his hand down his face. "I don't care. The only way I'll ever have a chance with her is if she sees me as more than her bodyguard. Please, Fons, I just want a fighting chance."

"Okay but we go somewhere out of town where none of Nikko's men might see you two together."

Houston thought for a second. "There's Edward's Steak House in Jersey City, and it's off in a quiet neighborhood. It won't take us long to get there. There's a theater close by, too. If we leave at 4 pm, we will have plenty of time for dinner and a movie."

"Okay, but you owe me one. No... make that two," Fons chuckled. Houston rushed out to the balcony where Sophie was reading.

"Ms. Star, I would like to invite you to dinner and a movie."

She chuckled. "That was a little formal, wasn't it?"

"Well, it's a first, *almost* date, so I thought it should be memorable." He displayed a sheepish grin and made a drumroll noise with his hands on the small table. "And the answer is...?"

"What is, YES?" Her *Jeopardy* reference was noted by him.

"And the crowd roars," he replied.

"You have until 4 pm, then your pumpkin will arrive with your prince charming."

"Oh, I thought I was going with you?"

Houston laughed. "Like I said, your prince charming."

"Well, I better get started. As I recall, it took Cinderella a long time to get ready." She started to walk to her room then turned and asked, "where are we going?"

"Jersey City, to Edward's Steak House and then to a movie."

"Sounds wonderful," Sophie said. Houston felt like a teenager going on his first date.

Houston wore black linen slacks and a white Topman classic stand up collared shirt with a leather bomber jacket. He went to knock on her door. "Your pumpkin has arrived."

Sophie stepped out wearing a Mac Duggal fit and flare, black and cream dress which hung a couple of inches above the knee, with a black, peep toe, low heeled shoe.

Houston whistled. "Cinderella has nothing on you."

"Except the glass slippers." She lifted her shoe. He grabbed her light jacket from the chair and carried it for her.

Nikko had gotten a message to Thomas. He needed some papers taken to Fitz that were in his desk at his condo. Franco was with him, so he figured it was a good time to put Nikko's things away that Sophie gave him. The FBI had been here and confiscated Nikko's computer. Thomas knew there would be nothing incriminating on it. It looks like they took some files too, but he found the papers he was looking for.

Thomas went to Nikko's room and started unpacking his suits in the walk-in closet. Thomas kept hearing that awful shriek from a smoke detector with a low battery. He sent Franco to look for it, but he noticed it sounded like it was coming from behind the closet wall. He started putting his ear to the walls and stopped where it was loudest. Then he started feeling every inch of the wall for a way to open the secret door. When his hand landed on a button, he pushed it, and the wall slid to the left. Inside, he found a light switch.

There were four monitors—two on a desk and two on a shelf built above the desk. There was a computer with an additional hard drive. He looked to the right, and there was Nikko's vault safe. He knew he had one but had never noticed it when he was at the condo. Now he knew why. He turned on the bank of monitors. All the screens were blank. He turned on the computer—still nothing. He checked the files and opened the one with the oldest date on it and waited for it to open. Up on the screen came a picture of Sophie's apartment. Then the door opens and in comes Nikko with Sophie. Thomas turned up the volume.

"Do you like it?" Nikko asked Sophie on the screen.

"I love it. I'm going to have a place like this someday," Sophie replied.

"How about having one right now?"

She looked at him. "I can't afford this."

"Well, this one was supposed to be mine, but I like the penthouse I have now. The location is great, and I prefer the design, so I can lease this one to you for just the maintenance fees and the taxes. Consider it a perk for working for me."

"Mr. Morano, I couldn't do that. It doesn't seem right," she responded.

"I told you to call me Nikko. And I insist. I need to know that you're safe, and this is a secure building."

Thomas stopped it there. He had a bad feeling about this. He opened one dated from just after they started seeing each other. He fast forwarded until he heard voices.

"Cody, please come with Chelsea to see my condo. You both have been putting it off for months." The person on the other end was speaking but he could only hear her side of the conversation. "No, that's not true. I've just been busy." She was listening again. "I know you don't like my cooking. I'll order in," she laughed. "You promise?" she waited. "Okay. Be here at eight."

Thomas closed that file then opened one from the next day. He fast forwarded it until he saw Sophie let Nikko in.

"I'm almost ready, Nikko. I just need to get my jacket."

"Who else are you seeing besides me, Sophie?"

She looked surprised by his question. "No one, Nikko. Even though we've only had a few dates, I'm not seeing anyone else."

Out of nowhere, he slapped her. She stumbled backwards, stunned, and put her hand to her face.

"Who is Cody?" Nikko asked sharply. It took her a minute to catch her breath.

"Cody is just a friend. I've known him a long time. I'm not dating him."

"I don't want you seeing him or talking to him again, do you understand me? If I am dating you, I don't want you seeing anyone else." Thomas saw something come over her face.

"I don't have a problem with being exclusive, but If you ever hit me again, I will pack my bags and be out of here," she threatened.

Nikko must have seen it, too, because he went to her and held her. "I'm sorry, Sophie. I'm just so crazy about you. I can control my jealousy, I promise. But tell me you'll never see him again."

"Okay, Nikko. But get it under control."

He closed that one and opened one from just before she disappeared. He fast forwarded it then he realized this was only one angle. He hit a few buttons and all the screens came up. He saw her in her bedroom getting out of her work clothes. She was headed to the bathroom to take a bath, then he saw that there was a split screen with her shower and tub on one of the monitors. He quickly stopped it. He wasn't going to violate her like that. He heard Franco behind him. "How long have you been standing there."

"Not long, boss. Is that what I think it is?"

Thomas yelled at him. "Fuori di qui!"

Franco turned around and went to the living room to wait. Thomas grabbed one of the boxes he just emptied and dumped all the hard drives and modem into it. He would take them home and destroy them all, tonight. *Nikko, how could you be such a pervert? She had no idea you were violating her this way.*

He didn't want to admit it, but his brother was sick. He was a stalker, and his obsession with Sophie went back years. He was so angry that he smashed the monitors and the computer, turned off the light, closed the door, and walked out with the box. He didn't know if he should tell Sophie about this. She was already scared of Nikko.

Agent Rodriguez drove while Houston and Sophie rode in the back on their date. It was awkward at first, but the mood was light, and they were having fun just talking about nothing. They got to the restaurant about 5 pm hoping to beat the rush. It was Wednesday, so they caught a break and got seated right away. Rodriguez opted to stay in the waiting area. He needed to give his buddy some room to work his magic. Sophie almost blew it for him because she felt bad about leaving him alone, but Rodriguez insisted he was on duty. Houston mouthed "thank you" to him as they left him.

Sophie ordered the salad with red French dressing, prime rib, and a baked potato. He ordered the soup du jour, rib eye steak, and mashed potatoes. He really preferred the garlic mashed potatoes, but he wanted to kiss her tonight. She was so easy to talk to, on any subject. He didn't realize how smart she really was.

"Do you want dessert?" He figured she would be like most women and say no.

"Is the pope Catholic?" He laughed. They shared cheesecake covered with strawberries.

"Okay you promised me a movie," Sophie pressed, "so now we have to negotiate."

"Negotiate what?"

"What kind of movie. No war movies or superheroes."

"Ugh! What's left?" Houston asked.

"Also, no law-and-order type films," Sophie pushed.

"Hey, now you're going too far. That only leaves a chick flick. How could I live that down when Rodriguez is here to make sure everyone finds out?"

Sophie took pity on him. "You have a point. Okay, use your phone to see what our choices are."

He looked up the theater, and she called it. There was a superhero movie, a war movie, a crime drama, a scary movie for teens, a comedy, and the obligatory chick flick.

"Well, definitely not the war movie or scary movie," Sophie said.

"Okay and I nix the chick flick and the crime drama. We have enough of our own," Houston joked.

"That leaves superhero, and comedy," Sophie said.

She nixed the superhero.

"Well, comedy it is. We could probably use a good laugh." He paid the bill and they headed to the theater.

They sat in the back of the balcony section, away from as many people as possible. Rodriguez sat two rows behind them and to the right. The movie was so cookie-cutter cliché they started making up their own lines. He had her laughing so hard, she had to run to the bathroom. He and Rodriguez followed behind and waited. When she came out, Houston asked if she wanted some popcorn. They went to the counter.

"Okay. I want popcorn with no butter," Sophie said.

"No way! That's just plain un-American."

"Then you have to buy me my own bag," she insisted. "And I want candy."

"What kind?"

"Raisinets, Whoppers, and Twizzlers. And I want a diet coke. I have to save my calories for the more important thing."

"Boy, and I thought you'd be a cheap date."

"I haven't had candy in weeks. We don't have any at the condo. Please?" Sophie batted her eyelashes at him in jest.

"Man am I a sucker," Houston smiled.

Rodriguez was a few feet away laughing his head off. Houston knew he was going to get a ribbing for this for weeks. They had too much to carry, so she asked for a sack. They went back to the movie and resumed their voice overs. She ate her Raisinets and a few Twizzlers, drank half of her drink, and put away a third of her popcorn.

Sophie threw popcorn at him a few times because of his dumb jokes, then he put his arm around her, and she laid her head on his shoulder. *Boy life doesn't get any better than this*, he thought. After the movie, they headed home. She insisted they not throw any of her goodies away; she wanted to take them home with her, so he packed them to the car.

Houston put his arm around her again and she lay her head on his shoulder, quiet. He was afraid she might be thinking again, which usually ended badly for him, but she had fallen asleep. He snuggled her closer and held onto her. He took her other hand that was on his knee and held it. He loved holding her hand. He loved having his arm around her. He loved the smell of flowers she wore.

Okay, I love her, now I said it, although it was to himself. He started praying. *Lord, you wouldn't give me such a precious gift just to take it away, would you? Please Lord. I trust you with my life.* But he knew there was a big chance she would have to leave in a hurry. His eyes watered as he thought about it. Rodriguez was looking in the rearview mirror and saw it. Houston looked up and caught his eyes in the mirror.

"I hope you know what you're doing, Houston."

"I know the risk I'm taking."

"Yeah, but I'm the one that will have to pick you up off the floor if she leaves."

"What are friends for, Fons?" He put on a sad smile.

Houston hated to wake her up when they got to the condo, but he didn't think she would want to be carried. When she got out, she said, "My goodies, Houston." He leaned back in to get them. When he straightened up, she put her arms around him, leaned her head against his back, and said, "Thank you for tonight. It was great." That sweet gesture made his heart skip a beat and made the thought of losing her hurt even more.

"It was my pleasure, princess."

"You *are* my prince charming." He turned, put his arm around her and they walked up to the condo.

Sophie said good night and headed to her bedroom. But Houston sat at the table. He couldn't stop the thought of never seeing her again. Fons did his best to encourage him, but he knew all too well that Houston was right. He might never see her again.

It was around 2 am when Sophie came out to the kitchen. She woke up craving sugar. She wanted her Whoppers. Rodriguez was on duty, doing paperwork at the table.

"You know he's crazy mad about you, Sophie."

"I know, Fons. I'm crazy about him, too. I'm not using him, I promise," Sophie said. He had a look of surprise on his face.

"Sophie, I never thought that for a minute. It's just I've never seen him lovesick like this before. What happens if you have to disappear?"

She sat at the table. "I don't know. Do you think I shouldn't go out with him anymore?"

"No, that would crush him. You know the old saying, 'It is better to have loved and lost then never to have loved at all.' I think that applies here."

"If I must go, will you take care of him, make sure he gets over it?"

"I'll make sure he doesn't pine away," he smiled.

"Well, a little pining is okay," Sophie smiled.

"You really are perfect for Houston. I hope it works out."

"Me too, Fons." She gave him some of her Whoppers then went back to her room.

There was that stupid grin on Houston's face again. As hard as he tried, it just wouldn't go. He was dressed for the day. Houston wasn't supposed to relieve Rodriguez until 8 am, but he had ulterior motives. He stepped over to the coffee maker.

"Hey, you're up early," Rodriguez said, looking at his watch.

"Yeah, I know it's only 6, but I thought I'd let you get to bed early."

Rodriguez lifted his eyebrows. "Alright, spill it. What do you want from me now?"

Houston sat down with a pleading look on his face. "I want to take Sophie go-cart racing. There's a place about an hour from here. I figure if you go to sleep now, you'd be up by 2, and we could leave at 4."

"You have this all figured out. What if she doesn't want to go?"

"I guess I'll have to live with no for an answer. Fons, I had so much fun with her last night. I can't get her off my mind."

"And that is why what you're doing is against regulations. You can't protect her when your all mushy like this."

Houston's smile widened. "Mushy?"

"Yes, that's the technical term. Mushy."

"That's why we won't go without you."

"All right. There really is no reason to sit around here. All the work is being done behind the scenes."

He patted Fons on his shoulder. "Thank you. I mean it."

Fons headed to bed. "Yeah, yeah."

Houston sat patiently waiting for Sophie to come out of her room. He knew she spent time in prayer in the morning, and he didn't want to knock on her door. She came out dressed for the day by 10 o'clock.

"Good morning, prince charming."

He smiled at her. "Good morning, princess."

Sophie stepped to the refrigerator to see what she could make them for breakfast.

"All we have is leftovers in here. I didn't realize we ate out so much. Oh, here, some eggs."

"I think there's bacon in the crisper, too," Houston added.

"I'll make the eggs and toast. You cook the bacon."

He got up. "Sounds like a plan to me."

"How do you like your eggs?" Sophie asked.

"I like them however you make them."

"Scrambled it is."

They made breakfast together and took their plates to the table. He grabbed them both some coffee.

"How would you like to go go-karting today?"

"I would love that. Will Rodriguez allow it?"

He had this mischievous look on his face. "I worked it out." They finished breakfast and cleaned up their mess.

Sophie went out to read on the balcony. She took the phone with her. He worked on his reports, seated where he could see her. He still had a job to do and that was to protect her.

The phone rang about noon. Sophie answered.

"Hello?"

"Ms. Star, this is Fitz. I have some news."

"Do you need to come by, or do you want to tell me over the phone?"

He thought for a moment. "The phone is fine. I think we have uncovered some mishandling of your case by the DA. It appears they have not handed over all the documents we asked for in discovery and one of them may have been doctored."

"Do you think it's enough to get the case thrown out?"

Fitz was trying not to get her hopes up. "I'm not sure yet. I'm meeting with the DA on Monday."

"That is certainly good news for me. What's happening with Nikko?" She had to find out if she still had some time.

"Nikko's case is a little more complicated. I have petitioned the court for a hearing concerning the lack of evidence on the murder charge, but the DA keeps stalling. I'm hoping to get it on the docket sometime next week," the attorney said. That gave her a few more days to breathe.

"Thanks for the update. Do you need me to do anything?"

"No. Just sit tight."

"I could call Thomas for you and tell him what's happening?"

"No, we're in contact every day."

"Mr. Fitz, thank you for all your work."

"You're welcome, Ms. Star, but it's what I get paid for." She could tell he loved his job. They said goodbye and she sat pondering the way things were working out. The DA must have come up with a convincing way to botch the case against her.

Houston saw she was on the phone but didn't want to just come out and ask who called. Technically, it was none of his business, it just felt like it to him. He had been praying about her leaving.

Houston considered taking his accumulated vacation time and going with her at least long enough to make sure she was safe and see where she was headed. Maybe he'd even quit and stay with her. He knew the Bible warned not to do anything without weighing the cost. But the cost of losing her was greater to him than quitting his job and disappearing. His only hesitation was his family. He loved his family and saw them often. He would drive to Trenton whenever he could and go to church with them. Never seeing them again would be difficult. *Lord, please give me wisdom*. He had one other dilemma. What if she didn't want him with her? That would hurt. She came inside, breaking off the battle that was raging in his mind.

"Fitz called and said the DA is doing as he promised. Fitz thinks he has some misconduct charges against the prosecution about not handing over documents properly. He is meeting with the DA on Monday. It's possible the charges will be dropped."

Houston knew this was a good thing for her but bad for him. "That will solve your concern about being a fugitive if you have to go."

"Yeah, at least until they purge the computer completely of my bogus charges. I figure it might take a year or so for that to be done. They have to close Nikko's case first."

"And Nikko has no plan to stick around if he can't get the charges dismissed," Houston reminded her.

"All of this will have been for nothing if he doesn't go to jail, Houston."

"That's not true, Sophie. You have done what you set out to do—tear down his organization. Putting him in jail is incidental. I know it won't feel that way to you. You want to make sure he can't ever get back into business, but if he has to leave the country, he won't be back in business, in this country, anyway. You have to let God determine the outcome."

She sat down folded her hands on the table. "You're right. It should be God's way. Otherwise, it's just revenge, and I don't want that to be my motive."

Houston put his hand on top of hers. "God sees your heart. You're a good woman, Sophie."

"I thought I had forgiven him, but the Lord is showing me I've hung on to a few things," she confessed.

Dangerous Obsession

CHAPTER SIXTEEN

After they ate leftovers for lunch, Sophie went to her room to find something to wear for their excursion. Agent Rodriguez got up and went to get a cup of coffee.

"Did you get enough sleep, Fons?"

"Like you care. You just want me ready for your date."

Houston laughed. "Well, yeah."

Fons took his coffee to his room. "I'll be ready by 4. Don't worry about me."

Sophie was wearing a pair of blue jeans and a dark blue pullover sweater. She was carrying her leather jacket. Her hair was in a ponytail with little make up on, just lipstick and mascara. She looked so young.

"I don't think I have seen you in blue jeans before."

"You either," she responded. While they waited, she gathered up her leftover candy.

"I can't leave without my treasure."

He laughed at her. "I bet you had a candy stash under your bed when you were a kid."

"I'm sure I did. How did you know?"

"I'm in law enforcement, remember? We know these things."

"Your chiding does not deter me one bit, Agent Townsend."

He laughed at her again. "Wouldn't want it to, Ms. Star. Just an observation."

Agent Rodriguez came out. "What are you two bickering about?"

"He was giving me a bad time because I want to take my candy."

"As long as you keep sharing it with me, I'm good with that."

Houston got a smirk on his face. "She shared with you? She wouldn't give me any last night."

"I guess I've just got something you don't," he retorted.

It took them a little longer to get to the go-kart track, because they had to get through town. Good thing it was only Thursday traffic. It was chilly out but not cold.

They got to the track and Houston paid for their ride while Fons stayed on the sidelines and watched. Houston and Sophie got in their go-karts, side by side, waiting to get up to the starting line.

Sophie hollered so he could hear with his helmet on. "What do I get for winning?"

"What makes you think you'll win?"

"I'm good at this. What do I get?"

"You get to choose the restaurant," Houston hollered back.

"Okay."

They got up to the starting line, the green light came on, and off they went. He was buzzing right along. He let her go ahead, then he waited for a spot to go around her and tried to leave her in the dust. She would have none of it. She was on his tail the whole way. Finally, on a straight stretch, she was able to get around him again and it was his turn to scramble. She only had to stay ahead another quarter mile. She could do it. Sophie swerved her cart back and forth so he couldn't pass her. She got over the finish line first and pulled to the side. She took her helmet off. He saw she was laughing. That was a sight he could live with the rest of his life.

"Two out of three," he said.

"Oh! A sore loser, are we?" She chuckled.

"No, just competitive."

"You're on!"

Houston won the next race, but the last one was a photo finish. Sophie pulled her kart over, took her helmet off, and ran to the operator. She held up the photo, jumping up and down.

It was so cute. Houston couldn't help but laugh. Rodriguez was at his perch watching over them. He couldn't help remembering the other women Houston dated. None of them made him act like this. Houston was the happiest he'd ever seen him. She was his perfect fit in every way. She challenged him, and that's what he needed. What he was dreading was the depths of his depression when she was gone. *I promised you I would bring him out of it, Sophie, but I'm not sure anyone will be able to.* But it was too late to save him from it, now. He might as well let Houston be happy while he could.

Sophie came rushing up to him. "I beat him Fons, fair and square."

Houston caught up to her, put his arm around her waist, and pulled her to him.

"You cheated!"

"Did not!"

"Did too!"

"You saw it, Fons. Tell him I didn't cheat."

He smiled. "She won fair and square."

Houston frowned at him. "Hey, what happened to the bro code?"

"I call 'em like I see 'em."

Sophie was clapping her hands. "Okay. For my reward, I choose where we eat." They headed to the car. Houston opened the door for her then went around to the other side. Rodriguez got in the driver's seat.

"Where to, Sophie?"

"I saw a Chinese Restaurant on our way here. With three of us, we can eat family style." Rodriguez looked at Houston in the rearview mirror. Houston met his eyes and nodded. He knew Fons didn't want to encroach on their time together, but he wanted Fons to join them.

They had a great time at dinner. Houston noticed Sophie was careful to always include Rodriguez in the conversations. Her sensitivity for other people's feelings just made her more attractive to him. His thoughts drifted to the horrible beating she endured from Nikko. How could anyone hurt such a gentle soul like Sophie? An anger started building up in him that he had never felt before. *Oh, Father, never let my anger or jealousy get out of control. I don't want to be that kind of man because then I wouldn't deserve her.* He forced his thoughts back to the conversation.

On the way home, he put his arm around her. She turned slightly, stretched, and gave him a quick kiss on the lips.

"Thank you for today," Sophie smiled. He was taken by surprise.

"Okay. Now, next time it's my turn," he chuckled.

"Something to look forward to." She gave a sly smile.

"Well, far be it from me to keep a lady waiting." He turned, put both hands on her face, and kissed her gently at first. Then he moved his hands around her back, pulling her closer to him, and let his desire for her come through in the kiss. "Wow," he said. "I've wanted to do that from the first day I saw you, and it was better than I imagined."

She smiled, "you're a good kisser."

"Next one's on you."

"I think I'll make you wait for it and let the anticipation grow."

"You are a wicked princess," he laughed.

196

"And you have need of patience, prince charming." She gave him a beautiful smile and rested her head against his shoulder. They got home before eleven, she said good night, and went to her room. Houston sat with Rodriguez for a while.

"Sophie got a call from Fitz today. The DA is keeping his promise. He is opening a way to get her case dropped."

"You know she has to leave soon, Houston."

"I'm thinking about going with her."

Rodriguez lifted his eyebrows shocked. "What about your job, your family? It will be like witness protection. You won't be able to come back."

"I don't know, Fons. I could just take my vacation and get her to where she's going safely and stay with her for a while. But I can tell you right now—I doubt I'd ever be able to say goodbye to her. I love her, Fons. A lot."

"I know you do. I can see it, and she is the perfect fit for you. But it's a big sacrifice leaving everything behind. Have you said anything to her about this?"

"No."

"How do you know she'll let you go with her."

"I don't, and I don't know how I'll take it if she says no." They talked for another half hour, and then Houston went to bed.

"Feel free to relieve me early anytime," Rodriguez joked.

Houston went to bed but had a tough time falling asleep. *What if she doesn't want me, Lord? How will I take it? Please give me strength. I trust you, Lord, to direct my path.*

In the morning, they made breakfast together again. "I think we need to go to the store. We can't eat the same thing every day," Sophie said.

"Not a problem. You start a grocery list, and it can't all be candy."

"Hey, you make your own list and leave mine to me," she teased him. That afternoon, when Rodriguez was awake, she came up to them at the table and, looking at Houston, said, "It's my turn to ask you on a date."

He smiled. "That's fair. Where are you taking me?"

"The ballet at the Metropolitan Opera House."

Houston almost choked on his coffee. "The ballet? Sophie, if the guys ever hear about this, I'll never live it down." Fons was laughing hard.

"So, does that mean I have to find another date?"

Houston sucked in a breath. "No, no. I'd love to go with you."

Sophie smiled. She knew she was torturing him, but he needed to extend his social experience. "You'll need a tuxedo." Fons was almost rolling on the floor. Houston slugged him on the arm.

"You too, Fons, unless you plan on neglecting your duty."

Fons suddenly stopped laughing, but Houston took it up. When they finally calmed down, Rodriguez said, "Sophie, we can't sit in the general seating."

"I know. A friend of mine has a private box. She never goes on Fridays, so we will have privacy. It starts at 8 pm" She headed back to her spot on the balcony while Houston and Fons figured out how to get their hands on some tuxedos.

"Smith just got married, and he's about my size. I bet he'll let me borrow his," Houston figured.

"What am I supposed to do?" Rodriguez blurted.

Houston thought for a minute. "I bet one of his grooms' men has one that would fit you."

"Once you make that call, you know word is going to get around," Fons said.

"I know, but she has been such a great sport on my dates. I can't do any less for her." Houston was back at the condo by 4 pm, tuxedos in hand.

By 6:45 pm, Houston and Rodriguez were ready and waiting on Sophie. When she came out of her room, he stood to meet her. She was in a red Jovani off the shoulder gown that draped to the floor with a slit on the left side that ran up to her knee. Her stiletto sandals had crystals on the strap across her toes. She carried a black satin clutch with a pearl clasp. A pearl ring and the matching three strand, freshwater pearl earrings set off her chignon at the nape of her neck. He noticed she hadn't been wearing the sapphire ring lately.

"How did you transform from the gorgeous girl next door from last night to this exquisite beauty standing before me?"

Sophie smiled, got right up in front of him, and put her hand flat on his chest. "You look very handsome yourself, prince charming." That touch made getting in that monkey suit worth it. He crooked his elbow, she slipped her hand in it, and off they went to the ballet.

Houston could see how much she was enjoying the performance, and he had to admit he liked it too, although he would deny it to his dying breath. After one of the male dancers made an extraordinary leap, he leaned over and whispered to her, "I could do that."

Sophie laughed. "I'd like to see it."

"You don't believe me?"

199

She turned to him. "No, now be quiet."

Houston started to stand. "If you don't believe me, I'll show you right now."

Sophie started laughing, then she slapped him on the shoulder. "Sit down and stop making me laugh."

But that was the problem. He never wanted to stop making her laugh. He pulled something out of his inside pocket and handed it to her. It was Twizzlers. She looked up at him with eyes sparkling and a big grin.

"Thank you, Houston." He reached for her hand and let her enjoy the rest of the performance. As they were leaving the box after the show, she turned to him, put her arm around his neck, and brought his face down to her so she could kiss him. "Thank you for my candy and for coming with me tonight. You were such a good sport."

"I think I deserve an extra kiss for the candy."

"When you're right, you're right." She reached up and kissed him again.

"Your turn."

Rodriguez was just outside the curtain that closed off the entrance to the box seat area. "What took you so long?" he teased Houston.

"None of your business," Houston said. Sophie laughed at the two friends. She loved to hear their banter.

On the way back to the condo Sophie asked, "can we stop by the bakery, Fons? I want some donuts for breakfast."

Rodriguez cringed. "Don't you think we're a little overdressed?" He was hoping he wouldn't be seen in public in the tux.

She laughed. "Are you embarrassed? You look very handsome." Fons smiled back through the rearview mirror at her.

Houston carried the donuts in and set them on the counter. He went to reach for one and she slapped his hand.

"Those are for the morning. Good night, guys." With that, she went to her room. Houston and Rodriguez couldn't get out of their tuxedos fast enough.

"I'll take them to the launderer tomorrow and then get them back to Smith. If we keep them around, she may come up with some other brilliant idea to make us wear them again."

"Good plan," Fons responded.

It was probably 1 am when she snuck out to grab a donut. By the time she saw Houston and Fons, it was too late to turn around. They already caught her with her fingers in the donut box.

"Caught ya!" They both chimed in together and laughed.

"Don't laugh too hard. I see you both are eating donuts, too."

"Guilty as charged," Houston confessed. She grabbed a glass of milk and sat with them while she ate her donut.

"I would really like to go to church on Sunday if you can make that happen, Agent Rodriguez."

"Do you have a church locally you want to attend?"

"No. I never went to church when I lived here."

"Sophie, my family goes to church in Trenton. It's only a little over an hour drive, and then we could have lunch with them," Houston suggested.

"I couldn't impose on your family like that, and they don't even know me."

"My family would love it," he answered.

She turned to Rodriguez. "Is it alright?"

"I can make it work," Agent Rodriguez said.

Houston added, "we'll have to leave here by 7 am to make sure we don't miss the 9 am service, though."

"That's not a problem for me. I'm Cinderella, not sleeping beauty," Sophie replied. She stood up and took her plate and glass to the sink, rinsed them, and put them in the dishwasher.

"Good night again." When she got back to her room, she remembered hearing a ping on her cell indicating she had a text. She hadn't wanted to be rude and check when they were on the date, but then she forgot about it. It was from Thomas.

'**Couldn't reach you by phone. Would like to take you to the theater tomorrow night to see Hamilton.**'

What was she going to do? She had to see this operation through. Thomas was the glue that kept it together. She couldn't say no, but it would hurt Houston to see her with Thomas. She knew that. She texted him back. '**Love to. What time?**'

Sophie waited to see if he might respond tonight. He usually stayed up late. Sure enough, the response came a few minutes later. '**7 pm, can't wait.**'

Sophie spent the next hour trying to figure out a way to not hurt Houston with this news.

Sophie slept late Saturday morning, not wanting to face telling Houston. She came out about 11 am. Houston was sitting on the balcony with a cup of coffee. Rodriguez was awake for some reason.

"You're still up?"

"Yeah. I got a few hours of sleep, but then command called wanting more intel on what's happening."

"Can I talk to you privately for a moment?" She pointed to the living room. They sat down.

"Thomas wants to take me to the theater tonight. I have to go, Fons. He is the glue to the rest of this operation." She shook her head. "I don't want to hurt Houston, but I know he will be if he sees us go out together."

"I know, but you have to tell him."

"I plan on telling him. I won't go behind his back. I just know if he sees Thomas pick me up, and I go out that door with him, it will hurt Houston deeply."

"You're right. It'll kill him inside. Even if in his head he knows that it's all part of the operation, his heart won't get it." Fons' face was grim.

"You have to make some excuse to send him to the warehouse before Thomas comes to pick me up."

"I'll figure something out."

"Thanks, Fons." Houston came in the balcony door.

"If you'd waited any longer, there would be no donuts left." He looked at Fons and changed his expression. "Has something happened?"

Sophie stood up. "Houston, can we go for a walk at that dog park?"

"Sure, Sophie." He got her light jacket and opened the door for her. She took his hand while they walked. When they came to a bench, she pulled him over to sit down.

"What's going on, Sophie?"

"You know this operation is not over, and Thomas is an important part of making it work."

"Just say it." He knew what was coming.

"He wants to take me to the theater tonight." Houston stood up and walked a few steps away from her.

"You know I have to go. It's just a part I'm playing. You know I have no romantic feelings for him. You know that, right?"

He turned back to her. "But he does have feelings for you, Sophie. He's in love with you."

203

She sighed. "The last few days with you have been some of the best of my life, but we have been living in a bubble. It's not real. I'm going to have to leave soon, and in order to protect myself, I have to make this plan work flawlessly." Sophie watched him as he came back to the bench and sat down. "I don't want you at the condo when he comes to pick me up. I couldn't take the look of hurt in your eyes. I'd break down," Sophie said.

"I'm not leaving the condo, Sophie." She felt him grow angry at her request.

"Are you going to tell me you can handle him taking my hand and leading me out that door?" He sagged on the bench without answering. She put her head on his shoulder.

"What if I could leave with you when you go?" His voice was so soft she could barely hear it.

"What do you mean leave with me?" She was looking him in the eye, questioning the statement.

"What if, when you finally had to run, I came with you?"

"Houston, I would never ask you to do that. What about your job, your family? I have no one. It's different for me. I can't let you sacrifice everything," Sophies tone left no room for debate.

"Then you wouldn't be alone. You'd have me."

"You don't know me well enough to make that kind of decision. What if you decided I wasn't worth the cost?"

"Sophie, I would follow you to the ends of the earth. I don't need my job. When dad's oil wells came in, he gave each of us kids a million dollars as a seed to start any kind of a life we wanted. He said we had known poverty long enough and it was time we knew wealth. I never told anyone because the men wouldn't think of me the same. But I can take care of us."

Sophie cupped her hand on his face. "I don't need you to take care of me. I have funds of my own, but that's the sweetest thing you could have said."

"I love you, Sophie."

"I love you too, Houston."

A shocked look came across his face. "You do?"

"Yes, of course I do. You're everything I could ever want in a man. You are my prince charming."

"I thought you didn't want me to come because you didn't care for me."

"No, I care for you too much to let you give up everything for me. You love your job."

He took her hand from his face and kissed the inside of her palm. "I love you more than my job. I could take a leave of absence and let command know you need protection until you're settled in your new life. They would set me up with a secure new identity. After you were safe, we could decide what to do from there. But I can tell you right now, I won't ever want to leave you."

"It's so tempting, Houston. We have a few days still. Give yourself time to think it over."

He stood up and reached out his hand for her. He pulled her close and kissed her with a hunger it would take a lifetime to quench. They headed back to the condo.

They didn't see Ben taking pictures. They hadn't noticed that he had been following them for days. When Nikko's men were released on bail, he gave Ben specific orders to follow Sophie. He wanted to know if she was planning to leave before he got out. *I'm not sure Nikko was expecting this,* Ben thought. He had to get these to Nikko, even though he knew what would happen next. He headed for the camera shop to have the roll developed and made into 8 X 10s. The impact would be worse at that size, but he knew it would be what Nikko wanted.

Dangerous Obsession

CHAPTER SEVENTEEN

Agent Rodriguez kept his promise and made sure Houston was gone. Houston knew it would be a bad idea to be there, and he needed to talk to Agent Hampton about leaving with Sophie and getting a secure new identity.

Agent Rodriguez answered the door in his suit and let Thomas and Franco in. He knocked on her door. "Ms. Star, Mr. Morano is here."

"Thank you." She came out in a black Raina Halo cocktail length flare skirt with red heels and red clutch. On her ears she wore her diamond studs and the sapphire ring.

Thomas went to her when she came out of her room. "You look beautiful as always."

He kissed her on the lips. She was taken aback. She didn't expect that. He took her hand, and they left. Franco and Rodriguez were leading the way. He had a private box which made her feel better. The show was entertaining, and Thomas kept the conversation enjoyable. He kept hold of her hand all night. All she could think of was that she had to let Thomas know she wasn't interested in him in that way, but she would be risking so much. After the show, they went for a late dinner, before they headed back to her condo.

"Sophie, it looks like Fitz may have found a way to get your case dropped."

"He told me. I'm so grateful."

"I want you to stay."

"Thomas, how can I do that? You know Nikko will come after me."

"I'll talk to him."

"Thomas, do you really think that will work?" He didn't answer. Sophie continued, "I've decided to sell my farm and network. I don't need the money, and I really don't ever want to be in this position again."

He took her hand, "that's great news."

"I may have a buyer. If it goes through, I think I may just leave town."

"Give me more time," Thomas pleaded. This time she didn't answer. They were quiet for a while. He ordered dessert for her. He knew what she liked.

"Thomas, do you ever think about God?"

His eyes looked in hers with surprise. "Of course. I was raised in the Catholic Church with my family. Nikko and I were both altar boys."

"That's not what I mean. Do you ever think about how much God loved us to send his son to take our sins on Himself so we could be with Him in Heaven?"

"Why are you asking me this, Sophie?"

"With all that's going on, I just want to know that we're all ready if something happens."

"I won't let anything happen to you."

"We will all die sometime, Thomas. We are all sinners, but Jesus will forgive our sins if we ask him. Don't you think sometimes it would be nice to just give it all over to Him, to just ask for forgiveness and trust Him?"

"Sophie, I'm a man who likes to be in control. I don't know if I could do that," he said, ending the conversation.

Sophie finished her dessert, and they headed out.

When the car stopped in front of her building, Thomas asked, "can I see you again next week?"

"Sure, Thomas. That would be nice."

Fons opened the car door, Thomas stepped out with her, gave her a kiss on the cheek and said goodnight. Before she turned to go inside, she said, "thanks for tonight. It was nice, but Thomas, you need to understand that there is no future for us. I don't want to lead you on."

"I told you I won't give up hope yet." Thomas got back in the car and Fons walked Sophie to the condo.

Houston was on the balcony waiting for them to come home. Sophie hurried to her room to change. She didn't want Houston to see her in date clothes. Rodriguez went out to the balcony to say hello.

"How was it?" he asked.

"I'm not going to discuss it with you, buddy."

"That's probably best," Houston responded.

Sophie came out of her room, she changed into blue jeans. He stood up and gave her a hug. Fons went to his room to change.

"I talked to my mom. She is thrilled to have you coming tomorrow." They sat down on the wicker settee.

"I will be so glad to be in church. I need it." They sat and talked for a long time. It was hard for her to let go of feeling she had betrayed him by going out with Thomas, but she tried to let Thomas know she wasn't interested.

Sophie finally said, "I'm tired Houston. I'm going to bed, but I'll be ready at seven," she stood up.

He grabbed her hand. "Sophie, I know you feel guilty about going out with Thomas, but I can handle it."

"Thank you, Houston. That helps a lot." She leaned down and kissed his cheek. "Your turn."

"That one doesn't count. Only the ones on the lips."

She smiled "who said you get to make the rules. We'll have to negotiate terms."

He gave a small laugh. Sophie knew he was trying to hide his hurt over this evening.

Sophie just wanted this day to end, but she couldn't sleep. She cried softly, telling the Lord, no matter what the cost to her, she would not accept another date with Thomas and hurt Houston like that again.

Rodriguez saw Sophie go to her room after he got out of his suit. He went to the balcony and asked Houston how he was doing.

"I'm okay, Fons. When I got back from command and the place was empty, my hurt feelings and jealousy were taking me over. Then I realized I needed my perspective changed. She stayed here because I asked her for time, a chance to see if we had something. At great risk to her life, she agreed. She should have been gone days ago. And here I was entertaining my petty jealousy and hurt feelings. I felt like a spoiled child. I asked forgiveness, and God gave me peace. I know I need to let her do whatever she has to in order to finish this. My part is to protect her and support her any way I can."

"I'm proud of you," Fons put his fist out to Houston, and they fist bumped.

"I told Agent Hampton I was going with her if Nikko gets bonded out and she had to leave. She'll still need protection until she gets settled."

"What did he say?"

"At first, he complained about the expense of continued 24-hour protection, but then he stopped mid-sentence. He said she had just performed a great service for this country and agreed that we should give her protection as long as she thinks it's necessary. If he hadn't agreed, I would have put in for my vacation or a leave of absence. He is setting me up with a secure new identity."

"Did you ever talk to her about this? You could be away from your family for a long time, Houston."

"I don't care. I'm not letting her go out there unprotected and alone. I did talk to her. She doesn't want me to make the sacrifice, but that's my decision to make, not hers."

"Okay, bud. I'm behind you whatever happens."

"Thanks, Fons." They just sat there for a while, quietly, before Houston got up and went to bed.

Nikko was on his cot when a guard handed him a manila envelope. His cellmate had been released yesterday, so he had some privacy, for a few days anyway. He was getting tired of waiting.

Nikko called Fitz earlier and told him he wanted out of here immediately. Fitz assured him he planned to go before a judge Monday and petition the court to drop the murder charge citing a lack of evidence. Then he could get him bonded out like his men.

Nikko took the envelope back to his cot, sat down, and opened the package. His face turned crimson as he looked through pictures of Houston holding hands with Sophie, kissing Sophie, laughing with Sophie. *His* Sophie. *His* fiancé, his wife, as far as he was concerned. Those were his lips to kiss, his hands to hold. He was going to kill that thug.

Nikko got up and started hitting the cot with his fists. His anger and jealousy surpassed anything he'd ever felt before, even more than when he nearly beat Sophie to death. Then he laid down on the cot and started planning what he was going to do.

Sophie felt better about things when she woke up. She was happy to be going to church. She was dressed on time and came out to find Houston and Rodriguez waiting for her. They made it to the church about 15 minutes early, and she could see his family waiting outside for them to arrive. His mother, Lily, came to her first even before hugging her son. She was still a beautiful woman, probably in her late fifty's. Her hair was blonde, she was maybe an inch taller than Sophie. She was slender and well proportioned. She gave Sophie a hug and said how happy she was to meet her. His father, Jack, came and did the same. He was Houston, only older. He had some gray in his hair, and he was maybe even an inch taller than Houston. You could see the family resemblance in his siblings, Spring, Ted, and Sam too. It was obvious Rodriguez was already a member of this family. He must have spent a lot of time here with Houston over the years.

Finally, they all filed into the church and sat a few rows from the front. There was something about sitting in the House of God, that always felt like coming home. Sophie hadn't realized it before, but she had felt like a vagabond for many years now. Nowhere she lived ever felt like home. The music was better than any concert. She recognized many of the songs from her church in Lake View. They had monitors up front like at her church, the words to the songs were on the screen for all to sing along.

The Pastor started his sermon. "I would like to give you a new perspective on the story of the prodigal son. The main scripture for my sermon is 2 Peter 3:9. The Lord is not slow in keeping his promise, as some understand slowness. Instead, he is patient with you, not wanting anyone to *perish*, but wishing everyone to come to repentance. The father in this story had two sons. He loved them both very much, but wanted them to stay out of choice, not a sense of obligation. So, he gave them their inheritance and told them they were free to leave. The one son, that most of us seem to refer to as the 'good son,' stayed. He loved his father and loved working the business with him. His family was there. He had no desire to go anywhere else. But the other son, the 'bad son,' had always had a wandering spirit. He wanted to know what was on the other side of the stream. He wanted adventure, risk, and excitement, so he said goodbye and went to see where life would take him. But he had no boundaries, and he ended up with the wrong crowd. The morals he was raised with meant nothing to him anymore. It was all about the adrenaline rush, whatever felt good at the moment.

"Eventually, all his money was gone. His friends had gone with it, and he was working tending pigs, ready to steal their food to eat. Now, he may have been in an *actual* pig pen, but some of us are in a *spiritual* pig pen. We can look like we are right with God on the outside, but in our hearts and minds, we are living in the gutter, looking at porn, stealing from our bosses. There are many 'pig pens' in life, but God is merciful.

"The bad son remembered that his father loved him. He was remorseful for having walked away from a man who would have given his life for him and instead allowed his flesh to rule. He had no right to his father's love anymore, but he just wanted to be close to it, to his father, like the old saying, 'I would rather be a servant in my Father's house than a prince in a castle.'

"During this time, his father went out each day to look for his son, longing for his son's return. He must have stood on that spot hour after hour, day after day, because the Bible says he saw his son in the distance and ran to him. What are the chances that was the first day he stood out there with open arms? The son fell into his arms and asked for his forgiveness. All he wanted now was to be a servant. He didn't deserve to be a son any longer.

"But when our Heavenly Father forgives us, he erases our sins. Under the blood of His Son, Jesus, they no longer exist. If we were to bring them up again, He wouldn't know what you were talking about. But we don't forget. We remember our brothers' sins. His brother had a problem with him being welcomed back as a son. That is how our fleshly minds work. Somehow, we decide who should be forgiven, whose sins are forgivable. But God forgives all sinners, all sins that are washed in the blood. The rapist, the murderer, the adulterer, we've decided in our hard hearts that their sins are too great. But if you were that murderer, wouldn't you want that forgiveness? We need not try to determine who is worthy of forgiveness. We need only be grateful that God didn't decide that *our* sins were the ones he wouldn't forgive."

The Pastor went on to make his final points, but Sophie couldn't hear anything else. She knew the Holy Spirit was dealing with her. She said she had forgiven Nikko, but she hadn't considered praying for his soul. She thought he was irredeemable. She had prayed for Thomas but never Nikko. Who was she to make that call? *Lord, forgive my pride. I repent for my unforgiveness.* Houston saw her crying and took her hand.

Houston knew he had failed God so many times, that he had thought of himself and his own selfish petty feelings before her needs. He didn't want to be that kind of man. He wanted to be like his Father; in fact, he wanted to be like both his Heavenly Father and his earthly father. He was so grateful the Lord had brought Sophie into his life.

After church, they headed to Houston's family home. It was a beautiful ranch style home made of brick. You could tell they spent a lot of time in the kitchen. It smelled of homemade bread. There was a breakfast bar with several stools that separated the kitchen from a long kitchen table.

Lunch was served in the formal dining room table in the next room. After grace was said, the best home cooked meal she could remember eating was being consumed. She hoped Houston didn't expect that from her. She was a terrible cook. It was almost a party atmosphere with all of them talking at once and laughing. She joined the fun but was observing the great relationship Houston enjoyed with his two brothers, Ted and Sam, and his sister, Spring. Spring's fiancé, Jonas, was out of town today.

After they ate, Sophie helped to clear the table. She was rinsing plates to put in the dishwasher when Lily, Houston's mom, saw the lost look in Sophie's eyes. She took her hand and led her to the porch just off the kitchen. She sat Sophie down and sat next to her.

"What's wrong, dear?"

"You have a wonderful family, Mrs. Townsend. You have raised an amazing son in Houston, but he has offered to do something for me that will be a great sacrifice to him. Seeing you here together, I know I can't let him do it. He's going to be upset when I tell him no, but I just can't let him do it."

"Please call me Lily, Sophie." She pondered what Sophie had just said. "There is one thing about my son—once he has decided something, no one can convince him otherwise. And I wouldn't want you to try to change it for him."

Sophie felt Lily had a pretty good idea she was referring to her son leaving for a long time.

"Houston is different from his siblings. He's the one most like his dad. Not just his dad's stubborn loyalty and protective nature, but his heart. I married Jack because I knew he would

215

treasure me and put the family's needs above his own. He treats me like the sun and moon revolve around me. That's the kind of love I wanted, and I love him the same way," Lily looked off into the distance as if she was remembering something and smiled.

"Houston told me your love story is one for the ages."

"Houston wants to love someone that way, but he's never met anyone who made his heart race. Until you."

Sophie turned to her surprised. "How could you know that?"

"Yesterday, when he called to say you all were coming, he told me a little about you. The way he talked about you, his heart was pouring out." Sophie hung her head. "You listen to me now, young lady. I have been praying my son would find the right woman for his whole life. You can't get in the way of what God has in store for him, and if God's will is that he leaves his family to care for you and build a family of his own, then we will just have to live with it."

"Miss Lily, I hear what you're saying, but I'm the one who will bear the responsibility of his sacrifice. I don't know if I can. I couldn't stand it if he ever regretted his decision. I told him I had the final say in this issue, not him."

Houston had come into the kitchen looking for Sophie. He saw that she was talking to his mother, so he went back to the others in the living room.

Sophie stood up, and Lily took her hands. "I'll be praying for you. Please consider what I told you."

"I will. I promise."

On the way home, her mind was being ravaged with the decision she had to make. Sophie knew it would be soon. If Fitz gets her case dropped tomorrow, then she might have to leave by Tuesday. She took a big chance waiting this long, but she didn't regret it. Sophie didn't regret falling for Houston, either. She never would. She was glad Houston was driving and Fons was up front with him. She didn't want to be near him right now. She had to think straight.

They were home by six with enough leftovers for a week. Sophie went to her room to change, and the men did the same. When she came out, Houston told her Fons had finally gone to sleep since they were home and safe.

Sophie went to the balcony to read, and Houston got on the phone to Agent Mathews. When he got off the phone, he came outside.

"I'm so glad you had a chance to meet my family. They loved having you there."

She padded the seat next to her. "Houston, we need to talk."

He sat down. "That sounds ominous."

Sophie looked in his eyes. "Houston, I love your family and, more importantly, you love your family. You would never be happy leaving them indefinitely. I can't let you come with me. It would be worse than death if I saw regret in your eyes within a few years."

"Sophie, I do love my family, and of course I would miss them, but not being with you would be like tearing my heart out. I'm not letting you go alone. Even if you don't love me, you need me to protect you."

Sophie could see he was hurt. "I do love you Houston, with my whole heart, which is why I've made my decision. I told you up front that I, alone, make this decision. Yes, I would be safer with you, but I know how to hide. I've proven that."

"It's a little arrogant to think that you know what's best for me, isn't it, Sophie? Do you know better than God?" His voice was raised and stern.

"No... no, of course not." This was the stubbornness his mother was talking about whenever he felt certain he was right.

"I have put my life in the hands of God, and He led me to you, gave me the task of protecting you, and that's exactly what I intend to do." He was standing now, pacing. "I've already gotten a secure new identity and cleared it with the agency. Even if you turn away from me for doing it, I plan on honoring my commitment to God and you."

Sophie broke down. He stood her up, took her in his arms, and kissed her. "I'm sorry I yelled at you, princess."

"No, that's not it. It's just so wonderful to be loved by a man I admire so much." He kissed her eyes, her nose.

"I can't begin to explain how much I love you."

She folded her arms into his chest and gave him a small smile. "You went out of turn."

"Remember, only the ones on the lips count," Houston chuckled.

She laid her head against his chest. He sat her down again. "If Nikko catches us, I know what he will do to me, but I can't imagine what he'll do to you," Sophie said. But she did know, and it scared her more than anything.

"I trust God, Sophie, for both of us. But as long as I'm breathing, I won't let him hurt you." They sat there for several hours without a word. By 9 pm she was emotionally exhausted. Sophie said good night and went to her room.

CHAPTER EIGHTEEN

While Sophie waited for the phone call from Fitz, she started packing. This time she could take some things with her. She limited it to one larger suitcase and a go-bag. She got all her documents together, both her passports, her bank information, and her computer and put it all in a large briefcase. She also had some jewelry she wanted to take and about $30,000 in cash. Sophie had her plans laid out. Since it was definite that Houston was coming, she would soon share it with him. She wasn't scared this time. She had someone she could trust to lean on. When she was finished, she walked out to the balcony with a cup of coffee.

"Good morning." Houston said with a huge smile.

"Good morning to you too," she responded.

Rodriguez came from the kitchen with coffee and some of Sunday's leftovers.

"What am I, chopped liver?" Rodriguez teased.

"Good morning, Fons," they responded in unison.

"That's better," he chuckled.

Sophie took Houston to the balcony. "I'm not going to try to sell the penthouse yet. It may be possible for us to come back someday. I'll leave everything here, except what little I'm taking, and I will keep the taxes paid from an overseas account. I may decide to sell later, but I have time to make that decision. Nikko knows I'm alive, so I'm not hiding in that sense. I just have to keep my location a secret," Sophie said. Houston nodded his agreement.

"It sounds like a good plan. I talked to Mathews today. He's the one creating my new identity. I am now Gage Turner."

She stuck her hand out. "Nice to meet you, Gage." He shook her hand.

"My pleasure, ma'am."

"Fitz should be calling anytime," Sophie reminded him.

"After he calls, I'm going to go get my papers and run over to my house and pack a bag," Houston said.

"Houston, I'm so sorry. I didn't even think about all your things. What will you do with them?"

"I'm going to have Fons go to Trenton and tell mom and dad I'll be gone for a while. I wrote her a letter giving her my bank account info and password and asking her to keep my mortgage payments up. I also asked her to check on the place occasionally. I have time to decide what to do from there."

Sophie put her arms around his neck and looked him in the eye. "I still hate this for you."

He kissed her eyes. "Not your choice, princess."

They went their separate ways to finish preparations. Depending on the disposition of Fritz's request to drop the murder charge on Nikko, they would either leave tonight or in the morning. He had rented a car online in his new name. Rodriguez would drive them to Easton, MD, and they would pick it up there and drive to Oklahoma City, OK, then take a flight from there on whatever airline that had two tickets available.

It was 4:30 when the phone finally rang.

"Hello?"

"Ms. Star, this is Albert Fitz. I have good news for you. It took most of the day, but the DA finally decided the bad press wouldn't be worth fighting the accusations against them. Your record is clean. They dropped the charges and expunged your record."

Sophie was genuinely pleased. She didn't think they would clear her record that fast, although expungement is not the same as having it wiped off the computer, but it would work until they could safely do that.

"That's the best news. Thank you, Mr. Fitz. Thank you so much. What about Nikko?"

"I took it in front of the Judge this afternoon. The DA really fought me but there was no way the Judge could overlook the lack of evidence. He should be release on bail later tonight or in the morning." He said goodbye and hung up.

Sophie started to panic; she could feel her stomach churning. She needed to tell Houston and Rodriguez. Houston saw the look on her face and went to her.

"What is it, Sophie?"

"Fitz called. They dropped my case and expunged my record," she took a breath.

"That's great news," Fons said.

"There's more isn't there, Sophie?" Houston knew what was coming.

"The Judge dropped the murder charge on Nikko. He is getting out on bail either tonight or in the morning."

Houston could see fear creeping up in her eyes. He grabbed her hand. "It's okay, Sophie. Our plan is in place. I'll leave right now to get my papers and clothes. I'll be back in a couple of hours, then we will be gone." He let go of her and headed for the door. She finished up in her room and took her luggage to the door.

Nikko called Ben. "They are letting me out on bail shortly. I need you to get a few guys together. I have an errand for you.

I'll tell you about it when you pick me up, but in the meantime, I need a few things."

"Sure, boss. It'll be good to have you back."

"Thanks, Ben. There's a packed SUV waiting for me at the long-term parking at the airport. I'll send you the GPS coordinates so you can find it. I need you to take it to the parking garage at Sophie's condo. You'll also need to pick up a rope ladder and then I need you to go to Stanley's lab and pick up some things he has waiting for me. Oh, we might need comms so we can communicate so grab some from the office. I'll call you as soon as I'm released."

"I'll have everything ready for you, Mr. Morano."

Houston picked up his new identity and briefed Agent Hampton then headed to his house. It wouldn't take much time for him to pack. He always had a go-bag ready, and he didn't need much...mainly his shorts, blue jeans, shirts, a few pairs of shoes. Most of the stuff he liked was already packed at Sophie's. He'd taken what he needed when he took this assignment.

Nikko got out within the hour, and Ben was there to meet him with a couple of Nikko's other men. Nikko had one of his men watching Sophie's condo, so he knew Houston had left and hadn't come back yet. He would wait for him by his parking space and deal with him.

"I am leaving town for a while, and I'm taking Sophie with me. She's not going to want to come willingly, and her goons are going to put up a fight. Right now, only Rodriguez is in the condo. I will take care of Houston when he gets back, but I need you to grab her and take out Rodriguez. Ben, I want you on the roof. The only way to breach her condo is to come through the balcony. There's a steam pipe on the roof strong enough to attach the rope ladder to, then you can scale down and breach. Have a man wait in the stairwell and one by the elevator. If she gets away from you, that's the only other way out. I will be downstairs waiting for all of you. Any questions?"

Ben answered, "no, that's pretty straight forward. What about Rodriguez?"

Nikko sounded annoyed. "What about him?"

"Dead or alive?"

"What do I care? But you better not harm one hair on Sophie. Is that clear?"

"Yes, sir."

"We all have comms. Keep them on so we're on the same page."

"Yes, sir."

Houston was just pulling into the parking garage. He checked the time. He was getting a little nervous. He needed to get Sophie out of here. In his rush he didn't use his standard security protocols when he opened his door. Out of nowhere, Nikko had an arm around his throat and plunged a needle in his neck. Houston's instincts kicked in, and he was about to defend himself when his body fell to the ground paralyzed. He couldn't move a muscle; only his eyes and eyelids would respond. He could hear but couldn't speak. Nikko dragged him to the back of the SUV. He opened the door and tossed the few items that were back there into the back seat and lifted Houston in and laid him out.

"I tried to warn you. Sophie belongs to me. But you thought you could take her from me."

Nikko tossed the used needle in the back next to Houston. "Let me tell you what's going to happen now. I just injected you with blue snake venom, and you are now paralyzed, as I'm sure you can tell. I had it modified so it wouldn't kill you. Death would be too merciful. I want you to listen to me take back what's mine while you agonize over the fact you can do nothing. It will take about 10 hours for it to wear off. We will be long gone, and for the rest of your life, you'll know that I won, and you lost. But first, I need you to learn a lesson. You should have never touched my fiancé."

Nikko took out his brass knuckles and swung hard into Houston's face. "Those lips touched hers. They were not yours to touch...they are mine! But never again." He swung again. The pain was excruciating, but he could do nothing to protect himself. Then Nikko grabbed a lug wrench from somewhere and with all his energy, swung down on Houston's left hand, crushing it. He tried to do the same to his right hand, but the angle was off a little. He still made contact. "These hands touched Sophie's hands. Those are my hands to touch, not yours!" The pain in Houston's hands was sending fire up his arm, but still, he couldn't move. Then Nikko spoke into his comm and said, "breach!"

Rodriguez was outside on the balcony with Sophie, waiting to take them to Easton, when he saw something move in his peripheral vision. He turned and saw Ben aiming a gun at him. He pulled out his Glock 17 and pushed Sophie toward the house. "Get inside, now!" She ran as Ben and Rodriguez exchanged fire. She heard Rodriguez yell into his comm.

"Shots fired! Shots fired! Send back up!" He kept pushing Sophie to the front door. With his eyes on the balcony door, he locked it to give them a few extra seconds. He shoved her to the side of the front door, looked through the peep hole, and then slowly poked his head out. He saw a man on each end of the hall. The stairs and elevator were covered. He saw Ben coming to the glass door, trying to open it. He was aiming at the lock. Rodriguez knew he had to get her out. He opened the front door again and shot blind in both directions. He knew the men would instinctively take cover. Then he swung the door open and ran while pulling Sophie behind him. He heard Ben blasting the lock on the glass door. One of the men poked his head out, and Rodriguez fired at him, then turned and fired the other direction. He had to take one of them down so he could get her out of here. Finally, the man by the stairwell stepped out to shoot and Rodriguez took him down.

Agent Rodriguez pulled her to the stairs and pushed her in. "Run." He heard her running. He stuck his head out the door, saw Ben coming, and shot him in the leg. The other man was still coming. He took the stairs three at a time to catch up with Sophie and waited on the landing. "Keep going to the garage, but don't go out the door." He was listening for the third man. He heard quiet footsteps coming closer. Rodriguez waited until the man turned the corner and shot him. He went down, but he still didn't know how many were waiting for them outside.

The "shots fired" call came in, and Agent Hampton was instantly alerted. He sent his men to the location and contacted the SRT. Paramedics were also automatically alerted to an "officer in distress" call. Hampton headed to his vehicle and turned on his lights. He had just gotten the word that Nikko had been released. He hadn't even had time to warn them.

Nikko could hear the fiasco upstairs through his ear bud. He heard Ben say she was coming down the stairs to the garage.

Rodriguez had her wait over to the side and opened the door slightly. He didn't see anyone out there, but he wasn't sure. Maybe he could wait for back up.

"What's the ETA on my back up?" he called into his comm.

"Seven minutes," came the reply.

Rodriguez heard another door open and footsteps of a man who sounded like he was limping. It had to be Ben. They were sitting ducks here. He stepped out to the garage and looked around, then he waved for her to come out. He started for his SUV parked next to Houston's vehicle. *Houston must be back*, he thought, but he was nowhere to be seen. He prayed Nikko hadn't killed him. Nikko was only a few feet from Sophie, so he stepped out and grabbed her, using her body for cover. Rodriguez turned; his weapon aimed at Nikko's head.

"Now, Rodriguez, you know you can't take that chance with Sophie right in front of me. Put your gun down." His voice was as calm as if he were speaking to his mother.

Rodriguez knew he had no choice. Sophie spoke. "Nikko, what are you doing?"

"I'm leaving, and I'm taking you with me."

He lifted his gun toward Rodriguez. She yelled, "No! if you kill him, I will never forgive you, Nikko! If you let him go, I won't fight you."

Sophie wanted to save him. Nikko was quiet for a moment. "Alright. I was going to use this on you in case you had an objection to coming with me. It just a sedative." He pulled it out of his pocket and gave it to her. "Shoot it in his jugular vein."

She went to Rodriguez and mouthed 'I'm sorry.'

He whispered, "we'll come for you, Sophie, I promise. We won't stop till we find you."

As she shot the sedative into his vein. Nikko flew into a rage. "Don't call her by her first name! That's the problem with you, Sophie! You let the help get too personal."

He turned to Rodriguez. "I guess I have to teach you some manners too."

He pulled out his brass knuckles, already bloody and gave a hard swing right into Fons's jaw. He went down hard. "The sedative will take effect in a minute or two."

Ben had just made it down the stairs and opened the door. "Where are the others?" Nikko asked.

"They're hit."

"Get them out of here. I don't want them picked up by the police." Ben took off to the elevator.

"Nikko, this is Houston's car. What did you do to him?!" Sophie was frantic.

"I didn't do anything to him; you did, Sophie. You let him touch you, kiss you. I thought you learned your lesson the first time. You know what I did to Jimmy. Come here...you need to see what you did."

Nikko had a vice like grip on her upper arm and directed her to the back of the SUV. He lifted the door. She gasped and started shaking. There was Houston in an unnatural position. He wasn't moving, but his eyes were open. His face was severely beaten with deep cuts, she supposed from those brass knuckles. But his hands were even worse. One looked completely crushed. She tried to reach out to touch him, but Nikko grabbed her. She started punching him, hitting him in the chest, the arms, and his face.

"Sophie, stop. You have to learn there are consequences to what you do."

She kept screaming and hitting him. Houston wanted to tell her, "Stop, he'll hurt you," but no words could come out. *Oh God. He was right. Death would have been merciful.* Hearing all this and not being able to save her was worse than death. He had heard everything—Sophie bargaining for Rodriguez's life and Nikko blaming her for what he had done. It was worse than the injuries.

Finally, Nikko grabbed her wrists, putting them behind her back, then held them in one hand. "I didn't want to have to do this, Sophie, but I can hear the sirens. We have to go."

Nikko used his other hand to knock her out. She didn't hit the ground because he had her wrists and pulled her body toward him to keep her upright. He shut the back of Houston's SUV and scooped her up, taking her to his vehicle. Houston's heart was being ripped out. *Sophie don't fight him. He'll hurt you. Just use your brain. I will come for you, I promise.* He was trying to speak, but he knew the words weren't coming out of his mouth. He had to try to say them, anyway. *I'm sorry, Sophie. I'm so sorry.*

Houston could hear the SRT and his fellow DEA agents. It would take some time for them to find him because they had to first try to rescue Sophie if she was still here. But it didn't matter. He just wanted to die. He couldn't live knowing that Nikko would torture her because he knew she would never comply. He lost Sophie, and he knew the chances of finding her were slim. Then, as clear as if it were spoken aloud, he heard, *but with God, all things are possible.*

A few seconds later he heard Agent Hampton's voice. "Over here. I need paramedics."

They must have found Rodriguez. Then someone spotted Houston. "Medic! I need a medic!" He didn't recognize the voice.

They loaded him on the gurney, then the medic went back and grabbed the needle. He figured the lab could find something to counter it.

When Houston woke up in the hospital, his mother was by his side. When she saw his eyes open, she came to his side.

"Houston, son, you're in the hospital. You're going to be alright." He could move his body some, but he was very groggy.

Agent Hampton came in. "Mrs. Townsend, do you mind if I speak to your son for a minute?"

"No, of course not." She turned back to Houston. "I'll be back in a few minutes." Agent Hampton pulled a chair up next to his bed.

"I know the doctor wants to get in here, but I have some questions I need answered. You were the one with the most contact with Nikko. First, I'm happy to tell you that they have found an antidote for the venom, so you should gradually be able to move again. The reconstructive surgery on your hand took over five hours. They said that, with therapy you should regain full use of it eventually. Now, can you speak yet?"

He struggled. "Some. Rodriguez?"

"He's good. They gave him a few stitches on his jaw, but the sedative wore off on its own. He said Sophie saved his life."

"She did. I heard it."

"Did he give you any idea where he was going?"

"No. He just said by the time I came out of it; he would be long gone."

"Was Sophie injured?"

"Nikko knocked her out because she was fighting him. That's all I saw."

Hampton rubbed his eyes. "I'm sorry, Houston. I tried to contact you as soon as I found out he got released, but it was already too late." Houston tried to get up, but he was still too drowsy. Hampton stopped him.

"I have to find her."

"You can't do anything in your condition. You must trust your team. We have all the transportation hubs covered, and we have units in the sky. We also put word out to our confidential informants. We will find her."

"Do you have officers in the hospital?"

"Yes."

"You need to get them out. If Nikko finds out we're undercover, that means her cover is blown, too."

"You're right. I'll take care of that now. I'll keep checking on you."

"Thanks."

Agent Hampton left and got all law enforcement out of the area.

CHAPTER NINETEEN

Lily stepped back in. Before she could say anything, the doctor entered the room.

"Mr. Townsend, you are doing remarkably well. I'd like you to move your right arm for me." He lifted it slowly, but it felt so heavy. "That's good. Now lift your legs one at a time." He complied but had the same hard time as he did with his arm. "We had an antidote for the venom. The paramedic's quick thinking in bringing in the needle, helped us out a great deal. Our lab isolated the substance, and found it was a modified form of blue snake venom. It's extremely deadly. The modification is what kept it from killing you. The antidote just helped you come out of it faster. You may still feel sluggish for a few more hours, but then you should be back to normal. You had several deep cuts on your face which required 34 stitches to repair. The facial trauma specialist who tended you said your cheek bone has a hairline fracture but that no bone fragments were displaced, so it should heal nicely on its own. You'll have to see him off and on so he can keep a close eye on it. As for your right hand, it is bruised and swollen, and you have a broken knuckle which we'll treat with ice packs and a hand brace. Then we'll let it heal on its own. Your left hand was a different story, though. The orthopedic surgeon put screws in three bones, but you are going to require a second surgery in a few weeks to clear away the scar tissue and bone fragments. We will keep it in the sling strapped to your chest right now until the swelling goes down, then we'll talk about a splint for protection. Do you have any questions?"

"When can I get out of here?"

"Not tonight, for sure. I'd like to keep you a few days and keep an eye on that hand, but we'll see how you're doing tomorrow."

"Thank you, doctor," Lily said. When he left the room, she gave her son some water. "Your dad and brothers are on their way."

"That's not necessary, Mom."

"Don't you dare say that. Caring for you *is* necessary. We share the good and the bad in this family."

"I'm sorry, Mom."

"Houston, I know that sometimes you can't really talk about the details of your job with us, but they're saying on the news that Sophie is a criminal and her king pin fiancé kidnapped her. I can tell you this — I don't believe that for a second. You need to tell me what's going on. I won't tell the others if you don't want me to."

Houston thought for a long time before he answered. "Before I do, Mom, what are they saying about me and Fons?"

Lily looked puzzled. "That her bodyguards were in the hospital with injuries from the struggle that ended in her being taken."

"That's good news, Mom."

Houston knew his mom would pray. He needed her to pray, so he told her the whole story, all the way from the beating Nikko gave her to her bargaining for Rodriguez's life. He had to stop a few times for water and to rest, but he got the whole story out.

"I won't tell the others, but I must say she is everything I thought she was. Sophie's an extraordinary woman with a soft heart, willing to give her life for others," Lily said.

"She's all that and more, Mom. I love her so much. This is killing me. When he took her, I was paralyzed, I couldn't do a

232

thing to save her. I just wanted to die." Tears were running down his cheeks.

Lily wiped them away and spoke to him sternly. "Don't ever say that son. Who else will search for her the way you will? God put you in her path for a reason, and God will direct you back to her." The door opened, and the rest of his family came in.

Sophie awoke to the sound of Nikko's voice, and Nikko knew it, but she didn't want to open her eyes because he would make her interact with him. She was sick with worry about Houston.

Nikko just kept talking. "I do have a confession to make. I've been with other women when you were gone, but I will never touch another woman now that your back. I know you'll be mad at me for a while, and I'm willing to wait for you. But don't make me wait too long. I have a honeymoon planned for you that we'll remember the rest of our lives. Uncle Tony came through for me, big time. I'm sorry I didn't have time to grab your luggage. I had some items taken to the cabin where we're going, so you'll have some change of clothes, but we'll stop somewhere, and you can shop to your heart's content." He went on to tell her that he planned on driving to the midpoint of their destination. He planned on staying a couple of days to let the law get tired of looking for them.

"They won't keep roadblocks up for more than a few days. They don't have the endless supply of funds that I do. When you decide you want to talk to me, just sit up. If you need to go to the bathroom or if you're hungry just say so."

Sophie wasn't ready to talk. She had to think. *Lord, what am I going to do? I can't let him take me out of the country. They'll never find me. I can't overpower him, and if I push him too far, I know what he'll do to me.* She tried to shut her mind down. Then, as big as day, the thought came to her—*use the intellect I gave you.* She responded, *okay, Lord. Lead me.*

Sophie sat up. "I need to use the bathroom." He pulled into the next gas station and came to a stop.

"We don't need any trouble. Just go to the pay window and ask for the key. I'll be right behind you."

Nikko opened the door for her since the child locks were activated in the back seat. She really wasn't going to cause trouble. Why should she be the cause of anyone else getting hurt?

Sophie went to the window. "May I have the bathroom key, please?" The young cashier handed it to her. Nikko followed her to the bathroom and went in with her.

"There is no stall in here. Can't I have some privacy?"

"I'll turn my back."

He really wasn't taking any chances. She finished, washed her hands, and handed him back the key. Nikko gave it back to the cashier and gave him a fifty-dollar bill. "Fill up on pump 8." She went back to the car but sat in the front seat. The gas tank drank up the whole fifty dollars. He got in, and they drove off.

Sophie pled with him as they sped down the road. "Why are you doing this? You know they dropped the charges against me. There's a good chance Fitz will get you off the hook, too."

"I talked to Fitz after the hearing. He told me the evidence against me is rock solid, except for the murder. He said they are offering a plea of six to ten. I would get out in five or sooner."

Sophie turned to look at him. "Then why go through this, Nikko?"

"Five years, Sophie. I can't go to jail for five years. First of all, you wouldn't wait for me, and second, I couldn't stand the thought of you out here without me."

"Nikko, how many times do I have to tell you that I won't ever be your fiancé or wife." She knew she was pushing him making that statement.

Nikko was getting upset. "Not *fiancé--wife*." She knew she shouldn't push him any further, but she was angry.

"I will never be your wife."

"I'm going to let that go because you're still mad over what happened to your boy toy. I wish I could say that it brought me no pleasure, Sophie..." He turned in his seat to glance at her quickly and smiled, "but I wouldn't want to tell a lie. I hope you've learned your lesson," Nikko snarked. Sophie turned her head to the window in disgust and stopped talking.

Sophie fell asleep at around 1 am and by 3 o'clock, he was pulling into a forest trail that led to a small cabin. She woke up when he turned off the main road. There were no houses anywhere, just forest. There was no place for her to run to if she could get away. He stopped in front of the cabin and told her to wait. He found the key under a rock in the yard and opened the door, then returned to let her out of the car. He led her inside. It was a surprisingly modern red cedar log cabin, and it was very aromatic, as well. Inside was a large rustic fireplace, a decently sized kitchen, and a comfortable living room.

"There are two bedrooms. I will let you have one of them by yourself for now. I had your room stocked with some necessities—a nightgown, some new underwear, some jeans and shirts, toiletries, and cosmetics. All the windows are nailed shut, and the only other way out is the front door. It has a key operated dead bolt so you can't open it. I know you're tired and so am I, so let me take you to your room. He led her to the first room on the left. It had an en suite bathroom and a big four post bed. It looked comfortable.

"I'll wait for you to change."

"What?" She was surprised.

"Go in the bathroom and take care of whatever you need to. I'll wait for you here."

"Why?"

He pulled out some cuffs. "Sophie, you are the smartest woman I know. I might have everything covered, but you could still find a way out."

She became indignant at the sight of the handcuffs. "I'm not letting you cuff me, Nikko."

"You don't have a choice." She stomped into the bathroom and slammed the door. She looked at herself in the mirror and saw the large bump and bruise on the side of her face. No wonder she had an earache. She looked for some Tylenol in the medicine cabinet.

She opened the door slightly. "I need Tylenol, Nikko. My head hurts."

"I'll get you some and a bottle of water." She heard him leave the room and go to the kitchen. She changed into some of the clothes he had provided. everything was the right size and the colors that she preferred. Nikko seemed to know everything about her. She brushed her teeth and braided her hair, then she came out. He was back from the kitchen with the Tylenol and a bottle of water.

"How will I go to the bathroom in the middle of the night?" She picked up the bottled water and medication.

"You won't, so maybe you better go again now."

Sophie was angry. "Nikko, this is ridiculous! Where would I go even if I could get out of here?"

Nikko responded, sternly, "well, maybe this is where you have to start earning back some privileges, because of your behavior."

She put her hands on her hips. "You can't punish me like I'm a child."

Nikko got in her face, grabbing the back of her hair in a fist. "If you don't want to be treated like a child, you will learn to listen to me. Now go to the bathroom. I want to go to bed."

Sophie went to the bathroom. When she came back, she got in bed, and he cuffed her right hand to the first post. Then he leaned down kissed her cheek and pulled the covers up over her.

"Good night, sweetheart." He turned the light out as he left and closed the door partway. She had never seen this side of him before. She always knew he was dangerous but now she saw he was also delusional and mentally unstable. Within a few minutes, she heard him go outside. It sounded like he was bringing things in from the SUV. Then he went to bed and all the lights were off.

Rodriguez snuck into Houston's room at 1 in the morning. When he opened the door, he saw Lily sleeping in the recliner, but Houston was awake.

Houston waved him in and whispered. "Come in, Fons. I wanted to see you."

"When do you go home?" Fons asked, picking up a chair and placing it close to the bed so they could whisper and not wake up Houston's mother.

"I'm trying to get out in the morning," Houston replied to his friend.

Fons looked down at the floor for a moment. "Did you know she saved my life, Houston? She offered herself so he wouldn't kill me. I know I'm ready to see Jesus, but the thought of being murdered still brings chills to my spine. I may be ready, but I'm not so sure I want to go yet. Who would have your back?" Fons looked up at Houston for a moment and gave a sly smile. "How do you repay someone for that?" He shook his head.

"I heard everything. I am so sorry I couldn't help you. I'm sick about it."

"Houston, he tortured you. What could you have done?"

"It ripped my heart out, Fons, what he was doing to her. Sophie tried to get to me, but he wouldn't let her touch me. She was so angry when she saw what he had done that she started hitting him until he had enough, and he knocked her out. I can't think about what she's going through right now." His voice broke and betrayed him. The tears he was holding back started to flow.

"Don't do that to yourself. You can pray and trust God. Don't let Nikko get in your head or else you'll be useless to her."

Houston closed his eyes. "You're right, of course. God is able to protect her better than I can. Where do we start? I'm leaving the hospital tomorrow whether they release me or not."

"Don't do that just yet. Wait until we have a lead to follow. Give yourself the best chance to recover your strength. You can't help her if you can't stay on your feet."

Fons stood up to leave. "I'll come by before I leave in the morning, and we'll talk this through."

A nurse came in to check on Houston. "What are you doing here?" The nurse asked Rodriguez curtly. Fons held up his hands in surrender.

"Nothing at all. I'm just leaving."

Loud noises coming from the kitchen finally woke Sophie. She was surprised she was able to sleep. She noticed Nikko had already taken the cuff off. She went to take a shower and get dressed then went to the kitchen and sat at the table.

"Good morning, sweetheart." he said with a smile. She realized how hungry she was when she saw the omelets he was making. Nikko was a great cook. He had worked as a sous chef in his family's restaurant since he was 16, then became one of the head chefs, working part time during college, until his dad felt he knew the business well enough to take over the management of it. He loved cooking, and he loved managing the restaurant. She wondered what would have happened if his father's other enterprises hadn't caught Nikko in their allure. He put an omelet with tomatoes, cheese, and bacon and a side of hash browns in front of her. He made a sausage, mushroom, and cheese omelet for himself. She said a prayer to herself and ate every bite.

He laughed. "Now that's the Sophie I remember."

"You know I've always loved your cooking."

"You know what they say...the way to a woman's heart is through her stomach."

"I think it's 'the way to a man's heart.'"

"What are you, sexist?" Nikko missed these little tête-à-têtes with her. Sophie was so witty. No other woman engaged him the way she did.

Sophie got serious but kept her voice calm. "I won't allow you to cuff me again, Nikko."

"Allow?" he interrupted. She knew that was a risky choice of words.

"Yes. If what you are trying to do is win me back, that is not the way to do it."

"Does that mean your open to coming with me voluntarily and marrying me?" he asked with hopeful expectation.

She weighed her words carefully. "I'm not willing to answer that yet but cuffing me does not make those prospects appealing."

Nikko hesitated for a moment. "Alright, Sophie. You always loved to negotiate everything, so let's negotiate. You promise me you won't run, and I won't cuff you."

"I can live with that," she stood up. "I'll wash the dishes since you cooked."

He laughed. "Like we could have eaten your cooking."

"I can cook breakfast just fine. It's the other meals that give me trouble," she said while clearing the table. The Lord told her to use her brain. She had to make him comfortable so he would make a mistake and share his escape plan. Maybe God would make a way for her to get that info to Houston.

"Then from now on, you make breakfast and I'll make the other meals." She stopped washing the dishes.

"But I love your omelets." He just laughed and went to the deck out front, leaving the door open. He was already beginning to let his guard down.

Lily was standing and praying at Houston's bedside, praying for his injuries to heal fast, to leave no scars inside or out, when he opened his eyes. He loved hearing his mother pray. He learned to pray himself from listening to her over the years.

"Mom, she took me to the ballet."

"That was random, son." She leaned down and kissed him on the cheek.

"I know. I just woke up thinking about it. You can't tell anyone, but I really enjoyed it. Or maybe it was just sitting next to her that I enjoyed."

She laughed. "Honey, that piece of news is too juicy to keep to myself. I'll have to tell your father, who you know will tell Sam, Ted, and Spring."

He closed his eyes and moaned. "When will I ever learn to keep my mouth shut?"

Lily patted him on the shoulder. "We are here to give each other a good laugh now and then. It's just your turn now."

"No one ever laughs at Spring."

"That's because you boys would have slugged anyone who did...other than family, of course."

Houston smiled. "That's true enough. It must have been hard for her always having us around."

"Don't be silly. She loved every minute of it."

He looked at her slyly. "Even when we grilled her boyfriends?"

"Well, maybe not that so much."

"Mom, will you brush my teeth for me. I don't want some stranger in my mouth."

"That's why I'm here dear, to help you until you can do those things for yourself."

Sophie was reading on the couch in the living room when the sermon she heard Sunday replayed in her mind. She knew God was dealing with her on how she had been judging Nikko, as if she had a right to decide who deserved to be redeemed. She had been undervaluing the huge price Jesus paid on the cross. The price for everyone, not just the ones she felt worthy, when she herself shouldn't have been forgiven. Sophie was having trouble letting go of the anger and fear. She knew forgiving Nikko didn't mean she had to accept what he was doing or that she couldn't fight with all she had to get away from him. She was struggling because she didn't want to let go of the anger that had become part of her. *Can't you see past your anger at the man and see his soul is in the balance?* That thought kept plaguing her. That was the problem; if Nikko asked God for forgiveness, what did she do then? How could she continue to despise a man who God had forgiven? She felt like she was the most selfish person in the world to want God to let someone go to hell because of what he did to her. When so much more was done to Christ, and he forgave them. Sophie started to cry.

Nikko saw her crying and came over to her. "Please don't cry Sophie. You'll see the benefits of my plan in due time."

"I'd like to go for a walk, Nikko."

"Sure. I'd do anything to make you happy."

He tried to take her hands. She instinctively jerked it away. "No, you won't, Nikko. You won't let me go home. I just want to go home. I don't want to leave the country," she pleaded.

"Sophie, listen to me. You are just angry. I told you I would protect you from yourself. Once you're no longer mad at me, you'll realize no one could ever love you or take care of you like I can. You're not thinking clearly."

Sophie said all she could. If she didn't do anything to make him jealous or angry, she could come out of this alive. But one thing she won't do is leave the country with him. If she did, she would be lost forever.

CHAPTER TWENTY

They walked in silence for a while. At some point she could hear what sounded like the surf.

"Are we by the ocean, Nikko?" Sophie asked. He questioned whether he should answer that, then decided it couldn't hurt.

"Yes." He always took her hand when they would go on walks, so she kept her hands in her jacket pockets. But she knew she had to do the right thing and talk to him about God.

"Nikko, do you ever think about God?"

He looked at her surprised. "You know Thomas and I went to Mass every Sunday with our family. We were even altar boys."

"I know that but I'm talking about something deeper than that. I'm talking about salvation, becoming a new creature in Christ, not some diluted version of that."

"When I was younger, I thought about God a lot. I even considered becoming a priest," he chuckled.

"I remember a sermon I heard about God's love. He created us to be His companions. When Adam and Eve disobeyed Him, they brought sin into His perfect world, which separated us from Him. But God loved us so much He wanted to make a way back which meant someone had to pay for the sins of the world. He sent His Son, Jesus. Before He came to earth, man's sins had to be covered by the blood of animal sacrifice. Jesus came as the final, ultimate sacrifice. On the Cross it was His shed blood that now covers our sins forever. 'When I am lifted up from the earth,

I will draw all men to Myself,' Jesus said. But the grave could not hold Him, He arose, proving to the world He was who He said He was. He doesn't ask us to be perfect before we ask for forgiveness, but He redeems us at whatever point in our lives that we are, and then he helps us to be what he intended us to be. We only have to want it. It's our choice," Sophie surprised herself at the mini sermon that came out of her mouth.

"Where is this coming from Sophie? I never heard you talk about God before." Nikko asked.

"I got to wondering what happens to us when we die. I can't believe we just rot in the ground. There has to be more, and I believe Jesus is that 'more.'"

"I haven't thought about God in years. My lifestyle doesn't really make room for it."

"I told Thomas that I'm selling my network and getting out of the life now. It's not worth it to me. I don't need more money, so why risk it?" Sophie said.

"Well, I'm out of it too, but not by choice. Everything was taken from me."

"But, Nikko, you loved working in the restaurant, and you are so good at it."

"I do love it, but it's not the same. When I was young, I always wanted to go with my papa on his deals. Thomas hated it, so papa would leave him home and it was just me and him. It was an adventure, it was exciting, there was a thrill to it, even a couple of times when it got dangerous. I loved it. That part has never left. I love the flavor of that life. The restaurant business doesn't do that for me. The only other thing that engages me is you, Sophie."

"But what if serving God could give you that thrill?"

"I often wondered. When I would turn on one of those Church channels and hear someone's testimony, they always sounded so energized about their life, they just wake up excited about where God would lead them next. I wondered if it could make me feel like that." He changed the subject abruptly. "I made you one of your favorites for dinner."

Sophie knew that meant this subject was over, but she was shocked at how open he was to hear it. Thomas had been distant when she tried to talk to him. It proves the truth of the scripture, "for God does not see as man sees, for man looks at the outward appearance but God looks at the heart." It was out of her hands now.

They were almost back to the cabin. "I need to call Thomas. I want him to get into the vault at my condo," Nikko said. Sophie had to figure out a way to talk to Thomas.

"I'd like to sit on the porch for a while," she said as they were walking up the steps.

He looked at her, quiet for a minute. "Can I trust you, Sophie?"

She wasn't sure what he was asking. "I already told you I won't run."

"No, I mean can I *trust* you?" This time she knew exactly what he meant.

Sophie didn't want to lie about this. "Nikko, it's too soon to ask me that. I'm still angry."

"That's an honest answer. I'll accept it, but I see you softening." He gave her a small smile and touched his hand to her cheek. "I'll get the satellite phone and come back out here."

Nikko dialed Thomas' number and sat on the wooden rocker. She was on the porch swing.

"Hello?"

"Thomas? It's Nikko." She could hear Thomas even where she was sitting, he was yelling so loud.

"What have you done?! You were out on bond, and now every federal law enforcement agency in the land is after you for kidnapping Sophie! Nikko what's wrong with you?"

He put the phone back to his ear. "I will explain if you give me a chance."

"This had better be good."

"When I met with Fitz yesterday before my bail hearing, he told me the evidence against me for the murder would never hold up, but the evidence against me on the raid was rock solid. They were willing to plead it down to six years on one condition."

"What was the condition?" Thomas asked.

"That I admit to killing Jimmy."

"Non buono."

"Si. Having a murder on my record would be a whole new ball game. It could do severe damage to the restaurant and the family. And mama, well, you know people would treat mama differently. That was reason enough, but I wouldn't have taken the deal anyway. I wasn't going to jail for six years. Five with good behavior."

Thomas let out a long breath. "I didn't know about the condition of the plea. I'm sorry, Nikko."

"Like I said, I wouldn't have taken it anyway. One of Sophie's goons was trying to take her away from me. By the time I got out of jail, she would have been gone; if not literally gone, she'd at least be with someone else. I couldn't live with that."

"Nikko, you'll never get her out of the country. Leave her and go. I will do anything to help you maintain your freedom, but not if you take Sophie," Thomas scolded him.

"Ascolta fratello, I know you think you're looking out for me, but there is no way I'm leaving without her."

"Nikko, she made it clear to you she doesn't want to be your wife."

"That's because she was mad at me, but she's getting over it and soon she'll realize I'm doing the right thing. No one will love her like me. You know that, Thomas."

Thomas knew there was no reasoning with him right now. If he got Nikko angry, his brother might take it out on her.

"Then let her tell me what she wants, Nikko." He took the phone from his ear and looked at Sophie. "I'm going to put our dinner in the oven. Talk to my brother. Tell him you're alright."

Thank you, God, she said to herself. She put the phone to her ear. "I don't have much time. Are Houston and Fons alright? He really hurt Houston badly, Thomas."

"Yes, he's in the hospital, but he'll be fine. Sophie, what about you? Can you tell me where you are?"

"I'm not really sure. We drove southbound until about 3 am, so maybe ten hours away? We're in a log cabin, and there's no other houses nearby as far as I can tell. I heard the ocean on our walk today. Thomas, you must come find me. The police will never be able to undo Nikko's puzzle. Get Houston and Rodriguez. You can trust them."

"Sophie, you have to stay calm. Don't force his hand. Just stay alive. We'll find you."

"I won't leave the country with him, I just *won't*. I'll fight him to my last breath. Once I'm out of the country, no one will ever find me, and you know it."

"No, don't fight him, Sophie. You know you can't win."

"He's coming back. Find me Thomas. Give him a reason to call you back tomorrow."

Nikko came back out. "He wants to talk to you again," Sophie told him while extending the phone. He took it and placed it to his ear. Thomas spoke.

"Nikko, I'm not convinced she is doing this of her own volition."

"Look, the reason I called you is that I need you to go to my condo and get into my vault. There's a million plus in there.

Transfer it to Uncle Tony. He has set up several international accounts in my new name. My vault is behind a secret door in my closet. You open it by...."

"I know how to open it, I figured it out the other day when you sent me to get the papers Fritz wanted. Nikko, I'm still not sure about this. I want you to promise to call me back tomorrow. I'll get papa's old contact in law enforcement to let me know if they have any leads on you."

"That's a good idea. I'll call you back around this time tomorrow. And don't worry about Sophie. I have the best world cruise planned for her. We're going on our honeymoon."

When Thomas heard that, he knew it was most likely a private yacht. Thomas sucked in a breath. He knew Sophie was right and he knew she figured it out too. "Don't forget to call me tomorrow, Nikko."

"Addio." Nikko hung up and headed back inside. "Dinner will be ready in 20 minutes, sweetheart, so go wash up."

Sophie got up from the swing. She knew God had to intervene, or they would never find her in time.

Lily was finished feeding Houston his dinner. His broken cheek caused him a lot of pain if he tried to chew, so she had ordered creamy potato soup, yogurt, applesauce, and chocolate pudding from the hospital kitchen. It was not nearly enough calories for a man his size and muscle mass, but losing a few pounds wasn't his biggest problem.

"Thanks for having dad bring me a pair of his pajama bottoms."

"I sent the clothes you were wearing home with dad so Spring could wash them. I'll have him bring them back tonight when he comes." As she was moving the rolling tray, the phone rang. Lily pushed the green button and placed it up to Houston's ear.

"Hello?"

"Mr. Townsend? This is Thomas." Houston sat up further in his hospital bed. "I talked to Nikko. I tried to get him to let Sophie go, but he won't do it. He let me talk to her. He was out of earshot, so she had a second alone with me. The first thing she asked was how you and Rodriguez were. I told her you were in the hospital but would recover. She's scared. Sophie begged me to find her. She said I could trust you and Rodriguez to help. Nikko told me that he was taking her on a 'world cruise' of some sort. My guess is that he wants to get them both into international waters. She told me she would never get on that vessel, which I'm sure is a private yacht registered in a country that doesn't extradite fugitives. She said she would fight him. I tried to talk her out of it, told her to just go along and that we would find her, but you know what she's afraid of. He seems patient right now, but he intends on marrying her — whether legally or in his mind, I don't know."

Houston broke his silence. "Mr. Morano, do you have any idea where we should start looking?"

There was silence for a moment. "No, he called from a secure phone so we can't ping it. My computer expert is trying to hack into the satellite video that goes over the east coast. If he can get it, we can search for the cabin and at least have a direction to go. Nikko's supposed to call me again tomorrow. I'll do my best to talk to Sophie. She's going to try to get me more information."

"I can start driving south," Houston said.

"No, stay in the hospital. We'll take my helicopter if we find anything."

"Okay, but I want to be with you."

"I agree. There aren't too many people I can trust with this. Understand one thing Mr. Townsend — we will get Sophie back, but we will not stop my brother from leaving the country, and we won't let the police know where he is when we find him. Is that perfectly clear?"

"All I want is my boss back. I don't care about the rest."

"I'll call you when we find something."

"Thank you, Mr. Morano. I know she trusts you."

He hung up. This was the first time Lily saw hope in his eyes.

"Mom, will you please call Fons on the land line. I don't want to use my undercover cell."

Houston gave her the number. He told Rodriguez what Thomas had told him. "Fons, call Agent Hampton and tell him that we will call him on conference call as soon as you get here, but he can't tell anyone." They ended the call.

"Mom, I need you to take this splint off my right hand. I need to try to work it so I can hold a gun."

She didn't move for a minute, then she looked her son in his eyes and stroked his hair. "I would generally not encourage such reckless regard for your health, but I know you. If you don't go after her, you won't be able to live with yourself. And I would rather you be able to defend yourself."

Lily went to the other side of the bed and took off the splint. His face registered his pain as he tried to move and exercise it. His dad came in with his clothes and while they were visiting, Lily put them in the closet.

When Rodriguez entered, Houston suggested his dad take his mom out to dinner to give her a break. Rodriguez called Agent Hampton on his private cell phone and put it on speaker.

"Sir, we have information. Nikko called Thomas. He couldn't get him to let Ms. Star go but he did get some valuable information." Houston relayed everything Thomas had told him.

Agent Rodriguez spoke up. "Sir, we need to run an off the books parallel mission,"

"We can do that. I'll bring in only a handful of the task force we used and of course Agent Cosby," Agent Hampton replied.

"Thomas is bringing us in on Ms. Star's request, so we'll know his every move," Rodriguez added.

Houston spoke up, "Thomas made it perfectly clear we were not to interfere with Nikko's plan to leave the country. But he was adamant that Ms. Star would not be going with him." He went on to tell him that Thomas wanted him to stay in the hospital until he got a lead on which direction to go.

"Agent Townsend, I'm worried about you trying to take this on. You were beaten ruthlessly." His boss was genuinely concerned.

"I appreciate that sir, but there is no way I'm leaving Ms. Star out on a limb. We were responsible for her protection, and we failed."

"I can appreciate all of that, but you know that's not how it happened."

"Thomas said Nikko was calling him back tomorrow. Let's hope he keeps his word." They worked on the details and ended their call.

"Houston, maybe I should stay here tonight. If Thomas calls with a lead, he'll want to go immediately."

"Good idea, Fons, and I can send mom home to get some real sleep." Lily and Jack returned from their dinner. They all visited for a while. Jack was getting ready to go when Houston stopped him.

"Dad, take mom home with you. Fons has volunteered to stay with me tonight. She's tired, and she needs to go home."

Lily began to say something, but she caught his eye and knew something was up. She went over to him, kissed his cheek, and whispered to him, "You be careful son. I know you can't lose her, but I can't lose you." She gave him a hug.

His dad came over and hugged him, as well. "You'll be alright, son?"

"Of course, Dad. I'm in a hospital. If I need help, there's plenty." He gave him a smile as they left.

Sophie woke up. She hadn't remembered feeling this rested in a long time. There had to be two layers of down over the mattress and another in the comforter that covered her. It felt like being cuddled in the soft arms of God. Then the realization hit her—this was a gift from God. He knew long ago exactly where she would be and exactly what she would be going through, and this was his way of letting her know that He was with her. *You're such a good God, thank you.*

As Sophie got ready for the day, she continued quietly singing praises to God. As she was stepping out of the room, a segment of a story by Corrie Ten Boom concerning forgiveness flooded her mind as if she were reading it again:

> *This man had been a guard at Ravensbruck concentration camp where we were sent. It was the first time since my release that I had seen him and my blood seemed to freeze..."You mentioned Ravensbruck in your talk," he was saying. "I was a guard there. But since that time," he went on, "I have become a Christian. I know that God has forgiven me for the cruel things I did there, but I would like to hear it from your lips as well. Fraulein—" again the hand came out— "will you forgive me?"*
>
> *And I stood there—I whose sins had to be forgiven again and again—and could not forgive.*

Betsie had died in that place – could he erase her slow terrible death simply for the asking? It could not have been many seconds that he stood there, hand held out, but to me it seemed hours as I wrestled with the most difficult thing I had ever had to do. For I had to do it – I knew that. The message that God forgives has a prior condition: that we forgive those who have injured us. "If you do not forgive men their trespasses," Jesus says, "neither will your Father in Heaven forgive your trespasses." – Matthew 6:15

Sophie felt so convicted. Corrie Ten Boom had suffered so much, had lost so much, but she forgave one of the guards who inflicted her pain and loss. And here *she* was being too stubborn to lay down her anger and fear. *Lord every time I think I have forgiven him you check my Spirit. The only answer is I must be hanging on to it in some part of my heart. Please help me.* She heard again from within her spirit, *can you look past the man and have compassion for his soul?* Her most honest answer was, *I don't know Lord. Please help me.*

Dangerous Obsession

CHAPTER TWENTY-ONE

After pulling herself back together Sophie went out to the kitchen and saw Nikko at the stove.

"I thought I was supposed to do breakfast?"

He laughed. "You offered, then rescinded your offer. But if you'd like to take over..." He offered her the spatula. She raised her hands. With a big smile he said, "I thought so."

"Since you're almost done, I'll just clean up."

"Yeah, right." They stuck with safe topics during breakfast.

"I'd like to take another walk today, Nikko."

"Sure. You know I love walking with you. Will you take your hand out of your pocket this time so I can hold it?" She knew that if she was going to continue to challenge him on the big things, like letting her go, or keeping herself uncuffed, she needed to make small concessions. She also didn't want him to sedate her to keep her in line — she would have no way to help Thomas and Houston find her if she was out cold the entire time. He was willing to accept a challenge if he saw a light at the end of the tunnel. Otherwise, he would take what he wanted by force. She had to think smart if she wanted to come out of this in one piece.

"Okay, Nikko, but don't let that give you the idea that I'm no longer angry at you or that I don't want to go home."

"I get it, but I'll take any step forward." While she was cleaning up, he was on his computer. *He must be talking to Ben*, she thought. She noticed that his mood had changed.

"Can I sit on the porch?"

He nodded. "I'll be out in a second." About 15 minutes later, he came outside. "I'm afraid our walk will have to wait."

Sophie worried he found out Thomas was coming after her. "What's happened?"

"I planned on us staying here until Friday morning. We have to meet the yacht on Saturday, but apparently some agency is using satellite imagery to search the east coast of North and South Carolina as well as Georgia. They either are getting smarter, or someone has leaked something."

"It's probably just standard procedure," she said.

"Maybe." He thought for a moment. "We have to leave, Sophie. Go to your room and get your things. There are a couple of suitcases in the closet. Take everything. I don't want any evidence that we were ever here."

Sophie had no idea what was in all the drawers. As she went through them, she found he had supplied everything she would need. She started putting things in the suitcases. When she opened the bottom drawer, she found boxes of jewelry. She opened them and found her own things. He must have taken them when he was staying at her condo. The boxes were filled with items that she loved but had to leave behind when she disappeared. She put on her small diamond hoops and one of the rings she liked, putting the rest in her suitcase. Then she had an idea—if she left a piece of her jewelry, Thomas would know it was hers and they would know they were on the right track. If Nikko checked her room and found it, she would just act like she dropped it. She placed a single gold ball earring on the floor next to the leg of the nightstand. She finished packing and brought her suitcases and toiletries to the living room.

"I see you finally found your jewelry," Nikko smiled.

"How did you get it?"

"When you were gone, I kept your condo for you. Sometimes I would stay there. You left these behind, so I put them in my safe so that no one would take them."

Sophie knew she couldn't tell him that she knew how he violated her privacy with the cameras. She felt blood rushing to her face. She had to leave it alone. Her anger would trigger his, and he would always win in that scenario. Instead, she just said, "it's nice to have them back."

"Grab whatever food you want to bring with us, and I'll put the suitcases in the SUV. Then I'll do a sweep and wipe down the cabin to be sure we don't leave a trail."

Sophie went to the refrigerator and took out the soda, orange juice, and bottles of water, and put them all in a small box sitting by the garbage can. From the cupboards she took the jerky for Nikko, the candy for her, and a few other snack items. She took the boxes out to the car and waited for Nikko to come.

Nikko took a package of Clorox wipes and rubbed all the common surfaces down, then he grabbed a large green garbage bag and put everything left in the refrigerator and cupboards into it. He dumped all the garbage and stripped the beds, putting everything in the garbage bags, as well. He went through all the drawers in Sophie's room to make sure nothing was left behind and did the same in the bathroom shower and medicine cabinet. He never noticed the earring lying by the leg of the nightstand.

Nikko took the bags to the SUV and put them in the back to dispose of in some dumpster down the road. He went back in, turned off all the lights, and locked the door. By the time he finished wiping away every trace of evidence and got behind the wheel, it was 7 o'clock on Wednesday night.

Thursday

In the morning, Houston was finishing up breakfast and had been trying to exercise his hand. He was getting some mobility back in his right hand. The swelling had gone down some, overnight. He didn't have his fine motor skills yet, but he felt that he would be able to brandish a gun. He was able to dress himself with relative ease. Although the nurses were not happy about it, he insisted on getting out of bed. He wanted to be ready at a moment's notice. Rodriguez had gotten trackers and belt buckles with mics in them from Agent Mathews, so they were prepared in case Thomas called.

Houston's undercover cell rang. "Hello?"

"Houston, this is Thomas. We got into the satellite late last night and targeted the most likely area. I think we got a hit. I've got the GPS coordinates, and I've sent Franco to pick you and Rodriguez up at the hospital. He'll take you to the helicopter. Be ready."

"Alright, Mr. Morano. We'll be outside in 10 minutes."

"That's good. Oh, and another thing—leave your cell phones there. There's a good chance that the DEA may be tracking you."

"Not a problem, but I'm taking my gun."

Thomas' voice went somber. "I understand you need to protect yourself and Ms. Star, but you should know now that if you kill my brother, I *will* kill you."

"Understood." He hung up, immediately called Agent Hampton, and filled him in.

"Since you won't have your phones, be sure you use those trackers and don't let anything interfere with the microphone in your belt buckle. There is no safe way to follow you once you're in the air. We will have to stay miles behind. When you're out of the chopper and close to the cabin, make sure you communicate it to us somehow so we can get closer."

Houston agreed, and replied, "Whatever you do, don't come in until we give you the signal phrase." The phrase they decided on was, "I wish we had brought more men." They were in the chopper in less than 30 minutes. It was 10 am when they lifted off.

They landed at a small airport where Thomas had an SUV waiting for them. They drove from there to the remote GPS location of the cabin. When they were a mile away, they pulled as far as they could off the remote dirt road and walked the rest of the way.

When they reached the cabin, it was obvious no one was there. Thomas had Franco break the lock on the door, and they went inside to see if Nikko and Sophie had been there. There was a faint smell of bleach. They spread out looking to find any indication that it was the right cabin. Houston searched the room with the large four post bed, going through the drawers then making his way to the bed. He sat on the bed and picked up the pillow, the scent was very faint, but Houston immediately recognized it as the perfume that Sophie wore. He also saw scratches on the first bedpost, thinking Nikko might have cuffed her to it. He sat on the bed with the pillow in his hand, dropped his head, and closed his eyes.

"Sophie, I'm so sorry we didn't get here in time. Lord, please take care of her." When he opened his eyes, he saw the earring on the floor. He picked it up. "Thomas, Fons, in here!"

When they came in, he showed them the earring. "This is hers I'm sure of it," Thomas said. "I bought it for her the first Christmas that she worked for us. That's the only jewelry I bought her except for a sapphire ring." Thomas put it in his pocket. "At least we know we're on the right track. Hopefully, we are not too far behind them."

"Where to now?" Franco asked.

"We'll head toward Florida, I think. If Nikko is taking a private yacht into international water, the Florida coast would be the fastest way to do so. Meanwhile, we will wait for more information to come in. Nikko was supposed to call me today. Maybe he still will." Franco closed the door behind them. As they walked to the SUV, Houston's mind went to the Sapphire ring that Sophie always wore—it was from Thomas. The only time he didn't see her wear it was when she was on a date with him. He didn't know how to process that. He wouldn't have known the difference, but her heart did, and she didn't want Thomas to have any part of her time with him, or at least that's how Houston was going to choose to interpret it.

Nikko and Sophie spent all of Wednesday night on the road, stopping for a few hours at a rest area so that Nikko could nap. By late afternoon on Thursday, Nikko and Sophie had been on the road for hours. She opened the bag of jerky for Nikko, but he was being awfully quiet. It wasn't a good sign when he was mulling things over like this. She didn't know what was gnawing at him. She knew he didn't like his plans being interrupted, but this seemed like more than that.

"Nikko, I have to go to the bathroom."

He looked at his gas gauge. "We need gas, too."

"I'll meet you back at the car when I'm done," she said.

"I'm going in with you." She was trying to keep things light. "You still don't trust me, huh?"

"You told me not to. Remember?" He must have been referring to the way she answered his question the other day. She went to open her door.

Nikko grabbed her wrist forcibly as his face contorted. "Don't you *ever* open your own door when I'm around."

That's when she knew—this was the Nikko that beat her, the jealous man who wanted total control of her, who violated her by spying on her in her own home. She was in danger, and suddenly became painfully aware of it. She had no idea what triggered it, but her insides were trembling. He opened her door and reached out his hand to help her out. She knew she better take it. He got the key to the washroom, and they went out back. Once they were both inside, he locked the door behind them. There were two stalls, so they each took one. After washing up, he took her inside the store. "What do you want to drink, Sophie?"

"A Lipton Peach Tea would be nice."

"They have donuts. Do you want one?"

"Yes." He glared at her. "Please," she added. *It's getting worse. That controlling spirit has ahold of him.* He paid for the food and gas, and they made their way back to the car. She stood outside for a moment to stretch her legs while he put the gas in. When he was done with the gas, Nikko opened her door and let her in the car. They drove around back to the dumpsters, and he got rid of the garbage bags in the back of the SUV. Then they were back on the road. She didn't talk. She didn't want to spark anything.

"You're not eating your donut." She picked it up and nibbled on it.

"I've been trying to figure out how they located us. Thomas is the only phone call I made. Maybe he's helping the FBI find you."

"Nikko, you know Thomas would never betray you."

He turned to her, and his face contorted again. "I didn't ask for your opinion, did I?"

"No," she said, timidly.

Nikko continued, "I was thinking about my conversation with him. He told me he would help me get out of the country but that I couldn't take you with me." He was quiet for a moment, and she knew what was coming. The tension was building, and she knew to stay quiet.

"I remembered something. When I handed you the phone and went inside, I heard the first bit of your conversation. The first thing you asked him was how your goons were. I didn't think about it until now. When will you learn, Sophie? You don't ask about another man, you don't think about another man, you don't look at another man. You belong to me!"

Then it came. Sophie didn't have time to brace herself as he hauled off and backhanded her, across her face. His knuckles forced her cheek to hit her teeth with enough force to break the skin inside her mouth. She screamed and covered her face with her hands to protect herself from more blows, but no more came.

"I just don't know how many times you have to learn the same lessons, Sophie. How could one woman be so stupid?"

Nikko wasn't remorseful like he normally was. He offered her no apology—he was stone cold. Sophie could taste the iron from her blood where her teeth had cut her cheek. She also knew a black eye was coming. She bent over her knees, head in her hands, and sobbed. She took some napkins from the console and spit out the blood in her mouth then set them in the door pocket. He handed her a bottle of water and pulled over to the side of the road.

"Rinse your mouth and spit it outside." She rinsed her mouth a couple of times and closed the door. "Let me see your face," Nikko commanded her. She turned to face him. "Good. I don't see another cut for the plastic surgeon to fix. I see you never got the scar removed from above your eye. I'll get that done when we're safe."

Nikko got back on the highway. She laid her seat back, turned her body to the passenger window, and laid there as she tried to stop crying. Exhausted from crying, she finally fell asleep.

Sophie woke when she felt the car pull over onto a dirt road. It was dark out, but she could make out the outlines of some camper trailers and tents. He drove another five or six miles past the last camper to an 'A' frame cabin and turned off the engine.

"Just so you know, I have rented every cabin within 2 miles of here so don't think someone can hear you if you scream. He went to the cabin door, unlocked it, and came back for her. For the second time in as many days, Sophie set foot into a deep woods prison.

This cabin was not nearly as nice as the last one. The main floor was open, with the kitchen located in the back of the room. The dining room and living room made up the rest of the floor plan. It looked like there could be a bathroom or utility room off the kitchen, but that door was closed so she couldn't tell. She sat down on the couch until Nikko was done bringing in their things.

He looked at her. "I'm tired. I'll get you set up in your room and take care of everything else in the morning."

Nikko grabbed her suitcases and led her up a small set of stairs to a landing at the top. Straight ahead of her was a bathroom with bedrooms located to both the left and the right. He took her into the room on the right and set down her things.

"Get cleaned up and dressed for bed. I'll wait for you."

When she came out of the bathroom, he had the cuffs in his hand. "Nikko, no."

"I'm tired. Don't you dare argue with me. You don't learn, Sophie."

She got on the bed, and he cuffed her right wrist to the headboard. He covered her up and partially closed the door as he left.

Sophie laid there silently, praying. *Lord, deliver him from that spirit.* She finally realized what was happening—there was a battle raging for Nikko Morano's soul.

Nikko never placed the call to Thomas like he had promised. At about the same time that Nikko and Sophie were settling into their new hideaway, Thomas, Franco, Houston, and Fons were still headed southbound in the direction of the Florida panhandle.

"Mr. Morano, we've been driving for hours. We don't even know if we are going in the right direction. I think we should get a hotel and wait until we have more to go on," Houston said, knowing they were at least five hours behind Nikko, wherever he was. Houston didn't want to go on a wild goose chase, he wanted some solid intel. His experience as an agent told him that sometimes it's just best to sit and wait.

"You're right, Houston. Franco, pull over at the next decent hotel." Franco spotted a billboard on the freeway advertising that there was an Embassy Suites off the next exit. "Embassy Suites, one mile sir. Is that good enough?"

"Yes. They should have a restaurant there, too. We can eat something after we check in."

By the time they got settled into their rooms, it was 10:45 on Thursday night. Houston and Rodriguez didn't have their phones, but they didn't dare use the house phone in case Thomas paid off the clerk to monitor any outgoing calls.

"Fons, I'm going to go out the stairwell exit door and find an outside phone to call Agent Hampton. I'm sure they're not far behind, but I need to see if they have anything new to go on."

"Okay. If Franco or Thomas stop by, I'll say you went to the snack machines, so don't be gone long and come back with some snacks. Houston ran down the stairs and out the rear exit. He had seen a gas station across the street with a minute mart attached and figured he'd try there first. The young man at the counter didn't look up when he came in. He went to the counter.

"Hey, I locked my keys and all my stuff in my car. Can I use your phone to call for help?"

He pointed to the land line and shrugged. "No skin off my nose."

That was easy, Houston thought. He called Agent Hampton and asked if he had any additional information. Houston told his supervisor that they were driving toward Florida until they received new information. In return, Agent Hampton told him the satellite images that they captured showed an SUV leaving the cabin around 7 pm on Wednesday night. They were able to visually track the SUV for a while, they last spotted them southbound on I-95, but that's when the satellite lost its direct line of sight.

"I have a team waiting for stores to open in the morning along that route," Hampton informed him. "We're going to see if any of the businesses have surveillance cameras out front. If we can identify the vehicle by lining up the time stamp on our satellite picture with any surveillance camera footage, maybe we can get a license plate and the freeway cameras can perform a real-time search for them."

"That's perfect, sir. How do we get it to Thomas? He needs to be the one to find them. Sophie's best hope is if Thomas can talk Nikko down."

"I agree with your assessment, Agent Townsend. We could get one of our informants to try to sell the information to one of Thomas' men."

"That's a great idea, sir. Are our trackers and audio working?

"Yes. We went into the cabin after you guys left. We didn't get anything more than you did. But we heard Thomas verify that was her earring you found. She's one smart lady, leaving that for you."

Houston smiled. "I have to get back before I'm missed. We can cut over state route 10 to get on I-95 once Thomas realizes that's the direction Nikko went. I'll call again as soon as I get a chance."

"Be careful, Agent Townsend. Remember you're still not at 100 percent. You only have use of one hand. Let Rodriguez take the lead on any physical encounters."

"Yes sir." Houston thanked the boy for the phone and ran back up the staircase, stopping by the snack machines before heading back to his room.

"That was a clever way to make me buy you snacks, Fons."

He smiled. "I do what I can."

CHAPTER TWENTY-TWO

Friday

When Sophie woke up, she was still cuffed to the bed. That was a bad sign. She sat up. She didn't have her watch on, but it sounded like someone was moving around downstairs.

"Nikko." She tried not to yell too loudly but just enough to get his attention. She heard him coming.

As he walked in the door, she could see his demeanor wasn't any better. "I need to go to the bathroom."

He uncuffed her. "Get dressed, come downstairs, and make us some breakfast."

Nikko went back to what he was doing. Sophie saw her face in the mirror. The eye was black and blue but not swollen all the way shut. Her cheek was swollen, and the cut in her mouth stung. She got in the shower and got dressed. She put her hair in a ponytail, but she didn't bother to put on makeup. She went downstairs to start breakfast.

He looked up at her. "When we're done with breakfast, go upstairs and take out that ridiculous ponytail. You know I don't like that look on you. And get some makeup on, too—you look terrible."

Sophie was surprised to see food in the refrigerator. Nikko must have made a trip to a convenience store before she woke up. She made scrambled eggs and bacon, setting his plate down in front of him and poured him some orange juice, doing the same for herself. Sophie responded to his conversation but didn't initiate any. After washing the dishes, she went upstairs, restyled her hair, and put on some makeup. It hurt rubbing the foundation on her swollen cheek and eye, but she didn't want to agitate him. She grabbed a book from her suitcase and went downstairs.

"Can I sit on the porch and read?"

He looked at her. "Well, at least you look presentable now, yeah."

He took her outside and took out the cuffs again. "Really, Nikko?"

"Don't push me, Sophie. I'm not in the mood." She sat in the wooden rocker, and he went back inside. It was very quiet here, wherever "here" was. The weather was warm, and the sun was out — something to be thankful for.

It was 9 am and word of Nikko's last known whereabouts hadn't gotten to Thomas yet. They were eating breakfast at the hotel restaurant and Franco was working on his computer.

Thomas' phone rang. "Ciao?"

"Mr. Morano, this is Kenny. I had an interesting visitor a few minutes ago. A man came looking for you. I've seen him around before; I think he may have done some things for your brother. Anyway, he gave me some information about Nikko and Sophie."

"Get to the point, Kenny."

"Well, he was hauled in for questioning at the DEA and while he was there, he heard an Agent talking to his partner about some satellite photos coming in. It had something to do with a kidnapping. He figured it must have been Nikko, so he brought me the information hoping to get a reward."

"What did he hear?"

"He said they had images of an SUV leaving a cabin in North Carolina and the satellite tracked it down I-95 moving south toward the Florida coast."

"Perfect. Give him a thousand dollars and tell him there is more where that came from if he can get us something else." Thomas hung up. He turned toward the other men.

"We have a lead. It seems that the DEA has been tracking Nikko by satellite. They followed his SUV when they left the cabin. Their last known location was southbound on I-95. We're on the right track."

Houston acted surprised. "That's great news, Mr. Morano. I'm pretty sure we can cut over on state route 10 and get onto I-95 to start looking."

They got up, paid their bill, and headed to their vehicle. Franco jumped eagerly into the driver's seat, and they started south again.

Nikko came outside and spoke to Sophie an hour later. He pulled up a wooden chair and sat down in front of her. "I guess it's time for me to tell you what the plan is. Uncle Tony bought a yacht and registered it with Switzerland. Even though they have an extradition treaty with the US, they never comply with it. We need to get out to international waters as quickly as possible."

He unlocked her cuffs as he continued talking. "The crew signed on for 6 months. After we are safe in international waters, we will go to the Bahamas where that crew will get off and we'll get a new crew for six more months. While in international waters, the captain can marry us. We'll stay out to sea for a year or so. The yacht has a helicopter landing pad, so we can call out a helicopter if we need to get off the yacht quickly. It will be our honeymoon cruise around the world. We can stop anywhere and go on land for sightseeing or shopping." He looked at her. She looked pale and ready to cry.

"Nikko, I don't want to leave the U.S., and I'm not ready to marry you. I told you that."

Sophie knew she was taking a risk, but she didn't care. He acted like he hadn't even heard her. He stood and pulled a ring box out of his pocket.

"I've been carrying this around too long waiting for you to get over your little tantrum. I'm done waiting, Sophie."

"You would rather force my decision now than give me the time I asked for to make the decision on my own? If you do that, my answer is no."

His face softened a little. "What is it you want from me before I put this ring on your finger?"

Sophie knew he was going to put it on her finger regardless, so if she could get him to compromise something, it was worth a try.

She thought for a moment. "Okay, Nikko. I'll put that ring on my finger if you promise me, you will not touch me until we are married."

Nikko stood and paced on the porch, but he wasn't angry. He walked back over to her, got down on one knee, pulled the ring out of the box, and slipped it on her finger. "I can live with that condition. My mother would approve."

She put on a small smile and let him hug her. He kissed her cheek. "After I make you lunch, I'll take you on a walk."

Sophie thought about King Saul. When the evil spirit would come on him, David would play his harp and the spirit would leave. She could see when a spirit took Nikko over, and when it left. It wasn't a subtle change.

Lunch was good, as always, and after she washed the dishes, he took her outside for a walk. She didn't jerk away when he took her hand.

"Nikko, I've been thinking more about what we discussed on our last walk."

He turned his head to her. "What's that, Sophie?"

"We talked about how Jesus died for our sins, how all that is required for eternal life is to ask Jesus to forgive our sins and cover them under His blood." She took a breath, but he didn't stop her like she expected. "When I die, I want to go to Heaven, Nikko, and I want to see you there too. The alternative is Hell, and based on what the Bible says about it, you don't want to spend eternity there."

A small chuckle came out of him. "Sophie, you have the sweetest heart of anyone I know. Of course, you'll make it to Heaven. But I'm not like you. I've lived an unscrupulous life. I can't just ask for forgiveness and have it all wiped away."

Sophie stopped and faced him. "Oh, but Nikko, you can! None of us is sinless in God's eyes. My sins are no different than yours in the sight of the Lord. That's why he had to send Jesus. Once we ask forgiveness, our sins are washed away under the blood never to be accounted to us again."

He tugged her hand slightly to get her walking again. "If I became a Christian, my whole life would change."

"That's right, Nikko, but that could be a good thing."

"You're still thinking I could open a restaurant somewhere and clear the slate between me and God?"

"Between you and God, yes. I don't know how all the legal stuff would shake out, but I know one thing—with God on your side, you can handle any troubles."

"I've often thought of things that I would have done differently, if it had been *me* that built Morano's. I think I would have had an authentic brick pizza oven that guests could see and maybe bottle our marinara sauce for sale. You know our customers ask for it all the time."

Sophie smiled. "Those are great ideas, Nikko!"

Back at the cabin, they were still talking about the restaurant while he made dinner." He turned to her. "You know, I could teach you to cook, Sophie."

Sophie laughed. "Have you ever heard of someone who is *tone deaf*? I think I'm like that but with food."

He chuckled. "You could be right. I remember your attempt to impress me with your cooking. We had to eat out that night."

"Not funny, Nikko." She managed a grin but ended up wincing from the pain.

Nikko put the plates on the table, and they ate. He reached his hand over and cupped her face.

"I'm sorry about your beautiful face, Sophie."

She didn't respond for fear of saying the wrong thing. After cleaning up together, he went back to his computer and she asked if she could go back out on the porch and read.

He looked up at her. "Can I trust you, Sophie?"

She looked at him. "You can trust me not to run."

He nodded his head and continued his work. It was a beautiful evening—the stars were bright, and there was just a slight cool breeze blowing through the dogwood trees. The scent of the air gently swept by her. She stayed outside until he called for her to come in at around 9:30. She sat down on the couch and continued to read.

It was dark when Franco nudged Thomas in his seat to pull his attention away from his phone. "Mr. Morano, we've been on I-95 going south for quite a while now. Where are we going?"

Thomas let out a breath. "I don't know. Keep going for a while, then we'll stop and hope someone comes through with more directions."

Nikko left his computer and sat down beside Sophie on the couch. "I never called Thomas back. I really need to know if he has any information on who tracked us." She stayed quiet. She didn't know where this was going. He picked up his satellite phone and dialed.

"Ciao?"

"Ciao, Thomas."

"You were supposed to call me yesterday," Thomas said. Nikko could hear the anger in his voice.

"I know, but we had to leave in a hurry. I got word that someone was using satellite imaging to look for us," Nikko said. Thomas was disheartened to learn that Nikko knew about the satellite tracking.

"I could have warned you if you had called. I heard that the FBI was doing a grid search of the east coast."

"Mi dispiace fratellino. I just got paranoid." Houston and Rodriguez were hoping the Agents following them could hear this side of the conversation.

"Nikko, dove sei?" Thomas asked.

"Right now, we're safe., we'll be on a yacht and out of the country soon."

"Nikko, you will never get away if you try to take her. Please, fratello, let her go. Set yourself up in your new location then send for her, but don't make her spend her life running with you."

Nikko thought for a moment. "Sophie's not mad at me anymore, Thomas. She put my ring back on."

Thomas knew she was just bargaining for her own protection. "Fratello, I'm begging you not to go through with this."

"Abbastanza, Thomas. What I need to know is if the FBI has caught my trail again."

"According to my sources, all they know is that you are going south. So, that means you need to be very careful. Maybe you should change your plans and pick up the yacht somewhere else. I can help with that if you send me its location."

"That may not be a bad idea. Let me think about it. I'll call you back tomorrow."

"Wait—Nikko, I want to talk to Sophie."

He was quiet for a minute then answered, "No, not tonight. I'll call you tomorrow. Good night, Thomas."

"Buona notte, Nikko."

When Thomas put his phone down, it seemed to Houston like it was forever before he relayed the conversation.

"They're holed up somewhere. Their destination is definitely a marina in Florida. I thought if I could convince him to change his plans, he would ask for my help and we could be waiting for them at the boat. At the least, we would have a few more days to locate him. He wouldn't let me talk to Sophie. I'm not sure what that means, but he said she's wearing his ring again."

Houston was relieved. "That was smart. It buys her some more time." It meant she was using her wits to stay alive.

"Yes, and I know Sophie, she will never marry him. We have to find her before..."

"Before what?" Rodriguez asked Thomas, cutting him off.

274

"before Nikko realizes that." Thomas told Franco to find them a hotel on I-95. "No sense in going any farther tonight."

After Nikko hung up, he turned to Sophie. "Thomas thinks I should switch up my plans since the FBI are so close." Sophie wasn't sure if she was supposed to respond.

"What do you want to do?" She asked him.

He rubbed his face with his hand. "I'm going to sleep on it. Are you ready for bed?" Nikko asked.

"Yes. I'm tired."

Nikko locked the deadbolt, took the key, and turned out all the downstairs lights. He went to her room and started to take out the cuffs.

"Nikko, no. I told you I wouldn't run."

He let out a long sigh. "Sophie, I'm not a fool. I know you're just placating me by putting on that ring and letting me hold your hand. I don't know what to believe." He sat down on her bed while she stood over by her suitcase.

Sophie went to him, knelt in front of him, and looked into his eyes. "Nikko, I have been honest with you from the start. I don't want to leave the country, and I'm not ready to marry you." She stopped for a moment, but he didn't respond. "I was so young when we met. I was attracted to you and the lifestyle you offered me. You had slapped me a couple of times, but I was naive and figured no relationship was perfect. At times, I still see that man who I saw then, but I can't be with a man I'm afraid of. You can't make me marry you. That's why I had to leave the hospital." *No, no, no*, she thought, *I shouldn't have said that.*

Nikko got up and took a few steps toward the door. She stood and moved to the edge of the bed, sitting where he had been.

"Who helped you get away?"

"No one helped me." There was no way of putting this genie back in the bottle.

"You are smart, Sophie, but you're not smarter than me. I couldn't find you, and I couldn't find out who helped you." He came to the bed and squeezed her face in his hand. "Who helped you, Sophie?"

He let her face go, shoving her back on the bed. She sat back up right away. He took the cuffs and put one on her wrist the other on the headboard. "I can't trust you to stay with me, and I'm not ready to let you go. The thought of you alive and not with me — well, it isn't going to happen. And just to be clear — " he got inches from her face now, " — I *can* make you marry me."

Nikko pulled the covers up over her and left, closing the door. She was still in her clothes. He hadn't even let her change. She just laid there thinking, *Houston, Thomas, anyone...please find me soon.*

It was hard for Houston not to take the lead on this. He was desperate to protect Sophie from Nikko. But he knew his best chance was with Thomas running the show, so he put his ego aside. Rodriguez made the nightly phone run to make sure command heard everything and find out if they got a license plate.

Fons walked into the hotel room. "The boss says they spotted the SUV on surveillance at a bank down I-95. We got a partial plate and they're running it through the DMV to come up with any vehicles matching that description. He's hoping to have something by morning."

"How will he get the information to us?" Houston asked.

"Hampton said once they have the whole plate number, they will go over freeway surveillance for the last 24 hours and try to find out where he's headed. Then he'll leak it again."

Rodriguez handed Houston a bag of pretzels, some Funyuns, and a Pepsi. They had no idea what Nikko would do. They tried to come up with some plausible scenarios, but it was useless.

Houston finally said, "Maybe Thomas can convince him to change his plans. Even an extra day would be helpful."

"God knows exactly where she is Houston. Trust Him."

Sophie woke up in the middle of the night. She was hearing a soft voice. She opened her eyes and saw Nikko sitting in a chair in the dark just looking at her, talking to her like she was awake. He didn't notice she opened her eyes, so she partially closed them so that it wasn't obvious that she was awake. Then she watched and listened.

"Sophie, I'm not letting you go. I could never marry anyone else. You've ruined me. If you were still alive, I would never get over you. If you died, I would grieve but at least I'd be free from this torment and could move on."

Nikko had made vague threats like that to her face off and on, but this sounded more like a decision. He walked closer to her bed, and she shut her eyes completely. He stoked her hair softly. "Sophie, wake up. I should have let you get in your pajamas." He unlocked the cuff and moved out of the way.

Sophie pretended to be roused from a dream. "Oh. Thank you, Nikko." Her mind was racing to figure out what she was going to do. He was losing hope that she would ever accept him. That meant she was dead to him, figuratively, and soon, maybe literally. In the morning, she would have to start changing her strategy. She had to stay alive long enough for them to find her. She came back after she changed her clothes, and he cuffed her again, covered her, and left.

Saturday

The men were done with breakfast and sat waiting in the lobby of the hotel for any clue where to go. Thomas and Franco were online and making calls. It was nearly 11 am before the first leaked information came through.

Franco's phone rang. "Hello?" They couldn't hear the other person. Franco's face was lifting. "How sure are you about this?" He waited. "I'll tell him. Thanks, Kenny!"

"What is it, Franco?" Thomas asked.

"That same informant has a friend at DMV who said that the FBI called requesting a partial license plate identification on a black SUV with New York plates. Apparently, they traced it using freeway cameras to an I-95 off ramp, exit 321. That's by Lake Panasoffkee. There are a lot of campsites and private cabins up there."

Houston stepped in. "Thomas, do you think you could get your man to hack into the satellite feed when it's over that area. This is the first solid lead we've had."

"Franco, call Nate and tell him what we have. We'll go as far as that exit so we can be close if we get anything."

They headed for the car while Franco was calling Nate. Houston finally had a glimmer of hope. *Hang on princess. we're coming*, he prayed more than thought. He knew the joint task force would be already on their way there waiting for satellite images of their own.

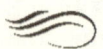

CHAPTER TWENTY-THREE

When she opened her eyes, Nikko was in her room waiting for her. He uncuffed her without a word.

Sophie needed to start fixing things. "Nikko, after I get dressed, can I make breakfast for you? I know it's not as good as yours, but it's my turn."

He nodded his head and went downstairs. She was finishing the pancakes when he came into the kitchen. He had been on the porch just sitting. Silence from him was a bad sign.

"Pancakes are ready. I made the blueberry kind that you like."

Sophie placed his plate on the table and grabbed some juice and coffee for him. She finished preparing her own plate and sat down with him.

"Thank you for letting me change last night." She waited, but he never responded.

Sophie reached over and took his hand. "Do you think we could go for a walk today?"

Nikko sighed the sigh of a man grieving. "Sure, why not?"

After she cleaned up, he took her outside. A few minutes into the walk, she took his hand. She wasn't sure what to say, so she just held it as they walked.

Finally, she said, "I really like the ideas you have for a more authentic Italian restaurant. I could do the books like I did before."

He yanked his hand out of hers. "Don't toy with me Sophie. You don't intend on being with me."

Whatever she said next had to be both careful and believable. "Nikko, none of us knows what tomorrow brings, and I'm here with you now, aren't I?" That was the best she could do.

"If I thought there was a chance you could change your mind about me..."

Sophie took his hand again. "As long as we have breath, anything is possible."

That statement startled him for a moment, but he kept walking. It took him a while, but he started talking about the restaurant again, almost getting excited. She added ideas and menu suggestions.

"You just don't want to have to pay for a meal ever again," he razzed her.

"Guilty as charged," she responded.

Nikko laughed at her. "Sweetheart, you really are going to have to learn to cook." Sophie didn't object to the endearment. She was making progress.

"Not as long as you're around," she smiled.

Sophie felt the impact that her statement had on him. She hated leading him on, but his mind had gone to a dark, dangerous place, and she needed to get him out of it.

"That's true enough. I love cooking for you." They made it back to the cabin, and he went back to his computer.

"Can I read outside?" He looked up at her. "Yes, but keep the door open."

Sophie was making headway. He didn't cuff her. He came out about noon and asked what she wanted for lunch.

"I love everything you cook, so you choose. Do you want me to make dinner?"

"Seriously, Sophie?" He laughed.

"No, really. I saw TV dinners in the freezer."

"Now I know you've lost your mind. They must be left over from the previous renter."

He went inside to start lunch. After the dishes were done, she went back outside.

"I love it out here, Nikko."

He came out to stand by her. "It is beautiful. But there are places in this world that would make this pale in comparison, and I would like to show them to you." She didn't respond. As he was turning to go inside, he heard a vehicle coming down the long driveway.

Nikko sprang into action, "get inside, now!" She did. It would be dangerous for whoever happened to be in that truck if she said anything to cause suspicion.

The pickup truck stopped, and a man got out. He looked like a local. He was an older man, wearing blue jeans, a plaid work shirt, and a baseball cap with a fish on it. Sophie could see through a slit in the curtain without being seen.

The man sauntered up to Nikko and addressed him in a deep southern drawl. "Howdy, mister. My name's Peter." He reached his hand out to Nikko, and Nikko shook it. "Sorry to bother ya'll, but I told old Frank I'd be checking on his cabins for him from time to time. You the feller who rented all of 'em?"

"Yes, sir. My name is Vinny. I needed some privacy to finish my research, and Frank gave me a fair deal."

"That's sounds like Frank. Money don't mean much to 'em. Well, if ya need anything a'tal, I live a mile east, as the crow flies." The man chuckled at his own idiom, then turned to head back to his car. "Y'all take care, now."

"Thank you for checking in." Nikko watched him leave, then went inside.

"Everything okay, Nikko?"

Nikko was still pensive and clearly a little shaken. "I'm not sure. He seemed real enough."

Nikko was on his computer with Ben until dinner. She could tell he was still jittery, unsettled. Later, while he was making dinner, he stopped to look at her and said, "sweetheart, I think you should pack your things. The FBI are right on our tail. I need to change my plans."

Sophie wasn't going to argue anymore. This wasn't the time. She just went upstairs and collected her things. It didn't take long since she never really took anything out. She brought her suitcases downstairs and put them by the door.

Nikko had dinner on the table. "Go ahead and eat. I need to call Uncle Tony." Sophie ate her meal and cleaned the kitchen. She covered his plate in plastic wrap and put it in the refrigerator in case he wanted to eat it later. She was trying to eavesdrop without being obvious.

"Uncle Tony, the FBI has been on my tail from the start. They must have my plates or something." Can we redirect the yacht and switch cars?" He went into the kitchen. "I can wait. I won't go anywhere until I hear from you," he hung up.

"I put your plate in the fridge. Can I heat it up for you?" She asked.

"That would be nice," he replied.

"What has you so spooked, Nikko?" She was curious. "Was it that old man?"

She took the plate out of the microwave and set it in front of him with a cup of coffee.

"No, not exactly. It just seems like the FBI have been right on top of us since the start. Changing plans is the best option. I'm waiting for Uncle Tony to make some different arrangements for us."

Nikko finished eating and went upstairs to get his things. He brought down the sheets and put them in a plastic bag, then went back up with the bleach wipes. She grabbed a few things from the kitchen and put them in a bag, then took them to the SUV. He finished wiping the downstairs area, dumped the rest of the food in the garbage bag, and brought it out to the car.

After loading everything up, he said, "we'll wait here on the porch for his call." They sat down and quietly waited.

If Nikko was indeed stationary, then the men were now only two hours behind and gaining precious time. Houston hadn't been able to contact Agent Hampton to get more intel, nor had Thomas gotten any new leaked information which probably meant the satellite hadn't produced anything yet. Sophie had been gone a long time now. Houston wondered what she was doing, how she was holding it together. He knew she was smart—she could outthink him if he didn't get wind of what she was doing.

Nikko's ringtone pierced through the still, Florida, Saturday-night air. "Uncle Tony, what have you got for me?" She watched his face as he listened. They were speaking Italian. "Send all that to my phone so I have it. Thank you. I'll call you tomorrow." He waited a few seconds until he heard the ping on his phone confirming that the information had been received. Nikko opened the SUV door for Sophie, she got in, and they were back on the road by 7:45 pm.

Thomas' phone rang. "Ciao?" Thomas put it on speaker since they were in the SUV, and Nate's voice came from the other end.

"I have the GPS on a cabin by Lake Panasoffkee that has an SUV matching Nikko's out front. I'll send it. Just to let you know, the last images are 3 hours old. I'm trying to get something more current right now, boss."

"Good. Keep me updated." By 8:45 pm, they were arriving at exit 321. According to the on-board navigation, they were about 25 minutes away from the cabin. Thomas told Franco to floor it.

Meanwhile, Nikko was being cautious. He didn't take the freeway, trying instead to stick with local access roads.

"Uncle Tony has a new car waiting for us at Edgewater Mall in Biloxi, Mississippi, right off state route 10. We'll pick it up and stop somewhere for the night. Then we'll head to New Orleans and board the yacht there on Monday morning. It's a couple of days later than I wanted but I don't want to take any chances."

"How do we find the car?" She wondered.

He gave me the GPS signal. It will be registered to my new alias, so no one should be able to track it.

"What is your new name, Nikko?" She looked at him.

"Vinny Marko."

"I like the name Vinny," she responded. "Did you get me one?" She had assumed he must have, or she wouldn't be able to get in and out of foreign ports.

"I'll tell you if you promise not to get mad."

"Nikko, what did you do?" Sophie furrowed her brows at him. He looked at her.

"It was in anticipation of our marriage. It's Twinkle Marko."

Sophie shot a look at him. "Twinkle? Are you kidding me?"

Dangerous Obsession

Nikko tried to keep a straight face. "I wanted it to remind you of Star."

She slapped his shoulder. He pretended to flinch like it hurt. "I will not go by the name of "Twinkle," do you hear me?"

Nikko started laughing. He could hardly contain himself.

Sophie glared at him. "Tell me you didn't."

He was trying to talk, but he was still laughing too hard. "No, of course not. It's Ruby Marko because you're such a jewel."

She slapped his arm again. "Nice save, Nikko. You're not out of the doghouse yet." Nikko chuckled.

About 4 hours in, they stopped for gas and a bathroom break and to get rid of the garbage in the back. He still went in with her, which means he still wasn't sure she wouldn't try something.

Just up ahead, the access road was closed for construction, and he had to get on state route 10. He got off about 20 miles later, though, and stayed on the side roads for another hour. He decided not to go into Biloxi until the next day — he was exhausted.

Nikko pulled off the freeway just west of Crestview, Florida, where he saw an advertisement for hotels up ahead. He drove until he found one that looked like a four-star hotel and got a room. He got Sophie settled, unplugged the phone in her room, and took it with him. He cuffed her to the bed then went and parked the car out of sight. It was nearly 1 o'clock in the morning when he finally retired to his bed.

The men stopped a mile from the cabin and sprinted up. It was dark, but the moon was out, so they didn't use their flashlights. They came upon the cabin, but there was no SUV, and the lights were all off. They went up the steps cautiously just

285

in case Nikko had hidden the vehicle and was waiting inside. This time, the door wasn't locked. They went inside, turned on their flashlights, and swept every room with their guns drawn.

Thomas came down to the kitchen, turned on the lights, and slammed his fist on the table. "How does he get away from us every time? He can't be that far ahead of us!"

Houston was pacing the floor. "He's getting better intel than we are."

Thomas called Nate back. "Tell me you have more for me. He's not here."

"Yeah, we have images of him leaving about 7:45 pm. I was able to track him on the access roads. He left going west on state route 10. The better news is that Kenny called with the license plate number."

Thomas realized Nikko had changed his plans like he suggested. "It's 9:15, so we're less than two hours behind him. We need to do everything we can to close that gap. Tell Kenny to keep the information coming. I don't care how much it costs. What else can you give me."

"West on 10 is all I have, but I'm going to hack into the Department of Transportation's cameras to try to track his plate."

Thomas thought for a moment. "We can't afford a wild goose chase when we're this close. We'll get back on I-95 north. We'll stop at the Florida border and wait for more information. He could have gotten off 10 and be going any direction by now. Maybe he'll call in the morning."

Houston went to the table. "We're closing the gap Mr. Morano. That's good news. Wherever he's going, he has to stay by the coast for the yacht."

Thomas sat down and lowered his head. "I know Houston, but we don't know what condition Sophie's in. The fact that he wouldn't let me talk to her worries me."

"Me too." Houston couldn't show Thomas his real feelings. It would hurt the mission, but this was eating him up inside.

Franco's phone rang as they were pulling off at a Tallahassee exit to get gas and wait for more directions.

"Yeah, Nate. What do you have?" He put Nate on the speaker phone again. "The camera picked them up about an hour east of Crestview, Florida, westbound on SR 10 at 11:45 pm. Everyone looked at their watches. It was just after midnight. Franco had been driving for hours so Houston offered to drive the next leg. They raced toward the coordinates they were given.

If only Nikko hadn't taken the phone cord, she could have tried to get ahold of Houston or Thomas. She knew they had to be close because Nikko never changes his plans. He came in, locked the door, and went to the bathroom. When he came out, he uncuffed her and let her get ready for bed.

When she came out, he said, "Sophie, I'm exhausted. I'm afraid I won't hear if you get up. I'm sorry but I have to cuff you."

Sophie didn't fight it. She didn't want a repeat of the other night. He kissed her forehead and went to bed. She lay there quietly praying for him and for someone to find her.

Sophie was beginning to see past the man to see his soul. She realized she had never really forgiven him. Sophie had said the words, which is the first step, but her heart and mind never got the message. *Forgive me Lord. You would have died even if he was the only soul, but I judged him to be unworthy when I was just as unworthy as he. Please forgive me.* With that on her lips, she fell asleep.

The men had been driving for a couple of hours. "Thomas, does your brother generally drive without stopping for sleep?" Houston started being concerned they would end up driving right past them.

"My brother is very fastidious. He doesn't like making mistakes or taking chances. My bet is that he stopped somewhere to sleep."

Rodriguez had an idea. "The last camera caught him on SR 10 just east of Crestview before midnight. He wouldn't want to stop anywhere right off the main exits because there would be too many cameras on the businesses. So, he would probably stop at an exit just past the city."

"That makes sense. What do you think of pulling over at one of these exits and driving around a while? If we don't see his vehicle, we can get a hotel and wait for more intel."

Thomas agreed. They got off two exits past Crestview proper. It was as good a guess as any. They drove around all the hotels and searched for Nikko's SUV. Having not spotted him after an hour or so, they got themselves a couple of rooms at a local motel. It was Houston's turn to find a phone and check in with Hampton. He found out that there were no more sightings of Nikko's SUV past Crestview. Armed with this rather promising news, he went to get some sleep.

Sunday

Nikko got up first and took his shower. He knew he could be in and out much faster than she could. When he came out, he saw her sitting up in bed waiting. He uncuffed her and she went to get ready. He got on the computer to check if the yacht was on schedule for Monday morning.

He was debating about calling Thomas. "Nikko, can we go to the Pancake House I saw on the way in last night? It's only a couple of blocks away — we could walk there." She was speaking through the bathroom door loud enough for him to hear.

"Talk to me when you're done." He hated talking through doors. She came out in clean jeans and a light cotton top. She had her makeup on, and her hair was washed and styled.

"Well, what's your answer?"

Nikko shook his head. "You know that food is mostly sugar."

Sophie folded her arms and stared at him. "Your point is?"

He laughed. "Alright. You're worse than a little kid. I'll walk our things to the SUV then come back for you."

"Why don't I just go with you and then we can walk to the restaurant? According to you, I'll need to work off a lot of calories anyway. Deal?" She put out her hand.

"Deal." But instead of shaking her hand, he kissed it. They got everything done and made it to the Pancake House by 8:20 am.

Thomas, Houston, and the others got up early and waited for word from Nate or Kenny, but none came. They decided that they would wait there for an hour, until 9:30, then go get breakfast and get back on the road going west. Houston had unstrapped his arm from his chest. He needed to stretch it.

Nikko and Sophie looked at their menus waiting for the waitress. The place was full, so it was going to take some time.

Finally, the waitress came. "What would you folks like this morning?"

Sophie was about to put in her order when Nikko spoke up. "She will have the strawberry waffle with the strawberries and whip cream on the side, a cup of hot chocolate, and a glass of water. And bring the carousel of syrups for her too. I will have steak and eggs with wheat toast, orange juice and coffee, and I'd like some peach jam for my toast."

He handed her the menus. He absolutely had to control her—she knew that. She wanted to get angry and act out, but she decided there was no point. He ordered exactly what she wanted. He really had paid attention to her the few years they were together. A bus boy brought their beverages, and they waited for their food to be served.

Nikko broke their silence first. "I think you are going to have to start working out with me if you insist on eating like this." He wasn't joking. He had no intention of having a wife that wasn't picture perfect. Again, she let the comment slide past her because she knew that she would never be spending her future with him no matter what she had to do.

"Where are we going from here, Nikko?"

"We'll be in Biloxi in about 2 hours and 30 minutes. That's where we'll change vehicles. Once we've done that, we can take our time, go shopping, whatever you want. It's only another hour and a half to New Orleans. The yacht won't be there until 10 am on Monday morning."

Their food came, and she ate every bite of it. He laughed at her. They were up front paying for the check when she noticed there was candy in their glass counter.

"I'd like some candy, Nikko."

"You can't possibly have room for candy."

"It's for later," she explained.

"Alright, but if you start bouncing off the car doors from all this sugar, I'm pulling over and you're doing pushups to get it out of your system."

"I can live with that." She asked the counter person for some Whoppers and Twizzlers. Nikko paid their bill. He opened the door for her, and she walked out. They walked at a slow pace toward the copse of trees that separated the freeway and businesses from a rural subdivision. The trees were a sound barrier for the residents.

Dangerous Obsession

CHAPTER TWENTY-FOUR

Thomas and the others were waiting at the hotel, no one had called or messaged the men, so they decided to get in the car and go to the Pancake House a couple of blocks down. The men pulled up in front of the Pancake house at 9:15., and Houston caught a glimpse of a couple walking toward the trees. He just smiled and headed for the restaurant door but stopped short a moment later. There was something about the way the woman walked that was too familiar.

"Thomas, it's them! Look over there!" He shouted to the others and took off running across the parking lot. The others followed close behind.

Sophie was trying to put the candy in her pocket and realized she missed it completely. Her Twizzlers fell to the ground. She had taken a couple of steps before she realized it and turned to go back for them. Nikko turned and stopped to wait for her. Then she froze. She spotted Houston running across the parking lot at a break-neck speed. Sophie started to take a step toward him when Nikko realized what was happening. He grabbed her upper arm and ran for the trees. She reached one arm out to Houston while Nikko was yanking on the other.

"Sophie!" Houston yelled.

"Nikko! Stop and let me talk to you," Thomas yelled after them.

Houston could see them at the edge of the tree line. Sophie tried to turn to Houston, but Nikko was too strong for her. She tripped and started to go headlong into the pavement, but he was able to keep her on her feet.

"If they make those trees, we'll lose them, Fons." He didn't expect a reply. He kept running.

Nikko got her beyond the trees and into the subdivision on the other side. His SUV was in the backyard of an abandoned home. They were only two blocks away, but the men were right on their tails.

Thomas and the others made it past the trees and headed for the houses, but Nikko and Sophie were nowhere in sight. They spread out and each took a street, searching yards and bushes. They couldn't be too far ahead of them.

Having reached his vehicle, Nikko unlocked the door and hurried Sophie into the front seat. He cuffed her to the hand hold above the door and got in. He pulled out slowly trying to see if any of them were close. He turned left on the street and headed out of the subdivision. As they turned the corner, they saw Houston with his back turned toward them as he searched in the wrong direction. Just as they were driving by, he turned. She looked him in the eye and mouthed, "I love you."

Houston started running after the vehicle. He pulled his gun and shot at the tires, but his hand wasn't working well enough to hit the moving targets. He couldn't risk shooting into the car. The others heard the shots and headed for Houston. He kept running after the SUV, trying to shoot the tires again while running. He thought he nicked one of the tires, so he kept chasing them. But when Nikko pulled out of the subdivision, it was too late. Nikko and Sophie were too far ahead.

"We need to get to the car. We know he's going west now. Maybe we can catch him," Houston panted as Thomas, Fons, and Franco caught up to him.

Though they were struggling for breath, they all ran back to where they had left their vehicle. As he was running back the same way they came, Houston noticed what it was she had gone back for—her Twizzlers were laying on the ground.

Oh, Sophie. I'm sorry I've failed you again.

The sight of her reaching out for him while Nikko dragged her away was seared into his brain. He also saw she was handcuffed when the SUV drove by. His heart was being torn to shreds, and he was helpless to do anything about it.

"Nikko, what are you doing? That was Thomas. He wanted to talk to you."

Nikko got off the access road and drove around looking for a place he could hide his vehicle. His tire was flat, but he had to find a place to hide before he could do anything about it. He knew there was a can of tire sealant in the roadside emergency kit—that would have to suffice for now. He pulled behind a Walmart Superstore and retrieved the kit from the storage compartment. It sealed and aired the tire. He would change it as soon as he felt safe.

"He isn't here to talk to me, Sophie. He's here to take you away," he barked at her.

"What are you talking about? He's your brother." She snapped back.

He calmed down and explained. "When Thomas called the first time, he told me he would do anything to help me get away, but he would not allow me to take you."

Sophie noticed they were driving the opposite way from the freeway. "What are we doing out here?"

"They're going to assume I'll get on the freeway and try to outrun them. If we wait it out for an hour or two, they'll be ahead of us, and we'll be safe. I know they have these plates. That has to be how they and the FBI are tracking us."

After driving about 20 minutes away from the freeway, he found an abandoned barn out in a field and pulled the SUV in, closing the barn doors.

"Nikko, please call Thomas. I'm sure you've misunderstood him. He is extremely loyal to you."

He thought about it. "I will, Sophie, in a little while."

"Uncuff me, Nikko," Sophie was irate.

He uncuffed her and then went to the back to change the tire. Sophie walked around the barn letting off steam. He changed the tire and put everything away in less than 25 minutes.

"Sit down, Sophie. You're driving me nuts. You're on a sugar high."

The men were in the SUV headed toward state route 10. Houston was driving while Thomas fumed. "This is ridiculous! We had them, and now we have no idea where to go. What are we going to do, just drive around thinking we'll run across them again by chance?" Thomas asked, frustrated.

Houston replied, "I know one thing. If I were him, I'd hide for a while and wait for us to leave the area."

"We can't just sit here. If he is on the road, he'll get too far ahead of us," Rodriguez said.

Thomas thought about the different opinions the men had. "Houston, drive for a half hour on 10 then pull off. If we get word that they're behind us, we can get back quickly. We'll get off and wait on the access road in case we see him go by. Otherwise, we'll wait for more information."

Sophie was sitting next to Nikko on a bale of hay swatting bugs off her. They had been sitting there for about forty-five minutes or so. He grabbed his satellite phone from the SUV and dialed Thomas. Nikko put it on speaker so she could hear but told her not to speak.

"Ciao?" Thomas answered on the second ring and put it on speaker.

"Thomas, how did you know where I was? Are you working with the FBI?" Nikko asked suspicious of his brother.

"No, of course not Nikko. I told you I would support you leaving if that's what you want. One of our men has resources and is giving us information and Nate is hacking into a Satellite to help us track you."

"How close are they?"

"I'm sure they are close. We came across you by accident. They don't know about this, at least not yet. I'm sure someone will call it in," Thomas advised him.

"I want you to stop following us, Thomas."

"I told you already that I won't let you take Sophie with you, Nikko. It's not right. It's kidnapping. You'll stay on the most wanted list, and I don't want that for you, fratello. What about mama? Are you going to just desert her like this?" Thomas tried to convince his brother to abandon this intrigue.

"Thomas, Uncle Tony has already activated my escape plan. You know that the details were worked out many years ago. It's a solid plan! I'll be able to see you and mama again, just not in the United States. You know she's been wanting to move back to Italy for years, but papa wouldn't leave."

"Nikko, please, let's talk face to face, solo io e te."

"I'm leaving Monday, Thomas. I'll call you again before I leave."

"Can I talk to Sophie?"

Sophie didn't wait. "I'm here Thomas." Nikko hung up and got angry at her.

"Why didn't you let me talk to him?"

Nikko stormed away. "Because you'll give away too much information."

"I won't, Nikko. I want to talk to him."

"I said no! Now, drop it."

Thomas slammed down the phone. "That was fruitless. I have no idea where he is."

Houston's heart stopped when he heard Sophie's voice for that split second.

"Well, that's not exactly true. Did you notice what we didn't hear?" Rodriguez interjected.

"Yeah, there was no road noise. It was quiet—no external voices, no music, no phones ringing, no gas station noises. It was totally quiet," Houston answered.

"What does that tell us?" Franco asked.

"It means they're not driving. They're stationary somewhere away from the city, away from the freeway," Rodriguez said.

"They drove away from the freeway rather than to it." Thomas understood the implications. Houston had no way of getting to a phone, so he said what he needed command to do as if talking to Thomas.

"Mr. Morano, do you think Nate can hack into some satellite footage of a 10-mile radius of the area where we caught up to them? I know I at least nicked one of his tires because it was going flat as he was leaving the subdivision. He had to pull off and either change it or put sealant in it. He probably pulled behind some building to get out of our line of sight knowing we would head for the freeway."

Thomas turned to Franco. "Call Nate and tell him what we need."

Nikko called his uncle. "Uncle Tony, the FBI is on top of me. I can't drive any further. Can you get a helicopter to my location? We need to get to New Orleans and hide out until the yacht gets there." He listened as his uncle responded. "We're in a field right now outside of Crestview, Florida. There's plenty of room for it to land here." He waited for his uncle to finish. "You think maybe within the hour?" He waited. "Good. Thank you, Uncle Tony." He hung up and walked over to were Sophie was. "I know this has been uncomfortable for you, but it's almost over. Once we're on the yacht, I'll have you pampered like a queen, I promise."

Sophie looked up at him. "Do you think I'm that shallow, Nikko? I don't care about being comfortable—I care about being free."

He squatted down before her. "But you will be free. We can go anywhere we want in the world."

"...anywhere but here," she snapped. "I want to talk to Thomas, and I want to say goodbye to him face-to-face before we leave." Sophie was trying to get some concessions from him while he was apologetic.

"The helicopter will be here in an hour. I'll let you talk to him before that," Nikko caved.

"Can I take a walk outside. It smells in here?"

He nodded. "I'll go with you."

Houston and Rodriguez stood outside the SUV, waiting for something to come in. The phone rang at 11:23 am.

"Hello?" Franco answered and put it on speaker.

"Is Mr. Morano there, Franco?" Nate asked.

"I'm here, Nate. Tell me what you know." Houston and Rodriguez walked toward Thomas' open window when they heard the phone.

"I was able to capture several images. The first was of his vehicle parked behind a huge Walmart Superstore by some dumpsters. Then the SUV was driving north away from the freeway into a farming area. The last image I got was a few minutes ago, but I couldn't see his SUV again. There is a barn in a field, though, and it looks like someone is outside walking. I have no idea if it's them, but we've lost the SUV somewhere in that area."

"Thanks, Nate. Send me the GPS coordinates." Thomas hung up the phone.

"Get in. That has to be them." Houston and Rodriguez were already getting in the vehicle. Based on the GPS coordinates, they would be at the barn in about 50 minutes.

As Nikko and Sophie were walking, she said, "You promised we could call Thomas. He is your brother and my friend, and according to you, I won't be seeing him for at least a year."

"He can take a helicopter out to the yacht anytime, Sophie."

What she really wanted was to talk to Houston, but she didn't dare say so. She was trying to come up with some way of letting them know where they were headed. They went back into the barn, and Nikko kept his promise and dialed Thomas. Before handing her the phone, he put it on speaker so he could keep track of what was said.

The phone rang. "Ciao?" Thomas answered, putting it on speaker as they were speeding back the way they came.

"Thomas," Sophie responded.

"Where are you? Are you alright?"

"She is not telling you where we are, Thomas. If you ask again, I'll hang up," Nikko butted in.

It was obvious they were on speaker so he would have to be more careful. "At least let her tell me she's alright," Thomas said. Nikko nodded to her.

"I am. I just wanted to say goodbye. I'm trying to get your brother to let us meet up before we leave to say goodbye in person. We could have one last meal together and eat your favorite cuisine. You always said it was never the same when we ate it in New York." She glanced at Nikko who was still listening intently.

"Che ne dici, Nikko?" Thomas asked. "Can we meet up for a last meal. I'd come alone."

"I'll have to think about it." Nikko could hear the faint whoosh, whoosh, sound of the helicopter, so he hurried her.

"Finish saying goodbye, Sophie."

"Goodbye, Thomas. Promise me you'll come see us on the yacht." Nikko hung up the phone and unloaded their items from the SUV in preparation for their helicopter ride.

The men finally arrived at the barn, jumped from their vehicle, and threw open the giant doors. There was Nikko's SUV, but Nikko and Sophie were nowhere to be found. They split up and searched outside hoping to find them somewhere, but to no avail.

"Rodriguez.," Houston called out "look at this!"

All the men ran over to a patch of grass where he was standing about 25 yards behind the barn. "This is clearly the rotor wash pattern from a helicopter landing," Houston informed them.

"Nikko called in a helicopter," Thomas was thinking out loud as they walked back to the barn. Houston and Fons searched the SUV.

"He hadn't decided on the helicopter right away because he changed the tire when he got here," Houston observed.

"Now where do we go from here?" Thomas asked more to himself than to anyone else.

Rodriguez turned to Thomas. "What cuisine is it Sophie was referring to? Maybe she was trying to give you a clue."

Thomas thought for a few moments, and replied, "We all went to the grand opening of a new Cajun restaurant in New York, but I complained because it was nothing like the food you can get in..."

"New Orleans!" Houston said aloud, overlapping Thomas' response.

"Their picking up the yacht in New Orleans!" Thomas shouted. "Franco, call Kenny and have him send a helicopter to these coordinates. We know where they are heading."

Houston smiled. *Excellent job, princess.*

They all grabbed their gear and waited outside while Franco arranged for the vehicles to be picked up.

Nikko and Sophie landed at a helipad close to Lake Borgne shortly before 2:00 in the afternoon. They needed to be close to Chef Harbor Marina. Uncle Tony set them up in a five-star hotel that had all the amenities so that they didn't have to leave the common area. Their suite had two bedrooms, a small kitchen, a living room, and a balcony.

Nikko decided Sophie needed a nap before they went to eat. Sophie looked worn out from the stress of the day. He brought her things to her room, disconnected the phone cord, and went out onto the balcony. She dropped down on the bed and started thinking. *I hope you caught my clue, Thomas. Oh, Lord, please give me a way out. Give me the right words so Nikko turns his life to you.* Then she fell asleep.

The men knew they were over two hours behind, but at least they had a definite destination for once—New Orleans. Franco was creating a list of all the marinas in the area. They would have to check them all.

"Franco, when we get in town, use that list to contact all the marinas and offer a reward for anyone who will contact us if any large yacht docks in the next 24 hours. Make sure the Dock Master passes it on to whoever relieves him."

"That's a good idea, sir."

Sophie woke up a few hours later. She couldn't shake the morose mood she was in. She knew she had to figure out how to get away from Nikko before he got her on that yacht, but he was so careful. She was never far enough away from him, without being cuffed to something, to make a run for it.

Nikko came into her room and saw she was awake. "Are you ready for an early dinner, sweetheart?"

"Sure, Nikko. Just let me change and clean up."

They went down to the restaurant in the hotel and were seated immediately. The normal dinner crowd probably didn't come until 7 or 8 pm. The maître d' that seated them had given them menus. The bus boy brought them water and offered them drinks. Nikko asked for a beer and ordered Sophie an iced tea.

She looked over the menu. There was a lot of fresh seafood. She was craving some lobster and steak, maybe with a house salad. The waiter came around to take their order.

Nikko spoke up. "The lady will have the seafood platter and clam chowder."

Sophie stopped him. "No, I want the lobster and rib eye with a house salad and French dressing."

Nikko was taken back by her assertiveness. He glared at Sophie while continuing to speak to the waiter. "As I was saying, she will have the seafood platter and clam chowder, and I will have the lobster tail and crab stuffed chicken."

The waiter was stuttering and visibly uncomfortable. He wasn't sure what to write down. Nikko looked at him. "That will be everything."

Nikko waited for the young man to leave, then, in a low whisper that spoke volumes, said, "don't ever embarrass me like that again!"

"You know what, Nikko, I don't care!" she quietly spat back. "I'm sick of you trying to control everything. I'm sick of it!" She spoke the last words a little too loudly and glanced around to see if anyone was looking at them.

"What is wrong with you?" He was genuinely disturbed by her behavior.

"What's wrong with me? You're forcing me to leave the country, you won't let me see the few people I consider friends, before I leave and now you won't even let me eat what I want."

"Calm down." Nikko gave her a stern look.

"How about you eat both meals since you ordered what you wanted, and I'll get something from the snack machine?"

Nikko let out a long sigh and waved for the waiter. "Give her whatever she wants. Go ahead, Sophie." She gave the waiter her order again.

Sophie didn't speak, and when the salad came, she ate very little of it. She was starting to get scared. There were only a few

304

hours until the yacht would be here, and she still didn't have an inkling of a plan to escape his grasp. The dinner entrée came, but she just pushed the food around.

"Sophie, quit moving your food around and eat. You made a scene about getting what you wanted, now you better eat it all!" She threw the cloth napkin on her plate and stood to leave.

Nikko grabbed her arm as she started past him. "Don't you *dare* move until I pay for our meals."

Dangerous Obsession

CHAPTER TWENTY-FIVE

Sophie had pushed him as far as she dared. He motioned to the waiter and settled the bill. Taking hold of her upper arm, he escorted her out of the restaurant and into the elevator. He was gripping her arm with no regard to how much it hurt her, and it hurt her a lot. She had no doubt there would be five large deep bruises there soon. He didn't loosen the grip on her arm until he shoved her into the suite.

"Now, you wan'na tell me what that little tantrum was all about?"

"You know very well. You just don't listen!" She walked out to the porch and sat on the padded chair. He followed her out. His voice turned placid, and he sat in front of her taking her hands into his own.

"Give me a chance, Sophie. When we get out of here, you will see what a great life I have planned for us. Just give me a little time. I've been thinking about what you said. I am tired of this criminal life. I want peace, and I want a family. Opening a restaurant would make me very happy."

"And I'm excited for you to live that life, but I don't want to live it with you." She tried to say it with as much compassion as she could.

He got up. "I'm not ready to let you go, Sophie."

She was losing all hope of escaping. She needed to do something. "If I agree to go with you, will you promise me, and I mean *promise* me, that you will not make me marry you until I'm ready, *if* that day ever comes? That also means you don't touch me until then, and if I'm not happy, you must swear to let me come home."

Nikko sat back down and took her hands once more. "How long, Sophie? How long are you going to string me along like this?"

Sophie got up. "String *you* along? You're the one who kidnapped me."

Nikko stood and faced her. "That might be true, but you have been toying with me ever since you came back to New York."

"That's a lie. I have tried to be as honest with you as I could."

"Yes, and then you would hold my hand and talk to me about the restaurant. You've been playing with me, Sophie! Don't deny it!" He blurted out.

"Nikko, I really do care about you. I was honest when I said I want to make it to Heaven and that I wanted to see you there too. But you want things from me, that I don't have in me to give you," she responded.

"That's why I need time. If you just give me time, Sophie, I know you'll feel the same way about me." He was pleading with her, almost begging her now.

"Not without those conditions." It was her only hope. He sat down and thought about it.

"I can promise not to force you to marry me and not to touch you until you're ready, but I'm not sure that I can swear to let you leave. The more I spend time with you, the more I know I can't live without you. Do you think I would tolerate any other woman treating me the way you do? I know I'm asking a lot of you, but I want to give you the world, Sophie Star."

She knew that was true. She had done every conceivable thing to make him not want her, but he kept taking it.

"No, Nikko. You must swear to me, that if after six months I want to come home, you will bring me home. If I don't feel the same way for you that you do for me by then, there is no chance that I ever will, which means that there is no chance for us." Sophie didn't know how she could survive as a prisoner for six months, but she needed there to be some end in sight for her to maintain the strength to keep going.

Nikko stepped back, somewhat dejected but just as determined as ever. "I'll give you my answer in the morning."

"That's fair." She went to sit back down. He sat beside her and put his arm around her.

"Sophie, you are so much work." They sat there for about an hour, relatively quiet. Then she broke the silence.

"I'm hungry."

Nikko laughed. "I'll order from room service. I don't want another scene. Tell me what you'd like to eat. I'm not paying for three meals again."

Sophie turned her face to him. "I'd actually like the seafood platter and clam chowder." He looked at her with an amused expression.

"You are incorrigible." He went to put in the order.

Thomas and the other men had been in town for hours, going from marina to marina. Not all marinas could dock a large yacht that could travel long distances without refueling. They had made the calls earlier to the Marina Managers on duty, but they couldn't be sure the information was being passed on from shift to shift. They pulled into the Chef Harbor Marina. Houston got out to talk to the Dock Master.

"Good evening, sir. I'm trying to locate a yacht that is supposed to be here in the morning. Do the captains of private yachts generally give you notice of their arrival times?"

"The well trained ones do. Are you the one who called my Marina Manager asking the same question?"

"Yes." He pointed to Thomas standing outside the SUV. "He's supposed to meet his brother, but he lost contact with him."

The Dock Master looked through his logs. "It looks like we got a call yesterday from a Swiss vessel that wanted to know if our waters and dock could take their size. We told them we are fully capable of handling them. They're set to dock between 8 and 10 am in slip 6. That one is for short stays. They plan on leaving by 11 am."

"Thank you so much. I will have Franco come and give you what he promised."

"I'm a Dock Master. I don't take money for doing my job except from my employer," he said, insulted.

"I didn't mean to offend you, sir. I can see you're a man of integrity. Thank you." He rushed out to tell the others.

"Thomas, this has to be the place. There is a Swiss yacht coming in between 8 and 10 am tomorrow." He repeated aloud everything that the Dock Master had told him. He didn't know if reception was good inside the Dock master's office, and he needed to be sure that Agent Hampton and the command center caught all the details. Besides, knowing Hampton, he would have wanted all the details repeated twice for accuracy.

"Now we have a place and a time. Let's find a room and get a plan," Thomas replied. They loaded into the SUV and headed to locate the nearest hotel.

Sophie took their plates back to the rolling cart and set it outside the door, then went back to the balcony.

"Thanks for dinner, Nikko."

"We'll have to be ready at 8:30 in the morning. Uncle Tony is going to text me the captain's phone number once he docks.

"I love sitting outside listening to the sounds of life during the day and watching the stars at night—just taking in the sights and smells of the ocean," she said randomly.

"Then you'll love it on the yacht, Sophie. Since there are no city lights or noises, the stars are so much brighter, and the sounds of the ocean are relaxing." He was still trying to make the idea appealing to her.

"I'm sure your right, Nikko." They sat out there for a few hours, not saying much, just listening to the city. They finally went to bed at 11 pm. Nikko cuffed her to her bed over her objection, but unless he slept in front of the door there would be no way to keep an eye on her and he was tired and wanted to sleep.

The men were at the table in Thomas' room with a satellite image of the marina opened on Franco's laptop.

"I'll wait until they're on the dock to approach him, and I need to go alone so he doesn't get spooked," Thomas instructed.

"Rodriguez and I can take cover over here." Houston was pointing to a maintenance shed that was right next to the dock.

"I'll be over here," Franco suggested, pointing to some bushes, off to the left.

Thomas leveled his gaze at the men, particularly Houston and Fons. "Under no circumstances is anyone to hinder Nikko from leaving. We are here only to make sure Sophie is not forced to go against her will. And if anyone of you kills my brother, *I will kill you*. Is that perfectly clear?"

"I will defend myself, Rodriguez, and Ms. Star if I have to, Mr. Morano," Houston fired back, failing to flinch at Thomas' threat.

Thomas stood his ground and reiterated, "I'm just letting you know that if you kill him, then I will kill you." They ended their discussion. Houston and Rodriguez went to their room.

"Fons, I'm going to find a phone and talk to Agent Hampton. We are going to need comms to keep informed of what the task force is doing." Houston headed out the door.

"Tell them they better stay out of sight until we have Sophie. And they can't contact the coast guard until we give the word, either, because this could end up being an alphabet soup disaster," Rodriguez added.

Agent Hampton was waiting for his call. "You heard sir?" Houston inquired.

"Yes. Agent Rodriguez is right about the alphabet soup. If SWAT gets called in, they will try to take over since we're in their jurisdiction. Then add NOPD to the mix. We're a special task force out of our jurisdiction, so we can't override their authority," Agent Hampton said.

"Sir, you can't let anyone get shot. Ms. Star is already carrying so much guilt about all of this. She would jump in front of a bullet to save either one of those brothers." Houston was worried things would get out of hand tomorrow.

"I'm sending Agent Timms over with the comms you asked for. Wait there at the gas station. We will all be in civilian clothes nearby in case you have trouble getting her back. Don't worry about Nikko. If he leaves on the boat, the Coast Guard will pick him up," Agent Hampton instructed him.

"Sir, I just don't see him giving her up. He may pull a gun. He has made a number of statements that lead me to believe that he wouldn't hesitate to kill her," Houston said.

"That is a legitimate concern, Houston. We will have a sniper in position and ready to act if it looks like things are going that way."

"Alright, sir. I better get back." Houston hung up and waited at the gas station until Agent Timms pulled up. "Houston, are you alright?"

"Yeah, but this has been brutal. I am scared for her, Timms," he said in a somber voice.

"One thing I've learned about Ms. Star—she is a critical thinker. If anyone can make it out of this, it will be her." Agent Timms was trying to encourage Houston. "Anyone who could get you and Rodriguez in a monkey suit, I'll bet on any day." They both smiled. Apparently, word about the ballet had already spread through the office.

Monday

"I ordered breakfast. It's out on the balcony, Sophie." Nikko told her as he uncuffed her. "I just got the text from my uncle. The yacht is running on schedule."

Sophie got dressed and went out to the balcony. She had spent most of the night praying. She sat down and ate her scrambled eggs, toast, and a slice of bacon.

"Nikko, there's no more time. What is your decision?" He knew what she was asking. He came close to her and sat down.

"I will keep my promises on the first two, but I just can't promise to let you leave if you don't want to stay," he said softly.

Sophie got up and went to her room. Ten minutes later, she came back out. Her hair was in a ponytail, and she had taken off her make up so her blackened eye and bruised cheek were showing. She also was wearing a sleeveless top that showed five very large dark bruises from last night among other slightly fading bruises.

"What on earth, Sophie? Get back in there and change," he said, fuming.

Sophie's eyes were piercing his with their ferocity. "No. if you can't make that promise to me then you are going to face what you have done to me. You need to see why I hesitate to marry you!" Sophie screamed at him.

Nikko came at her with his fist raised but stopped short when he saw her brace herself for impact. He suddenly saw Sophie like he had never seen her before. But in those fiery eyes, he also saw a reflection of himself and what he had truly become. Her hands were raised and ready to protect herself from his impending strike. Here was this little woman standing her ground to a man twice her size. How cowardly could he be? He dropped his fist and sank into a chair nearby with his face in his hands.

"Sophie, you are tearing me apart piece by piece. I want to be a better man for you, but I can't overcome these urges. You've made me a shell of a man."

"You are ten times the man you were before in my sight because now you see your own need to control yourself, and you did. None of us can be anything good without Christ. He is the one who gives us power to overcome our flesh. All you have to do is ask for forgiveness and let him take over your life, Nikko." She went to him and took his hands down from his face.

"I'll promise whatever you want, Sophie," Nikko said. She went back to her room, changed back into what she had been wearing, and put her makeup back on.

The task force was in place by 8 am. They wanted to be as inconspicuous as possible, so they were spread out. They all had comms to communicate and hear what was going on.

Houston and the other men were at breakfast with Thomas. He said he didn't want Nikko to see him until he got on the dock.

They decided that after breakfast they were going to wait in their car somewhere out of sight.

Back at Nikko's hotel room, someone knocked on the door. "I'll get that, Sophie." Nikko let the bell-hop in. The bell-hop gathered the suitcases and put them on the rolling cart.

"Please have a taxi waiting for us and load the suitcases." Nikko handed him a fifty-dollar bill.

"Thank you, Mr. Marko." After he closed the door, he turned to Sophie.

"Are you ready?" She didn't answer but simply headed toward the door. He gently took her upper arm, and they headed out of the hotel to the waiting taxi.

"How far is it to the Chef Harbor Marina?" He asked the driver.

"About ten minutes away, sir." Nikko called the captain and asked for the cabin boy to come for their luggage at the taxi drop off in about 10 minutes.

Thomas saw the taxi pull up, and the cabin boy grabbed the bags and headed to the yacht. Nikko got out of the taxi, paid the man, and went around to help Sophie out. He saw that he had her by the arm to keep her under his control.

"Let's go," Thomas said. "Just don't let him see you." When Houston and Rodriguez were in position and sure neither Thomas nor Franco could see them, they put in their comms.

Houston spoke quietly to command. "We have our comms in and are in place, command."

He heard two cracks which meant his message was heard. It had been almost a week since he had seen Sophie other than their brief run in at the Pancake House yesterday. He just wanted to run to her and take her away from all this, but that was too dangerous.

Nikko and Sophie were only a few feet onto the wharf toward the yacht when Thomas called out. "Nikko."

Nikko turned and saw Thomas stepping off the boardwalk and onto the pier about four feet behind him.

"What are you doing here, Thomas?"

"I've come to get Sophie, Nikko. I told you I wouldn't let you take her."

Thomas was trying to stay calm. Sophie was standing just ahead of Nikko, who still had his hand around her arm. Nikko turned back to the yacht and started walking. "Go home, Thomas," he shouted over his shoulder. "This isn't your business." Thomas caught up to him and grabbed his shoulder to turn him around.

"You *are* my business, Nikko. If you take her out of the country, the FBI will hound us and tear through all our businesses looking for evidence. You're going to leave the entire family behind to take the fall for *your* drug empire. That is *very much* my business, fratello."

Nikko looked him in the eye. "I can't leave her. I won't do it. We have made an agreement. If she's still doesn't want to be with me in six months, I'll let her go."

"Listen to yourself, Nikko. This is not normal. Men don't kidnap women they supposedly love. They let them choose what's best for themselves." Thomas was pleading with him.

"Sophie's confused right now. She doesn't know what's best for her—I do." There was a commotion behind Thomas. He turned to see police vehicles and a SWAT team pulling into the marina parking lot.

"You called the police on your brother, Thomas?!"

"No, Certo che no! Someone must have recognized you from the news. You have to go before they stop you, Nikko. Just leave her and go. I'll take care of her until you're safe somewhere. Then you can send for her." He looked at Sophie, who echoed his pleas.

"Please Nikko, go. If you leave me, they will look for you for a while but then they'll go on to someone else. If I'm with you, they won't stop looking."

His face was unmoving. "We had a deal, Sophie. Come on." Nikko continued to drag her toward the gangplank of the boat.

Houston was talking into his comm. "Command, you have to do something to stop the SWAT team. They don't know what's going on, and they're going to blow the whole operation or worse, get someone killed!"

Agent Hampton located the SWAT team leader. He held out his left hand to present his badge, and he held out his right hand for a courteous handshake.

"Agent Troy Hampton, New York Drug Enforcement Agency. I need to speak with whoever is in charge, stat."

The man in front of him shook Hampton's hand. "Agent Hampton, I'm Lt. Samuels with the NOPD Tactical Operations division. Several calls came into 911 about the kidnapper, Mr. Morano. His picture has been all over the news. But when we called your office to let you know, they said nothing about having men on the ground."

"So, you've heard about the raids on Mr. Morano's drug network?"

"Absolutely," the Lieutenant confirmed.

"Well, that was done by our joint task force. Mr. Morano jumped bail and kidnapped that young woman. We have been tracking him across the country. I should have contacted you last night to let you know we were in town. I apologize for that break in protocol, but we were trying to keep a low profile. Right now, I have several undercover agents out here in the fray. We need

317

to protect their cover, and we need to capture Nikko Morano alive and unharmed," Agent Hampton continued.

The lieutenant folded his arms over his chest. "I can let you take lead here, but I have a sniper posted and ready. If it looks like the hostage's life is in jeopardy, you understand we can't just stand by and do nothing. We have jurisdiction which means we also bear the responsibility if things go badly." Hampton thanked the man, gritting his teeth because he knew that he was right.

CHAPTER TWENTY-SIX

When Nikko spotted the officers massing in the parking lot, he immediately panicked and pulled his gun. "Nikko put that away, you'll get us all killed!" Thomas shouted to him.

"I'm not going to jail, Thomas."

"We have the best attorneys in the country. You need to cut your losses and trust them to do their job. You're out in plain sight now for the whole world to see. Do you really think that this will end well if you try to get on that boat? Don't let mama find out about this on the nightly news, Nikko. Let me help you." Thomas stepped up to take Sophie away from him. This startled Nikko who then raised his gun and leveled it at his brother.

"Stay back, Thomas."

"You won't shoot me, Nikko. I'm your brother!" He kept coming forward slowly until Thomas was standing right next to Sophie and Nikko. "Let her go, *ora.*"

Nikko was like a rat trapped in a cage. Letting go of Sophie for a moment, he punched Thomas and started running toward the yacht, grabbing Sophie's arm. Thomas caught up to him, turned him around and they started struggling. Nikko let go of her so he could handle Thomas. She started to run, but Nikko saw her, pushed his brother away, and raised the gun. "Sophie, stop." He shot the gun at the ground by her feet. She stopped dead in her tracks and turned around.

"Come back here!" Nikko yelled. Sophie started walking back slowly.

Houston had started to run to get her when she was free, but then Nikko shot his gun and he knew he couldn't reach her in time, so he stopped. The situation was becoming extremely volatile. Nearby, he overheard the SWAT team leader tell his sniper, "if you have a shot, take it. He's escalating."

Houston turned and hollered at Agent Hampton, "Sir, please! Stop them! She's too close!"

"I'm sorry, Agent Townsend — It's out of our hands now," he replied.

Thomas was still in the line of fire, as well. "Nikko put that down. They don't know that you won't really shoot us." Thomas was afraid his brother would end up dead. He lurched forward to tackle Nikko when a single shot rang out. Thomas fell to the ground.

Sophie screamed. "NO! DON'T SHOOT!" Nikko ran to Thomas, knelt by him, turned him over, and checked his pulse.

"They shot Thomas! I'll kill them!" He got up and was going to start firing toward the boardwalk, but he found Sophie directly in front of him, attempting to shield him from the sniper while she tried to calm him down. She could see Thomas was shot in the shoulder, but he was not dead.

"He's just shot in the shoulder, Nikko. He will be fine, but we still need to get him help. Put down your weapon so they don't shoot you."

Houston was watching his worst nightmare play out. He knew she would protect Nikko with her own life. The man who had almost beat her to death, who invaded her home with hidden cameras, who kidnapped her and still she was willing to give her life for his.

Lord, Houston prayed silently, *this is her living out your command to love our enemies and pray for those who persecute us.*

Protect her, Lord, and give me the faith that she has. He didn't dare make himself visible because if Nikko saw him, it would only agitate the situation. Franco had tried to get to Thomas where he lay on the pier, but one of the officers held him back.

A bullhorn blared, "This is the New Orleans Tactical Operations Team. Mr. Morano drop the gun and get down on your knees. You have one minute to comply, or we will have no choice but to use lethal force." Sophie turned to him, still blocking the view of any sniper.

"Nikko, please. We have to get Thomas help. There is no way we can outrun them. The Coast Guard will stop any attempt for us to leave. I care about you, and I can't stand to see you get hurt." He looked down at Thomas, and saw his brother needed help.

"Alright, Sophie, we'll do it your way." She turned to start walking side-by-side with him to the boardwalk when she suddenly realized that Nikko hadn't dropped his weapon yet.

"Nikko, throw down the..." A second shot rang out and stole the sound from the air around her head. She heard the unmistakable sound of a whizzing bullet making contact with a soft target. *Thud.* She turned around just in time to see Nikko being thrown backwards by a high velocity rifle round. "WHY!?" She knew she was screaming, but she couldn't hear herself. After a few moments, the air seemed to *whoosh* back into her ears.

"He was surrendering!" she screamed as she sunk to her knees and held his pallid face in her hands, laying his head on her lap. Houston was running to their side despite Agent Hampton's orders for him to stand down.

"Sophie," Nikko was struggling to talk, "is everything you told me about Jesus, true?"

"Yes, Nikko. He is the Son of God who died for our sins," Sophie said between her sobs.

"I believe it. What do I have to do?" His breathing was labored.

"All you have to do is repent and you will spend eternity with him in Heaven."

Nikko started praying out loud. "Lord, I am so unworthy of your forgiveness, but I believe you are the Son of God and that you died for me. Forgive me and all the terrible things I've done." Tears were running down his cheeks. "Cover all my sins with your blood and come into my heart. What else Sophie?" She could barely hear him now. She wiped the blood from the corners of his mouth.

"Nothing, Nikko. All you had to do was ask." She could tell he was almost gone. Houston reached her side prepared to pull her to safety, but when he heard Nikko praying, he stood back to give him time. The man's life was already lost, but now his soul was at stake.

SWAT team members and medics were approaching fast. Houston turned toward them and yelled, "hurry! We're losing him!"

Nikko feebly raised his hand to the sky as if reaching for something that only he could see. He tilted his gaze to Sophie and with his last breath said, "thank you." Nikko smiled and closed his eyes for the last time, under the hot Louisiana sun.

The medics finally reached them. Half rushed to Nikko and half to Thomas. While they were tending Thomas' wounds, she crawled over to him, but they wouldn't let her get near. Sophie was still sobbing; she had no strength left in her to stand. Houston cupped her shoulders and helped her get on her feet. Her knees were buckling—she couldn't stand on her own. Fons was there with them, helping walk her to an ambulance. Franco stayed with Thomas.

Agent Hamilton came to them. "Houston, you, and Rodriguez stay with her. Keep your covers intact. No one can know you two were a part of my team. I have no doubt Thomas would put a bounty on your heads."

"Yes, sir." Rodriguez answered for both.

"And Ms. Star, I'm so sorry it ended this way." She looked at him blankly but couldn't muster an answer. They got her in the ambulance and took her away.

At the hospital, Houston stayed with her in the emergency room, and Rodriguez waited outside for the ambulance with Thomas in it. One of the doctors came to see if she had any cuts or contusions, but he got called away when Thomas' ambulance came. They were in that little room for a couple of hours. Agent Hampton requested the emergency room doctor keep her overnight just to be safe, so she was taken to a room on the third floor.

Fons came in to keep Houston updated on Thomas' condition. "They took him into surgery to get the bullet out and repair the damage it caused. They expect him to fully recover after some rehab. Agent Hampton is on his way to talk with you."

Sophie had just been lying on the bed quietly crying since she had gotten to the hospital. They waited for Agent Hampton. Houston turned when the door opened. "Sir, what happened?"

"The sniper had a bead on Nikko and an order to fire. When Thomas made the move to rush him and get Sophie away, he got in the way of the bullet. Sophie had kept her body in front of Nikko so he couldn't shoot again, but with the 'fire at will' order still out there, the SWAT team sniper shot the minute she was out of the way. He had no idea Nikko was surrendering. With the erratic way Nikko was wielding that gun, he couldn't take any chances. He was just doing what any of us would do." Agent Hampton sympathized.

Houston nodded. "That's true sir, but what happens now?"

"Well, I know there will be an extensive investigation on all of our actions because the Morano family's attorneys have already called the DOJ wanting answers. They're threatening unlawful death lawsuits and anything else they can think of." He turned to Sophie who was only half listening.

"We will need your statement about the kidnapping."

She barely lifted her voice loud enough to be heard. "Nikko has already paid the ultimate price for his sins. I won't crucify him in the press. I will have no statement for you."

Agent Hampton was shocked. "That will put us in a tough spot considering that kidnapping you was part and parcel to his death, Ms. Star."

"He was also a fugitive who was walking toward police with a gun in his hand. I'm sure you will be able to make your case, Agent Hampton," Sophie was done talking.

"What are the team's orders, sir?"

"I'm sending everyone back to New York tonight. With the scrutiny on this case, I need all incident reports and verbal debriefing finished immediately so we can piece the events together. Reports from you and Rodriguez will stay confidential, but I still need them immediately. Since she refuses to make a statement, your reports will have to explain our actions."

"They release her tomorrow. I want to stay with her and escort her back safely," Houston requested.

"We're boarding a flight back to New York tonight. We'll get you on a commercial flight tomorrow, but I need at least one of you back in the home office ASAP. So, you decide who stays and who goes home. We still have a lot of clean up here before we leave."

"Sir, I don't want to fly her economy class in her condition. I'll pay for the upgrade to first class," Houston offered.

"Considering what Ms. Star has been through, I agree. I'll put in for first class tickets." Agent Hampton looked over at her.

He shook hands with the men, said goodbye to Sophie, and left the hospital for a long night of answering questions.

Fons offered to sit with Sophie so Houston could take a break, but he refused. He said he would come back with some food and coffee.

After everyone left the room, Sophie closed her eyes and slept. Houston sat by her, holding her hand in his good one, while a nurse changed the dressing on the other hand and strapped his sling across his chest again. When she whimpered in her sleep, he would kiss the palm of her hand or stroke her hair, shushing her fears away.

In the emergency room the nurse had noticed Sophie's tears had smeared the mascara all over her face, so she took some time to clean her up. Lying in front of him now, Houston could see the black and blue on her eye and cheek. The hospital gown revealed the five large bruises on her arm, and the bruises on her wrist were obviously from being cuffed. He'd seen that before when people would struggle trying to get out of their restraints. He had no idea what she had really been through, but he had no intention of letting her go through the aftermath alone. He prayed that she wouldn't shut him out. He wanted to help her heal, but most people's first instinct was to shut down.

Houston ate what Fons brought him. There was no question which one of them was staying, but he offered once more to give Houston a break before he left with the team. Houston refused to leave.

Tuesday

Sophie woke up with a start a few times throughout the night, but he stroked her hair and told her she was safe with him. In his heart, though, he wondered if that was true. He was the one who was supposed to protect her, and he failed. Nikko got to her, and it was his fault.

In the morning, the doctor released her. Her suitcases had been brought up to her room during the night. The yacht had been searched and released, but her and Nikko's items were taken off first. She got into a pair of tan slacks and a cotton button down shirt. She had her purse and a light jacket with her. Houston asked the officer that was driving them to the airport to take her suitcases and his bag to the SUV.

"I'm not leaving until I see that Thomas is alright. I want to talk to him," Sophie insisted.

"He's in ICU, but I'll see what I can do."

Houston headed off to find someone who would let her see Thomas. After about ten minutes, he came back and took her to him. She saw him hooked up to machines and bandaged up.

"Oh, Thomas. I'm so sorry you were hurt like this." She went to his side and took his good hand.

"What are *you* doing here, Sophie?" Thomas said sharply. She was stunned by his gruff tone.

"I came to make sure you're alright. I know they are transferring you to a hospital back home today so your own doctors can take care of you," she replied softly.

"I don't want you here." He yanked his hand away.

Sophie was thrown by his comment. "Thomas?"

"This is all your fault. Why did you come back, Sophie? You're toxic to everyone who loves you."

"I don't understand...," her voice quivered.

"If you had never come back, none of this would have happened and Nikko would still be alive. You were away from him, safe. You didn't have to come back. How do I tell my mother that her firstborn son is dead and all over a woman? It will absolutely kill her."

"Thomas, no. You can't really think that. You know I never wanted Nikko to die. I tried to get him to let me go and to leave on the yacht by himself," she pleaded.

"You led him on, Sophie, and you know it."

"No. I told him over and over I didn't want to go with him. I didn't want to marry him. But once he decided to kill me if he couldn't have me, I had to change my approach. I was just trying to stay alive."

Houston stepped in. "Thomas, I won't let you do this to her. You know very well what she was dealing with. Nikko was obsessed with her, even delusional sometimes. You can't blame her for this."

"My brother is dead, and if she hadn't come back for..." Thomas trailed off and looked at Sophie for a long moment. "What *did* you come back for, Sophie? You never answered me. Was it revenge? You wanted him dead for what he did to you. But all he wanted was for you to love him."

"Thomas, you don't actually believe that." She tried to reason with him.

"You can try to whitewash it any way you want, but he's stretched out in the morgue downstairs and here you are alive." Thomas' heart rate was going up and the machine was beeping. "Houston get her out of here. I don't want to see her face again." Sophie tried to speak, but he screamed this time, "Get out of here!"

Houston lifted her from the chair and walked her out, as the nurses were rushing in to check on Thomas. Houston practically carried her to the nearest place to sit down.

Sophie was sobbing. "I didn't want him dead. You know that, Houston. I would have taken the bullet if I could have."

"I saw you protecting him, Sophie. You didn't want anyone to die. Thomas is just grieving. He'll come to his senses eventually," Houston said, trying to comfort her.

But Sophie was not as hopeful as he was. "I don't think he'll change his mind. He loved Nikko so much. He always looked past Nikko's flaws—he only saw his brother. And he's right, Houston. I did get him killed. Why did I come back? What was this all for?"

Houston tried to talk to her, but she was shutting him out. She didn't speak again until she got on the plane.

"I should have never come back," she said. Houston's heart was crushed. If she hadn't come back, he would have never met her. He hoped she didn't really regret *everything* about returning to New York.

"You needed to take down Nikko's network. Look at all the good that's been done."

"Good? Good for who, Houston? Some other king pin will only come and take his place. What was the point? How pure were my motives? Honestly, looking back on it now, the whole thing feels very selfish of me."

Houston turned to her in his seat and made her look at him. In his most tenacious and righteous voice, he said, "You need to try to put this in perspective. If law enforcement felt that way, that their actions are completely pointless, then they wouldn't bother arresting criminals at all. We do it because it's the right thing to do—we do it because it is just. The results are in God's hands, and remember, God knows all the days of a man's life and He wants everyone to come to him—that's his ultimate goal. Everything else that happens is to promote that end. Your goal was to undo some of the hurt you brought the world by helping the Morano family build their empire and to get Nikko to a place where he could receive Christ. In that light, I'd say that your mission was a success. He's in Heaven now because you obeyed the Lord. Do you think anyone else on this planet could have accomplished that with Nikko?" Houston took a breath. "If Jesus went through, being crucified for our salvation, don't you think he would use *these* circumstances to that end?"

Sophie looked at him like a lightbulb had just gone off in her head. "You think God ordered all of this so Nikko could get saved?"

"I think God uses whatever happens by our free will and choice and works it out to allow someone the opportunity to hear about him and be saved. If Nikko had not chosen to repent, it would have been on him. But God was giving him an opportunity because He knew Nikko's life was coming to an end shortly. Our days are numbered. Our God knows everything, and you were willing to be used by Him, even though it cost you dearly, to ensure that Nikko could have a chance at eternal life."

"Wow, Houston. You don't know how much that helps me, but the things Thomas said to me...I don't know how I will get over that. God may have used me, but were my motives pure?"

"The fact that you would worry about it says that your heart is in the right place," Houston answered.

Sophie was quiet for a few minutes after that, which Houston knew meant she was still pondering on all that happened. Finally, she spoke up. "Thomas was right about one thing, Houston. I am toxic to everyone who loves me." She put her hand on his cheek. "Look at you. Your handsome face is all cut." Her touch melted his heart. She looked down at his wounded hands. "Your hands were crushed because you loved me. Thomas was shot because he loved me and wanted to protect me, and Nikko is dead for loving me." She was trying to convince herself he was better off without her.

"That's simply not true. All my injuries will heal, but those things happened because of Nikko's actions, Nikko's choices, not yours Sophie. Please don't shut me out." He could feel what was coming.

"I've made a decision. I'm leaving after I get some things taken care of in New York," she said with seemingly little emotion.

"Sophie, please don't shut me out of your life. Let me come with you." He was desperate.

"No."

"At least tell me where you're going," he was trying to get any morsel from her.

"No, but I'll be back to take care of you when you have the second surgery on your hand. You'll need help for a while."

Houston was going to try to stop her, convince her not to go, guilt her into staying, but he heard in his spirit—*let her go*. His mind was battling the thought and trying to convince himself it wasn't from God, but he knew better. It would be the hardest thing he ever did, but he would obey God. How could he not? To disobey God would make him unworthy of her anyway. They didn't talk again until the plane landed.

CHAPTER TWENTY-SEVEN

Sophie insisted on helping bring the luggage up so Houston wouldn't have to make more than one trip. He still had one hand strapped to his chest, making packing things difficult. When they got to the condo, she went directly out to the balcony, grabbed one of the couch pillows and laid down her head. Houston put her things in her room and came out to talk to her.

"I'll pack Fons' and my things and take them with me tonight. I'll stay until about 11:00, but since the operation is over and everyone knows I'm in love with you, I don't want to damage your reputation by staying here. Although I think you genuinely need someone watching over you right now."

Sophie heard but didn't respond, so he continued.

"I'll give you back your key, but I want to do wellness checks on you during the day, bring you dinner, and take care of you in the evenings until you leave. Will you promise to open the door for me, Sophie?"

She looked up at him. "Keep the key for now," she said softly.

Houston knew she wanted to be alone, so he went inside and packed up his things. It was dark outside, and he knew she hadn't eaten because she refused her food on the plane, so he reheated some of the Chinese takeout he had ordered. He had checked the refrigerator but everything in it was spoiled. They had been gone over a week now, and since the new locks had been installed, they hadn't given a key to the housecleaners.

Houston brought a plate out to her. She sat up and played with the food but didn't eat more than a bite or two. Finally, she stood up and spoke. "Thank you for dinner, Houston, but I'm tired and I'm going to bed."

"Good night, Sophie. I'll make sure everything is locked up when I leave." Houston had called the condo manager before they left New Orleans and asked him to supervise a repairman to come and fix the damaged balcony door.

Houston watched her go inside. He picked up their plates, took them in, and washed the dishes. Then he cleaned out the refrigerator, determined that tomorrow he would bring some fresh food that he could prepare for her. He took the garbage out then came back to haul out Fons' and his things. When he returned, he prayed for her until he left.

Wednesday

In the morning, Houston stopped by Sophie's as he was heading into work. Agent Hampton was pressuring the men to get their briefings done. He had quite a few reports to fill out.

He knocked but no one answered. He put his ear to the door but didn't hear any sound inside. He knocked again, hesitant to use the key, but when she didn't answer, he went inside and looked for her. She was still in bed. It looked like she hadn't been up at all. He figured she was exhausted from the entire ordeal and decided to give her privacy for that entire day. He had left some fruit and muffins on the kitchen counter, along with a bag of Whoppers candies. If she woke up and was hungry, she would have something there to eat.

Thursday

The next day, when Houston returned, he found the apartment in the same condition as when he had last been there. When he opened the bedroom door and softly called her name, she stirred in her bed a little but did not respond, a pile of tear-soaked tissues next to her on the nightstand. None of the food had been touched, the shower had not been used, and she was wearing the same pajamas. Thoroughly worried that she might not be able to break out of this rut, he decided to make a call.

"Max, I need a favor."

"What can I do for you, Houston?" He responded.

"It's Sophie. She's in bad shape, and I'm worried. She blames herself for Nikko's death, and Thomas unloaded a heap of guilt on her about it. She's depressed—she won't eat, and she just lays down and either sleeps or cries. I was wondering if I could get Bully to bring her out of it. Is he working right now?"

"We just finished an assignment. I was going to take him camping for a few days, but Sophie is a higher priority," Max responded.

"I'm on my way to work. I'm going to come back here and bring her lunch, though I know she probably won't eat it. Can you bring him down to the office for me?"

"Sure. I'll be there by 1 pm."

"Thanks Max." Houston was hoping Bully could nudge her into getting out of bed.

"Houston, it's not a problem. You know how much we care for Sophie." They ended their conversation, and Houston checked on her one more time before he left. He decided to leave the donuts on the table in case she woke up.

Houston came back with Bully around 1:30 pm. He knocked on the door. No one answered, and he heard no movement, so he unlocked the door. He checked the box of donuts he had brought earlier in the day to see if she had eaten, but they were all there. He filled Bully's water dish and put it down in the kitchen next to some of his dog toys. He left the bag of dog food on the counter and decided to feed him when he came back later that evening. His hope was that Sophie would get up to take him for a potty break.

If she would just get up, get some fresh air, let some endorphins flood her brain, it would probably help her snap out of this depression. He slowly opened the bedroom door and saw her in the same spot as before. He knew she had to have gotten up to at least go to the bathroom, but he couldn't tell. She looked like she hadn't moved. He removed Bully from his leash, and the dog jumped on the bed and laid down with his head on her legs. Houston left the bedroom door ajar just a little in case Bully needed out of the room for water.

At work, he was useless. All he did was watch the clock. When he was in briefings, his eyes were facing whoever was speaking, but his mind was on Sophie. If she didn't snap out of it, he was going to get her help. He waited for his watch to hit 5 pm then headed to the store for some dinner groceries to take to her condo. He knocked on the door, but she didn't answer. He heard Bully come to the door and bark. He used his key again and put the groceries away, grabbed the leash, and took Bully for a walk to the dog park.

"Bully, you have to work your magic. Sophie needs to know you're there. Just nudge her a little and make her get up." Bully was looking at him as if he knew what he was saying. They got back to the condo, Houston fed Bully on the balcony, and let him roam around out there for a while. He made up a salad and a pitcher of iced tea and put it in the refrigerator. His plan was to open the curtains in her room and try to get her up to eat. He

334

went in and got some light in there, sat down next to her on her bed, and tried to wake her.

"Sophie, it's me Houston. You need to get up and eat. If you don't, I'm taking you to the hospital. Do you hear me?"

She stirred, opened her eyes, and told him she wasn't hungry and that she just wanted to sleep.

"Get up Sophie and eat, or I'm carrying you to the hospital."

Sophie sat up. "Give me a minute then I'll come."

Houston left her room and waited. She came out 15 minutes later. Her face had been washed, her hair was combed, and she had on a new pair of pajamas. He knew that was a big step. She sat down at the table where the salad and iced tea were waiting for her. She played with her food and ate a couple of bites but didn't have anything to say.

Sophie noticed Bully on the balcony and smiled. "When did he get here?"

"I brought him by this afternoon. He's been sleeping in bed next to you. You didn't notice him?"

"Oh. I thought I felt something heavy on my legs. Thank you for bringing him, but I'm tired now. I'm going back to bed."

"Sophie, please stay up for a while. Play with him and get some fresh air. It will help with this depression."

"I just don't have it in me, Houston."

"You do, princess. You're one of the strongest people I know."

"Sorry to disappoint you." She went back to her room.

Houston knew getting her up was progress. He stayed until 11:00 pm and just before he left, took Bully for another walk, and then led him back to her bedroom. He left the door open so the dog could come in and out if he wanted to. Before Bully went into her room, he grabbed one of his toys and then got up on her bed. Houston saw him nudge her arm with his nose, and she put her hand on his head.

Good boy, Bully. Keep it up. He left feeling the first bit of hope since they got home.

Friday

Friday morning, Houston came with another box of donuts. He was sitting outside the front door on the floor, trying to wait her out and make her get up and take Bully for a bathroom break. She was too soft hearted to not consider him even in her worst state. He'd been sitting there for an hour. *Maybe I better take her to the hospital,* he thought, when his plan wasn't working.

He got up ready to put his key in the door when he heard a noise inside. He ran to the stairwell so she wouldn't see him. He peeked out and there she was, her hair in a ponytail, in blue jeans and a pullover sweatshirt. She was taking him for a walk.

"Thank you, Lord," he whispered. After they got in the elevator, he went into her apartment and left the donuts. He would come back at noon with lunch.

Houston was running late that afternoon, so when he got there at 1:30, much to his surprise, she answered the door when he knocked.

"We're out on the balcony, Houston." She led the way.

"I brought some lunch. Want to eat out there?" He was hoping he wouldn't have to fight to get her to eat.

"Sure." Sophie grabbed some glasses and the iced tea. He kept the conversation light and didn't press when she stopped talking. She didn't eat more than half of her food, but it was progress.

Houston cleaned up the mess and told her, "I'll bring takeout tonight for dinner. What kind would you like?"

"How about Boston Market?" She answered him.

"Boston Market it is. I'll be here around seven. Can you do me a favor and walk Bully? I don't want him to have to wait that long." He knew he was pushing her, but he hoped she wouldn't notice.

"Sure," she replied. He gave her a peck on the forehead and left for work. He could see her coming out of this. *Lord, you're so good to us. Thank you.*

When Houston came back with dinner and set it up outside, Sophie hadn't come back from her walk yet, but he was early. She came in, took off Bully's leash, fed him, washed her hands, and went to the balcony with Houston.

"Houston, I want to thank you for being here for me through all this. I don't know if I could have come out of it on my own. God surely had mercy on me, but it's time for me to go. I'm leaving tomorrow afternoon."

Houston couldn't say anything. He was deeply hurt. He was hoping beyond hope she had changed her mind. What could he say? He couldn't stop her and be obedient to God at the same time. He had to let her go.

"Alright, Sophie. I'll pick up Bully in the morning." He gave in. They ate but had little conversation.

"I can give you a ride to the airport," he offered.

"Thank you, but I have a town car coming. I'll be back for your surgery. It's a week from Tuesday, right?" She asked.

"Right," he responded. He knew she felt this obligation to him. He could have relieved her of that by insisting his mother planned on taking care of him, which she did, but he wasn't going to take the chance of never seeing her again. If obligation was what it took, he was okay with that.

Saturday

Houston came and got Bully at 10 o'clock. Sophie answered the door, and they went to the balcony. She sat on the wicker couch; he sat next to her.

"I hope you find what you need wherever you're going, Sophie."

"I just need time alone, Houston."

It took everything in him not to plead with her to let him go with her, not to shut him out, but he kept quiet. He stood up, put out his hand to help her up, and held her. He kissed her with a desperation he couldn't put into words, then handed her the key to her condo and said, "the next move is yours, Sophie."

Houston left with Bully without looking back. He didn't want her to see the tears rolling down his cheeks. He made it out the door and then leaned against the wall for support. It hurt so much.

Houston took Bully to Max's house. "Thanks, Max. Bully hasn't lost his magic touch."

"Hey, don't let him hear that! I don't want him to get a big head. He's a police officer just like you." Max smiled and rubbed Bully's head. "Aren't you boy?"

"Well maybe he can teach me a thing or two," Houston chuckled.

"I have a secret to tell if it's safe with you, Houston?"

"Of course, buddy. Anything."

"No one knows this, but Agent Kelly and I have been dating for about a year. We didn't tell anyone because we want to be able to work together when the opportunity arises, and you know the rules. One day we took a day trip to Governors Island with Bully and Titan. Unfortunately, we paid more attention to each other than the dogs and the next thing we knew Titan was pregnant. We never said who the father was, but we donated all the puppies to the K-9 unit.

Annie stipulated that she have the right to claim one of the puppies if she decided she wanted to. She would have to claim it before they start police training at 8 months. They are all at the K-9 kennel now, but they gave her 6 months to decide. I asked Annie last night how she felt about giving the dog to Sophie, and she loved the idea. The six months is almost up. What do you think?" Max asked.

"I think it's a great idea. Sophie is leaving town today, but she's coming back for my surgery. When will the puppy be ready to leave the kennel?" Houston asked excited.

He hadn't thought to give her a dog of her own. She responded well to dogs during stressful times — it would be a perfect gift.

"The puppies are almost 6 months old now so anytime. Do you think she'd want a boy?" Max asked.

"Oh, perfect. More competition," he laughed. "Thanks Max. I have to get back to work."

"I'll let Annie know." Houston left feeling better. He knew this was the right thing for her. Even if she went back to *wherever*, she needed the company and the protection.

After he left Max. Houston headed to Trenton, he needed to speak to his father. He made the phone call on the way. "Hello?" He had called his dad's cell phone.

"Hey, dad. I'm on my way home. I need to talk privately. Do you have time for me?"

"Of course, son. I'll be waiting for you in my shop. I'll tell your mom we need some private time."

"I'm just over an hour out." They said their goodbyes.

Sophie had a town car waiting for her when she touched down. She made it home by 9 o'clock at night, west coast time. Just being geographically away from New York lifted a heavy weight off her shoulders. The driver brought her suitcase in, and she gave him a good tip.

Sophie's neighbor, Suzie, had just gotten home from a date and saw the light on in Lexi's apartment. She went to knock on the door. Sophie opened it. It took Suzie a second to recognize her in her natural color hair, but when Sophie smiled, Suzie gave a little yelp and hugged her.

"I have missed you so much, Lexi!"

"Come in, Suzie. I've missed you too."

Sophie told her she had nothing in the house to offer her, so Suzie ran home and brought over some Lipton peach tea for them.

"Now, you have to tell me *everything*." Suzie planted herself on the couch with her legs folded under her.

Sophie smiled. She would have to edit all the undercover parts, but she could tell her that she went back to try to make some things right from her past and about meeting Houston. She also wanted to tell her how it ended with someone she once cared about dying but turned his life over to Christ before he died. So that's what she told her. She hadn't decided yet if she would tell Suzie, her real name. They talked till early morning. It felt good talking to a girlfriend.

Houston bypassed the house and went straight to his dad's shop.

"Hi, dad." He went to give his dad a hug. Jack directed Houston to the chairs in his shop.

"Sit, son. Tell me what's on your mind."

Houston opened his story with the fact that his father could tell no one what he was about to hear, other than his mother who already knew. Lives were at stake, Houston's included. Then he told him as much of the story as he felt he could and how it ended.

"Sophie was distraught, dad. She went into a depression like I've never seen; it frightened me. It was only through the mercy of God that she came out of it. I was getting ready to take her to the hospital. I tried to tell her that if it weren't for her, it was likely that Nikko would have never turned his life to Christ. It helped, but Nikko's brother, Thomas, laid a load of guilt on her and blamed her for his death. She just wasn't expecting that, nor did she deserve it. Thomas knew what Nikko had done.

"Dad, I think I loved her from the moment I saw her come out of Agent Hampton's office that first day. That feeling kept growing every day until I felt a bond with her like nothing I could ever imagine." He told his dad about the dates they had and how much fun she was. He even told him about the ballet. That made his dad laugh.

"Son, I know exactly how you feel. I loved Lily from the first moment I saw her. I was lucky she said yes to my proposal because I was going to beg and plead if she had hesitated. I knew I didn't want to spend one more minute without her. I often asked the Lord, when I had to be away, why he had put such a love in me for her. Being away was like torture, but when I married her, I vowed to take care of her and that meant going where the work was to feed her and our children.

"One day in prayer, the Lord opened my mind to the idea that He gave me that magnitude of love for her so that I would feel a tiny bit of the love He feels for His children. When we separate ourselves from Him, it hurts Him. That's why he paid such a horrendous price to give us a way back. He couldn't stand to be separated from us. It gave me a whole new depth of understanding regarding His love for us, and it intensified my love for Him. God made us for companionship, and we are made in his image, so it's natural for us to connect with others in a passionate way. There are other kinds of human connections. Look at Jonathan and David. They had a bond greater than brothers." His dad's story resonated with him.

"I recognized that your love for mom was the most beautiful love I had ever seen. Dad, I feel that way about Sophie, but she left me, she shut me out. I would have begged her to stay, but the Lord told me to let her go." Houston was leaning forward with his forearms on his knees and his head down.

"If for some reason you never do see her again, son, you have to know that having the opportunity in your life to love someone like that, was a gift. But I don't think it's over. Jesus knows what He's doing. He knew she needed time, and you need to know that you can't put anyone before Him, so He's doing what's best for both of you. When your mom and I married, we told each other that we would never put anything or anyone above each other except God." His dad leaned closer to his son. "Let me pray for you, son."

They prayed and talked until he heard his mother holler out the back door, "lunch is ready, and Sam's here. A little birdie told him you were in town."

His dad laughed. "And guess who that little birdie was?"

The food and company were great — both helped him to get through the pain.

CHAPTER TWENTY-EIGHT

Sunday

After church Sunday, Sophie had made an appointment to speak with Pastor Doug. But first she needed to speak with the man that had been running her office while she was gone. She ran to catch up with him, he was almost to his car.,

"Sophie, hi. I didn't realize you were back," he said.

"I just got back yesterday. I'd like to meet up with you tomorrow at the office and get caught up."

"I'll be there."

She said goodbye, then headed to her appointment with Pastor Doug.

The secretary was off today so she walked in his open office door. Pastor Doug noticed her hair color was different but just smiled and offered her a seat after saying hello.

"We've missed you around here, Lexi. Glad to have you back," he went around his desk and sat on the chair next to her.

"I'm glad to be back Pastor, but first let me tell you that my real name is Sophie Star." He didn't say anything, but his eyebrows went up.

"I need to have you keep everything I'm about to tell in professional confidence. No one can ever know. People's lives are at stake." She went on after he nodded. She told the entire story, sparing no details except for a few minor things that were of no consequence to the outcome.

"I was so shocked that Thomas reacted the way he did when he knew what the truth was. It spun me into a deep depression. Maybe I was wrong in going back — maybe it wasn't God leading me but me wanting revenge like Thomas said. Houston worked me through the depression, but I wanted to get away from everything and everyone." Sophie finished and looked up at Pastor Doug who had listened patiently as she recounted her story to him.

"Do you want my perspective on what you've told me?"

"Yes of course. I know you'll tell me the truth," she responded.

"You know that Christ died so that a way could be made back to the Father. We are his children. He made it simple, but we still can't seem to find the way. Do you think a God who sacrificed so much wouldn't use what you went through to bring one soul back to him?" He stopped for a moment.

"You think God was in all of this?" She questioned him.

The Bible says, "'(He)...is longsuffering to us-ward, not willing that any should perish, but that all should come to repentance' [2 Peter 3:9]. I think God uses the situations his children get into and works them around so that we can come back to Him. You said the man who died repented and gave his life to Christ before he died, didn't you?" He waited for her response.

"Yes. As he was laying in my arms bleeding, he asked if everything I told him about Jesus was true, then he repented and asked for Jesus to come into his heart."

"You think his soul wasn't worth what you went through?"

"No, of course not." She was surprised by the question.

"Do you think he would have come to God under *any other circumstances* or by anyone else's words? Do you think you could have handle things better than God? He knew that this man's

344

days were numbered. If he hadn't died that day by a bullet, his lifestyle would have caught up to him sooner rather than later," Pastor Doug said.

"I know God is all knowing, and we 'see through a glass, darkly'. And I don't think Nikko would have ever allowed anyone to talk to him the way I did." She remembered Houston telling her the same thing that the pastor just said.

"Then it sounds like, besides helping law enforcement in a big way, you did a wise thing. As the Bible says, 'remember this: Whoever turns a sinner from the error of their way will save them from death and cover over a multitude of sins'" [James 5:20].

The pastor gave her a chance to think about it for a moment then continued, "When it comes to Houston, you say you love him, but you only thought of how all this affected you. Christ didn't think of himself on the cross — He thought of you and me. Yes, you went through a great trauma, but he did too--in a different way. Can you imagine what a man like him went through — a protector, not able to protect? Think what it was like knowing what you were going through and not being able to save you. Men like Houston show their love and find their value, partly, in being able to do a job well, fix problems, and protect and serve others. And are particularly protective of the ones they love. That's why so many men like him go into the military or law enforcement. It's that need to protect. When someone they love rejects what they offer, or says they don't need their protection, it effectively shuts them out. It lessens their value in their own eyes. You're effectively saying that he has no value to you." He waited for a response.

"I know, I hurt him."

Pastor Doug saw a tear come to her eyes. He leaned forward. "I don't want, in any way, to make you feel that what you went through wasn't horrible. You needed to grieve, which it sounds like you already did in the days after. But if you don't let it go now, it will define you and taint the rest of your life. It will take time for all the residual effects to fall away, but recognize them for what they are, and don't let them shut you down. The Bible says, 'Brethren, I count not myself to have apprehended: but *this* one thing *I do*, forgetting those things which are behind, and reaching forth unto those things which are before'" [Phil 3:13]. He stood. "Can I pray for you?"

Sophie stood. "Yes, please. And I want to thank you. You've helped me see things from a different perspective, Pastor." They ended in prayer.

Monday

It was Monday, and all that Houston was doing at work was checking his phone to make sure he hadn't accidentally turned off the ringer. Rodriguez tried to talk to him, but he answered only in grunts and nods.

Fons finally got disgusted. "Houston, bud, you need to snap out of this. You knew she was going to leave, and you went into this with your eyes open. Give her some time. It's only been a couple of days."

"I know, I said I knew what I was getting into, but this is killing me, Fons. I have no idea where she is or even if she made it there safely."

"Then you need to pray and give it over to God because you are not handling this very well," Fons responded impatiently.

Houston tried to concentrate on his job and improve his attitude after that. He knew Fons was right. It was almost 5 pm when his phone rang. He jetted up to his feet and checked his caller ID. "It's Sophie!" he exclaimed to Fons loudly. The other men looked over at him and smiled — they all knew what he was going through.

"Aren't you going to answer it, dummy?" Rodriguez laughed at him. Agent Hampton came out wondering what was going on. The room answered in unison, "It's Sophie." He went back in his office with a smile on his face.

"Hello?" He sounded like a two-year-old boy, so he cleared his throat and tried again, manlier.

"Hello?"

"Houston, it's Sophie. Do you have time for me?"

"Of course! Are you alright?" He looked around and saw everyone staring at him. He frowned at them and sat down.

"Yes, I'm fine, but I need you to forgive me. You have been so good to me, taking care of me through that horrible pit of depression, bringing me out of it, and I thanked you by shutting you out," she confessed.

"Sophie, you were just trying to protect yourself." He defended her actions.

"No, Houston. I was only thinking of myself, and I know I hurt you. I understand if you don't want anything to do with me," she regretted how she treated him. He saw Fons unashamedly listening intently to his conversation with a smile on his face.

"Of course, I forgive you. I love you," he said.

"Then can I ask you a favor?"

"Yes. I'll do anything you need."

"Can you come and help me get things done so I can come home?" She asked.

Houston jetted out of his seat again. "You're coming home?" He said it too loudly, and everyone looked over, again laughing.

"Just tell me where you are. I'll be on the first flight in the morning." He didn't care if he had to charter a plane — he was going to be there tomorrow.

"Get a ticket for Portland, OR. I'll pick you up. I live about an hour north." He was writing down the information.

"No, I don't expect you to do that. I'll rent a car. Just give me your address."

Sophie gave him the address and they hung up. There was that stupid grin on his face again, but nothing was going to remove it at this point. Houston went straight to Agent Hampton's office. Within a few minutes, Agent Hampton came out, stepped over to Sarah's desk and told her to get the paperwork ready for Houston to get his vacation time. Then he said loudly so that everyone in the office could hear, "he needs to go get his girl and bring her home." The office erupted with applause.

Houston went back to his desk and looked at Fons. "I know I'm leaving you with a lot of work because of these stupid lawsuits the Moranos are filing, but I'll make it up to you."

"It's not a problem. Sophie really is a perfect fit for you. Don't blow it," he said smiling.

"I won't. I promise." Houston cleared off his desk and dialed his dad. He was going home to pack and get his airline ticket, but first he wanted to tell his dad.

Tuesday

The plane was landing, and Houston's left arm that was in the sling, and strapped to his chest was aching. Since he left the hospital earlier than the doctor suggested, he did his best to keep it in a sling whenever he could. He would sleep with it and travel in a car or plane with it on. He knew his hand was healing because, before, if it weren't in the sling all the time, his hand would throb to his heartbeat—now it rarely did. His second surgery to clear away the scar tissue and bone fragments was in a week. His hand would be in a cast for six weeks and then he would have to endure physical therapy.

Houston was trying to focus on anything *except for* the fact that he still had an hour drive before he saw Sophie. He wished he hadn't told her not to pick him up, but he did, so now he needed to live with it.

The passengers filed out of the plane, and he stopped to take his sling off. He always scanned the faces in crowds for trouble like any good law enforcement officer. As he was passing security, his eyes stopped on the most beautiful sight he had ever seen. *Sophie.* Houston ran to her but stopped short right in front of her. He had told her that last day in New York that the next move was hers, and he meant it.

Sophie threw her arms around his neck and kissed him. He dropped his bag and wrapped his arms around her, melting into her kiss. When she leaned back, she put the flat of her hand on his chest and patted it. "The next move is yours," she said with a sly smile. He grabbed his bag, and they went to retrieve his gun in the luggage area at the firearms window.

Sophie handed him the keys, gave him some directions, and they left the airport. She told him about her business and the duplex she bought and how many things she had to get done before they left. As they drove north on I-5, they approached Woodland, WA. Sophie asked Houston to pull off the exit so they could eat at the Oak Tree restaurant.

"We're not far from Lake View," she said as they went to have a nice dinner.

As they waited for their food, Sophie filled Houston in on her progress. "I found someone interested in buying my accounting firm, but I promised them I would spend three days going over the files and the computer programs with them, which means I can't pack or get anything else done. That is where you come in," she smiled.

After dinner, as they were leaving the restaurant, Sophie continued telling him all that needed to happen before they left.

"Can you find a lawyer for me that will transfer the deed of my duplex to the Church? I want it to allow Suzie to pay only half her monthly rent and to manage the premises in return. I also want a clause that says she can stay for as long as she wants to live there. I will leave my furniture in the apartment, and I want my clothes, personal papers, and electronics shipped to New York. I would like everything else boxed up and taken to the Salvation Army. If you call my church, they always have a day worker who is willing to help for a little pay. I'm happy to pay someone."

Sophie, take a breath. "We can figure all this out. There is no rush. I'll stay as long as you need me. Anyway, it sounds like you have it all organized in your head. I can do all those things for you, no problem," Houston smiled.

"Oh, and you have to call me Lexi here. Only Pastor Doug knows my real name."

Houston was using his right hand to drive because his left was still wrapped like a mummy, so she couldn't hold his hand. Sophie reached over and ran her fingers through the hair at the nape of his neck, then just let it rest there. Her touch felt so good. He had thought he would never feel it again.

"I have a room at the Red Lion, is that far from your apartment?" He asked.

"It's okay for tonight. But in the morning, I'll take you to a hotel just two blocks from my place. That way we can share my car. If that's alright with you?" Sophie asked. Houston nodded.

They pulled up to her apartment, and he grabbed something from his bag. They went in and talked strategy so that they could accomplish the most with their time. Then he handed her a present. Sophie dumped it out on the table and screeched with glee when 30 assorted candies bars came out of the bag.

Sophie kissed him. "Thank you. I loved Halloween as a kid. That deserves two kisses." She kissed him again.

"That was the response I was hoping for," he laughed.

Sunday

It was Sunday afternoon. They were on the plane back to New York, in first class. Houston insisted when he booked the airline tickets that they were going to fly in style. Sophie managed to close the deal on the accounting business with a pretty hefty profit, but Houston had done the real work. He was extremely efficient and organized. By that morning, there was nothing left to do but go to church. Pastor Doug spent a little time with Houston privately.

The Church board thanked Sophie for her donation, but it was the least she could do to repay them for the impact this Church had on her life.

They treated her friends to a farewell lunch and had a great time. Houston insisted on paying. Sophie would have objected but she remembered what Pastor Doug had said about men like Houston needing to take care of those they love. Houston really was amazing, and she told him so often. She was sad to be leaving this little community, Suzie most of all, but her future was with Houston in New York, or at least she hoped it was.

Dangerous Obsession

EPILOGUE
THREE MONTHS LATER

Sophie was in the kitchen filling up her spray bottle with water so she could spray her new plants. She had decorated the balcony to feel more like a home. Houston was outside throwing the ball to Bully Jr., their new puppy. She'd never forget the day before Houston's operation, when she went to answer the knock on the door. Standing there was Houston holding this huge puppy with its belly exposed, squirming, its legs dangling.

The look on Houston's face was priceless when he said, 'he followed me home. Can we keep him, please?' Bully Jr. was the spitting image of his father, hence the name. Houston told her the whole story, and she couldn't have been more pleased.

Jack took Bully Jr. home while his son was in the hospital because Sophie insisted on staying by Houston's side the entire time. His mom took care of the things which Houston was too embarrassed to have Sophie do, but she did everything else. He had done so much for her, she felt she owed it to him, and she loved caring for him.

Houston struggled with the painful therapy, but Sophie stayed through every minute of it. And if he missed one repetition or tried to stop one minute short, she would chew him out up one side and down the other. But it paid off because the prognosis was excellent that he would recover his full range of motion.

Sophie was spraying the plants when Houston asked, "would you like to go see a movie tonight, after dinner, *So*?"

Sophie turned to him and put her hands on her hips. "I told you not to call me '*So*'. I am not an adverb."

Then she got this mischievous look on her face, and he knew what was coming. Sophie moved closer and sprayed him. Houston hadn't moved fast enough and got it right in the face. He started chasing her. She was giggling and of course, Bully Jr. had to interject himself in the fun, barking and chasing them. She turned suddenly and reached out her arm with the sprayer.

"Stop, or I'll shoot!"

Houston backed off, putting his hands in a surrender position. "Put the sprayer down, ma'am. We can negotiate this," he laughed.

"You have nothing to negotiate with," she responded.

Houston reached into his pocket and pulled out a package of Twizzlers he had bought for her. "Put it down, and I'll give you these." He extended the candy toward her. She looked at the Twizzlers then at the sprayer. A naughty smile crossed her face, and she snatched them out of his hand and ran. He ran after her and wrapped his arms around her from behind.

"You cheated," he said.

"Did not," she replied.

"Well, you're my prisoner now!" Instantly, he realized what he had said and let her go, putting his hands up. "I'm sorry Sophie. I didn't mean it like that."

Houston tried to be careful not to trigger painful memories. Sophie cupped her hand on his face.

"Houston, you don't have to walk on eggshells with me. There are things that bother me sometimes, but I can handle it. God has given me distance from the pain. I want you to be comfortable enough not to worry about things like that, okay?"

He put his arms around her and kissed her neck. "What would a smart, beautiful, kind woman like yourself say if a handsome, law enforcement type got on one knee and proposed in the very near future?"

"I think that woman would think that the handsome, amazing, law enforcement type was a very smart man." Sophie looked in his eyes and smiled.

Houston had been wanting to propose for months, but he had paid a fancy jewelry store to design a ring unique to her taste and it hadn't come in yet. He could hardly wait.

"Well, you haven't answered my question about the movie yet, *So*. I guess that means the next move is yours!" He started running to get a head start on the sprayer...

~To be continued~

Dangerous Obsession

FROM THE AUTHOR

I hope you enjoyed reading Sophie's story. My objective was to illustrate how far God's love and mercies will go in order to bring one lost sheep home.

I want to acknowledge Corrie Ten Boom for the quote I used in this book.
I highly recommend her book "The Hiding Place."

Above all I want to thank God for sending his Son Jesus to make a way for our salvation and my Pastors who taught me the power in the undiluted Word of God.

L J

www.ingramcontent.com/pod-product-compliance
Lightning Source LLC
Chambersburg PA
CBHW020520260626
47156CB00006B/2065